S.S. BAZINET

BROTHER'S BLOOD

BOOK FOUR

The Vampire Reclamation Project

Renata Press
Albuquerque, New Mexico

This book is a work of fiction. Names, characters, places, businesses, organizations and events are either the product of the author's imagination or are used fictitiously. Any resemblance to actual persons, living or dead, events or locales is entirely coincidental.

Published by Renata Press
Albuquerque, New Mexico
www.renatapress.com

Visit the author's website:
www.ssbazinet.com

ISBN-13: 978-1-937279-19-6

For all those who enjoy

a journey into the light!

Acknowledgments

I've had so much support from so many. In bringing this book to publication, I'm so grateful to Laura Christine, my beloved, genius editor. My profound thanks go to Gene Hoglan, who spent so much time meticulously going over the manuscript. I am so appreciative of his loving dedication to detail. I am also so grateful to my other extraordinary earth angels, Gabriel, Anna Marie and George, Julia Ann and Rick. They are all blessings, and I am so fortunate to have them in my life!

One

Rolphe stood at his studio window, peering out with weary eyes. It was raining. Nature was blessing Paris with its holy waters. They washed the magnificent city, cleansing the sidewalks and structures in a heavy downpour. As the rain tapped out a melody of renewal on Rolphe's window, he knew that nothing would ever cleanse his soul. He'd been able to sidestep that fact for most of his life, but not now. As he tried to outdistance his fate, hell was already nipping at his heels.

The week before he'd nearly drained a man of his blood. Only the intervention from an outside force had stopped him and saved the man's life. But robbing a man of his blood or even his life wasn't new for Rolphe. His inability to resist his base nature was an engine that propelled his life. But this man was different. His blood was different. It wasn't something that could be consumed and forgotten. This man's blood demanded retribution.

After his trip to London, Rolphe had returned home in a daze of increasing misery. The fires were already burning in his body. His limbs were already consumed with pain. It was a new and fearful experience. During his long life, he'd always been strong. His six-foot-five inch frame was heavy boned and made to withstand whatever he came up against . . . until now.

The blood he'd recently imbibed not only cursed him with bodily afflictions, it threatened to put an end to Rolphe's earthly existence. What would follow was too much to bear. His wicked ways were so numerous and unforgivable that his soul would surely be damned for eternity.

Two

Arel came awake, opened his eyes, glanced around William's guest bedroom and quickly closed them again. Even though he felt so weak he could barely lift a finger, inwardly he was screaming. He couldn't believe that he was still alive. Why couldn't his body let go? Why did his heart insist on beating when he longed to leave the earth behind?

As if that weren't enough of a burden, he had to worry about William. The man was just as stubborn as his body. He sat by Arel's bed, hour after hour, day in and day out. Surely it had been a week since Arel had been attacked by the villain, Rolphe. Why wouldn't William get on with his life? He had an ex-angel, the beautiful Annabel, by his side now. She was the one who needed tending. The idea of being a human was new and challenging for her. Why didn't William help Annabel instead of thinking he had a duty to Arel?

Arel also had Michael to deal with. The angel was like some kind of faithful sentinel who kept trying to get through Arel's carefully erected shields. Like William, he wanted to help. At first, Arel thought the angel was doing him a favor. Keeping up his shields took a lot of energy. He hoped the extra strain would deplete his life force. No such luck. Like his body, his energy reserves managed to hold. So there he lay, wanting to die and being foiled by his body and good-intentioned helpers.

But what his helpers didn't know was that they were keeping a potential monster alive. Arel had glimpsed the future and knew he wanted no part of it. If he thought he'd misused his power in the past, it was nothing compared to what he was capable of doing if he lived. No, he had to find a way to convince William and Michael to let him go before the worst happened.

Three

Peggy stood in the kitchen of her suburban home. She was clutching her phone, waiting for it to ring her party. She was in Chicago. The person she was trying to contact was in London. Happily, Tim was there with her while she made the call. When she looked up at him, he gave her a nodding smile. He was her tall, handsome rock. He was the person who never wavered, even when she panicked. But his support wasn't enough to help her at the moment. "I swear, Tim, if I don't get some answers, I'm getting the next plane out."

Tim's gray eyes remained steady. "You can't keep doing this to yourself, Peg. Arel has changed. He knows how to handle himself. Besides, he has William and Michael to look out for him."

Peggy held the phone closer. "I know you're right, but these visions I've been having are off-the-charts scary."

"They've been scary before, and Arel has always come out just fine."

"Shh, it's ringing," she whispered. "I'll put it on speaker so that you can hear too." She held up her hand again. "Hello, Michael? This is Peggy. I'm calling because we want to check on Arel. We haven't heard from him. Is something wrong? And please, don't sugarcoat the facts."

A few minutes later, Peggy hung up the phone and narrowed her brows. The conversation had been a very short one. "That was a waste of time."

"What do you mean? Michael told us that he and William are taking care of Arel."

"Oh Tim," Peggy said with a sigh. "Can't you hear what he didn't say? Michael is worried too."

Tim walked over to the coffee maker and poured a generous amount of hot liquid into a large mug. "Maybe you're right, but we've known Michael for some time now. He's very capable of handling tough situations."

Peggy joined him and held out her cup. "I guess, but in the meantime what am I supposed to do with what I've been feeling?"

Tim filled her cup and replaced the carafe in the coffee maker. "I thought you said you practiced some meditation techniques that helped."

"Yes, but I haven't used them recently."

Tim smiled. "Maybe it's time to get the candles out again. You need your sleep."

"Can you believe Arel was the one who got us meditating in the first place?"

"He was very persuasive from what I recall."

Peggy took a sip of her coffee and smiled. "And then he slept through the entire first session, the rascal."

"He was pretty burnt in those days, trying to take care of Carol and Kevin when Carol was in danger of losing their baby."

"And as soon as Arel insisted that they stay at his house, Kevin got that horrible case of stomach flu and kept throwing up."

"Kevin said he missed the toilet a couple of times. I can't imagine Arel cleaning up that kind of mess. You know how uptight he is about his house."

Peggy's smile broadened. "Poor guy went from being a reclusive bachelor to chief cook and bottle washer."

"And don't forget card shark. I came home penniless on many an occasion."

"Yes, but you know you care about him."

Tim patted his stomach. "He's a darn fine cook when he throws a dinner party."

Peggy sat down at the kitchen table and straightened a placemat. "But there haven't been many parties for a while."

"We have to have some faith, Peg. Arel is stronger than he looks. I'm sure of it."

"I hope so."

Tim put his mug on the counter and walked over to Peggy. He started to massage her shoulders. "I know so."

Peggy was about to let out another sigh and grabbed her phone instead. "I almost forgot. I'm supposed to call Carol and Kevin. I promised to let them know if I found out anything from Michael."

* * *

Carol put the phone back in the cradle and walked over to the living room sofa. Kevin looked up from his newspaper. When their eyes met, he quickly folded it and tossed it aside. He wore jeans, an old football jersey, and an expectant expression as he patted the seat next to him. Carol sat down and grabbed hold of his arm. "Peggy said that Michael repeated what we already knew. Arel is still sick."

"He should be better by now."

"You coached him, Kevin. I hope you're right about him having hidden strengths."

"Yeah, but he's also temperamental. If he gets into one of his moods, he can go down for the count if you let him."

"He didn't look good when he left here. I hope his health doesn't deteriorate again. Remember what he was like when we met him?"

"Talk about working with a downer outlook. It wasn't easy trying to help him."

"At least he has two friends with him. Michael is great, and as for William—"

"Please, Carol, do I have to hear about how wonderful William is?"

"Well, he is."

Kevin gave her a sideways glance. "I'm very grateful that the guy helped you to know how amazing you are."

"Thank you. I appreciate the compliment."

"Ever since William's visit, I can't keep up with you."

"Really? Have I changed that much?"

"You know you have. When you took that ride with Carey on his motorcycle—"

"Please, Kevin, we just went around the block."

14

"You wouldn't have gone near a bike before you started being the 'new' Carol."

"I must admit that having confidence in myself is great."

"Maybe I need some of that confidence if I'm going to compete with William."

Carol knew he was kidding, but Kevin had gone through some hard times when he didn't know how to help her. She'd been so depressed after a miscarriage. She tugged Kevin's arm and snuggled close. "William might have helped me get my perspective back, but you're the one I married."

"You don't regret it, do you?"

"Of course not. Stop saying things like that."

Kevin shrugged. "I keep remembering our time in Paris. You loved visiting the art galleries and stuff like that, but I don't always feel excited about the same things. Do you think I'm boring?"

Carol stared up at him and started laughing. "You're not boring, and I'd never visit another art gallery if it meant not having you in my life."

"I met a lot of gals when I was dating, but when I saw you, I knew I'd hit the jackpot."

Carol thought back to her first impression of Kevin. He stood at her door, practically filling it up with his masculine body. But it was his smile that made her melt. "You have the biggest heart of anyone I know, Kevin Bailey, so stop doubting yourself when I mention William."

"What about the rest of me? I hope I'm not just a guy with a big heart."

Carol squeezed his arm again. "Believe me, I wouldn't have shopped for hours yesterday, looking for just the right lingerie if there wasn't more to you than just a good heart."

Kevin's face flushed with embarrassment. He was still getting used to Carol's new choices when it came to nighttime apparel. When he recovered a little, he glanced at her with anticipation.

"Do you think you could model that lingerie for me tonight?"

Carol responded with a playful sparkle in her green eyes. "I think that could be arranged."

Four

William didn't know where he was. The soft glow that lit up the wispy landscape reminded him of something very familiar. Was he having another near-death experience? The thought was quickly dismissed when he noticed Arel leisurely strolling down a path nearby. This wasn't some heavenly afterlife. He had simply fallen asleep and been shanghaied again. He was in a dreamscape that belonged to Arel. The man had become very proficient at doing whatever he liked when he slept, including summoning William to join him when he liked.

"Arel, I don't appreciate the way you take liberties when I'm sleeping, but I am happy to get a chance to talk to you."

Arel smiled back. "I know. That's why I arranged this meeting."

Ever since Arel had been shot in a London park, he'd been failing physically. Besides suffering the effects of blood loss, the wound in his arm was festering. In spite of Michael's efforts to help, Arel's life force was slipping away. After a week, he was running a high fever and remained unconscious most of the time. So it was a relief to see the man up and about, even if it was in a dream William hadn't initiated. "For someone who's on death's door, you look very fit in spirit form."

"Exactly. You need to stop worrying about me."

"Arel, this isn't the real world. In reality, you're dying."

Arel gestured William over to an ornate bench and sat down. "We should talk."

"Just tell me why you're still clinging to your ridiculous death wish."

16

Arel crossed his arms. "A better question is why you won't let yourself enjoy your life. You don't need to concern yourself with me. You have Annabel and a bright future. You could start a family."

"I thought we were family. Isn't that what you wanted when you tossed me out of heaven? You wanted a brother, right?"

Arel looked down at his hands, clasping them together with stiff, white-knuckled fingers. "I've done so many inexcusable things. I keep misusing my power over and over."

"We've both made mistakes, but that's all behind us now."

"No, it's not."

"What do you mean?"

"Look around you, Will. I was able to bring you here without your permission. Do you think that's the kind of thing a friend does to a friend or a brother?"

"It was important to both of us that we talked this thing out. That's why you did what you did."

"Even if that's true, it's not the point. You might be able to live with your mistakes, but I can't."

"You're kidding. After all this time, you're still hanging on to your ridiculous attitude. That's the big mistake."

Arel stared back with dark, golden eyes, as if he couldn't connect with what William was trying his best to explain. On the plus side, he appeared as his handsome self again. With his dark, wavy mane and fine, genteel features, he'd always been a person who attracted women. However, he'd routinely backed away from them, giving them a frown instead of a smile. Now, he frowned back at William.

William stiffened with irritation. "Why can't you lighten up, Arel? Look at the positive side for once."

The statement made Arel laugh. He got up and began to pace. "You have no idea about what I'm dealing with. You mean well, but you're playing with fire. I can't tell you how I know this, but you're asking me to put your life in danger."

"In case you haven't noticed, I have a little power too. I was able to save your butt, wasn't I?"

Arel turned and glared back with hard, flashing eyes. Their golden color turned into pools of anger and sudden indignation. "You shouldn't have done that!"

Arel's sudden outburst shook the heavens. William was forced to grab hold of the bench to keep from being dislodged. But instead of being frightened, he stood up and approached Arel. He grabbed hold of his shoulders. "Stop acting like a child. We're in this thing together now. You made sure of that when you gave me Michael's blood. So don't think you can simply back out when you please!"

Arel struggled, trying to free himself, but he didn't seem to have the strength. He went from looking fit and robust to shivering and weak. "Please, Will, let me go. It's the only way you're going to have a decent life, or any life at all. Please! I'm so scared about what I might do next."

William tightened his grip. "No, you're not skipping out! Like I said, we're going to get through this!"

"I'm sorry, William. I'm sorry for everything, and I wish I could stop what's happening to me."

"What's happening? Tell me."

"Please for both our sakes, let me die, please!"

As Arel pleaded, the scene began to dissolve. William woke up in his bed, clinging to his blanket. The dream left him feeling as if he was helpless to change anything, especially Arel's mind. He was also wondering why Arel looked so scared. Before he could figure out the reason, he heard Annabel calling out his name. When he opened his eyes, she was staring down at him.

* * *

"William, wake up!" Annabel sat on William's bed trying to rouse the man she loved. He was in a deep sleep, scowling and calling out so loudly that Annabel's heart was racing. What if he was slipping away too, like Arel? She shook his shoulder again, this time more forcefully. When William's lids finally fluttered open, she let out a gasp of gratitude. "Thank goodness."

William blinked back with lined brows. "What is it? Is it Arel? Is he worse?"

"No, he's the same."

"Then what?"

Annabel sat back, trying to calm her breath. "I'm sorry, but I was concerned."

"Concerned?"

"Michael said you needed to rest. But you've been sleeping for hours. Then you started having nightmares."

William shut his eyes. "I'm fine now."

"Are you sure?"

"I'm positive."

"You've been stressed for days."

William opened his eyes again, targeting Annabel with a fierce frown. "Because of our house guest. Or haven't you noticed the mess Arel's gotten himself in?"

Annabel bit her lip. "And what about you? With all the stress you've had—"

"You're letting everything frighten you. But Annabel, you took off your wings and stepped into the world of humans. That means you have to toughen up a bit. Do you understand what I'm saying?"

Annabel looked away. "Are you angry at me?"

William took a deep breath and sighed. "Of course not. Why would I be angry at you?"

"Sometimes I don't know what to do. I only know that I love you."

"I love you too. That's why I'm trying to help Arel. Once he's well, and he's safely back home in Chicago, we can enjoy what we have."

"I know that you care, but Michael says—"

"Michael's an angel. He can't do anything when Arel's like this. It's up to me to find a way to get him back." He paused and stared at her with softer eyes. "Annabel, you have to understand my position."

Annabel did understand. Arel was deathly ill and needed help, but the man had his shields up, very powerful shields. Michael had to respect Arel's closed-door policy. Her beautiful William lived by different rules. "But what if you can't help him? What then?"

William reached out and caressed her cheek. "Please Annabel, have a little faith in me. I've helped him before. I'll find a way."

Five

After Rolphe's return to Paris, he'd been going over his life. It wasn't that he liked to think about the past, but he couldn't stop the memories that surfaced. Perhaps it had to do with the blood. Most of his recollections were unwanted, especially when they involved the family he'd once had. As a young man, he'd lost his wife and two sons to an epidemic.

But one memory was beautiful. It came from his childhood. Rolphe recalled a special day when he was a boy of six. He'd been so innocent at that age. He loved his family and the warm bed that he shared with his brothers. But he was an active child, and he often woke before the others. On one particular morning, he came awake to the predawn sound of a bird chirping. He lay still and listened to its song. It made him curious. What was the bird trying to tell him? Why did it sound so happy?

As the singing continued, Rolphe slipped from his bed and quietly let himself out of the house. He hoped to search out the bird. Instead, he found the sun. It's bold, bright face was just inching up over the distant hills. Rolphe instantly understood that the bird was singing to the radiant orb, welcoming its return.

As the sun rose slowly over the ridge, its rays renewed everything it touched with a blazing light. Rolphe had never seen a more beautiful sight. He continued to gaze at the sun, letting more questions fill his mind. Who created such a wonder? Who had the power to guide something so splendid through the sky each day and put it to bed each night?

When the idea of God sprung forth from his heart, he smiled. He'd been taught about the deity, but the word didn't mean anything concrete. It remained just a thought. It took the magnificent sunrise to illuminate his mind. For the first time in his short life, he understood what greatness he was privy to. Behind the workings of the heavens and earth, there was a Divine Being.

He watched as the sun's fingers traveled over the fields, and across the road. He was anxious for the sun to anoint him too. He wanted it to fill his body with warmth and light like it lit up the wheat, turning the ripening heads to gold.

When the sun reached his face, he knew it was baptizing him for a second time. He had already been washed with the waters that took away sin. This was a baptism that would awaken him more fully, just like it did for all of earth's creatures. Everything stirred from its slumber when the sun gave its light. The cock crowed, and the bees came out to welcome another day of gathering honey. Rolphe knew he had a part to play too. He promised to honor the life he'd been given.

As the years passed, he didn't remain in his exalted state. His choices sent him in the opposite direction. He began to defile life's gift. But now, as he stood in his studio, he knew he'd come to the end of the road. Before he died, he wanted to honor what was beautiful in the world one last time.

He began to paint what he'd seen as a child. He worked tirelessly, mixing his colors, applying careful brush strokes to the canvas. With every ounce of strength he possessed, he seized hold of his youthful experience and the unbounded joy that he'd felt as a young boy.

Once the painting was finished, he studied it with the appraising eye of an artist who'd worked at his craft for more than a quarter of a century. He was satisfied with what he saw. A radiant sun rose into the heavens. Its light, like something issued from the hand of God, consecrated a young child who stood in the foreground. Animals gathered round, giving thanks like the boy. The painting was a glorious tribute to what was wondrous and sacred in life.

Now, after looking at the painting for days, he was tempted to destroy it. Instead of helping him, it became another reminder of what he'd lost and why he should be punished. But what good would it do to destroy something of beauty? Would it change who he was and what was going to happen to him? Still, he had to get away from the painting and from his despair. That's when he thought about the gypsy woman who'd made him a vampire.

Chessa was an amazing teacher who had many talents. She even showed Rolphe how to leave his body. Together, they traveled to a world that could only be reached by a focused mind. He hadn't thought about that world for a very long time. After Chessa's death, it slipped away and became a memory too. But what if it was still there? The idea was intriguing.

The more Rolphe contemplated getting away from his loathsome situation, the more he longed to leave normal reality behind. With an intention to find Chessa's world again, he laid down on the tiled floor. For a long moment, he remained very still. He relaxed and let the cold, hard surface soothe the heat that ate away at his body. When he felt a little better, he spread out his long limbs and tried to remember the steps he'd been taught. One of the most important was to withdraw his attention from the room. He needed to let go of what he considered the real world and picture an alternate realm that he'd visited long ago.

Once he achieved his objective, not only could he travel to that alternate world, he could also leave behind the idea of being a man. In the world Chessa had showed him, he could become whatever he wished. He could become an animal, a wolf that didn't have the same moral restraints. Perhaps if he was very lucky, he could leave behind his sins.

* * *

Arel almost smiled when the swirling ethers around him slowed. For once his powers came in handy. He'd reached his destination. As he adjusted to where he was, his astral body began to feel very much like the physical one that he'd left behind. He could sniff at the air and note its musty odor. His sight worked perfectly too. If he held his hand in front of his face, it looked very normal.

Using astral travel to find Rolphe was a desperate answer to a desperate need. After Arel's meeting with William in a dream, he knew he'd never convince William to let him go. That's when he decided to search out Rolphe. Rolphe was someone who had no problem with ending a life. And since they were linked by the blood exchange, Arel had no problem finding the man. Each person had a unique energy signature. It was easy to search out the signature that belonged to Rolphe.

As Arel took stock of where he'd ended up, he was confused. Rolphe lived in Paris. So why did he feel like he was a very long way from that beautiful city? As he questioned his whereabouts, he heard a low, menacing growl.

"Rolphe?" His murmured whisper was met by another growl. This one was louder and more aggressive than the first. He jumped back instinctively and hit his head on a hard, uneven surface. "Dammit! What now?"

As Arel's eyes adjusted to the dim light, he made out rocky walls. When he looked down, he saw a dirt floor. "A cave? I'm in a cave?"

Another growl answered him. It quickly turned into a vicious snarl. All curiosity about his strange whereabouts was abandoned. His sense of danger escalated so fast he had to steady himself against the stony wall behind him. Astral body or not, his heart was pounding out a very clear message. If he wanted to die, he'd come to the right place.

The theory was reinforced when a grotesque beast came out of the shadows. It stopped about twenty feet away. As Arel stared at it, he gasped. "What a hideous creature!"

The four-legged beast was so big that its green eyes were level with his own. It appeared to be an enormous wolf, but not the kind pictured on nature posters. Those wolves were noble, handsome animals. This oversized monster was ill-formed and mangy, with a huge head. As it continued to glare back at Arel, copious amounts of frothy drool dripped from its powerful jaws.

Arel felt the irony of the situation. He was standing in some wretched place, trembling. But the reason he wanted to die was because he felt too powerful. Whenever he'd allowed his abilities to surface, he'd been awed and terrified by what he could do. So why would he let some flea-bitten beast scare him? And what about the beast itself? His intention was to find Rolphe. Had he done something wrong to arrive in a cave and encounter a wolf?

As soon as he calmed himself a little, he was able to connect with the creature's mind. That's when he practically snarled himself. He was looking at Rolphe in wolf's clothing. The wolf's repulsiveness was a reflection of how Rolphe felt about himself.

Arel almost had a moment of pity, almost. "Well, aren't you a pretty sight, Rolphe?" he asked as he stepped forward. "Have all your sins caught up with you?"

The wolf's ragged ears pricked forward to listen. When its hateful eyes softened just a bit, Arel knew Rolphe could comprehend what he was saying.

Arel let out a contemptuous laugh. "I guess we have a lot in common. Neither one of us has been able to get beyond our transgressions."

The wolf lowered its head and whined in agreement. It seemed to be genuinely touched by Arel's observations. But the moment of remorse didn't last. As if a switch was triggered, its penitent attitude was quickly discarded and boldness was restored. The creature stepped closer and began to lick its chops. Sin or no sin, the wolf looked hungry. Its body was quivering with need and anticipation.

Arel was momentarily put off by its actions. Obviously, Rolphe had a different take on how to handle his wrongdoings. Arel usually did a lot of mental self-flagellation. Rolphe, on the other hand, seemed beyond such lofty pursuits. His eyes were those of a predator that had one agenda, to satisfy itself.

Arel swallowed hard. It was time to make a decision. Did he really want some filthy beast to finish him off? Did he want its stinking breath to foul his lungs as he took his last breath? Did he want to know what it was like to have his throat ripped out?

He knew it would be the worst kind of death. He was prepared to slip away from life on William's guest bed or even in some apartment in Paris, but he didn't want some ghastly creature chewing on his bones. Then he paused as another thought crept in.

"Oh hell and damnation, I'm missing the point!" he hissed.

He was worried about how to die, but a more important issue was at stake. Rolphe had Michael's blood too. What if he used its power to go on killing forever?

And I'm the one responsible for giving him that blood.

It was a horrible thought. It was so horrible that his mind filled with outrage at his own foolishness. Then, it raced ahead, thinking about what Rolphe might do in the future. How many innocents would Rolphe kill?

The man had to be stopped. But Rolphe wasn't a man at the moment, was he? He was a wolf getting ready to spring into action.

Arel felt himself change too. His anger began to fan out from his gut. As it spread throughout his body, he stiffened with resolve. There was no way he was going to allow Rolphe to prey on anyone ever again. He let out a snort of loathing, intent on making his wishes known. "If you know what's good for you, you'll back off, you hellish monster!"

The wolf glared back with its own disdain. Instead of retreating, it slunk another step closer. It licked at its drool again, obviously salivating over the meal that had presented itself.

Its insolent actions intensified Arel's need to rectify the situation. The facts were plain and simple. He could have used his power to stop Rolphe that night in the park. Rolphe might have used the opportunity to feast on Arel's blood, but Arel was the one in charge. Dying had been his choice.

He took in more of the damp, fetid air before he made his second declaration. "I could exterminate you in an instant, you fool! Don't you dare think you can have your way again. Do you understand?"

His question echoed off the walls, making Arel glance around again, impressed with how forceful he could sound. But the wolf seemed amused more than impressed. Its eyes flickered with mirth as it began to close the distance between them. When it was within striking distance, it suddenly went down into a low crouch, muscles tensing again as it prepared for a final assault.

Arel's knees went weak for just an instant. Facing a ferocious beast was new for him. Then he remembered how many times he'd told himself that Michael had made a terrible mistake giving him his blood. In Arel's mind, that angelic act had loosed a demon on the world.

And I better loose that demon now if I don't want to end up being dog chow for this heinous creature!

He stood up straighter, managing to get a firm grip on his self-confidence. He had thrown William out of heaven. Now he was visiting a hellish world with a fellow reprobate. The thought added fuel to the fire in his gut. He'd always turned that fire on himself, often burning up with fever. What would happen if he used it on Rolphe? In this setting, he knew the wolf would experience more that an elevated temperature.

The wolf went rigid instantly.

Arel blinked back a couple of times before he understood what the wolf was telling him.

So, you can read my mind. Is that right, Rolphe?

This time, when the wolf lowered its head, it was a gesture of submission. Rolphe seemed to quickly understand that Arel had the upper hand and the power to inflict pain.

Six

William squinted, looking for some kind of movement. Arel lay so still in the bed that it wasn't clear if he was even breathing. Michael was in a chair next to the bed, keeping watch. He was almost as motionless as Arel, but as William stared at him, Michael shifted in his seat and stood up. William took it as his opportunity to reach out to the angel. "Michael, will you help me to get Arel back before it's too late?"

Michael didn't answer. Instead, he gestured for William to follow him out into the hall. Once they were a few feet down the corridor, he turned to William. "Maybe you need a little background before you make that decision."

"What kind of background?"

"In many lifetimes that you've spent together, you've both lost your way, but neither of you totally gave up. Unfortunately, Arel has reached a point where he's mired in despair."

William waved off Michael's explanation. "He was despairing as a young man. It's nothing new."

"But this is different. Arel never had so much power before. Now, his ability to call in the darkness is much greater. If he succeeds in believing that his light is gone—"

William gave Michael a questioning glance. "Hold on. That doesn't compute. From what I've learned from Raphael, it's impossible to lose that light. It comes from our soul, correct?"

Michael smiled back indulgently. "You're bypassing an important element, free will. As a human being, you're given the opportunity to make choices. When a person experiences fear and lets it guide his or her decisions, they begin to close off their connection to their true self. You might say they put blinders on where their soul is concerned. Many humans live in that condition."

"And what about Arel? He's gone beyond the norm. I've seen him in action. He's become quite a show-off when it comes to his abilities."

"When a person has great power at his disposal and that person denies his connection to his soul, they can suffer much greater consequences. That person can experience what some would refer to as hell."

"So what? Arel courted that place before you gave him your blood."

"Yes, but now he's powerful enough to keep himself there if he chooses. He's completely cut himself off from my help."

William walked back to the doorway and looked in on Arel. With death at his doorstep and his link to the physical practically nil, the man's usually troubled face was unlined. It reminded William of the man's ability to lose himself to his virtues. In those special times, Arel could be selfless and totally giving. When William was at his lowest, Arel had been willing to damn himself to help William escape his misery.

"Excuse my language, Michael, but why does Arel have to be such a stubborn bastard? Why is he pushing everyone away?"

"Arel doesn't want to pull you down too. He really does want you to be happy."

"Believe me, I want that too, but he's giving up too easily."

"When he recalls his interference in your life, he's truly afraid. He's made grave, even deadly mistakes. Remember, you did almost die. He can't see beyond those mistakes."

"He should stop thinking about me as a victim. We're only victims if we allow ourselves to go that route. That's how this situation with Rolphe started. At first, Arel's power frightened me. I let myself think I couldn't handle my interactions with him. So I got in touch with Rolphe. Talk about mistakes! That was a colossal one. But it was my mistake, not Arel's."

Michael smiled. "You're very good at taking responsibility. That's an excellent quality to have in life, especially if you use it properly."

"Right, I make mistakes, learn from them, and I move on. But Arel doesn't seem to have that capacity."

"You've had a lot more practice. When Arel wanted my blood, he'd been hiding from the world for a very long time."

William laughed. "I can just imagine what you were dealing with. He was still a complete idiot, wasn't he?"

"He definitely had his limitations, but I believed he could overcome them."

"So help me get him back."

Michael hesitated. His eyes flickered over William's body, scanning William from head to toe. Then he looked away.

William took offense. "Don't you believe in me, Michael?"

"Yes, but you're asking me to help you enter a realm that's foreign and treacherous. If you're injured there, your physical body will feel the same effects. You've never dealt with a situation like this one before."

"Please, we've already discussed all that. Arel is with Rolphe. Together, they're licking their wounds in some god-forsaken alternate reality, right?"

"It's a little more complicated than that. In Arel's despondent condition, he's allowed himself to be aligned with Rolphe's negativity. It's a dynamic that decreases Arel's ability to make good decisions. It also increases the bleakness and futility he's experiencing."

"So what you're saying is that Arel is probably irrational."

"You've summed up the situation very well. But you left out a very important consideration. You don't know how to use your power independently yet. If you can't convince Arel to listen to you, and something goes wrong, it could mean your life."

William took a deep breath. "Then I better get Arel to listen to me."

"I'll be able to accompany you on your journey. Hopefully, Arel will drop his shields. If he doesn't, you'll be on your own."

"Right."

Michael sobered as he gave William a final once-over. "Are you absolutely sure about this? What about Annabel?"

William glanced around, checking on Annabel's whereabouts. He remembered she'd gone downstairs to check on their pet mice. "I love her, but—"

"Have you talked to her?"

"William?" Annabel's voice rang out from the doorway to the lower level stairs. "William, what's going on?"

William turned and managed a smile. "We were just discussing Arel."

Annabel quickly hurried over. When she took hold of William's arm, her hand was trembling. "No, there's more to it than you're telling me. Please, be honest. You're going after him, aren't you?"

"It's his only chance. I have to do this."

"But why? Arel has done his best, but he's tired." Annabel stiffened and stared back with a frown. "He doesn't want you to save him."

"But Annabel, what if you'd said that to Arel when I died? I wouldn't be standing here, would I?"

"That was different."

"How?"

Annabel put her arms around herself and stared down at the floor. "I'm just afraid of losing you. Is that so wrong, to want to keep you safe?"

"No, it's not wrong. But I want Arel to survive too. Please, don't ask me to make your security more important than saving his life."

Annabel tightened her grip on her arms and glanced up. "I'd never do that."

Seven

William lay on his bed with his eyes closed. His intention was clear. He wanted to find Arel's wandering, astral body. Michael explained that it was hidden in a place that was as near as William's breath and as distant as a world which housed only spirits. With that confusing bit of information, Michael also agreed to be William's guide. The angel used his deep, reassuring voice to propel William onward towards his destination.

As William listened to Michael's words, he began to get drowsy. His lids were so heavy that he couldn't lift them. With each second that ticked by, he could feel his body becoming denser and more confining. Just before he drifted off, something inside of him broke loose. It took a moment to realize that he was floating over the bed. He was still himself, but there was no solidity to his form. Happily, after several similar experiences, he was getting the hang of being out-of-body. He felt light and free again. Michael was floating next to him. William used a thought to communicate with the angel.

I'm starting to enjoy these trips.

Michael's response was immediate.

Hold on to that feeling.

William didn't have a chance to ask what Michael meant. Without any idea about what to do next, he was flying. Well, not exactly flying. He was moving through the ethers so fast that everything became a blur. He felt drawn to a certain location, but he didn't know how to get there. Michael's voice continued to help him relax.

Trust that your intention will guide you.

31

William tried his best to comply, but he felt so disorientated and out of control that he almost panicked. It was only when everything began to slow down that he could relax a little. As his normal perception returned, he realized that he was hovering above a bleak, inhospitable landscape. Its dark, foreboding energy hit his wispy form in menacing waves.

Turn back, now!

William's rational mind was quick to issue a warning. It was accompanied by an acute discomfort that rippled through his misty form.

Michael seemed to know what he was experiencing and sent him a message.

Maybe you should heed what your mind is telling you.

Before William allowed himself to consider the advice, he thought about Arel's plight. How could he let the man damn himself to some hellish existence? Arel would never abandon him. He stared back at the view below. It wasn't pleasant. Heavy clouds hung in a dark, threatening sky. It formed a backdrop for a glowering mountain range. Charred by some ghastly inferno, its sharp features and steep pillars of gloom were set high above a valley of stony, blackened ground.

William's descent into the barren valley was quick. By the time he arrived on the surface, his form had begun to solidify. Soon he weaved unsteadily on the rough ground, trying to acclimate. Michael stood a few feet away. In the otherwise dismal setting, the angel emitted a soft light.

You're glowing.

When Michael pointed and smiled back, William realized that he glowed too, but the effect didn't last very long. It began to diminish as his form took on more density. Soon he could clasp his arm with a hand that felt very real. When he tried to use his voice, his words were too loud, disturbing the scorched silence around him. He lowered it to a coarse whisper.

"You weren't kidding when you said Arel can construct a version of hell."

Michael's form took on more physicality too, but he retained a certain amount of illumination. "This isn't Arel's work. This is Rolphe's vision of this world."

William glanced around. "Where are they?"

Michael pointed towards an area just ahead of where they stood. There was a ground level fracture in the face of a rocky formation. "It's hard to tell it's there, but there's an opening that leads back into a cave."

William began moving forward and stopped abruptly. He stared down at himself. His normal attire had morphed. He wore leather boots and breeches. His upper body was clothed in a rough, hand-loomed shirt. A strange talisman hung around his neck. His long hair caught the wind.

"What now?" he asked as he turned to Michael. He jumped back in surprise. The angel was clad in a suit of golden armor. The outfit reminded William of Michael's true nature.

Michael's eyes were spirited, but he didn't comment.

William took in a lungful of heavy air and sighed. "Pray tell, oh heavenly messenger, why are we dressed like this?"

"Rolphe has a flair for the dramatic. He seems to have created a scenario that reflects that aspect of himself. When we began to interact with this world, we took on its qualities in regard to how we look."

William stared at the weapon hanging by Michael's side. A very imposing sword was housed in a fancy scabbard. Its golden pommel, grip and cross-guard caught the light coming off of Michael. Armor or not, the angel retained a radiance that made the dreary surroundings even more depressing.

William pointed at Michael's sword. "Do you think you'll need to use that?"

Michael withdrew the long blade and made several sweeping gestures, testing the weapon's assembly and balance. "Rolphe's early life was seeped in religion. He has a deep respect for angels. I think that's why I'm outfitted in this way."

William didn't have a sword, but he patted down his clothes. He hoped he'd discover a knife or some other weapon. When he came up empty-handed, he thought about Rolphe and what a formidable opponent he was. "Listen, Michael, if anything happens to me, tell Annabel how sorry I am."

"It's not too late to turn back. You have no obligation to—"

"I understand, but I'll see this through," William said as he started walking again. "It's going to take more than hell to stop me."

But Rolphe's version of hell was a cold one. A sharp change in the weather greeted their arrival at the cave entrance. A howling wind made every breath an effort. William shivered as the damp, freezing air buffeted his loose-fitting shirt and icy fingers of cold caressed his skin. He had to shield his eyes from the gritty dirt that filled the fouled air. When he spoke to Michael, he made sure to cover his mouth. "The only thing missing in this place is Arel's 'Home Sweet Home' sign."

* * *

Annabel sat in her bedroom, barely able to breathe. Her arms were wrapped tight around her body. Her eyes were downcast, but she didn't notice the thick, soft carpet that covered the floor. When she had first been William's in-the-flesh angel, she'd sometimes sat in the room, experiencing the world through physical senses. She even took off her shoes. The feel of the deep-cut pile on her bare feet was exciting, so interesting, even enjoyable. Coming from the ethereal realms, she welcomed the new sensations. They felt expansive. In those early days, she welcomed the adventure of having a body.

Now, she didn't have time to think about bare feet or how enjoyable the senses could be. Her speech came out in a moan. "Oh, my William, where are you?"

A gentle tap on her shoulder brought her out of her lament. She looked up at her visitor. "Raphael!"

The tall angel smiled back. "William asked me to stay with you while he's attending to some tasks."

Annabel jumped up and glared at him. "He's not attending to tasks! He's left me!"

Her loud, unpleasant shriek scared her. She hadn't thought about what to say. Her outburst came out on its own. She fell back into the chair and grabbed hold of herself again. She was sure she was falling apart, an ex-angel who'd made a terrible mistake by giving up her wings. Her breath came in gasps instead of shallow sips. She had to swallow the lump that was stuck in her throat. Her body was trembling. "I'm sorry," she finally managed.

Raphael crouched down next to her. He wore a white t-shirt and jeans, but his clothes couldn't cover up his striking, almost beautiful face or the overly-bright sparkle in his eyes. "Dear friend, can you look at me?"

Annabel shook her head. She'd gone back to staring at the rug and holding herself in a tight hug. "I'm going to lose him, Raphael. We've barely had any time together, and William is going to leave this world and cross over."

Raphael tipped up her chin. "You can't be sure of that."

"But that's how I feel!" Again, she'd raised her voice when she hadn't meant to.

"I understand."

"No, you don't, Arel tried to warn me about being a human. He said that angels have no idea about what a person feels. Now, I understand how right he was. I thought being in love like other humans was going to be wonderful, but—"

Raphael reached out for her hand. "Let me help you."

Annabel couldn't respond. She felt like the rusty tin man in the Wizard of Oz. When she thought about William dying and leaving her alone, she couldn't move. "What's wrong with this body I'm in? It's always doing things I don't want it to do?"

Raphael stood up. "Your body is your friend. It's letting you know that you're caught up in your fears."

"Friend? It doesn't feel like a friend! I don't like these feelings!"

Raphael gave her a compassionate nod. "You have to take the good with the not-so-good when you're in the physical."

"My body felt relaxed and happy when I had my wings. Sometimes I wonder if it's the same body."

"Remember, you have a different way of viewing life now."

"I don't know how to go on like this. It's not just my body that's out of control. My thoughts keep going in circles. I know that William shouldn't have gone after Arel. Angel or not, that's the one thing I know for sure."

Eight

William took a moment to catch his breath once he was inside the cave entrance. Although he'd escaped the harsh, punishing winds, he was still shivering. He checked out Michael's condition and frowned. "I can't believe the cold isn't affecting you."

Michael shook his head. "As I explained, Rolphe sees us as God's blessed ones. The harshness of the elements don't apply to me."

"What role do you think I'm playing in his crazy world?"

"How do you feel?"

William glared back. "Rolphe's dream or whatever it is, has me nearly frozen and feeling like I'd like to take that sword you have and kick the bastard's—" William paused and let out a disgusted laugh. "Listen to me. I'm sounding like Arel. I think this place has me rattled."

Michael gave William's shoulder a gentle shaking. The action also had a warming effect. William's body stopped trembling so violently.

Michael smiled. "You can't let yourself buy into Rolphe's rules. Try to stay as flexible and forward thinking as possible. You'll also have to control your negative emotions. This place is fueled by them. You don't want your energy to fortify that negativity."

"I just want to finish this." William turned to a dim, narrow passageway. The path ahead was rough and stony. He slowly made his way towards a tiny finger of illumination in a bend ahead. He'd only gone a half-dozen yards when Michael grabbed his shoulder again.

William turned to look at him. "What now?"

"I can't go any further," Michael announced. "But it's not Rolphe's energy. Arel has set up his own energy barriers."

"So I guess I'm on my own."

"When you see Arel, insist that he take down the barriers at once."

William paused. "You think I'm making a mistake. I'm sure you're right. Arel is probably too far gone—"

"He has a very adept mind when it comes to focus. He was able to use that focus to hold on to guilt and anger for a very long time. Now, he perceives himself and his power through that same lens."

"He seems so afraid of his power."

"His confidence can't keep up with what he's capable of doing."

"You gave him your blood. Didn't you know this would happen?"

"My blood was only a catalyst. But you're right. I took a chance. Now it's your turn to decide on the best course of action."

"The better part of me tells me to turn back."

"That part of you is giving you good advice. Arel's shields are powerful for a reason. He wants what he wants. If you challenge him—"

"He'll what?"

"I'm not sure, but please be very cautious."

William looked towards the narrow passage that led to Arel's whereabouts. No matter what his mind was telling him, anger and determination made him start walking again. "I'll be careful, but I want to see this through."

"William!" Michael called after him. "Arel isn't thinking clearly. Arguing with him isn't going to help."

William nearly laughed at Michael's admonition. He didn't need an angel to tell him about Arel's pigheadedness. But he couldn't think about Arel at the moment. He had to pay attention to where he was stepping. With barely any light, he groped along the cold, wet walls. He stumbled twice as he made his way deep into the cavern. He nearly chipped a tooth on a boulder that jutted out in his path.

"Damn, Rolphe, who are you hiding from?" he protested. "This is your world. Arel has barriers everywhere. I don't think you had to tunnel in this far."

When he saw a brighter light ahead, he hoped he'd reached his destination. "Finally." The word was barely out when he tripped a third time and went down hard. Cursing under his breath, he forced himself up and rubbed a bruised knee. The pain and another icy blast of cold made him want to give in to his temper. Thankfully, he was well versed in self-discipline. He shut his eyes long enough to let Michael's voice fill his mind.

You can do this, William.

William had despised Michael the moment they'd met. He didn't believe in angels or the power that Arel rambled on about. His attitude changed when he witnessed Arel's amazing abilities to heal or hurt. But more importantly, he'd discovered his own power. It was new and exciting, barely tested and unstable. Michael and Raphael had to help with his control, but he was learning. Now, he was on his own, navigating Rolphe's demented world. Once again, his mind screamed out a protest.

Turn back. Arel will never let you in.

William had always listened to reason. He'd lived a very successful life by staying rational. Yet, his reason had been challenged and tossed aside after he sipped a bit of Arel's blood. Insanity followed. He'd even stabbed himself to save Annabel. But overall, his life had changed for the better. He had a beautiful ex-angel who loved him. He could walk in the sun again, and he could feel a light growing brighter within. Arel was at the center of that change, and William had to try to keep him from throwing his life away.

He held on to the thought as he rounded a sharp bend on the path. Suddenly the narrow space gave way to a much larger opening. Its air was smoky and even heavier than the air in the passage. Its dark, earthen walls were coated with residue from too many fires. William scanned the space and was taken back. He'd found Arel. The man sat against a wall. He didn't look much better than he did in his sick bed.

A bulky, purple cloak sat heavy on Arel's thin, trembling shoulders. A fur rug of sorts protected him from the damp floor of the cave. A crude wood fire was blazing in front of him. His eyes glowed as he stared at its bright embers.

William stepped forward. "Arel?"

When Arel looked up and saw William, his face remained sullen and dark for a moment. Then he returned a weak smile. "Oh William, my misguided friend, won't you ever learn?"

Nine

Rolphe had always enjoyed indulging in the alternate world that Chessa had shared with him. She had also introduced Rolphe to psychic abilities that he'd never dreamed possible. He'd been raised to plow and plant. As a young soldier, he learned to kill. But his world had remained very small until he met Chessa. Fortunately, he was an apt student when she shared her knowledge with him. When he learned how to leave his body, Chessa was pleased. Together, they traveled to a new and amazing place. It was an incredible, fairy's realm where they could play. Waterfalls and lush greenery abounded. Bright pools invited moonlit swims. They could even enjoy the sunny skies. Their private world had different rules than those on the earth.

Rolphe glanced around the ill-lit cave. When Chessa was killed, their paradise lost all of its splendor. At one time, the cave had been a crystalline structure. No king or queen ever experienced anything as magnificent. When Chessa danced around the campfire in her gypsy skirts, the walls and ceiling were alive with flashing rainbows of color that seemed to be dancing too. The sight was so beautiful that Rolphe couldn't hold back his tears. Like his ancestors who played the balalaika and danced when they were happy, he wasn't ashamed to show his emotions. Chessa chided him and called him a child in a mocking voice. But he didn't hold it against her. Chessa didn't have the capacity to feel as deeply as he felt. She was more interested in her wild nature.

At times, they assumed other forms, frequently taking on the bodies of magnificent wolves. Chessa's fur was as black as the night. Even her eyes were like fiery coals. Rolphe was her submissive companion. His fur was silver and gray. Yet both of them were huge, winsome creatures that roamed the grassy hills and flowered meadows. They reveled in their animal strength and primal desires.

Chessa could make Rolphe forget about how he conducted his life. Her wild attitude didn't allow for guilt. She simply took what she wanted. After Chessa's death, Rolphe couldn't be quite as unfeeling as Chessa, but he did manage to live with his sins.

That changed when he imbibed Arel's blood. The amazing substance could fill a person with bliss. Rolphe couldn't get enough when he took in great gulps of it on that fateful night. Yet, afterwards, when it made its way through his body, it opened inner doors. It ferreted out his transgressions and thrust them into the light. The sins he planned on paying for when he died came alive. Faces of those he'd killed and maimed haunted him.

He had to flee such misery and sought sanctuary in Chessa's world. But he couldn't run away from what he was. He brought all the ugliness with him. It expressed itself in his hideous wolf's body. It carved out a world that was dark and foul.

Yet, there was solace in being an animal. Even if he couldn't escape who he was as a man, as an animal he could view himself from a simpler mindset. Like Chessa, he could put away his guilt. As he lay in the darkness and nursed the sores on his mangy body, he remembered the taste of blood and salivated.

When Arel showed up, Rolphe rejoiced at his good fortune. He'd fill himself again. Unfortunately, his intruder didn't cooperate with Rolphe's plans for an impromptu dinner. Even though Arel appeared weak and frail, he let Rolphe know who had the power. Rolphe soon realized that Arel could easily punish him.

But I need his blood again! I need it to help quench my thirst and fill my empty belly.

It was an enticing thought, but Rolphe didn't know how to accomplish his goal. After Arel set himself up as the one in charge, Rolphe was forced to retreat into the shadows and wait for his ill fortune to change. He'd almost given up on tasting blood again when an unexpected possibility presented itself. Another visitor arrived. As soon as Rolphe was aware of a man's presence, his ragged, wolf ears pricked forward. Remaining as quiet as possible, Rolphe raised his snout and sniffed the air. He let his mind attune itself to the new intruder.

BROTHER'S BLOOD

This one is not as strong as Arel. I can feel his weakness.

Rolphe licked his massive jaws in anticipation. He wouldn't go hungry much longer.

* * *

Huddled over with cold, wishing he had his down jacket, Arel couldn't get warm. He sat in a cavernous space with his teeth chattering. A few pieces of wood and kindling, thrown on an open camp fire, couldn't thaw out his icy surroundings or his body. He longed for the comforts of central heating. Instead, a ridiculous cloak was supposed to stave off the chill, damp air. He couldn't believe he was dressed in clothes fit for the middle ages, but this was Rolphe's world. Arel could control Rolphe's animal self, but he didn't know how to change the rest of his environment. Even in his astral body, he appeared weak and sick as his emotions plummeted.

He'd failed at life. Now he was a failure at the art of dying. From everything Michael had said, it should have been an easy transition. A person simply let go of one kind of existence and moved into another. William had managed it so easily when he died. He was quickly walking around in a wispy beautiful heaven, happy and content.

Then I showed up and forced him back to earth. Sorry about that, Will!

Maybe if he had died in the London park, he would have been able to achieve a better kind of crossing over. But he doubted it. Looking back on that night, his death wish was almost as strong as his desire to get Rolphe out of the picture. Yet he didn't have the courage to put an end to his life. That was when he had a brilliant idea. He could take advantage of the situation. He could use Rolphe. The ravenous ogre could be the lethal weapon that killed him.

Looking back, Arel knew he'd been wrong to drag Rolphe into the equation. A person doesn't go to heaven when he uses people like that. Now, he was paying the price. He was stuck with not only his own misdeeds, but he'd also created a terrible bond. He'd linked himself to a person who was even more dismal.

Arel had entertained a lot of negative thinking, but Rolphe took the prize when it came to darkness and misery. The man had a long history of violence. As he aged, Rolphe had thoughtfully branded

41

himself a sinner. But that was as far as Rolphe got. In an attitude of hopelessness and need, the man didn't fight temptation. He proclaimed himself unworthy of redemption, so he had nothing to lose if he sinned again.

Now, they were both stuck in a miserable cave that gave Rolphe some respite. The man had taken on the repulsive form of a mangy animal, and Arel was keeping him company. Still, there was purpose. Rolphe would never be allowed to hurt or kill again. Arel would make sure of it. It was the one positive thought that kept him going. Then William appeared.

The man rounded a corner of the cave opening and called out Arel's name. It was a shock to hear William's voice. Arel felt their time together was over. William was finding his freedom. He didn't need Arel to drag him down. Yet Arel couldn't help but smile when he saw William. The guy was dressed like Robin Hood and was more dashing than ever. He was obviously trying to be some kind of hero. "Oh William, my misguided friend, won't you ever learn?"

* * *

After successfully finding Arel, William's first duty was to relay Michael's message. He took a couple of steps into the cave and gave voice to the angel's instruction. "Arel, Michael says that you have to lower your shields."

After his initial recognition, Arel avoided William's eyes. He stared at the fire. "William, what are you doing here?"

Instead of answering, William repeated his request. "Arel, will you do what I asked? Michael says—"

Arel looked up. "I have to tell you something, and I don't want any interference."

"Michael doesn't intend to interfere, but—"

"Please Will, let me talk for just one minute. Can't I have sixty seconds of your time?"

William glanced around the cave. His body was immediately on guard. Something about the place made his skin crawl. "I don't like what I'm feeling, Arel."

Arel stood up and almost lost his balance. His thin fingers trembled as he held on to his cloak. "It's okay. It's Rolphe, but he's not going to hurt you. He knows I'm the boss in this horrid place."

William narrowed his brows. Arel didn't look like he could fight off an attack from an irate puppy much less a bloodthirsty maniac. "Fine, just tell me what's so important. I want to get out of here."

"I've created an ogre," Arel lamented. He stumbled over to the wall behind him. "I gave my blood, or should I say Michael's blood, to a person who's beyond caring about anyone or anything."

William sucked in a breath. Whatever he was sensing didn't feel like a man's energy. A scary, intimidating presence was hidden in the darkness. "So let's get Michael in here—"

"William, what have I done? When I think about Rolphe, I'm at my wit's end. You might have killed people, but you're capable of change. Rolphe isn't. So tell me what to do. I can't let Rolphe loose on the world, not if he inherits the power I have."

William squinted, trying to understand what he was dealing with. While Arel was faltering about on the other side of the cave, William was picking up on something very close. The slightest movement caught his attention. It came from a shadowy area a few yards away. "Arel, I understand, but this isn't the place to discuss your options, please—"

Arel gave him a quick, sorrowful glance and turned to the wall again. He put his head down on the damp surface and moaned. "Options? The only option I have is to disable the man in some way. If that doesn't work, I'll have to kill him." As if Arel had to emphasize the severity of the situation and his dilemma, he began to bang his forehead against the stony wall. "But I don't want that, Will. I'm not the killing type."

"You're not listening to me!" William's plea was genuine. No matter what Arel said about being in control, whatever was stalking him was so close he could smell it. It reminded him of damp fur mixed with a horrible case of bad breath. He made a last ditch effort to reach Arel. "I'm in trouble here!"

He called out, but Arel was in his own world, ranting again, oblivious to William's situation. "Arel, you have to drop your shields!"

While he was trying to get Arel's attention, he tried to summon his own power. There was only one problem. He didn't know how to go about the task. Sure he could put himself into a light trance state and let his healing powers restore a mouse. But this situation called for something much more impressive. As he tried to think, he saw a hideous creature emerge into the dim light.

"Arel! Help me!" William's shriek for assistance barely left his lips when the repulsive beast was in motion. From William's vantage point, the only thing he saw coming was an enormous, dark form with yellowed teeth and glowing green eyes. He managed one more screeching outcry. "Michael!"

The angel's name was still echoing on the cave walls when the creature closed the gap between them. Time slowed as William saw it go airborne. Drool and spittle sprayed out in all directions from its powerful, open jaws. When the beast landed on him, its weight and thrust slammed him backwards. As his head and body hit the rough cave floor, time returned to normal. He was under attack. A ferocious animal was on top of him, snarling and trying to kill him. William fought back, desperately hoping to protect his throat. But he couldn't stop the vicious animal from repeatedly biting his hands.

In spite of the beast's growls and his own screams of pain, William heard Arel shouting. Arel's body looked frail, but his voice was so loud and panicked that it made the cave shake. His petition was clear. "Michael, save William!"

Michael appeared at once, wielding his sword, but he didn't get a chance to use it. Arel had already rushed over to where William lay, struggling to survive. Going into a madman kind of frenzy, Arel heaved a heavy rock down on the beast's head. As soon as he did, the attack came to an end. In the same instant, the creature disappeared. So did the cave and everything else when William blacked out a moment later.

* * *

Rolphe opened his eyes and groaned. He was lying on the floor of his studio. He tried to move, but the room was spinning. The back of his head was a massive source of pain. But how could that be? He'd been off in the fantasy world. So how could something that happened in the cave affect him when he returned to his normal reality? He fingered the back of his head and winced. When he retrieved his hand, it was covered in blood. He didn't know how, but his injury was proof that the rules must have changed. It was a frightening prospect. Not even Chessa could blur the lines between two worlds.

His brows narrowed as another name came to mind. "That bastard, Arel, must be responsible!"

He didn't have time to think about his powerful foe. He had to take care of his wound before he lost too much blood. As he tried to gather his strength, he glanced at the big pillow next to his easel. Dantela, his beautiful kitten, stared back at him. "My little friend, I'm in trouble," he moaned.

Dantela stood up, arched her back in a careful stretch, and jumped off her soft accommodations. Mewing, she quickly padded over to where Rolphe was spread out on the floor. She paused and sniffed at his bloody fingers. She was about to lick one of them when Rolphe pulled back. "No! It's cursed blood, Dantela!"

Dantela leaped backwards and ran for her cat carrier. Rolphe had covered the enclosure with a heavy throw and added a soft blanket to the interior. Dantela frequently used the space for a nap or to hide herself when she got upset. Now, she peered out at Rolphe with wide, blue eyes.

Rolphe slowly rolled over and got to his knees. When he felt stable enough, he crawled over to the cat carrier and locked the door. "Sorry, little one, but you have to stay here while I clean up this mess."

It took him a few minutes before he felt well enough to stand. When he did, he weaved his way to the bathroom. The sink provided something to hold on to as he tried to clear his mind. Later, after he managed to bandage his head, he remained at the sink. The events in the cave began to replay in sequence. He had attacked William. He was just getting down to the business of ripping William's throat out when something interrupted his plans. A shout of protest rang out in the cave. The impact of the sound was so great that the cave shook. After that, something came down on his head. Thankfully, in his massive wolf form, he had a thick skull. On the other hand, the pain was enough to send him reeling back into his human body in the studio.

As he relived the events, he looked in the mirror. He blinked a couple of times at the person looking back. His eyes still had a primitive, animal glint in them. He immediately wanted to return to his dark sanctuary, but a cringing sensation in his gut told him that it was a useless wish.

"But why? Why can't I go back to my cave?" he hissed through clenched teeth. He tried to envision the dark, comforting place where he'd hidden himself. He even tried to visit the refuge again. After several tries, he stepped back in disbelief.

"It's gone! My cave, even the world where it existed, is all gone!" He slowly backed up against a wall and sunk down to the floor. His breath came in gasps of disbelief. The truth came out in a burst of anger. "Arel destroyed it all! He has that much power!"

There was only one bright spot that helped him get past his loss. William's blood had changed since he'd first tasted it. William was young and brash when Rolphe met him. The man's need for answers and power exceeded his common sense. His blood reflected his foolhardy nature. Now, it was comparable to Arel's blood, an intoxicating substance that had Rolphe longing for more. When he thought about the euphoric liquid filling his mouth and his gut, he was sure it would help him forget the fires of hell that waited for him. It would blot out his sins, at least for a little while.

Ten

It had been two days since William's return from the cave. During that time, Raphael had helped to heal his wounds. His hands sustained the worst of his injuries. Wolf teeth were perfect for punishing human flesh and extremities. He sat on the living room sofa and examined each of his fingers, testing its flexibility and wellness. All in all, he felt lucky. He could have died in his unfortunate exploit. He'd made it back alive, but his usual stable constitution was a bit shaken.

"Will?"

William's name, spoken so quietly, made him jerk up. "Arel, finally, good to see you."

Arel nodded and slowly made his way over to a chair. "I wanted to say goodbye."

"Goodbye? But we haven't even had a chance to talk. Michael kept me barred from your room."

Arel looked down, clasping his hands in his lap. "I asked him to keep you away. I needed time to come back to this reality. Later, all my energy went into getting well enough to go home."

"You're going back to Chicago?"

"Yes. My flight leaves later today."

"If you need more time—"

"You're very kind, but I have to get back."

William studied the way Arel took short breaths, the kind elderly people took when they were sick. His skin was ashen. His face was too thin, with hollow cheeks and sunken eyes. "I hope you're better soon."

Arel nodded again. "Thank you for all that you've done. You've pulled me back from the brink. I'm grateful."

"Are you sure about that? I don't mean the grateful part, but the part about being back from death's door. I know you wanted to exit this world."

"You were very brave to do what you did, Will." Arel raised his eyes for a brief moment, then lowered them quickly. "As usual, I was a fool to think I could solve anything. It seems my only function is to make more problems for you."

"That wasn't your intention."

William stated what he knew to be true. He'd gone over Arel's actions and motivations. Arel had never wanted to hurt him, quite the opposite.

Arel started to stand up and couldn't manage it. Michael rushed over. The angel had been standing just outside the room. He took Arel's arm and helped him up.

William wanted to say something and had to stop. It was like some information link between them had been severed. Even the cave incident began to feel dreamlike. He stood up too and held out his hand to Arel.

Arel shook his head. "No, Will. It's better that we avoid all contact from now on. Get on with your life with Annabel. Put all of this behind you. It was just a nightmare." As he spoke, Arel brought his gaze in line with William's. For the first time since Arel came into the room, his eyes came alive. They glowed with kindness, but they were so bright that they seemed totally out of place in Arel's frail body.

After only a moment of staring back, William had to sit down himself. He tried to figure out why he felt so strange. Why couldn't he manage any thought? By the time he could engage his mind again, Arel had already left the room. He was still frowning and confused when Annabel came in to join him. She sat down next to him on the sofa.

"Is something wrong?" she asked. "I purposely stayed in the other room so you could talk to Arel alone."

William shrugged. "I don't know what's going on, but Arel is leaving."

Annabel looked away, eyes forward. She retrieved a tissue from her pocket and blew her nose. "I love him dearly, you know that. But after everything that's happened, maybe it's for the best that he goes home."

William knew Annabel had been frantic after his cave expedition. She'd come into the bedroom and found him lying on the covers with bloody hands and a large bump on his head. Her fears escalated when he remained unconscious for several minutes. Raphael had to escort her out of the room until she could calm down. After that, she did her best to stay in a supportive role, but it was obvious that she continued to fear for his safety.

"Everything is going to be alright," he said in a firm voice.

"Good." Annabel's one-word reply was barely audible.

He glanced over at her and then touched her forehead. "Are you getting a worry line?"

Annabel rubbed her brow. "What's a worry line?"

He put his arm around her shoulders. "It's something that's telling you that you need to relax."

Annabel laid her head against him. "William, do you wish we hadn't fallen in love?"

"What?"

"Do you regret allowing me into your life? Because I never wanted to make things harder for you. I just don't know how to stop this feeling I have."

"What feeling?"

"That I'm another liability. So many times, when I was still an angel, you talked about having to take care of Arel. Now you have me causing you more grief."

"It's two very different situations."

Annabel pulled away from him and sat up. "Are you sure? Because I'll understand if you want me to leave. I don't exactly know what I'll do with myself, but I'm learning to let Raphael and Michael in again. They can help me."

He pulled her back into his arms. "You're not going anywhere. Besides, you're actually doing very well considering what goes on around here."

Annabel smiled weakly. "Really? You think so?"

"Yes, and I'll do everything I can to get things stabilized."

Annabel reached over and carefully lifted his hand to her lips. She kissed each one of his fingers and then held his hand to her breast. "Wings or not, my only desire right now is to protect you. I can't stand the idea that some beast had hold of you."

"I wasn't too crazy about the idea myself. However, Arel did come through in the end. And from what Michael tells me, Arel also took care of Rolphe's little hangout. But that's all behind us now."

"Good, then maybe we can do all the wonderful things you told me about. You called it 'enjoying life to the fullest'."

He sighed. "That's exactly what I plan to do."

Eleven

When Arel got back to Chicago, there were no friendly welcomes or cozy visits with friends. For the first few days, he kept his homecoming a secret. He couldn't let his friends see him looking so weak and pale. By the fourth day, he felt more himself. With Michael's help, he was stronger and getting back some of his energy. He considered himself well enough to come out of hiding.

In the past, his friends insisted that they wanted to be there for him. He'd been surprised by how much their support helped. In his present condition, he probably needed another dose of friendship. With that in mind, he invited the two couples over for a visit. He was pleased when his invitations were quickly accepted. However, everyone chided him for not telling them about his homecoming. It was their way of letting him know that he'd been missed.

On the night of the event, he wondered if he'd been too rash. Michael encouraged him to be open minded, but he didn't know if he could be people-friendly. He'd spent too much time in a cave with a vicious beast to entertain many happy expectations. Plus, his body was still very tired and worn. As he made his way from his bedroom and down the hall, each step forward was an effort. He tried to rally his energy, but it was strangely bound up with what had happened when he'd had to save William from the beastly Rolphe. He leaned against the wall, trying to calm himself as he started to relive the nightmare.

Michael quickly stepped in. "Arel, do you want to go into the living room and wait for your guests there?"

"What?"

51

"Arel, are you okay?" Michael asked in a louder voice.

Arel looked up, trying to bring himself back to the moment. "Sorry, Michael, I got side-tracked again." He took a breath and navigated the last few feet to the hall mirror. He had to use all his willpower to push the nightmare with William away. Staring at his reflection, he hoped he was presentable. "I'm looking better, right?"

Michael smiled. "Yes, you have a bit more color."

"Good, because I don't want Peggy fretting over me. She gets so upset all the time. It's tiresome."

"That's what friends do when they care."

Arel frowned at the ashen image he saw in the mirror. "I told William to leave me alone, but would he listen? No, he almost got himself killed. I keep remembering his screams—"

"But he didn't die. You made sure of that."

"It was too close a call, and you know it. I was my usual self-indulgent self. I was going on about my problems while William was desperately trying to—" Arel leaned forward on the table and gasped. "Anyway, the bottom line is that William is never going to be in that position again."

Michael pointed to the living room. "Try not to think about it now. Your guests will be here soon. While you're relaxing, I'll get the door when they arrive."

Arel nodded and started towards the living room. He'd only gone a few feet when he paused. "That reprobate, Rolphe, is feeling better too. I guess I didn't hit him hard enough."

"You need to conserve your energy instead of constantly monitoring everything Rolphe does. Your body needs to recuperate."

"Really? I might have dropped the ball with Will, but what I told him was the truth. Rolphe is a monster. If I don't keep him in line, who will?"

Before Michael could reply, the doorbell rang.

Arel grimaced. "Inviting friends over was a mistake. They belong in a different world, one that's safe and normal. Maybe you should tell them to go home."

Michael smiled. "You belong in that world, too. You're just tired and getting back on your feet. Things will get better."

Arel laughed and shook his head. "Oh, how I wish that were true."

Peggy walked up to Arel's front door, holding on to Tim's arm. "Don't let me get started, please."

Tim smiled back. "Honey, relax. I said I'd help you get through this, and I will."

Peggy raised her hand to ring the bell and hesitated. "I'm so tired of being the one who's always worrying, especially about Arel. He makes me feel like I'm the biggest buttinsky ever."

Tim pulled her away from the door. "Forget all that. When I come home from work and see you, I know that I'm the luckiest person in the world."

Peggy took a deep breath. "Thank you. I'll try to remember that."

Tim bent down and kissed her forehead. "Right. Now let's have a nice time. We haven't seen Arel for a while. We can catch up on what he and William have been doing."

Peggy nodded and rang the doorbell. "Here goes nothing."

When the door opened, Michael gave them a welcoming smile. "It's so nice to see you both again. Show yourselves into the living room. Arel is waiting for you there."

Peggy stepped into the foyer and paused. Michael had always been so sympathetic when it came to her needs. Without thinking, she grabbed hold of the front of his button-down shirt. "How's Arel doing? Is he feeling better now?"

Michael hesitated. "Yes, but he's still recovering. He was very ill so it's taking time—"

Peggy's fingers tightened on Michael's shirt. "You never said what the problem was. Did he have a bad case of the flu or was it—"

Tim stepped forward and put a hand over Peggy's. "Sweetheart, why don't we say hello to Arel."

Peggy flushed with embarrassment. "Oh my, I'm sorry, Michael." She let go of his shirt and tried to smooth out the wrinkles from her tight, grasping fingers. "I guess I'm just happy he's home."

When Michael smiled again, she hurried towards the living room. She hadn't been in Arel's house for more than thirty seconds, and she'd broken her promise to mind her own business. No matter what, she wouldn't say another word about Arel's health or lack of it.

He was home and had the energy to invite them over. That's all she'd think about. She looked back at Tim, determined to change her ways.

Her resolve hit a wall as soon as she saw Arel. He sat in a recliner, looking frail and deathly pale. Peggy's first thought was that he was one step away from life support. When he looked up at her, she nearly cried out. His normally, striking eyes were vacant and dull. No wonder she'd been worried. The person who had recently traveled to London was gone. She hardly recognized his replacement.

Fortunately, in the strained silence, Tim offered his hand to Arel and made small talk. When it was her turn to say something, all she could manage was, "We missed you."

She turned away after that, hoping Arel didn't see the tears that were welling up. As she took her seat on the sofa, she quickly wiped them away and looked at Tim instead. "Honey, tell Arel about Sara's latest tooth."

Arel interrupted. "You usually bring little Sara over with you. Is she okay?"

Tim smiled. "Yes, she's fine, but we thought it would be better if we got a sitter. Carol and Kevin agreed. They got a sitter too. We all wanted time to catch up on what you've been doing."

"Doing? Not much." Arel looked at Michael. "Right, Michael?"

Michael came over, smiled at Arel and sat down in his chair by the window. "Arel's activities have been hampered by his illness."

Arel nodded but didn't comment.

Tim gave the room a quick inspection. "Where's Carey?"

Michael spoke up when Arel hesitated. "Arel wanted Carey to get away from the weather and have some fun. Since Carey loves the water, Arel found a place in Florida where Carey can take a short course in scuba diving."

"That was nice of you, Arel," Tim said.

Peggy nodded, but she wasn't buying Michael's explanation about Carey. A scuba diving course? Really? Still, she was proud of herself when she offered only a short comment. "Very nice," she said in barely a whisper.

Arel gave her a strange look, as if he wasn't buying her act either. When he spoke, he looked down at the chair arm and fingered the fabric. "And what about you, Peggy, how have you been?"

Peggy clenched her hands together and had to fight back an overwhelming desire to blurt out the truth. She was having one bad dream after another, night after night. They were all centered on Arel and the danger he was in. Now, she had to hide the truth instead of voicing her concerns. She managed a quick lie. "Nothing new here."

The sound of the doorbell saved her from answering any more questions. "That must be Carol and Kevin," she said as she sprinted to the foyer. Her exit was a little too fast, but she couldn't help her response. She was holding in so many emotions that she felt like she'd explode if she had to sit quietly for another second.

On the other hand, she felt a sense of triumph. Arel looked terrible. She was beset with nightmares. In spite of it all, she'd kept her feelings to herself. All of her deep concerns remained safely tucked away in some inner, closeted space. She even managed a smile as she let Carol and Kevin into the foyer. She took their coats and gestured to the living room. "Hi guys, nice to see you. Go on in."

* * *

When Kevin arrived at Arel's house, he was content. Carol had fixed one of his favorite dinners, pot roast and mashed potatoes. He sat down next to her on the sofa, appreciating how her culinary skills kept improving. He was just getting settled when he spied the canapés on the coffee table. He immediately reached out for one. Full or not, who could resist smoked salmon pate or crab squares? "These look great, Arel," he said, looking up at his host. His face flushed. Not only hadn't he taken the time to greet Arel before digging into the food, but when he saw Arel's physical condition, he dropped his canapé. "What the hell happened to you?"

Carol sat up straighter and joined in. "Have we come at a bad time?"

Kevin pulled back from the food and crossed his arms. His gaze traveled over Arel's body in another quick sweep. "Arel, old buddy, you look like you're waiting for the undertaker."

As soon as he made the comment, he felt a tug on his sleeve. Peggy, who sat on his other side, gave him a polite smile. "It's none of our business," she said quietly.

Kevin returned a look of surprise. Peggy's entire world consisted of other people's business. "Sis, he looks bad, admit it."

Peggy leaned into Tim's shoulder. "Still, we have to respect Arel's privacy. Isn't that right, Tim?"

Tim nodded. "Yes, that's right."

Kevin frowned back. He didn't know what was going on, but both Peggy and Tim were acting very strange. "But sis, aren't you—"

Peggy glared back. "Kevin please, eat your cracker."

Kevin snapped his jaws shut, not knowing what else to do. He was known for blurting out his views without thinking. Maybe, in this case, he'd keep silent for the moment. But as the evening dragged on and everybody discounted the obvious, that Arel looked horrible, his curiosity and concern mounted.

Later, when he and Carol returned home, he needed some answers. After they took care of the sitter and got ready for bed, he turned to Carol for help. "I don't understand the rest of you. How could all of you ignore Arel's condition? Don't you care about him?"

Carol sighed. "Of course, I care."

"You didn't act like it when we were visiting. You barely said anything to him. You and Peggy kept looking at each other and acting like a couple of mummies."

"It's because Peggy begged me to help her. She's desperate."

"Help her do what?"

"Peggy doesn't want to interfere in other people's lives anymore. She made Tim and I promise to support her. Maybe she's right. Arel does seem to resent people who question his need for privacy."

"It's one thing to be a busy body. It's another thing to ignore a friend in trouble."

"I'm not trying to ignore Arel. I'm trying to respect what other people want. In Peggy's case, she needs to feel like she's not some crazy person who's always quizzing people because she's worried."

"I know Peggy. She needs to vent. If she doesn't express herself, she could blow sky high."

Carol smiled. "Don't exaggerate."

Kevin crossed his arms. "You don't know what you're dealing with, but as her brother, I do."

"What do you mean?"

Kevin let out a huff and climbed into bed. "Never mind. Maybe I'm wrong. But, Carol, I swear if I'm not wrong, when Peggy loses it, she's going to be in worse shape than ever."

"And what about Arel? What do you think we should do?"

"I'll call him tomorrow and see what's going on."

* * *

Arel used the wall for support as he slowly made his way down the hall to his bedroom. "Lock up, Michael. We can take care of the dishes in the morning."

Michael turned the lock on the door. "Are you sure? There are just a few glasses and some plates to put in the dishwasher."

"That can wait."

"Is there something you need?" Michael asked.

Arel paused. "I just want you to know that I'm staying out of people's heads, except for Rolphe's."

"I see."

"Yes, but I wonder what's going on with everybody. Did you notice how quiet Peggy was and how she corrected Kevin? He was concerned about me, and she shut him down a couple of times."

"I agree. Peggy was acting out of character."

"I thought she would be the first one to voice her opinion about my condition. Doesn't she care about me anymore?"

Michael smiled. "I'm sure she does."

"She doesn't act like it. Kevin was right. I look like the grim reaper missed a pickup."

"Peggy did what you've been asking her to do for a long time."

"Ignore me?"

"I thought that's what you wanted, to have time to yourself. Isn't that why you sent Carey away? You didn't want him around while you were recovering."

"Of course I didn't want him around. He looks up to me. I'm supposed to be a father figure. But I can't be there for him. I'm too toxic. Everything I touch turns to crap. I don't want to wreck his young, impressionable mind." He hesitated and looked away. "It's just that it would be nice to know that my other friends are there for me. They didn't even bring over the babies. What's that about?"

"Tim explained that the babies can be a distraction. They wanted time to catch up."

"Catch up? Tim asked what I've been doing. After that, not one of them seemed interested. They talked around me like I wasn't there. What a great evening!"

"Arel, you're getting yourself upset."

"And why shouldn't I be? If one of them was sick or unhappy, I'd find out why. I'd dig a little deeper."

"But—"

"I don't want any 'buts,' Michael. I nearly killed my one, true friend, the brother who does care. So I'm staying away from him. But I thought the rest of the people in my life would be there to welcome me back. Now I see how wrong I was. The whole lot has demonstrated where they stand. They're pulling away. They've found more important things to do with their lives than be bothered by a loser like me."

"A loser?"

"Yes, look at me. Every time I come back from a trip, I've got some problem. Then there was that whole episode when William was here. Peggy and Carol made it clear that I wasn't wanted."

"I thought you got that straightened out. It was a misunderstanding."

"All that I know is that they're pushing me away. But that's fine. Let them do whatever. I have to deal with more important issues."

"You mean Rolphe?"

"Of course."

"Arel, as I told you earlier, your body can't heal if you continue doing what you're doing."

"What choice do I have? As Rolphe recovers from that little blow I gave him, he's become fixated on William. He wants Will's blood. Maybe if I can convince him that it's a useless quest, he'll drop it. Maybe your blood will do what it's supposed to do and purge him of his viciousness."

"Arel, you know it's more complicated than that. Rolphe has to want to change. Otherwise, my blood can't help him. Right now, it's intensifying his emotions."

"Well then, Michael, you better pray that I can keep him in line."

"I understand the situation. But I'm very concerned. You're not just monitoring Rolphe. You've been doing a lot of out-of-body travel. You're exhausting yourself. Your physical vessel is getting weaker by the day. It won't hold out much longer."

"Dammit, Michael! Why can't you stop criticizing me?"

"I'm sorry."

Arel glanced at the angel with softer, contrite eyes. "Oh hell, listen to me. I'm taking my anger out on you. But I'm the person who gave Rolphe your blood. His sins, and that's the way he views his evil deeds, are on my head. Whatever he does to harm another will be my fault. So I'll never stop what I'm doing. I'll fight the man to my last breath before I let him get to William again."

"The way your health is declining, that day could come sooner than later."

Arel straightened up and started down the hall again. "So I'll have to think of something more drastic, won't I?"

Twelve

Rolphe's dream began as an intoxicating fantasy. He was feasting on William's blood. After getting a taste of it in the cave, he salivated every time he remembered how even a little had soothed some of his pain. His stomach ached for more, and his thirst grew every minute that he was denied. In the dream, he was able to satisfy his voracious hunger. As William's blood bubbled from an artery, Rolphe filled himself. He took in great, gluttonous quantities. The rapturous experience blotted out all his fear. He was lifted to a place where he was beyond reproach and blame.

He was so absorbed in his bounty that he failed to notice that an intruder had entered the dreamscape. When he saw Arel, the man was already upon him, grabbing hold of Rolphe's shirt and flinging him across the room as easily as dispatching a puppy from a food dish.

Rolphe woke up as soon as he slammed against a wall. The pain in his head was overwhelming. He'd been badly hurt in his dream. And like the cave incident, it affected him physically in the real world.

His head was feeling better after his first encounter with Arel. Now, it suffered from another terrible pounding. He had to remain very still on his sofa, not daring to move for fear of more blinding pain. But inside, his rage was bubbling up like William's blood. What Arel was doing wasn't fair. "He has no right to punish me when I'm dreaming," he hissed.

"Oh, but I do," a voice called out.

In spite of the pain, Rolphe made himself sit up. He held his head as his eyes darted about the room. His gaze steadied when he saw a ghostly form. It appeared across from him, sitting calmly on a chair. Its features slowly came into view. "Arel! Again!"

Arel was like some watchdog from Hades. He was always around, even when Rolphe dozed off. Most people wouldn't have been aware of him, but Rolphe had a gift. He could see what normal people missed. He took the opportunity to tell the man what he thought. "You don't have the right to punish me! You're not God!"

Arel smiled. "That's right, but you're going to meet your maker very soon if I have any say in the matter."

Rolphe glowered back for only an instant before he looked away. Arel was right. Hell was waiting for him. "You know, the first time I saw you in London, I thought you were the most beautiful being I'd ever laid eyes on. If you had told me that you were one of God's messengers, I would have believed it. Now, I keep asking myself, how did I err so completely? You have no compassion or kindness, only hatred and punishment."

"Because you're evil, Rolphe. You cling to your evil ways. You refuse to change."

"I can't! I've been this way for too long. I don't know anything else!"

Arel's eyes narrowed, becoming golden slits of wrath. "Then don't expect any kindness on my part. And I'm warning you, leave William out of your sordid thoughts and despicable dreams. Is that clear?"

Before Rolphe had a chance to answer, Arel's form faded and was gone. But his absence made Rolphe wonder about Arel's threat. Why was Arel so intent on protecting William? Why was the man with the delicious blood so important to him? When someone worried about another, it was a weakness that might be exploited. Rolphe began to feel better in spite of his painful head. He was going to find a way to exploit that weakness.

* * *

Annabel sat on the sofa and studied the ball of yarn in her lap. Michael had advised her to find a hobby. It would help take her mind off her fears. She decided to try knitting. She ran her fingers over the fuzzy, blue wool, then took a quick peek at William. He sat on the other end of the sofa, supposedly reading his book. It was hard to keep her mind on counting stitches when he looked so troubled. Arel and Michael had returned to Chicago, but William acted as if they hadn't taken all their problems with them. He was often preoccupied and distant.

Annabel had different ideas about what William should be doing. When she visited the nearby park, she saw people laughing and having a nice time. They strolled by, arm in arm, enjoying the day. She wondered when she and William would stroll in the park. Would there ever come a time when the two of them were free to enjoy their lives too? Or would William be pulled back into another life-threatening situation? The thought made her snatch up the knitting needles.

"Are you enjoying your new past time?" William asked.

"I'm not sure." She found the long, metal knitting rods difficult to handle. Keeping them at the proper angle was almost impossible. "Maybe I should have tried crocheting."

William put his book aside and came over. He sat down and gave her an understanding smile. "I once knew someone who was an expert at knitting. I think this is the right way," he said as he repositioned the needles in her hands.

Annabel frowned and sat back. "Who was this expert? Someone I might know?"

William smiled as he went back to his seat and began to read again. "Nobody you know. It was just a person from my youth. She was a servant who worked in my father's house."

"Oh, I see. Was she an older servant?"

William turned a page and paused. His eyes softened as if he'd just seen a beautiful flower. "Actually, she was rather young and quite attractive."

"Really?" Annabel tried to put the point of her knitting needle through a tight loop of yarn on the other needle. The yarn resisted, and the needle slipped. She couldn't manage her task. She was too distracted by a new feeling she was having. It was one of extreme annoyance when William mentioned another woman.

William gave her a quick glance and laughed. "I've never seen that look on you before, but I've seen it on other women I've known."

Annabel put her knitting aside and crossed her arms. "So now I'm like other women? I thought you said I was special."

"Oh my, you've been visited by the green-eyed monster."

Annabel sat up straighter. "The what?"

"Sorry Annabel, but you're jealous."

Annabel uncrossed her arms, her brows deep in furrows. Was William right? As an angel, she'd observed women who kept a very close eye on their partner. They watched for any sign that their man was straying. It was an obnoxious vice when she viewed it from her human standpoint. She stood up and stared at William. "That's it! I refuse to sit here day in and day out, getting more and more dependent on you."

William stood up too, came over and put his hands on her shoulders. "Try not to get yourself upset."

"I'm disappointed in myself."

"You're doing very well."

"You really believe that?"

"Yes."

She took a deep breath. Besides suggesting a hobby, Michael had also told her that she couldn't hurry the integration process. Going from angel to human could take quite a while. In the meantime, she had to concentrate on maintaining as much patience as possible.

She tried to smile and changed the subject. "I have a request? Is it alright to give the three control mice to a nice lady I met?"

William stood back. "Control mice?"

"Yes, don't you remember? They're the three extra mice I purchased to use in your experiment. You wanted to know about your power to effect—"

"Oh, that. It seems like a thousand years ago."

Annabel studied his face and how his eyes went distant. "I remember your instructions perfectly. 'No one is to touch the control mice.' That's what you told Arel and me. Your voice was very stern when you explained how we had to adhere to the rules you'd set up. You were determined to understand and measure your abilities."

William came back to himself and laughed. "What was I thinking? Control mice? Measuring our abilities? With the power we're dealing with?"

"But we all enjoyed interacting with the mice."

"Maybe, but the only thing that came out of it was that Wolfie ate that poison and nearly died."

Annabel didn't want to think about almost losing the adorable little mouse. "Anyway, when I was at the pet shop, this lady said she was looking for some mice for her two boys. The store is temporarily out of them, and she was delighted when I told her about our situation."

"No baby mice? There must be too many pet snakes to feed."

"William, please."

"Sorry, but that's the way life is, Annabel. It's no use ignoring facts."

Annabel took another breath. "William, I love all six of our mice, but with everything that's happened—" She paused again. "It'll be easier to take care of just three. With the other three, well, I think they'll have a better home with the little boys."

"Good, anything we can do to make life simpler is welcome at this stage."

"What stage are you talking about?"

William hesitated. "Nothing is settled with Arel. In fact, his health is declining again."

"How do you know that? I thought he asked that you sever all ties."

William avoided looking at her and went quiet.

She knew what his silence indicated. It was easy for William to tap into Arel's thoughts and vice versa.

William glanced up with a frown. "Do you know why he's in the shape that he's in? He's terrified, Annabel."

"What are you talking about?"

"He's trying to deal with Rolphe."

"I thought that was all settled. Arel took care of him."

William began to rub one of the many scars on his hand. "He delivered a blow, yes, but Rolphe won't be stopped that easily."

Annabel respected William's concern about Arel, but that didn't lessen her fears. What if William got involved in something dangerous again? Fortunately, she stopped herself from saying the wrong thing. "I'm sorry the situation is so difficult."

When William didn't comment, she shifted the conversation to another topic that needed discussing. She'd put off her questions long enough. "William?"

64

"Yes?"

"Why haven't you wanted . . . I mean, what's keeping you from—" Annabel felt her mouth go dry. Angels didn't have personal agendas. It was easy to be open and communicative. Without that mindset, she faltered.

"What is it? Talk to me."

She glanced at his pale, blue eyes and back at the rug. "Remember when you kissed me? Why don't you kiss me anymore? Why haven't you invited me into your bed? Are your actions part of some human ritual I don't know about? Are we supposed to wait before we engage in—"

William clasped her hands and held them securely between his own. "Believe me, I want all those things. But I don't want to rush you. You were an angel for a long time. When we make love, I want it to be special, very special. Right now, I'm too scattered to love you the way you should be loved. I have to figure out what to do about this situation with Arel and Rolphe."

"Please, William, let Arel handle it."

"He can't. He's giving it everything he has, and it's killing him. All because he's trying to protect me."

"Is Rolphe still a threat to you?"

"Rolphe is not a nice guy."

"And if Arel dies, what then?"

William's eyes sparked with defiance. "I won't let that happen."

"But if you couldn't prevent it, will Rolphe come after you?"

"If he does, it won't be like it was in the cave. I'm learning to use more of my power."

Annabel stepped back and sighed. Day by day, she could feel herself settling deeper into her body. It was a dense, heavy feeling. Just the idea of handling her constant emotional upheavals was like a baby lifting weights. "I'm so incapable when it comes to doing anything useful. As your angel, I was supposed to help you, but I selfishly abandoned my job."

William smiled. "It's okay. I have Raphael in my corner. We both know he'll be there for me."

"Yes, Raphael—"

William grabbed her hand and pulled her toward the hall. "Let's visit the mice. You told me that petting them relieves stress."

Annabel let him lead her towards the stairs. William was right. Maybe she needed to lighten up a little. "I found some new treats. The little guys are getting very spoiled, but maybe they'll like them."

"If they don't, I'll remind them about how lucky they are. They could have ended up being snake dinners."

Annabel knew William was just trying to tease her with such remarks, but she couldn't stop herself from thinking the worst. William had almost ended up being Rolphe's dinner. She'd have to talk to Raphael and make sure the angel was clear about what his duties entailed. Grilling an angel was a ridiculous idea, but as a frightened human, she felt like ridiculous ideas were becoming the norm.

Thirteen

After his return from another astral trip to Rolphe's world, Arel settled back into his physical body without too much effort. It was getting to be a familiar routine. Unfortunately, he made the mistake of moving too quickly and paid the price. His arm exploded in pain. The bullet wound had started to heal while he was in London. It was feeling much better until his recent encounters with Rolphe. With all the negativity they shared, his injured arm and what it represented started to fester and burn all over again.

Arel grimaced when a fresh trickle of blood soaked through the bandage. He grabbed a towel and tried to be careful as he wrapped his arm, but every movement was agonizing. Only the thought of keeping Rolphe in line shifted his focus away from the physical pain.

His frown deepened when he thought about the impact he was having on the man. No matter how much Arel punished Rolphe, he couldn't force his tough adversary into submission. Yet every battle, even if victorious, took tremendous energy. After more than a week, Arel's reserves were running on empty. His breath was shallow and quick. He was barely able to move from where he sat. He didn't dare take to his bed. He'd never have the energy to get up again.

He tried to clear his thoughts and let out a wheezing breath. What would happen if he was too weak to continue? The idea made his rage flare and fester like his arm. His emotional storm was interrupted when Michael stepped into the room. He gave the angel a brief glance. "What is it?"

"Peggy is here to see you."

Arel slumped deeper into his chair. He had no time or energy for his neighbor's intrusions. "Tell her . . . I can't see her."

He'd barely issued the order when Michael was pushed aside by a very petite person. When the redhead stepped forward and trained her eyes in his direction, Arel shrank back. His visitor had the fiercest frown that he'd ever seen on a woman.

But he was becoming an expert at reading minds. Behind Peggy's anger, there was a tremendous current of hurt and bewilderment. It was obvious that no matter how she'd acted during her visit the week before, she cared about their relationship.

* * *

The distance between Peggy and Tim's two-story residence and Arel's rancher could be measured in feet. But the emotional distance between Peggy and Arel was something that Peggy defined in more graphic terms. Arel was being a selfish isolationist who didn't communicate with or even care about her or her concerns. After all the love and attention she'd extended to him, he continued to act as if she didn't exist. No, there was more to it than that. Arel had invited Peggy and Tim over one time since his return from London. After that, he'd refused Peggy's calls and shut her out of his life completely.

Peggy had stuck to her guns. She would not interfere in Arel's life ever again. But that promise only lasted a few days. She started to crumble after that. Her inability to stay committed to her objective came from her constant nightmares and waking up every morning feeling exhausted. How could she forget about Arel when her dreams were telling her that he was in trouble, life-threatening trouble?

The repetitive nightmares reminded her of the early days, when she'd just met Arel. That's when her dreams about Arel's safety started. And she'd been right to worry. Arel almost died before he accepted her help. But he hadn't always been like that. In a past lifetime that they had shared, Arel had been Peggy's biggest supporter, a brother who was willing to give his life to save her.

This time around, Peggy had wanted to be just as loving and supportive of Arel. But the man resented the help she offered. She'd made allowances for his behavior for a long time. She knew he'd suffered horribly in that past life they shared. By being a loving brother, he'd been put to death in a most ghastly way.

But, this was another time and another life. Peggy's patience only went so far. She was too tired and worn to approach Arel with an understanding attitude. In fact, as she marched up the front steps to his porch, she decided to sever their relationship. Arel gave her no choice. If he always insisted on pushing her away, she had to accept it. But she couldn't do it quietly. She could barely contain the emotional tempest that was swirling inside her brain. Her bruised and battered feelings needed expression. She was going to let Arel know what an ignorant cad he could be.

She had hardly knocked on Arel's door when Michael opened it. When she insisted on seeing Arel, he didn't offer any objections. He asked her to follow him to the lower level. She was surprised. Michael was a wonderful person who always had time for her, but he usually made excuses for Arel. This time he seemed eager for her to reach her objective. He wasted no time in quickly traversing the stairs and going directly to the lower level living room. Without hesitation, he announced Peggy's presence to the thin man who sat in the library area.

Peggy was grateful that Michael was so obliging, but his mannerly conduct didn't stop her from pushing him aside and glaring at Arel. She was about to unload all her frustrations on him when she stopped herself and forgot everything she'd come to say.

"Oh my heavens, you poor thing!" she cried as she ran over to where Arel sat. He was skeleton thin again, a bundle of bones with a bloody towel wrapped around his arm. "We've got to get you to the hospital!"

Arel shook his head. "It won't help." His voice was barely a whisper as he tried to catch his breath.

Before she could say anything more, Arel reached out slowly and touched her face. The effort was too much for him. His limp hand dropped to his lap, but he did get out a few words of apology. "I'm sorry . . . so sorry for everything."

Peggy immediately snatched up his hand and held it close. In the space of a moment, she knew Arel was right about medical help. Deep in her bones, she knew something beyond the physical was destroying the man in front of her. "You're not alone, sweetie. Somehow, Kevin, Carol, Tim and I are going to find a way to help you, just like before. Remember?"

Arel tried to smile. "I wish you could, but—" He paused and shut his eyes. His chest wheezed every time he took a breath.

Peggy looked back at Michael. "Please, help me get him into bed. Then tell me what's going on."

* * *

Rolphe glanced around at his living room. Could it be true? Could Arel be gone? He shut his eyes and used his psychic senses to explore the space. For the first time since his cave had been destroyed, his head felt clear of interference. He walked over to the chair where he'd often glimpsed Arel's ghostly form. The man would sit there for hours in his wispy body, watching. But he wasn't there now. After a quick search of all his other rooms, Rolphe knew his home was Arel-free.

He let out a relieved sigh and looked at Dantela. The kitten was on her pillow, cleaning a paw. Ever since Rolphe had returned from London, Dantela usually kept her distance. Now, she stared back and let out a quiet meow. Rolphe walked over to where she lay and scooped her up. He held her high above his head and did a little dance of triumph, ignoring his headache.

"Dantela! I'm free! That bully has left! I'm sure of it!"

Dantela mewed again as she looked down at him. She'd never been afraid of Rolphe's happy moods. It was his unexpected, angry outbursts that sent her running for her cat carrier. Rolphe lowered her to his chest and carefully ran his hand over her soft, fragile body. "I'm sorry if I've frightened you. I haven't been myself for a while, but that's going to change if Arel doesn't return."

He replaced the kitten on her pillow and began to pace. He didn't know if his good fortune was temporary or permanent, but he was confident that he could find out. If he turned the tables on Arel, he might be able to learn why Arel had left. He went to a cabinet and got out his incense and a candle. The items often helped him to get into a meditative state. With Arel around, his mind had been too frazzled to relax enough to use his powers properly. Now he had a chance to check out Arel's whereabouts.

He had to sit for several minutes, letting the candle flame sooth his mind. When he managed a tranquil state, he searched out his foe.

When he connected with Arel's energy, a relieved smile crept across his face. Arel wasn't only gone, the man was gravely ill. His power was failing.

The thought was so exciting that Rolphe couldn't help but celebrate. "Oh, what a glorious day this is, Dantela. Soon I won't just be dreaming of a feast, I'll be dining on William's blood. And Arel won't be able to lift a finger to stop me." He paused savoring the moment and the thought a meal that he'd soon be enjoying. His moment of victory shifted slightly. "But before that happens, I'll give Arel a taste of what it feels like to be tortured day and night."

Fourteen

William put his phone on the table and walked over to his recliner. He'd never heard Carol sound so upset. She'd practically pleaded with him to return to Chicago. Then Peggy got hold of the phone. Her method of communication was more direct. There was no pleading. She had simply informed William of his duty to come to Arel's rescue. The man was barely lucid most of the time.

As William considered his options, Annabel came over to stand next to him. She'd listened in on his conversation with Carol and Peggy. She was doing the hands-clasped-tight-around-herself again. It was becoming a habit whenever she got upset. "Try to relax," he whispered, hoping to calm her.

His advice seemed to have the opposite effect. Her grasping fingers tightened on her arms. "William, go to Chicago if you're needed, but please don't get mixed up with Rolphe! Arel brought this on himself."

Instead of addressing Annabel's comments, William remained still and mute. He couldn't let himself be swayed by anyone's emotions. Carol, Peggy and Annabel didn't know what Arel was dealing with. William had a very good idea about what was going on, but he had to tread carefully or he'd end up like Arel. "If it will ease your mind, I'll talk to Raphael about the situation."

"Good, at least you're not stubborn like Arel. You don't try to fix everything yourself."

William turned and stared at her with probing eyes. "You don't have much respect for Arel, do you?"

Annabel backed up. "I care about him, but maybe you're right. I think he's made a lot of foolish mistakes."

"Is that the angel in you talking or the human?"

Annabel blushed. "When I was an angel, I never judged Arel, but when I look at him now—"

"You're letting your fear get the better of you."

"Maybe I am, but—" Annabel turned away. "I can't help what I'm feeling."

"You've spent eons as an angel. And now, after all that time you're telling me to do what, let fear be my guiding light?"

Annabel returned the briefest glance. "Maybe it sounds pathetic, but you need to protect yourself from this mess Arel has gotten into. Otherwise—"

"Is that all you care about, Annabel? My safety?"

"I'm sorry, but the answer is 'yes.'"

William looked away too. "I guess I should be grateful that you're still honest, but you don't inspire any confidence when it comes to the angelic side of things."

"What do you mean?"

"Maybe Arel was right. He was beginning to think that angels aren't the best advisers after all. Obviously they live in an entirely different world than humans."

Annabel faced him again. "You can't judge them so critically just because I used to be one."

"Why not? If you can judge Arel, then I can judge your old buddies."

"Please, William, don't be like that. I'm the only weak one. Michael and Raphael would never give in to fear, even if they took off their wings."

"You don't know that. I was becoming a believer, but after listening to you, I think I've given angels too much credit."

"You're saying that because you're upset."

William sat down in the recliner. "Maybe, but I know that your appraisal of Arel is offensive. He was there for me when I was in pain. He was willing to damn his soul to help me. For a guy who's so foolish, I think he did a pretty good job at being a friend."

Annabel glared back. "Then he almost let Rolphe kill you in the cave! That's not what I call a friend."

"Give him a break. He's been fighting night and day to keep me safe ever since."

"But he's the one who gave Rolphe his blood to begin with, William! He's the one who got this mess started!"

"No! I was the fool who contacted Rolphe. I was the one who got Rolphe gunning for both of us. If it weren't for Arel, Rolphe might have murdered me and you in our beds! Think about that before you want me to abandon Arel."

Annabel took a ragged breath. "You're right. I'm sorry. I'm sorry for everything, especially for being so critical. I just get so scared that something is going to happen to you."

William got up and went over to her. He pulled her into his arms. When he held her close, he felt her heart racing. "I'm sorry too. I know that you're doing your best. Being a human is a drastic change for you."

"Maybe I wasn't such a great angel either." Annabel looked up and frowned again. "Angels don't get involved personally. I failed as an angel, and now I'm failing as a human being."

William laughed and squeezed her tighter. "Don't underestimate yourself. I think both Arel and I are different than most. We're quite a challenge for any angel. Just ask Michael. As for being a human being, you were thrown into very deep water when you took off your wings. Unfortunately, those waters might get even deeper and a lot rougher."

Annabel pushed him back and put her hands on her hips. "Listen, William, I know you have to do what you have to do, but you better come out of this in one piece or—"

William studied the woman he'd chosen to love after a lifetime of being alone. She suddenly looked much more spirited, and he liked the way her face lit up when she threatened him. "Or what?"

"Or you'll find out that Arel isn't the only one who can follow people into the afterlife. Is that clear?"

William grinned and gave her a small salute. "Yes, ma'am."

* * *

After Annabel left to do some shopping, William sat in his downstairs recliner. He needed to think, to use the quiet to figure out his best course of action.

"Do you still want a cowardly angel's advice?" Raphael asked as he stood at the base of the stairs.

William looked up and saw that his visitor was smiling. "I never accused you of cowardice. I simply wondered about angelic reliability. When it comes to understanding human dilemmas, what does your kind know?"

Raphael's face shone even brighter. "We do have an advantage. Our minds aren't muddled by emotions. And we can see the bigger picture."

"After talking to Annabel, I wonder. She was an angel. Now, she's one of the most frightened people I've known."

Raphael walked over to the mouse cage and peered in. "Would it be okay if I pet them?"

William shrugged. "Whatever, but don't give them any treats. They're getting too fat."

Raphael's smile broadened as he unlocked the cage door and carefully lowered his hand to the cage floor. The big, white mouse named Squeaky continued to run on a wheel. The other two mice scampered over. They both jumped into his hand at the same time. Raphael looked over at William as if he was unsure about how to proceed. "Is it okay to take both of them out?"

William got up and joined Raphael. "They're feeling frisky today. I'll take Wolfie, and you can hold Arel's mouse, Whiskers. He's the tan and white one."

Raphael withdrew his hand with both mice still clinging to it and let William take the brown one. "I'm happy to see that Whiskers is better."

William had his hand cupped over Wolfie as he returned to his recliner. "The poor little bugger was affected by Arel's energy when he was staying here. Happily, now that Arel is gone, Whiskers is back to his old self again."

Raphael sat down on the sofa. "About Annabel, I don't think you've been fully informed about her background."

William glanced up. "She was an angel. What more is there to know?"

"Well, that's a little like labeling you as simply being a human. But there's more to who you are than that. It's the same with angels. We're each individuals with a history of experiences. In Annabel's case, she doesn't have a long history when it comes to interacting with people. When Michael invited her to help you, she was rather new to her role in some respects."

"I don't think I understand what you're saying."

"Don't get me wrong. Annabel's very wise and quick to adapt. She also knows all about your world. You could say that she has her Ph.D. in human observation. But in actual practice, she never delved deeply into experiencing the negative aspects of humanity. Michael believed she'd be able to bring a fresh perspective to your situation, especially since you have angelic blood."

William frowned. "So you're saying I was assigned a naïve angel?"

Raphael didn't hesitate. "Annabel was a very exquisite angel, but Michael never expected the two of you to fall in love."

William's frown softened. "Michael didn't expect me to be so charming. I suppose Annabel couldn't resist me."

Raphael laughed. "It's more than charm, William. Someday, perhaps you'll understand more about who you are. Perhaps you'll understand more about Arel's true nature too."

"Yes, Arel, for a moment I almost forgot about the mess he's in."

"Michael and I will help in any way that we can."

William let out a heavy sigh and slowly ran a finger over Wolfie's small head. As he did, the mouse went from being feisty and searching for hidden treats to almost instant relaxation. Within a few seconds, his eyes began to close.

Raphael seemed to have a similar effect on Whiskers. The small mouse curled up in his hand and began to doze.

William finally spoke up. "It looks like I'm going to do some traveling."

Raphael stared back expectantly. "You're not going to Chicago, are you? You're going to Paris."

"Maybe, but you can't tell Annabel. Is that clear? She's scared enough already."

"William, are you sure? Confronting Rolphe in person could be more dangerous than your last adventure to the cave."

"Arel had his shields up that time, and Michael couldn't help. That won't be the case with Rolphe. You can come along, right?"

"Yes, but—"

"I don't want to hear any buts, Raphael. I want to put a stop to Rolphe's scheming. I want to make sure he stops dreaming about my blood, once and for all."

"William, I'm sorry, but I can't interfere if you decide to fight Rolphe."

"What if Rolphe attacks me?"

"I'll do everything I can to protect your life."

Before William could respond, his phone chirped. He stood up, put Wolfie back in his cage, and retrieved his phone. "Well, speak of the devil, Rolphe has sent me a message."

Raphael returned Whiskers to the cage too. "Do you want to tell me what he wants?"

William handed the phone to the angel. "He wants to meet with me."

Raphael stared at the text message. "Before you agree to meet him, I suggest you and I work on getting you ready."

"I agree. Let's get started."

Fifteen

When Rolphe passed by a hall mirror, he grimaced. His acute frustration was showing. His normally heavy, dark features looked even more severe. Not only did he have a morbid expression, he looked thinner. His hair had more gray and his body ached. "Arel's put me through hell. Now, the blackguard is hiding."

When Rolphe used his psychic gift to search out Arel, he'd assumed it was his turn to punish and brutalize. That was a short-lived dream. Arel wasn't as powerless as Rolphe had first thought. No matter how hard he tried, whenever Rolphe attempted to enter Arel's world, he didn't get very far. Arel knew how to shield himself. Trying to break through one of the man's energy barriers was like breaking into a bank vault.

Rolphe didn't give up easily. In one session, he was sweating profusely and screaming out obscenities before he decided to back off. The best he could do was prowl the exterior walls, looking for a weak spot in Arel's defenses. Unfortunately, Arel's fortifications were solid and unyielding.

Rolphe sought solace in his studio. He sat down and studied a blank canvas on his easel. If only he could paint, it would help. He could get some of his resentment out. He even envisioned loading up a paint roller with black paint and having a go at the entire room. At least he'd give his mood expression. It took time and patience for his more practical side to kick in. He had to retreat enough to come up with a new plan. It was obvious that if he was going to defeat Arel, he'd have to learn to play by his rules. "Or maybe I can bypass Arel and go for what he values most."

In the agonizing time that Arel had haunted and penalized him, Rolphe had learned quite a bit about Arel and his relationship with William. Arel thought of William as a brother. Arel even put William's life above his own. If Rolphe really wanted to punish Arel, he had to take out William. And since Rolphe already fantasized about the idea of sucking William dry, killing him would be a double pleasure.

The thought was enough to ease the tension in Rolphe's brow. He looked over at Dantela with understanding eyes. The kitten was in her cat carrier again, still hiding from the anger and rage that had poured out of Rolphe earlier. He'd gone on a rampage when he discovered that he couldn't get to Arel. But that kind of behavior had to stop. If he was going to carry out the plan that he was formulating, he'd have to keep his emotions in check. All his energy would have to go into a new way of conducting himself, one that involved Arel's potent tools, energy shields.

Rolphe stood up and walked over to the cat carrier. Getting down on all fours, he reached in and scooped up Dantela. He held her close to his face and rubbed her fur against his cheek. When he spoke to her, he made sure to keep his voice low and calm. "Don't worry, it'll be over soon, my little feline friend. Arel is already licking his wounds. Finding out that William is dead will finish him off. Then things will go back to normal. You won't have to be scared anymore. I'll even take you over to Myra's place. You know how much she loves you. We'll have a celebration. What do you think about that?"

Dantela relaxed a little and let out a soft meow.

Rolphe bent down and returned the kitten to the cat carrier. "In the meantime, I'll figure out how to trick William into letting his guard down."

* * *

Arel kept trying to fight his way out of a fog. It was so dense, he couldn't see in front of him. He couldn't think. His mind kept slipping, unable to grab hold of where he was. The only thing he had going was his shields. He had to protect himself. It was the one fact he could retain with some degree of clarity. He tried to understand what he was up against, but any answers were as elusive as the fog. Yet, it was clear that something was lurking just beyond the barriers he'd erected. Whatever or whoever it was, wanted him dead.

If that wasn't bad enough, another fear wouldn't go away. Like nails scraping his blank, chalkboard mind, it was a painful feeling. But more than that, he felt compelled to take action. Someone else was in danger, life-threatening danger. Yet, no matter how hard he tried to find out who it was, he couldn't remember a name or a face. As he searched over and over for a clue, he felt himself getting weaker. If he didn't stop and conserve his energy, he wouldn't be able to maintain his shields. He had to forget everything and focus all his strength on staying alive.

* * *

Peggy refused to leave Arel's bedside. She couldn't. If her link to Arel was broken, he wouldn't survive. She was sure of it.

"Peggy, please, listen to me, go home," Carol pleaded. "You've been here for ten hours straight. You have to get some rest. I'll stay with Arel. Plus Michael is here."

Peggy had heard the same advice from Tim and Kevin. But she had to ignore them all. "I won't desert him, Carol," she countered. Her reply was purposefully defiant, but she couldn't completely keep a note of weariness from spoiling its impact. When she'd started her vigil she was already exhausted. Now, her usually bright, brown eyes were red with fatigue.

Carol scowled back. "I'll go make you some tea. While I'm gone, maybe Michael can talk some sense into you."

Michael sat on the other side of Arel's bed. He smiled at Peggy after Carol left the room. "She's right. Please rest for a little while. I'll keep watch. I promise."

Peggy frowned back. "You've been here as long as I have. Shouldn't you take a break?"

Michael shrugged. "I don't need much sleep. I'm fine."

Peggy studied Michael's unlined face. "I have to admit, you look okay. But that's not the point. I can feel how weak Arel is. It's almost like we have a lifeline between us. If I leave, I'm afraid he won't make it back to us."

"You have to have faith in him," Michael whispered. "That's the best thing you can do if you want him to rally."

"I don't understand."

"Put yourself in his place. If you were ailing, wouldn't you want the people around you to see you as strong and capable? Wouldn't you want them to believe you could find your way back to wellness?"

"But I've had so many nightmares. In all of them, Arel is up against some terrible ogre. Maybe he isn't strong enough."

"Is that what you really believe about Arel? Haven't you seen how capable he can be?"

Peggy remembered Michael when she'd met him. He'd been Arel's friend and guardian, helping him back from ill-health and severe depression. "You've never stopped believing in him.

Michael smiled again. "Never, not for an instant."

"Are you sure I shouldn't stay? If I leave and something happens to—"

"Arel knows you're there for him. Now, he has to use his own strength to come back to the people he considers his family."

"Family? I don't think I know how to be Arel's family. When he returned from his trip, I was hurt because he treats me like a pest. So I ignored my intuition and the nightmares. I knew he was in danger, but my pride kept me away. What kind of family member acts like that?"

"You were trying your best under the circumstances. We both know that Arel likes his solitude."

Peggy laughed. "He thinks he's so wise, but I swear, sometimes I think he and Kevin can both be as dense as door knobs."

"I thought I was improving," a voice called out from the doorway.

"Kevin!" Peggy got up and hurried over to greet her brother. "And you brought the baby."

Kevin cradled his son, Ariel, as he leaned in to kiss Peggy's cheek. "How's our boy, Arel, doing? Any change?"

"No, I'm afraid not."

Kevin walked over to the foot of Arel's bed and looked at Michael. "Any clue yet about what's going on?"

"Arel has a tendency to exhaust himself and then some." Michael looked at Peggy. "Your sister has a similar approach."

Kevin smiled at Peggy. "Yeah, tell me about it. I may be dense as a door knob, but Peggy is the zealot. She's been single-handedly trying to take charge of all our lives since we were kids. Nevertheless, I couldn't ask for a better sister."

"Thanks, and you're a great brother," Peggy said as she tied the baby's shoelace.

"Good, and as your wonderful brother, I'm here to tell you that Tim is getting desperate. He wants you to come home and sleep before you pass out too."

Peggy glanced at Michael. "Do you really think I should?"

Michael nodded. "If anything changes, I'll let you know. In the meantime, please, take care of yourself and try not to worry."

* * *

After Peggy and Kevin left, Michael checked on Arel, scanning his energy fields. As he did, Arel let out a moan and opened his eyes. "You're awake," Michael said with a smile. "I didn't think—"

"Michael?" Arel tried to reach out to the angel with a shaky hand.

Michael quickly grabbed hold and gave Arel's trembling limb a firm squeeze. "I'm here."

Arel blinked several times. "Where is 'here'? I'm so confused."

"You're at home, safe in your bed."

"Really?" Arel's gaze traveled over the room and settled on Michael's face again. "What's wrong with me? Why can't I think clearly or remember anything?"

Michael hesitated. How could he tell Arel the truth without making him withdraw even further? On some level, Arel was protecting his fragile mind-set. He needed to forget everything for a while. The man had been misusing his power by terrorizing Rolphe. With his record of guilt and self-condemnation, he didn't need to be reminded of his misdeeds when he was so weak. "Arel, you were shot in London. You're trying to recover. You need to rest."

Arel pulled his hand away. It dropped to the bed as he made a fist. "But Michael, someone is in trouble. I feel it in my gut. I want to help, but I don't know how."

"You trust me, don't you?"

"Yes, I guess I do."

"Then let me in. Take down the barriers between us."

Arel's golden eyes flared. "I can't do that! I can't drop my shields. It's too dangerous."

"Of course, I understand. But maybe you could make an exception in my case."

Arel groaned again and shut his eyes. "I don't deserve your help."

"What do you mean?"

"I can't explain it. I just know what I'm saying is true. I feel myself drifting away from you, Michael. I'm afraid I'm going—"

"Arel?" Michael watched as Arel did indeed drift away, back into a scary landscape of nightmares and fear. When Michael tried to go after him, Arel's shields were stronger than ever.

"Michael, did I just hear Arel?"

Michael turned and saw Carol coming over. "You're still here?"

Carol went to the opposite side of the bed and straightened out the bedclothes. "Yes, after Kevin left, I was tidying up the house a little. You know, clearing out the dishwasher, that sort of thing. So did Arel wake up?"

"Yes, but just for a couple of minutes."

Carol frowned and sat down in the seat Peggy had occupied. "I have some questions, Michael. Help me understand why he's been going downhill ever since William was here. He used to be so interested in the babies and having dinner parties for us all. We were becoming a happy family. Then it all changed."

"You're right. However, you've made some personal changes that have been good, haven't you?"

Carol's cheeks glowed with a happy flush of embarrassment. "Yes, when William was here, he had a way of making me believe I could depend on myself. I think Kevin gets a little resentful, but William was great. He helped me find a way out when I felt stuck."

"I've talked to Kevin. Even if he's a bit envious, he seems to like the changes too. He looked very happy when he stopped by earlier."

"I wish Arel looked happy again. Peggy thinks he might be in danger because of some nightmare monster she's been dreaming about, but I wonder. Do you think that his ego got crushed when Peggy and I doted over William? Doesn't Arel realize how much we love him?"

Michael eyed Arel with raised brows. "He does have a rather fragile self-image. But neither you nor Peggy did anything wrong."

"Wrong or not, I just hope Arel knows how wonderful he is."

Arel's hand moved ever so slightly in Carol's direction. It was enough to make her jump up and grab hold of it. "Arel? Can you hear me?" she asked, leaning over him.

Arel's eyes fluttered open. He stared back for a long moment before answering. "Carol, what are you doing here?"

Carol brushed his cheek with a kiss. "I'm worrying about you of course. Peggy was here for ten hours straight, worried out of her mind. It was everything we could do to make her go home and rest."

"Really? I didn't think anyone cared—"

Carol squeezed Arel's hand. "Of course we care! None of us can believe you got yourself shot. Michael had to explain it all. How you were in some deserted London park at night, not being careful. Then you didn't even tell anyone. You sat there the night we came over, never letting any of us know you were wounded."

"Oh that."

"Do you know how upset we all got when we found out the truth?"

"I thought you all had better things to do than fuss over me."

"That's ridiculous. You always minimize our feelings. Please stop doing that."

Arel smiled. "I guess I don't have a choice."

Carol put Arel's hand on the blanket and sat down in her chair again. "Now I want you to rest. I'll be right here if you need anything."

Arel shook his head. "That's not necessary. Michael—"

Carol stood up and frowned back. "Are you starting again? Michael needs a break too. So like it or not, one of us is going to stick around until you're better, is that clear?"

Arel's eyes sparkled a little brighter when he looked at Michael. He even made a little shooing gesture with his hand. "You heard the lady, Michael. Take a break."

Michael started out of the room and paused. "By the way, Carey is going to be back tonight, Arel. When he heard you weren't well, he insisted on coming home."

Carol beamed back her approval. "Excellent, between all of us, Arel won't have a chance to be unhappy."

Arel blinked up at her. "I don't know what to say."

"Don't say anything," Carol insisted. "Just let all of us pamper you until you're back to your happy self."

Sixteen

Arel dozed off and on for the next few hours, but every time he opened his eyes Carol was there. She sat by his bed reading or tapping away on her touchscreen tablet. His mind was still very fuzzy, but there was something about Carol's pretty, innocent face that drew him in. She exuded a sense of home and well-being.

He realized how long it had been since he'd felt like he could relax. He'd existed in a world of sharp edges and treacherous drop-offs, where everything he cared about could disappear. That world kept his heart racing and his fingers grasping for some small niche of safety.

Carol's gaze filled him with a softer, nurturing energy. Arel's little godchild, Ariel, was lucky to have her tucking him into bed each night. Arel's mother had been far too busy with her social life to admit Arel even existed. Her cutting remarks made it plain that he was an unwanted intruder, a late-in-life child who had no right to spoil her well-ordered world. His father expressed his view of Arel more violently, often using his cane to show Arel just how unwanted he was. Arel grew up knowing that family meant pain.

That concept changed when Arel allowed new people into his life. Carol, Peggy, Kevin and Tim all proved themselves so consistently that Arel had no choice but to surrender to their care and concern. He'd even begun to expect life to be lighter, happier. So what made him forget that these people thought of him as one of their own? How did he drift so far from the friendship and the gentle bond that they offered?

He couldn't attempt any answers. He was too worn. All that he could do was consent to being in the present moment, to fall under the spell of Carol's kind attentions. When she saw that he was awake and smiled, he tried to smile back. He used muscles that were stiff with months of frowning and an urgent need to stay alert and guarded. But in the end, his weak attempt to return her sweet gesture encouraged Carol. She began to talk to him.

"We called William. We let him know that you weren't well," she said as she put an icepack on his fevered brow. "He said to tell you to stop worrying. In fact, he was quite adamant about you taking care of yourself."

Arel looked back at her, not knowing what to say. The name she'd mentioned didn't compute. "William?" he mumbled.

Carol laughed. "Yes, William. But I don't want you to think that any of us could ever care about him quite as much as we care about you. I don't know if you heard what I told Michael earlier, but I think you got the wrong idea when he was here."

Arel frowned. How could he reply to Carol's statement when he didn't remember the person she was talking about? As she continued on, the name, William, finally clicked physically. He felt a small ping go off deep inside. He retreated at once, knowing he didn't have the strength to search deeper. He stared back at Carol, holding on to the ease in her voice, the way she reached out and squeezed his hand again. It was enough to stabilize his mood. Sleep, that blessed state of renewal, called to him once more. "So tired," he explained as he shut his eyes.

* * *

Gabriel, aka Carey, sat on the sofa in the upstairs living room. His face was tan and glowed with the vitality of youth. It also glowed with his angelic spirit. Michael had asked Gabriel to help Arel when the man was bent on giving up. Gabriel had been successful in his mission, but he didn't reveal his true identity when he took on physical form. In Arel's mind, Gabriel was a wayward, young man named Carey. From the beginning of their relationship, Arel had assumed a paternal role. It worked for the angel. As Carey's fatherly role model, Arel had opportunities to learn about his strengths and weaknesses, just like any parent. Now, with Arel so ill, Carey hoped to find a way to help. He stared at his fellow angel, Michael, and knew his own job was easier than Michael's. "You look like you've been in the trenches," he said with a smile.

Michael hesitated. "Arel has practically done himself in recently."

Carey folded his hands over his chest and stretched out his legs. "I can't believe how quickly he sent me away."

Michael smiled. "You're like his son. He doesn't want to corrupt you with his weaknesses. As you know, he's been in a tailspin, even suicidal, claiming that he's tired of making horrible mistakes."

"He almost got his wish after being shot. Rolphe nearly killed him."

"Thankfully, William came through and turned the tide to a more positive outcome. On the down side, Arel has made it his mission to protect William, no matter what."

"So far, his protection methods have been quite brutal from what I've seen."

"Yes, and Rolphe is only more determined with his pursuits."

"Any ideas about how to proceed?"

"We both know that Rolphe has practiced and honed his psychic abilities for a very long time. He's also been studying Arel's tactics, especially the idea of shields."

"Great, if the guy lures William into a trap and has barriers set up, how are we supposed to intervene?"

Michael sat back with a sigh. "Very good question."

Seventeen

Standing by the kitchen table, Rolphe gripped the vintage goblet with one hand and held his stomach with the other. The glass was empty except for a few drops of dark-red liquid pooled at the bottom of the crystal interior. Rolphe had ingested his dinner too quickly, gulping it down in two swallows. Now, he felt sick.

He kept a plentiful supply of blood on hand. Sometimes, in his younger days, he'd get drunk on the stuff. Of course, in his younger days, blood came directly from the source. At one time, he could overindulge in the warm, satisfying stuff. He could take too much from a victim and still manage to avoid consequences. But times changed. A suspicious death was investigated more thoroughly in the current environment. Clever policemen who had very modern equipment at their disposal were very dedicated to assigning blame.

Rolphe knew when to switch to a more practical way of meeting his needs. It wasn't that difficult. He'd changed too. His primal drives had dwindled with age. He'd learned to be content with units of blood sold by reputable suppliers. Still, it was a compromise. Sometimes the taste of the stuff he purchased was off, depending on the blood donor's physical condition. Fortunately, the batch he'd recently acquired was excellent, even in terms of Rolphe's discerning palette. So why did his stomach ache? Why did he feel so queasy?

He walked his glass over to the sink and gave it a quick rinse. He was about to go back to the living room and paused. He had to steady himself on the counter. His stomach's contents were churning. Bile was rising in his throat. He was going to throw up. He no sooner had the thought when the vomiting started. Draped over the sink, he heaved out every ounce of blood he'd swallowed. It came out in a gush, splattering the white, ceramic sink with a putrid, dark liquid. Afterwards, he dry-heaved a couple of more times.

When he felt somewhat well again, he rinsed the sink, disgusted by the sickening stuff that he'd vomited. He was also curious. Why couldn't he tolerate perfectly good blood? This was the third time he'd vomited out his dinner.

He put a hand to his stomach again. After being made a vampire, blood became more than just a food source, it became a substitute for vodka. When he attacked a victim and drank himself into oblivion, it wasn't the blood itself that made him gluttonous. It was a need to forget about his life and how miserable he was. Chessa was different. She could drink whatever she wanted after her need for blood was satisfied. But Rolphe couldn't tolerate alcohol.

His stomach lurched again. Was his body trying to tell him something? Could he be allergic to regular blood now? His physical discomfort turned to a gripping fear about his future. If he couldn't drink blood, how would he survive?

Rolphe rubbed his belly thinking about his options. William came to mind. Maybe he needed something different, something special. William's blood was extraordinary, just like Arel's. The supply in Rolphe's freezer was foul in comparison. Maybe that's why he was so ravenous when he thought about William.

He walked to his sofa and sat down. William hadn't responded to his text yet. When the man did reply, Rolphe had to be ready. He had to work on a plan he'd envisioned. When he finally persuaded William to come to Paris, every detail in his trap had to be perfect.

* * *

Annabel had hold of her arms as she walked into the living room. She needed to confront William again. She glared at him as she made her announcement. "I want to talk to you."

William sat on the sofa. His brows were narrowed as if he was deep in thought. When he looked up, his eyes returned an uneasy look. "Yes, what is it?"

Annabel took a couple of steps into the room and cleared her throat. She found it hard to swallow, but she was determined to be heard. "You're a liar, William. You lied to me about what you're planning. How could you do that?"

"What do you mean?"

"You said that you were going to Chicago. But I just talked to Carol, and she said you never mentioned anything of the sort. That can only mean one thing. You're going to Paris, to see that maniac, Rolphe."

William's jaw tightened, but he kept his eyes steady when he met her gaze. "I'm not trying to hurt you. In fact, deceit is something new for me. But you've given me no choice."

"So you're lying to protect me? Is that your excuse?"

"I'm not trying to make excuses. I'm hoping to save you from undo misery."

Annabel noticed how controlled William's voice was compared to her own. Why did she let herself resort to yelling when she was afraid or angry? She stepped back, determined to keep her emotions in check. "You're treating me like a child."

"I'm trying to spare you."

Annabel's scowl deepened. Her hands released the grip she had on her arms and slipped down to her hips. "Don't you understand that you're the one who's being a juvenile? A thoughtful adult doesn't constantly put his or her life in danger."

William blinked back, then looked away. "Again, I'm sorry, but it is my life, and I'll do what I think best."

Annabel straightened her posture and lifted her chin. Making the small adjustments to her body helped to calm her nerves just the slightest bit. She knew William was correct. A human being had free will. She had no right to interfere in William's life, but that fact didn't make her feel any better. Expressing herself didn't help either. Maybe she *was* acting like a child. "Fine, you have to follow your path, and I'll do what I have to do."

William's eyes flickered for a moment, but his body remained still and composed. "And what does that mean exactly?"

Annabel turned and started out of the room without answering.

William called after her. "Annabel, I asked you a question, and I'd appreciate an answer."

She paused long enough to give William a backwards glance. "I don't know. I need some time to think."

She walked quickly down the hall. By the time she reached her room and shut the door, she was shaking again. She was always getting scared or angry or both. The worst part was that she knew she wasn't helping William. She simply put him on the defensive more and more of the time.

She went over to her window and looked out. The sky was overcast and moody too. Soon the clouds would probably burst open and drench the city with a downpour. But Annabel was tired of her outbursts. She had to find a way to love William without being afraid all the time. It seemed like an impossible task, but one she had to undertake for both their sakes.

* * *

William listened as Annabel shut her door just loud enough to let him know she was very upset. He'd almost let himself get angry after her comment about his behavior. Why was she talking to Carol? Why did she have to involve herself in something that was his decision alone? Yet, the more he thought about it, the better he felt.

His discussion with Annabel had been an opportunity to express his feelings. Love or no love, he needed his freedom. He would not allow his relationship with Annabel to slide into some kind of trap where personal liberty was a thing of the past. What chance did they have to be happy together with that kind of bond? Besides, he didn't have time for discussions with Annabel. Time was running out. The situation with Rolphe was becoming a real threat, and it wasn't just about Arel anymore.

William retreated to his bedroom and retrieved his laptop from a bedside cabinet. He wanted to go over Rolphe's latest email. The man repeatedly urged William to communicate with him. William read the message over again, paused, and concentrated. He wanted to use a more direct link to Rolphe and Rolphe's thoughts. But his ability to read another person's mind was sketchy at best. His psychic abilities needed a lot of work. With Arel it was easier. They seemed to share a link, similar to that of identical twins.

As far as other people were concerned, Arel was much more proficient at using his gifts. William suspected Rolphe was pretty good at it too. The man had traveled to another dimension that was real enough for William to visit.

On the plus side, William was learning to fortify his shields in case Rolphe attacked him. It wasn't as easy as William first thought. Even normal people often had their shields up, but these shields were something different. William needed practice and a lot of energy to erect the type of structures that Arel had going.

Unfortunately, he didn't have time to perfect what was definitely an art. Rolphe was getting stronger every day. The man had not only survived Arel's efforts to beat him into submission, he had also learned some of Arel's tricks. He was almost as capable at shielding himself as Arel. He was also pinging William's mind repeatedly, looking for a way in. What if the man became strong enough to attack William and even Annabel, using Arel's method?

Rolphe claimed he wanted a truce. William didn't believe him, but what choice did he have in the matter? Perhaps he could reason with the man. Or he could kill Rolphe. The thought didn't go very far. The angelic blood he had in his veins had finally done its job. He'd fought it, like Rolphe, but in the end he'd given up his desire to destroy when he felt like it.

He opened his laptop. It was time to decide on his travel plans. With Raphael by his side, he hoped to be relatively safe when he met with Rolphe. As he checked out details involved with his trip to Paris, a knock on his door made him look up. The door opened, and Annabel peeked in. She didn't look angry anymore, but he didn't know what to say to her.

Annabel gave him a little smile and opened the door wider. "William, I'm sorry for being so upset with you a few minutes ago. I'm just learning about relationships. And I think I must be making lots of mistakes. But I want to tell you that I don't regret loving you, no matter how stupid I feel at times or how hopeless I act or how scared I am. And no matter what happens to either of us, I'll always think of you as the most incredible man I could have met. And I'll always love you." She looked down and quickly swiped away a tear. "So anyway, that's all I have to say, except please be careful."

William hesitated. He tried to smile back, but he couldn't manage it. He couldn't let himself think about Annabel and how much he loved her. If he did, he might pack their bags and run off with her to some place where they could forget all the craziness. But running wasn't the way he approached life. If he started running, he'd never find any peace. He'd always met bullies and tyrants head on. If he faltered now, he'd lose all respect for himself.

Annabel seemed to understand what he was thinking. She patted her face dry and lifted her chin again. "I'm proud of you, my darling," she whispered as she let herself out and closed the door.

Eighteen

William stood on the dimly lit Parisian street corner, checking his phone and the message that just came in. It was the third one he'd received since he'd arrived in the city. Rolphe was playing with him, not giving him a home address directly, but sending him from one location to another. This time the message simply said, "Nice to meet again."

William was about to turn around and bumped into something hard and unmoving. When he looked up, Rolphe was there, standing behind him.

"Hello, William," Rolphe said in a deep, steady voice. "So nice of you to come to Paris. Let's get a cab and talk."

* * *

When Arel woke up this time, he felt like he'd come out of a suffocating dream. Everything he'd experienced was muffled and hazy. He opened and closed his eyes with relief. His mind was working again. Before he had a chance to enjoy the moment, he saw Peggy. She stood next to his bed, frowning down at him. "How long have you been here this time?" he asked. "Carol said you've been holding ten-hour vigils. Is that right?"

Peggy smiled. "How are you?"

"I'm feeling much better. The fog is clearing."

She grabbed his hand. "I'm sorry."

"For what? You've never done anything wrong."

"No, it's not that, but—"

"What is it?"

Peggy hesitated. "I don't want to always burden you with my wild dreams. But I think this is important."

"We both know you've been very tuned-in at times. You've saved me on a number of occasions."

Peggy's eyes dropped to the covers as she took in a breathless gasp. "It's not you this time, Arel. I had a terrible nightmare about William."

"A nightmare about...William?" As soon as Arel said the name and shut his eyes, a kaleidoscope of images filled his mind. A London park, a horrible, stinking cave, and a vicious wolf all flashed in a series of fast moving images. When the slideshow slowed, William came into view. It was the glorious, glowing William who had saved Arel in the park.

Arel smiled at the memory, but William's image suddenly disappeared. Everything came to a standstill when a final image came into view. A large, hulking man filled Arel's mind. Rolphe, with his shaggy, thick hair and heavy, dark beard sat in a cab. But he wasn't alone. As the image pulled back, William sat next to him, looking like a kid next to an ogre. When Arel realized what he was being shown, he grabbed for his chest. His heart had been fine for a long time, but now it felt like it was seizing again.

"What is it, Arel?" Peggy demanded. "Do you see it, too? Do you see that villain who has hold of William?"

Arel opened his eyes and pushed Peggy back. "Hurry! Get Michael! Tell him to come here, now!"

As Peggy obeyed and ran from the room, Arel threw back the covers. The room spun around, but he didn't have time for dizziness or his heart acting up. He didn't have time, period. Shutting his eyes, he tried to leave his body. He had to get to Rolphe in his astral form. He didn't get very far. He didn't have the focus he needed nor the energy. When he tried to tune into William again, there was nothing there. No mind to connect to. Nothing.

* * *

Rolphe scowled at William as they approached his flat and stopped in front of the entrance. "Get rid of him," he demanded.

96

"What?" William paused and frowned. "Who are you talking about?"

Rolphe put his key in the lock and threw open the door. "The angel! Get rid of him now. He's not welcome in my home."

William stepped back. "And why don't you want one of the Creator's own in your home?"

"God and I haven't had anything to do with each other for a very long time. When I die, your angel can send me to hell, but until that time, I don't want him here."

"Well, I do," William insisted.

"Of course you do. In fact, you have a sweet, little green-eyed angel back in London, don't you?"

William's eyes flared, but he didn't respond.

Rolphe smiled at William's ability to hold in his emotions. He'd have to work a little to get the reaction he wanted. "So tell me, is your new, lady love special? You know what I mean. How does she compare to the whores you've had in your bed?"

William held his ground. "I didn't come here to talk about anything but this truce you want."

"Maybe your little gal can be part of the bargain. Maybe I can meet her too."

"How dare you think in those terms."

This time Rolphe saw that he'd gotten a rise out of William. The man's voice remained in control, but the tense muscles in his face were a giveaway. He poked William in the chest, pushing him slightly off-balance. "Why shouldn't I think what I want? You always have. When we met all those years ago, you thought about nothing but yourself. You lusted after power. You were willing to sacrifice everything to have a taste of me. Now get rid of the angel, or I'll do something you won't like."

William stepped forward again, his face flush with color. "What's that?"

"Since you had a taste of me, I think it only fair that I have a taste of that little dearie of yours, the one who shops for mouse food."

William clenched his fists as his outrage peaked. "You bastard! I'll send you to hell myself!"

The angel Rolphe had referred to, had been silently standing to the side. As the situation escalated, he spoke up. "William, don't let him goad you into doing something—"

The advice came too late. William was seething when he lunged at Rolphe. But Rolphe was ready for him. As William rushed forward, Rolphe jumped aside and backhanded William as he passed. The blow was hard enough to throw William to the floor inside the apartment. He landed on the rug in a sprawl. When he stirred and started to get up, Rolphe was already grabbing him by his jacket and delivering another blow to William's jaw. Rolphe's powerful follow-through was enough to render William unconscious.

Rolphe looked back at the door with a wide grin. William's angel stood outside. He was helpless to enter. Rolphe's powerful shields were up, barring him from the apartment. Rolphe quickly closed the door before any nosy neighbors came by. He looked back at William's body with a feeling of pride at what he'd accomplished.

After all of his struggles with Arel, he had bagged his quarry. "Lucky for me, William is a love-sick puppy, or I might have had more of a battle on my hands." All in all, the execution of his plan had been flawless.

Nineteen

Arel never imagined how much pain Carol was capable of inflicting. When she tightened her grip on his wounded arm, his knees started to buckle. It took all his willpower to stay upright.

Their battle started when he realized William was in trouble or worse, dead. Arel had to act quickly, but Carol had come into the room just as Peggy was rushing out to get Michael. Peggy's orders were brief. "Take care of Arel!"

Carol thought that meant getting Arel back into bed. Arel's only thought was to help William, and he fought off her efforts. When she grabbed his arm, he almost fainted. She finally let him go when she understood what she was doing. Her face was instantly red with remorse.

But Arel didn't have time for her apologies. With more focus, he'd had a glimpse of William's plight. The man was unconscious, and Rolphe was sucking the life blood out of him. The image was followed by Michael rushing into the room. Arel exchanged a quick glance with the angel, letting him know what needed to be done.

Michael ushered Carol and Peggy out of the room with his petition. "Please, ladies, can I speak to Arel privately?"

Once they were alone, Arel reached out to Michael. "My energy is so low. I can't stop Rolphe."

Michael gave him a knowing nod. "Rolphe has a kitten named Dantela. Connect with her."

"What? I'm supposed to connect with the bastard's cat while he's killing William?"

"There's no time to explain. Just do it, please."

99

Arel didn't always heed Michael's advice, but he knew the angel wouldn't steer him in the wrong direction. Besides, in this case he had no other option but to close his eyes and obey. With Michael's help and the angel's boost of energy, he was able to more fully tune into Rolphe's flat in Paris. He almost despaired when he saw Rolphe. The tall, massive man had William's wrist to his mouth. He was feasting on William's motionless body. The voracious hulk seemed intent on taking every last ounce of his victim's blood.

"Arel! Forget Rolphe. Look for the cat!" Michael insisted.

Michael's stern directive was enough to make Arel start scanning for Dantela. The large room was dark, with heavy drapes shutting out most of the light. It took a moment to locate the young feline in the shadows. A flick of her tail helped. The kitten was a delicate, little ball of black fur with white tipped paws. Her beautiful, blue eyes were like beacons of light in an otherwise dreary scene. Arel didn't know how to communicate with the animal so he simply yelled out the first words that came to mind. "Dantela! Help William!"

His order barely crossed the astral airways when Dantela sprang into action. She'd been positioned in a crouch, watching her master. In the next moment, she was running. She covered the distance between herself and Rolphe so quickly that Arel was amazed at her speed. In a final leap, she landed on Rolphe's face, sinking her claws and teeth into his cheek.

Rolphe's reaction was just as fast. His head jerked up as he let out a loud bellow of pain and fury. Letting go of William, he grabbed hold of Dantela and flung the young cat across the room. She hit a wall with a thud and landed in a heap.

Arel started yelling when he realized that the kitten was probably dead. "You monster, Rolphe! Is that all you know? How to kill everything that's good in the world?"

Rolphe's next movements were sluggish. He blinked a couple of times, as if he was returning from a dream. Slowly, his dull, almost black eyes wandered over to where Dantela lay. Still looking slightly dazed, he forced himself into a standing position. His gait was hesitant as he made his way to the kitten. For a long moment, he stared down at her. "Dantela?"

As he continued to study the little animal, his eyes filled with recognition and sadness. He bent over and lifted the cat's limp head. "My little one, what have I done to you?"

Arel was watching Rolphe when he felt Michael tap him on the shoulder.

"Arel, try to help William."

Arel's focus went back to where William lay. "Tell me what to do?"

"Find a way to connect to him."

Arel shut his eyes and tried, but he couldn't reach William. "He's too far gone!"

Michael shook his head. "No, he's holding on. I'm sure of it. Keep trying to reach him."

* * *

William awoke in a bedroom with faded wallpaper and furniture that belonged in an antique shop. He opened and closed his eyes a couple of times, trying to focus. The last thing he remembered for sure was being knocked senseless by Rolphe. He didn't know how he ended up on the lumpy bed. Since he was still breathing, he assumed he'd been saved from Rolphe's clutches.

If thinking was challenging, moving his body was even more difficult. Lifting his hand was an impossible chore. Even shifting a finger was too much. His physical vessel was leaden and cold.

"Help is on the way." It was Raphael's voice, but William was too weak to turn his head and look for the angel.

"I'll come to the other side of the bed where you can see me," Raphael said as he moved into William's line of vision.

William tried to speak, but he couldn't manage that either. He used another means of communication with the angel, the telepathic kind.

How am I still alive?

Raphael sat down on the bed. "You did have some help, but you've lost so much blood. I'm doing what I can for your body on an energetic level."

William could feel his facial muscles trying to frown and failing to accomplish the task. His emotions were a different matter. When he thought about Annabel, he wished he could tell her that he loved her one more time. They hadn't had much time together as a couple. He didn't want her to think that she had given up her wings only to

101

be afraid. He'd been hoping to show her how wonderful the world could be. But his wish was pushed aside when Rolphe came to mind.

Just the thought of the ogre threatening Annabel made something inside of William break loose. Even if his physical body was cold as stone, a seething wrath set his mind on fire.

Raphael, take care of Annabel! Promise that you won't let that fiend get his hands on her! Promise me!

"I promise. But you don't have to worry about that now. Rolphe's run off. He's in hiding."

I wish I could have killed him!

Raphael paused. "When you wanted to take out Rolphe at any cost, you shut me out too. I'm so sorry that I couldn't help you."

William knew that the angel was right. He'd always been careful with his emotions. He'd always made sure to stay rational before taking any action. Being in love had made him careless.

I don't know if I can hold on much longer. I feel like I might pass out and never wake up. If that happens, tell Annabel how sorry I am.

"I will," Raphael promised. "But Arel is on his way. He'll be here soon."

Arel? He can't help, not in the shape he's in.

"Do you really think he'd let anything stop him from helping you?"

William felt his heart beat just a little faster. The thought of Arel leaving his sick bed and coming to Paris felt too good to be true. But he couldn't keep his eyes open any longer. He also knew why he felt himself slipping out of the world. He recognized the symptoms that accompanied massive blood loss. The world went black again.

Twenty

Arel sat in the backseat of a cab, ignoring the Parisian scenery. He'd had to use his psychic ability and Michael's assistance to find Rolphe's flat. He'd traveled to Paris as quickly as he could, taking the first flight out that he could book. He suspected that Michael and his helpers worked their magic in getting him on a plane within hours of Rolphe's attack.

Arel had considered contacting Annabel and enlisting her help since she was closer to Paris. But the former angel knew nothing about traveling or handling a crisis. In fact, Arel didn't know if Annabel even had a passport. Secondly, he wouldn't be able to tell Annabel where Rolphe's flat was located. He could get there in his astral body, but he didn't know the physical address. He had to let William's energy signature guide him. He'd tuned into the general location with no problem. It was the exact street and building that were more of a challenge. After an hour of searching, he knew he was getting very close.

"Arrêtez-vous! Pull over!" he yelled out. Thankfully, he'd learned French as a university student. He surprised himself when he realized he still retained enough of the language to make himself understood.

After he paid the driver and exited the cab, he felt drawn to cross the street. Looking up, he examined the aging building and felt a thrill. William was in one of the flats. He felt breathless and had to stop. He had to take some deep breaths and get more air in his lungs. Twelve hours before, he'd been bed-ridden himself. He was sure it was more of Michael's magic that kept him going.

"Your shields are down. You've let me in."

Arel smiled when he heard Michael's voice. The angel's cheerful message buoyed him up just as his energy was failing. He quickly let himself into Rolphe's apartment building. He hurried up two flights of stairs, ignoring the stale, heavy air. Like a hound on the trail of his quarry, he let himself be guided to a door that was halfway down a hallway. When he tried the knob, the door opened.

He stood in the living room, suddenly overcome. Rolphe's home was just as he'd seen it in his astral visits. When he'd been there before, the flat had a dreamlike feel to it. Now, everything was solid and real. It was an eerie and unnerving experience.

He recognized the oversized sofa, the piano, and the paneled wall where the little cat, Dantela, had met her fate. When he looked down at the carpet, the place where William was attacked, he saw a dark stain. It was William's blood. But where was William now?

Arel came out of his stupor and started to run through the flat, searching the rooms. He found William in a dingy, back bedroom. The man's skin was gray and ashen, and his head was at an odd angle like a damaged puppet that someone had carelessly thrown on the worn, burgundy covers. For a moment, Arel was afraid William's neck was broken. It was such a horrible thought that he had to grab hold of the door jamb to steady himself. He could feel Michael's presence close by, reminding him not to indulge in such damning thoughts.

He quickly pulled himself together and rushed over to the bed. When he grabbed William's hand, it was stiff with cold. He had another terrible thought. Maybe William was already dead. He put his fingers to William's neck and felt for a pulse. After a long moment, he sighed with relief. That's when he saw a note pinned crudely to William's shirt.

He snatched it up and read it aloud. "Arel, if your friend is still alive when you get here, there are medical supplies in the kitchen, and blood in the refrigerator."

The note was unsigned, but Arel knew that Rolphe had left it. The man had also bandaged William's wrist. It reminded Arel of something Rolphe had told him when they met in a London park. Rolphe had once helped to patch up his comrades' wounds when he was a soldier.

Arel crumpled up the note and threw it aside. "But the ogre was too much of a coward to stay and help William himself."

He made a fast trip to the kitchen and saw the medical supplies that Rolphe had left. Everything that was needed for an IV setup was on the counter. He opened the refrigerator and saw a dozen units of blood on the shelf.

"What should I do, Michael?" he asked. "Should I get William to a hospital or try to help him here?"

Before he got a response, he already knew the answer. He had to avoid getting the authorities involved. William's blood, like his own, wasn't normal. William had done extensive studies to understand its properties and declared their blood to be in a class of its own. If investigated, there'd be questions and possible ramifications that could make life difficult for William.

But maybe there's a better way. I have power! I've helped save William once before! I can do it again.

Michael's voice chimed in. "And you can use the blood that Rolphe left."

"You're right, Michael. I've watched William in the lab. Setting up an IV is easy." He hesitated. "All I have to do is keep from fainting when I look at it."

Handling or even seeing blood could send him over the edge if he was stressed. Unfortunately, with William ready to cross over, his stress level was at an all-time high.

Gathering up the medical supplies and a unit of blood, he hurried back to the bedroom. "Oh god, Will, I promise you that I'll do my best. I just hope that it's enough."

* * *

Annabel sat in her bedroom, holding her phone close to her heart. She'd tried to call William a dozen times and didn't get an answer. She'd left countless messages too. With her heart always racing and her body consumed by constant anxiety and stress, the challenge of facing life on her own seemed impossible. But she wouldn't give up.

She went to the kitchen for a cup of tea. She needed something to distract herself. Her mind felt like it was running on a mouse wheel. It kept going round and round, continually bringing up reasons why life was overwhelming. The facts were difficult to ignore. In the short time since she given up her wings, Arel had been

105

shot and William had nearly been gobbled up by a hideous wolf in a cave. Now, William was risking his life again. She didn't dare use her intuitive powers to tune into his whereabouts or the condition he was in. What if she found out the worst? Would her already fragile nerves snap if she learned that he was fatally injured?

She paused as she reached out a trembling hand for the kettle. Her thoughts returned to her phone and why William wasn't answering her calls. In the end, some small part of her rallied. She had to believe that she was strong. She had to hold on to hope and courage no matter what her emotions were telling her.

* * *

William floated out-of-body near the ceiling. At some point, he'd slipped away from his physical form. Now, he was fixated on what was happening to that physical part of himself. Arel was trying to set up an IV. William let out a moan as he watched. "I can't believe my life is in his hands. His shaky, incompetent hands. Look at him trying to find a vein!"

Raphael and Michael were on either side of William, offering their encouragement.

"Try not to worry," Raphael said in a light-hearted tone. "Arel is going to do just fine. Isn't that right, Michael?"

Michael returned a noncommittal glance. "Arel is new at this, but I'm sure he'll figure it out."

William frowned. "Please! He's doing it all wrong! The needle isn't at the correct angle. My arm is going to end up a pin cushion. I'll soon be dead at this rate."

Raphael shrugged. "What do you suggest we do?"

William hesitated. He didn't think he could get so upset while he was in his astral form, but he was wrong. He'd never felt quite so nervous or frustrated. "Listen, both of you, if you could just get Arel to calm down and do this thing the right way, I might have a chance."

"Do you think he should enlist proper medical care?" Raphael asked.

William sighed. "No, he was right not to go that route. If some over-curious people learned too much about my blood, I could end up being a science project or worse. It's a horrible alternative to contemplate, but I guess Arel is still my best bet."

As if Arel heard his name being bandied about, he looked up at the ceiling and squinted. "Will, are you there? If you are, I could use some help. I guess I should have listened a little more when you tried to teach me a few things in your lab. But if there's any way you can help now, I'm ready to listen."

William gave Michael an anxious scowl. "Get down there now, please. Show him what to do. At this point, I don't think I have the patience to communicate clearly."

Michael offered a weak smile. "I see. There's only one problem. I've never handled this type of situation either. Maybe you better tell me what to do."

* * *

Rolphe didn't know where to go after what he'd done. It was one thing to attack William, but he'd almost killed his beautiful Dantela. The kitten was like his child. He adored her. She was the only steady element in his life that was good and pure, just like his two boys had been good and pure.

Dantela's intervention surprised him. Instead of behaving like a thinking, rational person, he'd been in more of an animal mode, reacting like an animal when something threatened its food. Afterwards, when he started to come back to himself, he couldn't believe what he'd done. Remorse was a poor way of explaining how devastated he felt.

There was also something in William's blood that punished him. Its damning properties made themselves known while he was standing over Dantela's limp body. He was thinking that he'd killed his small friend when a bout of nausea grabbed hold. It came on so quickly he had to run to the bathroom. Holding his gut, he didn't make it to the commode. Nothing could hold back the rush of blood that spewed out of him. It anointed the walls and the fixtures. Everything was covered with the gruesome evidence of what he'd done to William.

When the vomiting was over, Rolphe was left staring at himself in a mirror. The glass was splattered with blood. But that wasn't the worst part of it. Rolphe saw a horrifying beast looking back at him. Blood dripped from his mouth and nose, and his face was frozen in a predatory snarl.

The sight had frightened him so badly that he'd rushed back to William and quickly bound his wrist, trying to make sure that the man didn't lose any more blood. Then he snatched up William's body in a kind of blind panic. As he carried the man to his bedroom, he was reminded of the time he'd carried his wife and children to a common grave. The village where they'd died had suffered from a pandemic. There wasn't time for proper burials. Only this time, it wasn't disease that was the killer. Rolphe was responsible for trying to snuff out a life.

The memory affected Rolphe so profoundly that his panic escalated. He had to escape what he'd done. After he dumped William's body on the bed, he ran from the room.

He quickly showered off the blood that matted his beard. While he was in the shower, he could feel Arel's energy. It haunted him with accusation and blame. Searching for some small gesture of atonement, he called one of his contacts and procured some medical equipment and blood. He left it behind in case William survived.

A blessing came later when he realized that Dantela wasn't dead. That's when he fled to Myra's apartment, cat carrier in hand. Myra was a trusting woman whom he'd known for years. It was easy to convince her that the kitten had had an accident. When he asked to stay with her for a little while, she responded with an open heart. She seemed to understand how much he loved Dantela and that he needed a friend.

Twenty-One

William opened his eyes and blinked a couple of times. He lifted one hand, then the other. His body worked. When he checked out his surroundings, he felt more relief. He wasn't in Rolphe's flat. His room was well-appointed with beautiful, period furniture and large, airy windows. He ran his hand over the soft, white bed linens just as Arel came into the room.

"Will, what a relief to see you awake," Arel said with a smile.

William couldn't manage to smile back. He was better physically, but after being brutalized by Rolphe, he experienced a feeling he hadn't known before. He couldn't put it into words, but he felt like hiding. He stared at Arel with a sense of loss and weakness. "I've faced death before, but this was different."

Arel sat down on the side of the bed. "I have to forget what you went through, at least for a little while. If I don't, I'm going to find Rolphe and kill him. Then I'll probably spend the rest of my life in jail."

William looked away without commenting. Just hearing Rolphe's name made his heart pound. Even worse was the overwhelming sense of helplessness.

Arel put a hand on his shoulder. "I'm so sorry about what happened. I should have—"

"Stop it." William took a deep breath and tried to smile again and failed. "You did everything you could. You tried your best—"

"I should have never gone back home. I should have come to Paris and—"

"And done what, Arel? Put Rolphe in a cage?"

"That's where he belongs! Behind bars!"

William shivered. "I'm cold. Can you turn up the heat?"

"Of course." Arel stood up too quickly and had to steady himself on a chair by the bed. "Just give me a minute."

William noticed the dark circles under Arel's eyes and the strain that had hold of his thin face. "You still look like hell. You need to take care of yourself."

Arel sat down again. "Listen, I've called Annabel and told her that you're going to be okay. Poor thing is pretty worried, but Raphael is with her."

"Thank you. I've been very worried about her too."

"There's something else I want to discuss."

"What's that?"

"I want both of you to come back with me to Chicago. Annabel has already agreed if you say it's okay."

William looked down at his hands. He had a death grip on the edge of the comforter. But the idea of leaving for Chicago made him breathe a little easier. "Maybe that's a good idea. Annabel deserves a break from all this madness."

Arel nodded. "I agree. So is it okay if I book a flight back for the three of us?"

William swallowed hard, unable to respond. There was something wrong with his emotions. They were out of whack, like he wanted to start bawling for no reason.

Arel seemed to understand. "Will, your body's been through hell. I've been researching stuff these past couple of days. After what's happened, it's going to take some time for you to get back to your old self again. In the meantime you have to be patient."

William tugged on the covers, trying to stop a chill that was making his teeth chatter. "Your right, I need a change of scenery. Go book those tickets."

* * *

Arel had barely paid any attention to his own physical condition since he'd come to Paris. It was only when William was out of danger that he allowed himself a few minutes of rest in his hotel room. As he sat on the French classical sofa, he longed for the comfort of his recliner back home. He glanced up with irritation at Michael. The tall angel was standing by the window, obviously enjoying the view. "Michael, please, close the drapes. With this pounding headache, the light is killing my eyes."

Michael did as he was told and sat down. "Don't you think it would be wise to get some sleep?"

"No, not now. I'm staying tuned in to William in case he needs me." He focused on Michael's eyes. They were always bright and kind. "Thank you for all that you've done to help William. His body is doing well. It's his emotional state that worries me."

"He's been through quite a traumatic event."

"I think he's suffering from PTSD, post-traumatic stress disorder. After some research, I've learned that it's common after going through something so horrible. Maybe Annabel has it too. After all, it has to be a shock to be an angel one minute and a human being the next."

Michael frowned. "Did you ever think that you might also be suffering from trauma?"

Arel paused for a long moment, rubbing his hand back and forth over the sofa's green and yellow brocade fabric. His headache was almost overpowering his ability to think, but Michael's question made him narrow his eyes in concentration. "Do you think so? I did live in a very closed world for all those years before you came along."

"Yes, and I remember how afraid you were after what you experienced as a child and young man."

"You mean like my father trying to kill me repeatedly?" Arel's fingers closed on the sofa arm. "And don't forget, I also thought I was cursed. I lived in hell thinking I was a monster. Then I found out that my supposed 'vampire' condition was caused by a virus. When William told me that, I thought I'd go insane thinking about the misconceptions I'd had and how much of my life I'd wasted. I'm lucky I didn't jump off a ledge trying to deal with that bit of information."

"The point is that in spite of all you've been through, you've had the courage to keep going."

Arel leaned forward with elbows on knees, holding his head in his hands. "You always try to help, Michael, but don't forget that I've also been a bastard. I might have asked for your blood, but I forced it on William. He never asked for any of this. He was happy with his life. He was a strong, capable man who never backed down from a

111

challenge. I took all that away from him and forced him to go through hell. And the nightmare never stops. After the latest episode in this unending drama, he's lying in his bed, riddled with fear. He flinches every time the maid's cart passes the door."

"He has gone through a lot—"

"Did you see Rolphe's bathroom? There was blood everywhere. The walls, the fixtures, the floor—"

"I know."

"That was William's blood!"

Michael nodded. "Rolphe couldn't stomach it."

Arel jerked his head up and winced. He had to use the sofa arm to steady himself. "William almost died. Meanwhile his blood was splattered uselessly over some stinking dump. It's not right. When I get my hands on Rolphe—"

"Arel?"

"What?"

"You have to forget about Rolphe. William isn't out of the woods. He needs you to stay calm, not keep talking about the man who left him devastated."

Arel's eyes became dark, golden pools of concentrated fury. "When I found William in Rolphe's flat, he was as cold as a corpse. I keep trying to make things right, and it never helps—"

"Arel, please, you have to stop making yourself responsible for everyone's pain. You did it with Justina, but William doesn't want that. Give yourself a break. You've always tried to do your best."

"My best?" Arel pushed himself off the sofa and slowly walked over to where Michael was sitting. "Look at me, Michael, and tell me something. If this is my best, what kind of deficient human being am I?"

Michael stood up and put his hands on Arel's shoulders. "You're not deficient, dear friend. You have to stop believing that."

Arel grabbed the angel's arms and held them tight. "Please, Michael, stop this nightmare I've gotten William into. I don't care about what happens to me anymore, but you have to find a way out for William, please. He loves Annabel. They need a chance to live a happy life."

Michael's gaze softened as he smiled back. "Keep believing that they can. Believe you can be happy too."

"I wish I could. I wish life would stand still long enough to find a different path than the one I'm on."

"There is a different path. It's always there, waiting for you. But you have to let go of your guilt and seeing yourself as a failure. In the days ahead, William is going to need you to believe in yourself, to be the strong one when he falters. If you want a way out of what's happened, you have to be willing to believe there's something better in life and give it a chance."

* * *

After Rolphe's attack on William, he realized that his blood lust was gone. It was purged away when he vomited out William's blood. He never wanted to taste another drop of the stuff again. Just the thought of imbibing any kind of blood made his stomach sour. If he didn't quickly think of something else, he ended up dry heaving.

As the days went by, his body suffered more and more. Besides the constant body aches, he had an insistent pain in his chest. Myra asked him why he kept rubbing the area. What could he say? He didn't want to worry her, but he knew his heart was acting up. It had always been a strong vessel. Now, it was telling him that his days on earth were running out. He decided to spend them alone. That meant returning to his flat. He gave Myra a hasty excuse for leaving. "Would you take care of Dantela for a little while?" he asked her as he put his arms around her waist.

"You're leaving? But I like having you here," Myra said. Her voice was tinged with disappointment. "Are you going out of town again?"

"I'm going on a long journey, my dear lady. I'm not sure when I'll be back. Will Dantela be too much of a bother?"

"You know that she won't." Myra reached up and ran her hand over his beard. "Where did all this grey hair come from? Promise that you'll take care of yourself. You don't look well."

Rolphe didn't reply. He bent down and kissed her forehead instead.

"What's wrong?" she asked. "I've never seen your eyes look so sad before."

"I was just thinking. I don't deserve anyone as good and beautiful as you." He gave her a light kiss on the lips and released her quickly. After he left Myra's apartment, he hurried to the stairs. His chest hurt and the pain was getting worse. He had to get back to his flat as quickly as possible. He also needed to contact William again.

Twenty-Two

Arel woke up to the sound of someone knocking on the door to his hotel room. He looked at the clock on the side table. He'd been asleep for almost four hours. "Coming," he called out as he threw back the covers. Before he got to the door, he saw the airline tickets on the desk. He, Annabel and William were flying back to Chicago later that morning. Annabel had joined them the day before and had spent the night with William. When Arel opened the door, he saw her with her hand up, getting ready to knock again.

"William isn't well!"

Annabel blurted out the words before Arel had a chance to greet her. "What's wrong with him?" he asked as he slipped into his robe and grabbed his room key. "Did he get sick during the night?"

Annabel went back to her room and opened the door. "I don't know. I fell asleep in a chair reading. When I woke up, he wasn't in bed. Hurry, please, I'm worried about him."

Arel followed her into the room and looked around the living area.

"In there," Annabel said, pointing to the bathroom.

Arel hurried over to the closed door and tried the knob. It wouldn't turn. "William? It's Arel. What's wrong?"

When there was no answer, Annabel came over and knocked on the door. "William? It's Annabel. Dearest, please let us in. We're going to Chicago today. You have to get ready."

After a moment, the knob turned and the door cracked open.

Arel pushed it open a little more and looked in. William was standing a couple of feet away, backed up against the vanity. When he tuned into William's mind, all he felt was panic. As he searched a little more thoroughly, he grimaced. "Oh no, not again."

"Oh, yes," William nodded, clearly shaken. "He's in my head, Arel. Rolphe is looking for me."

Arel turned to Annabel. "Get your things together while I help William. I want to be out of here in a half hour."

* * *

Arel sat on the plane, sandwiched between William and Annabel. William was nursing his third drink and appearing very relaxed. Annabel had her eyes closed, looking a little like a beautiful, modern Madonna. At some point in their relationship, William had obtained a passport for her. Arel was grateful for that detail. Now the ex-angel was deep in meditation and oblivious to everything that was happening around her. Arel wasn't so lucky. He was sure his face was frozen into a kind of man-meets-monster grimace.

He should have been proud of himself. His plan had worked. When they arrived at the airport, William was terrified. Arel's only option seemed to be a questionable one. He had to use his special ability to take on another person's negative energy. He'd kind of sucked up all of William's fears, at least temporarily. It was an overwhelming experience. He'd thought a lot about what William went through, but feeling his horror directly was almost too much.

The positive side was that William got through security looking like a normal passenger. It was Arel who barely made the flight. The security check went smoothly enough. Arel was able to control his reaction to borrowed visions of being helpless. Michael helped. He'd flooded Arel's physical vessel with his calming energy.

Under the sway of heavenly intervention, Arel shuffled through the airport check points with a minimum of fuss. It was the fainting on the other side that drew attention. But even that embarrassing event was overcome. William, not knowing that Arel had purged him of all thoughts of Rolphe, was able to assist. He'd been very kind and managed to get wheelchair assistance for Arel.

When the plane finally left the runway and was flying towards Chicago, Arel was left with a couple of problems. He had to keep William in a calm state. That meant preventing the man's mind from going ballistic again and generating more negative thoughts. He also had to find a way to get rid of the churning mass of fear in his own gut. His insides contained a vortex of William's worst nightmares, including acute anxiety and blind panic.

Arel's first problem kind of solved itself. With Michael sending William a steady stream of suggestions, William began ordering drinks. Since he hadn't indulged in alcohol in a very long time, his body was soon under the influence. His mind went along for the ride. He even began to smile.

Michael also came to Arel's aid. Once Arel found a way to see past his "borrowed" paranoia, he dropped his shields. Michael was able to draw off most of the negativity that Arel was harboring.

Afterwards, Arel still couldn't relax. He'd begun to generate his own negativity. That's when William insisted that Arel order some drinks too. Arel was sure he couldn't stomach the stuff, but William was so adamant that Arel complied. After downing several drinks, he felt himself swimming in an alcoholic stupor.

It turned out that both he and William were happy drunks. Arel didn't remember much about their flight, but when the plane landed, he was surprised by some of his fellow passengers. A number of them smiled at him and told him he and William were real comedians.

The drinks and Michael's amazing, secret additive were starting to wear off by the time their cab got to Arel's home in the suburbs. As Arel began to think a little more clearly, he remembered Annabel. She was sitting in the front seat of the cab, maintaining complete silence as the vehicle pulled into the driveway.

Arel climbed out of the cab holding his head and announcing that William needed to throw up. As soon as he delivered his message about William, his stomach went into spasms. Then the vomiting started. William followed suit with his own performance.

When Arel looked up, all white-faced and reeling, he noticed that his friends were gathered round on the driveway. Peggy, Tim, Carol, Kevin and two babies were there to greet them. All the adults stood staring at him with confused looks and open mouths. For some reason, he didn't care. He felt better than he'd felt in a long time.

Tim took charge immediately. "Peggy, why don't you take Annabel and Carol and the babies to our house while we get these two settled in."

Peggy reached out to Annabel. "I'm Peggy. Welcome to Chicago. You'll have to tell me all about your travels, you poor thing."

Twenty-Three

It was a bright and sunny morning, but Kevin was feeling less than sunny as he stood in Arel's kitchen. He was tired, and his nerves were shot. He'd had lots of experience with drunks in his college days. He didn't judge their behavior. After all, he'd tied a few on himself when he was younger. But he'd never had to take care of his inebriated buddies for any length of time.

That changed when Arel and William came home. The two men had needed constant tending. Tim took the first shift. Kevin took the second. He eyed his charges with a critical scowl as they sat at the kitchen table arguing.

"Why in the name of all that's good and holy, did you let me order that second and third drink?" William grumbled as he held both of his temples. "My head is a blinding field of pain and my stomach is still doing flip flops."

"Why are you yelling?" Arel shouted. "Besides, Michael and I had no choice. We couldn't take a chance on you going nuts again."

Kevin walked over and put two glasses on the table. "Shut up, both of you and drink this." He'd made the men his special recipe for hangovers, but he was out of patience. As soon as the alcohol had started to retreat from William and Arel's brains, they had complained and quarreled.

Michael and Carey had tried to help, but they found that Tim and Kevin seemed to know a lot more about what to do with drunken comrades. They had bowed out and let the two men handle Arel and William.

When Michael and Carey came into the kitchen and gave Kevin a polite smile, he didn't smile back. "So where did you two disappear to when I was cleaning up vomit?"

Michael's eyes shifted uneasily. "You were doing so well—"

Kevin glared back and threw down the towel he'd used to wipe up William's spilled coffee. "Fine, but they're all yours now. I'm going home, getting showered and going to work. And by the way, William threw up two more times. His clothes are in the washer. Put them in the dryer when the cycle is finished."

As Kevin started out of the kitchen, William grabbed his hand. "Thanks. You're a real friend."

"Yeah, yeah, yeah," Kevin said as he quickly headed for the front door.

* * *

Arel missed Kevin as soon as he left. After all of the recent events, the man's presence brought in an element of stability. Kevin embodied a quality that Arel was never privy to. Kevin was a regular guy. Sure he had his worries, but after dealing with them, he was back to a life that revolved around a wife and family. He enjoyed a routine, that day-to-day existence that he could depend on.

Arel couldn't maintain anything of the sort. He was always on a roller coaster. The constant highs and lows drove him to the edge. Luckily, there was another person he could depend on to cheer him up. When he met Carey, he knew the kid was like Kevin. He was normal.

Arel smiled when he saw the young man rummaging in the refrigerator. Carey loved his motorcycle, surfing, and food. "There are some donuts in the breadbox, Carey. Tim dropped them off before he went to work. Help yourself."

Carey grabbed a plate and smiled. "Thanks."

Arel watched Carey put several pastries on his plate. "Better take it easy on the sweets. Do you want me to fix you some eggs instead?"

Carey shook his head and stuffed a half donut in his mouth. After a quick swallow he frowned. "Kevin looked pretty worn when he was leaving. What happened to the poor guy?"

120

Arel stared at William accusingly. Somewhere during the trip home and getting drunk, their relationship had reverted to its usual argumentative nature. The respite allowed Arel to forget William's trauma, at least for the time being. "It was a rough night. William kept throwing up on himself."

William squinted back. "Like you didn't drive Kevin nuts with your constant whining? 'Kevin, could you clean that up before it stains the carpet. Kevin, the washer is off balance, redo the load. Kevin, get me a pillow, I'm too dizzy to get it myself.'" He paused and let out a sarcastic laugh. "You were horrible. I don't know how you have any friends."

Before Arel had a chance to respond, he saw Annabel standing in the doorway. She gave him a quick smile.

"I see you two are feeling better," she said as she shut the door behind her.

Arel went suddenly pale as he gazed up at her. After coming home and suffering from a hangover, he'd forgotten about Annabel. Now, her presence sent him into an instant panic. His brief moment of ease and banter with William slipped away as his mind buzzed with questions. How was he going to explain Annabel to Carey?

Innocent, normal Carey had met Annabel once before. On Arel's reunion trip to see William in New York, Carey had come along. Annabel hitched a ride with them. But Carey didn't know Annabel was an angel. He didn't even know Michael was an angel. So how would Arel explain Annabel's presence to the young man?

His hands gripped the chair arms as he braced himself for another emotional hell-ride. He tried desperately to come up with a logical explanation, but his thoughts were like flighty birds escaping a cat, too erratic to make any sense.

Carey seemed to notice Arel's apprehension. He came over and smiled down at him. "I think it's time that I confess something, Arel," he said.

Arel blinked back, still trying to find the right words to defuse his dilemma. "Confess what?"

Carey paused and glanced at Michael. "I'm not exactly who I've pretended to be. Annabel and I have worked together for a while."

Arel leaned forward. He tried to understand what Carey was saying, but the young man wasn't making any sense. "Worked together? What do you mean?"

Annabel came over to Arel and kissed his cheek. "His real name is Gabriel."

Arel slowly raised a hand to his cheek and frowned. "Gabriel? Isn't that an angel's name?" After a long moment, his eyes widened in disbelief. "Are you telling me—"

Michael patted Carey's shoulder. "He's one of us, Arel."

"What?" Arel stood up slowly, forgetting his hangover and his recent complaints. He couldn't stop staring at Carey. During the time that he'd known the young man, he'd tried his best to be a good parental figure. He'd seen himself as a person who could help the young man find his way in life. "I thought . . . you seemed like a real—" His voice trailed off as the truth began to sink in. He rubbed his forehead, hoping the gesture could bring some clarity to his muddled thoughts.

Finally, he held on the table for support and looked around the room. "Let me get this straight. I'm standing here thinking I know what's going on, but that's because I'm thinking I'm sane. But sanity isn't in my cards. I look at each of you and guess what I see, two angels, a former angel and a man who was a vampire. Does that seem reasonable to any of you?"

"I'm sorry," Carey said. "Concealing my identity seemed like the best idea at the time. Like you just said—"

Arel clenched his fists. "You scared the hell out of me with all your crap. I nearly had a heart attack when I hit you on that damn motorcycle. I tried to be a father you didn't have. All the while you were playing some rebellious kid who was driving me nuts. And now I find out that you're what? A liar? Or maybe you're an illusion. In reality, I could be locked up in a mental hospital and be hallucinating all of this."

William massaged his temples. "Arel, please stop making everything a big deal. If anybody has a reason to complain, it's me. I was doing just fine before you decided on revenge. Now look at my life. My health's been so bad that I died. But that wasn't enough for you. You tossed me out of heaven. You scared the hell out of me to the point that I got Rolphe involved. Then you go and give the bastard your blood and he nearly kills me, twice. But am I blaming you? No, I know I have to take responsibility for my life. And you have to take responsibility for yours. So don't cop out and say we're all your hallucinations."

Arel collapsed back into his chair. "I'm sorry, Will. I agree with everything you just said. But I don't know how to handle all this. I'm dealing with soul trips to the other side, angels who slip in and out of human form, mind merges, fighting a maniac on the astral plane, and countless other unexplainable events. Maybe you can deal with this craziness, but I can't."

William shrugged. "What choice do you have?"

Arel got to his feet again and went to the back door. "I don't know. I'm too tired to think about it. I'm going to Carol and Kevin's house. They have a spare room, and they appear to be normal, at least for the time being. You and Annabel can use the downstairs apartment while you're here."

* * *

William scowled at the empty chair where Arel had been sitting. He hadn't thought about it much, but Arel had been by his side for days. After the nightmare with Rolphe, the man had done everything he could to support William, including helping him with his fears. When they were on their way to the airport, William was in a panic. He didn't think he'd be able to get on a plane. Once again, Arel performed one of his tricks. William didn't know what Arel did to him, but he suddenly felt calm and relaxed.

Now, Arel was bowing out, at least for the time being. It left William wondering if he'd be able to cope. What if his nightmares started up? He didn't have long to think about it. Arel was barely out of sight when something dark and unwanted started pinging William's mind. Rolphe was back, haunting him again.

Twenty-Four

Peggy handed a stack of plates to Tim. "Thanks for helping me as soon as you got home from work. I know it's been a long week."

Tim started out of the kitchen and paused. "No problem. I'm just glad that William and Arel don't get drunk very often. That Monday night fiasco was a little brutal."

Peggy picked up a handful of silverware and followed Tim into the dining room. "That was the strangest thing. We've never seen Arel eat or drink before. Then lo and behold, he comes home high as a kite."

Tim looked up from his task and frowned. "I remember Arel explaining that he has special dietary needs, but you're right, we never see him eating. What's with that?"

Peggy shrugged. "Who knows, but we have bigger worries. After dinner, when Arel, William and Annabel drop in, we have to get Arel back on track. Carol says that he shuts himself up in their spare bedroom and barely comes out. If it weren't for his interest in little Ariel, he'd be a complete hermit."

"What about William and Annabel? Have you seen them around?"

Peggy straightened a napkin and smiled. "Annabel's gone shopping with Carol and me a couple of times. She's wonderful. Both of the kids love her to pieces. It's hard to keep them in their car seats when she's around. They keep wanting her to hold them. As for William, I don't know what to say. Like Arel, he's always got an excuse for staying home."

"How did you convince the two of them to come out of their shells and join us tonight?"

"It's simple. I wouldn't take 'no' for an answer. I told them that this evening is all about welcoming Annabel into our family, and they had to come. Both said they'd join us after dinner."

Peggy started back into the kitchen when the doorbell rang. "Would you get the door, sweetie? That's Carol and Kevin."

* * *

Peggy smiled to herself as she grabbed the coffee carafe and checked its contents. The dinner had been a success. Even Kevin, who had a bottomless pit for a stomach, looked sufficiently full and happy. Afterwards, Annabel, William, and Arel arrived and joined the party.

As Peggy was about to go back into the living room to top off Carol's coffee, Annabel came into the kitchen.

"Do you need some help cleaning up?" Annabel asked.

"No, thank you. I want everyone to relax. Tim and I will take care of cleaning up later."

Annabel edged her way over to the counter and looked at the turkey. "Really, Peggy, I'd love to help. I—"

Peggy noticed the way Annabel's eyes were flitting from the turkey to the mashed potatoes to the gravy. "Annabel, can I offer you anything? There are lots of leftovers."

Annabel blushed and backed away from the counter. "Oh, no, I wouldn't want to be a bother."

"A bother? Annabel, please, I love when people enjoy my cooking."

"Really? Everything does look wonderful."

Peggy quickly put down the carafe and went to the cupboards. She retrieved a plate and tried to hand it to Annabel. "Please, help yourself. The more you eat, the less I have to put away."

Annabel put her hands behind her back. "Maybe I'm being too forward. I shouldn't have barged in—"

Peggy put the plate on the table and smiled. "Sweetie, you're part of this family now. I want you to act like it. And if there's anything you need, I insist that you tell me about it."

125

Annabel bit her lip, but her eyes welled up with tears anyway. "You're very kind, Peggy, but I don't think I know how to fit in."

Peggy quickly put her arm around Annabel's shoulders. "You poor thing, you're shaking."

"I'm fine. I think I'm just a bit hungry."

"Hungry? Didn't you have dinner?"

"I had something at lunchtime. I guess I forgot about dinner."

"What did you have for lunch?"

"Carey and I shared a sandwich, but—"

"Shared a sandwich? That's it?"

"Well, Arel isn't there, and no one's gone shopping, so—"

Peggy blinked back. For once, she didn't know what to say. All that she knew was that Annabel was clearly unable to voice her needs. "Don't worry about that now. We'll get it all straightened out, I promise."

"Please, Peggy, I don't want to put more pressure on anyone. Arel and William are both very stressed right now."

Peggy walked Annabel over to the kitchen table and pointed to a chair. "Let's forget about them. Just sit down and let me get you some dinner. Later, let's talk about things so that your stay at Arel's goes a little better."

Annabel's movements were hesitant as she obediently took a seat, but her eyes did spark a little when she asked a question. "Could you also put some food in a container for Carey? I know he'd love something too."

Peggy thought about how much Carey's appetite reminded her of Kevin's need for food. "I have tons here. I'll get you both fixed up."

Peggy wasted no time getting Annabel settled with generous helpings of turkey, potatoes, peas and some dessert. "Just relax and enjoy your meal, Annabel. While you're eating, I'll be in the living room."

Annabel's face was practically glowing as she skewered a large bite of turkey. "Thank you for your kindness, Peggy."

Peggy went back to her guests in the living room, impressed with how quickly Annabel was gulping down her food. It made her think that she needed to talk to William privately. He needed to be aware of Annabel's situation. However, when she leaned over his shoulder and surprised him, he nearly jumped out of his chair. Before she got a chance to apologize, he excused himself and quickly fled from the room.

"What's wrong with William?" Carol asked with concern.

Kevin frowned. "Yeah, he went white as a sheet when Peggy tapped his arm."

Arel stood up and looked around the room. "Sorry everyone, but I need to explain something. You see William was recently assaulted by a mugger when he was in Paris. It was an unexpected and vicious incident. He's still recovering."

Carol gasped. "That's horrible."

Arel grabbed hold of the back of the recliner that William had been sitting in. "I've been trying to help, but I don't think I'm doing a very good job. I guess—"

Peggy put her hand over Arel's. She thought about the scary man she'd seen in the horrible dreams she'd had about William. "So what I saw in those nightmares came true?"

Arel nodded.

Carol got up and put a hand on Arel's shoulder. "Is that why you had to rush off, even though you weren't well yourself?"

Arel nodded again. "I want to help Will, but I guess my nerves are kind of—"

Carol sighed. "You're home now, and William is safe here. But you need to let us know what's going on. You can't try to handle everything yourself."

Peggy scowled and let out a sigh. "I know this isn't the best time to bring it up, but—"

Arel gave her an anxious look. "What now?"

"Did you know that Annabel is practically starving to death?"

Arel grimaced. "Starving?"

Peggy glanced back at the kitchen. "Poor thing is stuck in your house with no food. From what I gather, she doesn't know how to drive. So she can't get to the supermarket. She says she walks to a grocery back in London."

Arel swallowed hard. "I completely forgot about her."

Carol gave him a tight hug. "You and William both need to recuperate. In the meantime, the rest of us will help out, right?" She directed her gaze at Kevin and Tim.

Both men shrugged and nodded in agreement.

Kevin reached for an after dinner mint. "Listen, Arel, don't worry about Annabel. Tomorrow's Saturday. I'll take her shopping. We'll fill up your freezer and cupboards."

Arel glanced up. "I'll come with you. I don't want Annabel to think I don't care about her."

Twenty-Five

Annabel's smile couldn't get any bigger. Kevin had driven her to a supermarket that was huge. It dwarfed the small shop she frequented in London. The enormous produce area was amazing. She'd never seen so many kinds of fruits and vegetables. She was also impressed with all the aisles of baking goods, canned goods, frozen food and snacks. But her mouth really started watering when they approached the dessert aisle. She looked back at Kevin and Arel in a breathless, blush of happiness. "I love this place. Thank you for bringing me here!"

Kevin smiled back at her, but it was obvious that Arel wasn't as enthusiastic about their outing. He looked slightly annoyed as he and Kevin pushed their overflowing grocery carts down the long corridors of food. When Arel asked Annabel why she needed so many boxes of cereal and a twenty pound turkey, she had a good excuse. She told him that they wouldn't have to make as many trips to the store if they stocked up. She didn't want him to know the truth. The past week had been difficult, even scary with so little food in the house. On a couple of nights, her empty stomach had growled in protest, and she had a hard time sleeping. But everyone was too busy to notice. Michael was trying to help Arel, and Carey spent a lot of time with William. She wanted to help William too, but he seemed to do better when she wasn't around. Maybe he felt guilty about not being able to be there for her.

Glancing right and left at all the wonderful cakes and pies, she could forget about their problems. She could think about one of the benefits of having a body, that amazing activity called eating.

As she hung over a case of large, beautifully decorated cakes, she realized that Arel was staring at her. "Aren't they all so lovely?" she asked as she fingered the plastic cover of a triple chocolate cake. "Oh my, this one has raspberry crème filling."

Arel cleared his throat. "Yes, they're all very nice, but they're also high in sugar and calories."

Annabel turned and stared back at him, noticing the frown lines in Arel's brow. "Are you saying that I shouldn't eat cake?"

Arel shrugged. "Well—"

Kevin pushed Arel aside and stepped forward. "A little cake isn't going to hurt anything. Which one would you like, Annabel?"

Annabel didn't know what to say. It was clear that Arel disapproved of many of her choices. She'd seen him scowl a number of times as they made their way through the store. His eyes were particularly stern when she snatched up the potato chips, ice cream, and a handful of candy bars. Just remembering his censure made her pull back from the sweets she'd been eying. "It's okay. We can forget the cake."

"Nonsense," Kevin said. He reached into the case and retrieved the chocolate cake. "But maybe we should go to the check out. Arel might not have room for anything more. Besides, I'll take you shopping anytime you want to go, Annabel."

"You will?"

"Of course. I'm here all the time anyway." Kevin patted his stomach. "In case you didn't notice, little Ariel and I have big appetites."

Annabel observed the way Kevin's eyes lit up when he mentioned food. "That makes me feel better. I was beginning to think it was wrong to like eating so much."

Her comment seemed to make Arel come back from his distracted state. His eyes softened immediately. "Annabel, I would never want you to think there's anything wrong with a healthy appetite. You just have to watch what you eat."

Annabel rubbed her arms, aware of how frightened she suddenly felt. What if she was making terrible choices? She knew so little about how to take care of her body properly, what to eat or how much to exercise. She'd never had to think about those things when she was an angel. She stared down at the shiny, tiled floor. "Just put it all back, please. Get whatever you think best."

130

Kevin gave Arel a nudge. "Sometimes, you're such a spoilsport."

Arel glared back. "I'm trying to be helpful."

Kevin stiffened. "You're making Annabel feel bad."

As the two men bantered back and forth, Annabel had a queasy feeling in her stomach. The store didn't feel like a fun place to be anymore. "I'm going to the car. I'll wait for you there."

As she began to hurry to the front of the store, she heard Arel calling to her.

"Annabel, please, come back here!"

"No!" she yelled. She regretted her loud outburst immediately. She sounded like the little girl they'd passed in the snack aisle. The child was having a temper tantrum when she didn't get a cookie from her father.

By the time Annabel got to Kevin's car, she felt more in control of herself. She even had a little more clarity about the life she'd chosen. She wasn't a child. She was an adult who could make her own decisions. So why was she letting herself be so submissive? As an angel she'd been confident, even when things weren't going well.

Looking up at the bright, blue sky, she took a deep breath and tried to remember how much there was to appreciate as a person with a physical vessel. And it was up to her to take charge of her life. She needed to stop waiting for William to get himself together.

The thought of what they'd enjoyed for a brief time and then lost, made her eyes tear up. But crying wasn't going to change anything. She took a tissue out of her pocket and dabbed at her cheeks. She had to plan for a better future. Even if she couldn't count on William, she had to embrace her life and find a way to like being human.

When she got home, she knew she needed time to think things over. Arel was right to seek refuge at Carol and Kevin's house. He could get away from reminders of what was troubling him. Maybe she needed time away from William. Once she had the thought, she decided it was the right one. After she helped to put the groceries away, she went directly to the lower level apartment. William was there to greet her and followed her into the bedroom.

"Look, Annabel, I got a call from Arel when he was at the store, and he explained everything. I'm sure he didn't mean to upset you. From what he told me, he's simply concerned about your health."

Annabel crossed her arms. "Wasn't that nice of him?"

William paused. "Anyway, I'm sorry about—"

"Don't apologize, please. You and Arel have made it very clear that you know better than me. But I'm beginning to have a few ideas of my own. In fact, after thinking things over, I've made a decision. I'm returning to London. I'm going to learn how to make it on my own. I'm sure I can find a job doing something, even if it's washing dishes."

"Washing dishes?"

Annabel straightened up and threw back her shoulders. "What's the problem with washing dishes?"

"Oh please—"

"What is it? Do you still think I'm incapable of handling the most menial of jobs?"

"What are you talking about?"

"Remember your laundry? You told me I was folding your socks the wrong way. And when it came to your undershirts, I thought you'd have a fit because I couldn't make them look as perfect as you wanted. So how could I possibly take on a challenging job that involved cleaning up dirty pots and pans?"

William scowled back. "Are you listening to yourself? Everything you're bringing up is ridiculous."

Annabel went to the closet, grabbed her suitcase and threw it on the bed. "Yes, I guess you're right about that too. I'm a ridiculous, unstable ex-angel. But I've learned a lot since that first day when I gave up my wings. And one of the most important things I've learned is that I don't need you or Arel thinking I'm incompetent."

"I never said you were incompetent, except for the laundry. And you have to admit that you did seem clueless. Or maybe you were just stubborn. I don't know—"

Annabel went to the dresser and paused. "Fine, forget about all that. As you said, it's not important. So let's discuss something that is important."

"What's that?"

"Do you even think about me anymore? When I walk past you, do you notice my presence?"

William sat down on the bed. "With all that's happened recently, I've had other things on my mind. You can understand that."

Annabel opened a drawer and removed some of her clothes. "Yes, I understand. And I'm sorry about everything that you've gone through."

"But?"

"Even if you're having a hard time, you could talk to me. But you're so wrapped up in your problems that I don't exist for you."

William let out a scoffing laugh. "Of course you exist for me. I love you."

Annabel smiled as she put her clothes in her suitcase. "I know that you think you do. And I know you want the best for me. It's just that I have a different way of looking at love and what it means to be with someone."

William got to his feet and glared down at her. "When Rolphe said he might hurt you, I was ready to kill him. Isn't that enough?"

Annabel closed her suitcase. "Sadly no, it's not. My kind of love involves more than wanting to kill someone."

"So risking my life didn't mean a damn thing?"

"I'm sure it has a lot of meaning for you. And I wouldn't want to minimize that. But you're not in Paris now, William. You're here. I'm here. And yet, you haven't even held my hand or shown any sign of wanting to be with me." She hesitated, feeling her stomach twist as she reflected on William's lack of affection. "But I have to put that behind me. I talked to Peggy last night, and she said I could stay with them if I needed to. So that's where I'll be until I can get a flight back to London."

William avoided looking at her, but when he finally brought his eyes in line with hers, they were hard and distant. "Fine, if that's what you want, go. Maybe this whole thing has been a mistake."

Annabel grabbed her suitcase. "Yes, I think you're right about that too."

Twenty-Six

Arel moved back home after the food-shortage fiasco, but he soon regretted his decision. The house felt cold and inhospitable with Annabel gone and William being sulky and ill-tempered. Of course, he understood William's plight. The man had recently had an almost fatal run-in with Rolphe. Next, his relationship with Annabel fell apart.

When Arel walked into the living room, William sat in a chair looking like he was trying to distract himself from both issues. His brows were lined and his eyes were focused on what he was reading.

"It's nice to see you upstairs for a change," Arel said.

William didn't look up when he replied. "The décor in your downstairs apartment is a little heavy."

Arel shrugged. When I moved here, I needed the warmth of darker woods. They were comforting. Since then, I've redone the upstairs in lighter colors."

"All I know is when I'm lying in your bed, I feel like I'm in a Hollywood set for a turn-of-the-century novel."

"We can exchange bedrooms. The upstairs master is quite bright and modern." He paused, trying to think about what he wanted to say. "William, we have more important things to discuss than my furniture choices."

William put his book aside. "What is it?"

"About Rolphe—"

"I don't want to talk about him."

"Maybe not, but this thing with him concerns us both. So tell me how you're doing?"

William looked down at his clasped hands. "If you have to know, he's still . . . here." William pointed to his head. "I've tried to use your shielding techniques, and they're worthless."

Arel frowned. "I don't understand it. They work for me."

"Yes, well, Rolphe didn't have you for dinner, at least not against your wishes. Since his little feasting episode, I can't get ahead of him. When he starts in, I lose it, okay? Is there anything else you want to know?"

Arel went to the front window and stared out. A large crow was sitting on a barren, tree branch. Its black eyes were sharp and staring back. It was an uncomfortable moment, as if the bird were trying to accuse Arel of some misdeed. But which one? His original act of revenge on William? Tossing him out of heaven? Giving Rolphe his blood? There were too many mistakes to think about. "William, I'm not trying to pressure you, but I have to find out where we're at, that's all."

"There's no 'we', Arel. You're doing fine. Your color is coming back, and you're looking stronger. Carey said your arm is quickly getting back to normal."

"Yes, healing quickly is one of the few perks that I've gotten out of this whole business with Michael. Of course, I need to heal up fast so I can face the next hurdle."

"What next hurdle? What's going on now? Is Rolphe coming to Chicago?"

Arel's jaw went rigid. "No! Never!"

"How can you be so sure?"

Arel walked over to a recliner and sat down. "Because I'm going back to Paris."

"Are you crazy? Do you want to end up like me?"

Arel smiled. "Remember what I did in the cave? I'm not going to end up like you. I'm going to make sure you're safe once and for all."

"I'll go with you—"

"And do what? This is a one-man job, and when it's done, life can go back to normal."

"The only way life can go back to normal is for Rolphe to be out of the picture permanently."

"I agree."

"You say that like you're going to—" William narrowed his brows into a tight furrow. "Are you planning on killing him? I thought you were against taking another person's life."

"Rolphe isn't just a normal person anymore. He's got my blood, Michael's blood. If I can't stop him any other way, then that's how it has to be."

William stood up and came over. "Arel, please, you don't know what you're talking about."

Arel stiffened. "If there's no other way, I'll go to Paris, purchase a gun, and kill him. It's as simple as that."

William started laughing. "You are so absurd sometimes."

Arel glared back. "You don't think I can do it?"

"How many people have you killed, Arel, besides me, of course?"

"I never meant to harm you . . . well, I did in the beginning, but not since I came to my senses."

"Yes, and when you took your revenge, how did you do it? You used Michael's blood. You did the same thing with Rolphe. You didn't go out and buy a gun. So what makes you think you can show up at Rolphe's flat and shoot him? It's not your style."

"I've changed."

"Yes, I suppose you have. Using that boulder on Rolphe's head in the cave was impressive. Since it affected him on a physical level, he must have had a hell of a headache after that."

Arel rubbed the recliner arm anxiously. "I've done a lot more since then."

More recently, Arel's astral encounters with Rolphe also ended in violent punishments. When the man persisted in wanting William's blood, Arel kept increasing their severity. "I never thought I'd sink so low, but I did."

"Yes, but you've never killed outright and in cold blood. It's not the same. Besides, with your track record with guilt, killing someone outright could finish you off."

"I've never talked about it, but I have killed a lot of rats in cold blood."

William backed away. "Please Arel, I don't want to hear about your rat-killing days."

Arel retrieved a handkerchief and mopped his forehead. He hadn't thought about his forays into dark alleys in a long time. His stomach went queasy as he remembered his victims. "They're God's creatures too, Will. Please don't think it was easy taking their lives. I just didn't know any other way."

"Exactly my point. You're ready to keel over at the thought of what you did to a rat. How do you think you're going to feel if you kill a man?"

Arel tightened his fists trying to still their shakiness. "I can't let that stop me. I've made Rolphe the abomination that he is. I'm responsible for the hell he's created and will create."

William sat down on the sofa and let out a heavy sigh. "I can see the future so clearly, Arel. You're going to end up like Humpty Dumpty. If you kill Rolphe, no one is going to be able to put you back together again."

* * *

Arel laid a wool jacket across the other clothes in his suitcase. He was almost finished packing. He'd be leaving for the airport in an hour. William's warning was still fresh and disturbing, but he had to focus on his reason for visiting Paris, not his fear. A knock on the door made him forget everything for the moment and stiffen. Carey stood in the doorway. The young man, who was really an angel, still looked like he had when Arel met him. Dressed in worn-out jeans and a faded t-shirt, Carey remained the picture of a fervent youth with a defiant attitude. "You can drop the act, Carey. I don't have time for playing a fool who thinks he's handing out fatherly advice."

"So you're still angry with me?"

"What do you expect?"

"I was hoping that you'd remember how I tried to help you through a difficult time."

"I'm sure an angel's intentions are always pure, but don't expect human beings to appreciate finding out they're pawns in some ethereal game."

"I've never thought of my interaction with you as part of a game. Before I came into the picture, you decided to end it all. I thought I could give you a reason to go on."

"If you, Michael and William hadn't needed to save me, none of this hell would be happening. I would have simply drowned myself in a river when I was a young man. Then when I think about Annabel, I'm doubly sorry that you showed up in my life. If I'd crashed my car into a tree and died, William would never have come to New York, and Annabel would still be an angel happily playing her harp on a cloud. Instead, she's starving to death and crying her eyes out."

"And if I'd never showed up, where would you be?"

"How should I know? Heaven? Hell? I haven't a clue. I only know I wouldn't be here, plotting how to finish off Rolphe."

"Arel, I know something for certain. I know that you wanted this life. You wanted a chance for true happiness, for the joy that every man, woman and child is entitled to."

"If that's true, why did I pick the family I was born into? Why did my brother die and leave me to my father's rage? Why did I fall in love with Justina, only to have her kill herself? Where's the joy in all of that?"

"Aren't you leaving out some of the good parts? There were people in your life who loved you. Your brother and your grandmother were two of them. William loved you too. So did Justina. But you've chosen to forget the positive aspects of all those relationships. You've only held on to the pain. You've played all the wrongs over and over in your mind until you can't see anything but a deadly solution to it all."

Arel sat down on the bed. He crossed his arms and started to laugh. "Wow, that's quite a speech. And I thought you were just a pain-in-the-ass kid."

Carey came over and frowned. "Look at me, Arel. I wasn't just playing a role any more than a human plays a role. The only difference is that I remember more about my true nature. But there were times when I even forgot that. I felt like I was your son, and I liked the feeling. I liked how you looked out for me and tried so hard to help me make the best decisions. I liked the cherry pies you brought home for me. You broke your own rules about eating sweets because you wanted me to be happy. And I was. Maybe you think an angel is some robot programmed to always be the same, but we learn and grow through experience too. And I love what I learned being a person you cared about. So I hope you don't kick me out because you think I'm playing a game."

Arel shrugged. "I never quite understood Michael. There were a few times when I realized how much he cared, but I think I ignored that part. Like you just pointed out, I think I've ignored a lot."

Carey crouched down in front of Arel. "Take me with you to Paris! I don't have any answers about what will happen there, but maybe I can repay your kindness in some way."

"Paris? Absolutely not!"

"Why?"

Arel studied Carey's face. His handsome, not-quite-mature features were framed by winsome light-brown, curly hair. His expression was open and beseeching. Even if he was an angel, he was also the most charming and manipulative of beings.

"Please, Arel, I'm not trying to manipulate you. I truly want to be there with you, to face whatever you find in Paris. Please give me that chance."

Arel sighed and looked at his watch. "Even if I could, I can't get you a passport—"

Carey smiled. "Don't worry about that. I'll meet you there. However, I would like you to ferry some of my clothes and stuff. My duffle bag is out in the hall."

Twenty-Seven

William sat in the living room, listening. The house was quiet. Arel and Carey were off to Paris. Annabel was staying at Peggy and Tim's. So what was he supposed to do? He wasn't one to dwell on his problems, but he didn't feel like going back home, not yet. He needed time to cope with what had happened to him. He also found it difficult to manage his thoughts, especially those that concerned Rolphe. When he heard a knock at the front door, he welcomed the distraction. Even an unexpected visitor might provide a change of pace. When he answered the door, he smiled. "Peggy, what a nice surprise."

"Really?" The small woman gave him a look of wonder. "I mean I didn't expect . . . I mean after the other night, I—"

William frowned as he remembered how nervous he'd been when Peggy had touched him without warning. "The other night? Oh yes, my hasty departure from your living room. I'm sorry. I've been a little out of sorts lately. But please come in."

Peggy hesitated, looking suddenly uncomfortable. "Are you sure? I don't want to be an imposition."

He held the door open and stepped back. "It's nice to have company."

Peggy cautiously stepped into the foyer, clasping her hands. "Actually, I wondered if Arel was around."

"Arel? He's not here. He said something about an errand he had to attend to." William didn't know if he should disclose what that "something" was to Peggy. He knew she already worried a lot about Arel's welfare. If the woman knew he was off on a mission that might do him in permanently, she could go down for the count.

140

"Can I help in any way?" he asked as he gestured the petite redhead into the living room.

Peggy settled down on the edge of a recliner. "Oh, I guess not."

"Peggy, what's bothering you? I thought, after my last visit, that you and I were friends."

Peggy smiled and looked down as she twisted a button on her sweater. "Do you remember what I said when you were going back to London? I hoped you'd think of us, Tim and me, as family. Carol and Kevin feel the same way."

William did remember. In fact, he'd thought about Peggy's offer many times since. He smiled back. "Well then, as family, what can I do for you?"

"It's the baby. Sara's sleeping, and I thought that Arel could come over and watch her for an hour. There's a new coffee shop close by, and I wanted to try out their special French pastries with Annabel. I think she needs to get out a little more. You know, away from the house and the daily chores."

"I see. Of course, I'd be happy to sit with Sara, but I don't know anything about babies."

"Oh, that's not a problem. As I said, she usually takes a long nap in the afternoon. And I'll have my phone with me. If she wakes up, I can be back in five minutes."

* * *

Being a babysitter was something William hadn't contemplated. But sitting in Peggy's living room wasn't any more challenging than sitting on Arel's sofa. In fact, he enjoyed the change. Peggy's taste in decorating wasn't his style, but he appreciated the hominess. There was something very relaxing about the overstuffed furniture, the colorful assortment of pillows on the couch, and the Americana artwork on the walls. As he admired a farm scene with a number of cows in a field, he remembered how much he'd enjoyed the outdoors as a boy. As he continued to look around the room, he saw a stray teddy bear that had escaped the toy bin. From what he'd heard from Carol, it was probably a present from Arel. It seemed that the man was forever finding new bears for both little Ariel and Sara.

William got up and sighed. "The guy should stick to entertaining babies, not go off to Paris to snuff out a villain."

He picked up the stuffed toy and was about to return it to its proper place when he heard a sound. It was a little cry, very faint, but clearly an indication that baby Sara wasn't sleeping as peacefully as Peggy had indicated. When he heard a second whimper, he started to retrieve his phone. He was sorry to interrupt Peggy and Annabel's outing, but he'd told Peggy the truth. He knew nothing about baby care.

A loud scream of distress stopped him before he got his phone out of his pocket. Without thinking, he turned and dashed for the stairs. It was an automatic reflex. Thrown into an instant state of alarm, he took the steps two at a time. A second round of screaming had him rushing into the baby's room. Little Sara was sitting in her crib. She was crying so loud William wondered if someone had harmed the child. Looking around and not seeing anyone, he hurried to the crib.

"It's okay," he said in a whisper, remembering when he'd been a boy and found a frightened fawn. The baby looked up at him and held out her hands. Tears were coursing down her pink cheeks as she waited to be comforted. He had no choice. He had to pick her up. Once the child was in his arms, she threw herself against him, grasping at his shirt.

It was an amazing experience to hold such a tiny, little person. Sara was so light and delicate. He patted her back carefully. "It's alright. Your mommy will be back in a few minutes."

He realized that he was swaying back and forth and doing little, bouncy movements. Again, it felt very natural. After a couple of moments, the baby started to calm down. It was only then that William realized how fast his own heart was beating. But as he continued to comfort the baby, he felt better too. He also thought about Annabel, and how he hadn't been there for her in days. He'd been shocked when she'd walked out on him.

"Oh, little Sara, I've been in a fog."

The baby rubbed her tears against his shoulder and looked up. She stared at him with demanding eyes. That's when he thought about Peggy mentioning that there was a bottle in the refrigerator. Her instructions were very simple. If, by chance, the baby did wake up before she got back, he could warm up some milk.

He went back down the stairs cautiously, thinking about the fragility of the child he was holding. Yet, when he tuned into little Sara's mindset, it felt much stronger than her body. He found it easy to read her thoughts and desires. It was clear that he was there to hold her, feed her, and treat her like the little princess her daddy proclaimed her to be.

Later, as William sat on the sofa, feeding Sara her bottle, he felt some of his stress melting away. He'd never given the possibility of having children any serious thought until that moment.

* * *

Annabel enjoyed her outing with Peggy. The little eatery where they had coffee and croissants was a new found treasure. The shop itself was bright and cheerfully decorated. The servers were very polite. Best of all, the desserts were scrumptious. Peggy wanted to try seconds and suggested a round of éclairs, but Annabel resisted.

She left the shop feeling proud of herself. Her life was more balanced after only a couple of days. In fact, after being with Peggy and Tim, she felt like she might get the hang of being human. The couple's life was so different than what she'd known with William. The constant worry and stress wasn't nearly as bad. Of course, a lot of the stress revolved around Arel.

On the drive home with Peggy, she wanted the woman's opinion of the man. "You've known Arel for some time. Is he always so intense?"

Peggy flashed a frowning smile. "We met through Carol. And the beginning of our friendship was a little rocky."

"Why was that?"

"Arel was very guarded, and I didn't help the situation. I think I frightened the poor guy on a number of occasions. Then he became deathly ill. We were all worried that he was going to die. But he took a chance on trusting us. Maybe it was because he didn't think he'd make it either. In the end, he got better, and we've been close ever since."

Annabel noticed the warmth in Peggy's tone when she talked about Arel. "He's lucky to live next to you."

"And we're lucky to have him. I think he saved Kevin and Carol's marriage at one point. Believe me, there's no one as dedicated as Arel when it comes to helping one of us."

Annabel smiled as they pulled into the driveway. "Thank you for everything. This little outing was so much fun."

Peggy climbed out of the car. "I hope William did okay."

Annabel felt her heart do a little flutter when she thought about seeing William again. When he came over to babysit, they hadn't had time to do anything but exchange quick greetings. Now, she hoped they'd have a few moments to talk again, maybe even take a walk.

She followed Peggy into the house with a quiet anticipation. Then she saw William in the living room. He was holding the baby. When he looked up and their eyes met, she held her breath. She knew without a doubt that she still loved him completely, and from the way he smiled at her, she knew that he still loved her.

Twenty-Eight

Arel woke up with Carey standing over him and shaking his shoulders. He winced and tried to remember where he was. Finally, it clicked, he was in Paris. After his long flight and getting hassled in customs, he'd been too tired to do anything but check into a hotel and get some sleep. "Carey, what's going on?"

"You were having a nightmare."

He moaned. "I was dreaming about William again, about Rolphe attacking him." He rubbed his eyes and blinked a couple times, trying to get his bearings.

"It's okay. William is fine, remember?"

Arel let the information sink in before he gave Carey his full attention. "You look as energetic as always."

Carey's smile broadened. "With my kind of travel, I guess I don't have to worry about jet lag."

"And you don't have to worry about your stuff either."

"You're talking about my duffle bag."

"Do you know it took an extra hour waiting for customs to process what you had me bring along? And it weighs a ton."

"Sorry, I packed my books and a few other heavier items."

"Why would you bring your books?"

"They're like the cherry pie, I enjoy them."

"Carey, you have a phone that's capable of holding goodness knows how many books."

"It's not the same, especially for me. Physical items help me to relate better."

Arel closed his eyes. "Why do I bother arguing with you? You and Michael always have an answer for everything."

"Did somebody mention me?" a voice asked.

Arel glanced over at the window. "Michael, I didn't know you'd be here too."

Michael came over. "I didn't think you'd mind since you invited Carey along."

"He invited himself. But maybe I'll need you both. William is convinced that I'm headed for a break down."

Carey frowned. "I hope not. We're just starting over."

Michael sat down on a chair close to the bed, stretching out his legs. "About William—"

Arel pushed himself up on an elbow and glared at Michael. "What happened? I thought Carey said—"

Michael smiled. "He's fine. In fact, he and Annabel are back together."

"That's a relief," Arel said with a weak smile. He was happy for the couple. On the other hand, he wondered if he'd ever find love again. He'd been doing a bit of soul searching on the plane. He didn't like what he observed about himself. In short, he was a constant complainer who was always on edge. Even if there was good reason for his attitude, what woman in her right mind would ever want to get involved with him? He let out a wistful sigh adding self-pity to his list of shortcomings.

Carey nudged him out of his somber musings.

"Hey, Arel? This is kind of exciting, isn't it? You, me and Michael, all showing up at Rolphe's door. He might be a little surprised, don't you think?"

Arel nodded. "Yes, I think the vicious brute will be very surprised. I haven't been able to get through to him and change his mind, but he has quite a respect for the Creator's henchmen."

Carey pulled back. "Arel, please, Michael and I aren't henchmen."

Arel laughed. "You know that, and I know that, but Rolphe doesn't know that."

* * *

After Rolphe returned to his own apartment, he'd steadily been going downhill. In the past, Rolphe certainly had his bouts with guilt, but they came and went. The guilt didn't get stuck in his chest. It didn't become the impossible burden that it was now. Between the effects of ingesting Arel's blood and the William fiasco, he felt like he'd been thrown into a whole new arena of retribution. Not only were his former victims haunting him, but his dead sons were there too. Their ghostly forms would appear out of nowhere. Their faces were anxious and questioning. They seemed to be asking Rolphe how the father they had adored could have turned into such an ogre.

At one time, maybe he could have dealt with it all. Maybe his body could have remained as strong as ever if it weren't for those last moments with William. The man lay on Rolphe's bed, looking broken. Yet, even in his near-death state, William emanated a strange, eerie glow that Rolphe saw very clearly with his gift of sight.

He understood what the light signified. He'd seen a similar brilliance when he'd glimpsed an angel or two as a child. He knew that William and Arel weren't angels, but they were exceptional, none the less. Maybe they were God's chosen humans who were there to remind Rolphe of his evil nature in a way he couldn't ignore.

He couldn't ignore another fact. Punishment couldn't be put off until the afterlife. Rolphe's body was rapidly deteriorating. His chest pain was getting worse, and he felt a consuming weakness settling into his bones. With each day, he was slipping physically as well as emotionally.

That's why he'd been trying so desperately to contact William. Maybe if he could make amends, he could save himself. But William wouldn't listen long enough to let Rolphe apologize. He didn't get a chance to beg forgiveness. As he continued to lose ground, he hardly had the willpower to try.

When someone knocked on his door, he didn't know if he had the strength to answer it. But whoever was there was persistent. They continued banging away. He pushed himself off the sofa and slowly shuffled to the small entrance hall. He steadied himself enough to undo the locks and throw open the door. That's when time stopped and his psychic senses came alive more powerfully than ever. He stared at his visitors with wide eyes and gaping mouth.

"Holy mother," he managed to gasp. Seeing a couple of angels as a child was one thing, having two of them show up at his flat was too much. Their bright auras lit up the entire hallway. But it was Arel who was even more frightening. His golden eyes had transformed

147

into blazing pools of hatred. They were targeting him, letting him know that there was no escape from the man's wrath and punishment.

Rolphe tried to respond. More than anything, he wanted to escape the terrible spectacle in front of him. Instead, a squeezing pain took hold of his heart. He stumbled back a few steps, trying to stay upright, but the pain in his chest was paralyzing and he began to fall.

* * *

Arel stood at Rolphe's door, trying not to think about what he was going to do to the man. With Michael and Carey on either side of him, he felt a little calmer. He even tried to put his rage aside long enough to think more rationally. After all, he wasn't afraid of Rolphe. Since he'd had time to recuperate, he was his powerful self again.

Using his fist, he knocked loudly on Rolphe's door. He only waited a short few moments before he knocked again. "Open up, you bastard!"

He had to wait for a minute, but eventually, the door swung open. Seeing Rolphe in the flesh was a shock at first. His bulk took up most of Arel's line of vision. The man was huge. But when Arel looked at the man's eyes, they were those of a terrified child. Before Arel could say anything, Rolphe was stumbling backwards, holding his chest. Then he was falling, slamming to the floor, like a great oak felled by the woodman's ax.

Opened-mouthed, Arel looked at Michael. "What the—?"

Michael stepped forward and knelt down by Rolphe. "He's having a heart attack."

Arel hesitated, too stunned to know how to proceed. This wasn't the way he'd imagined his confrontation. Rolphe hadn't been lying on the floor dying. He'd been his usual depraved self, trying to get the upper hand.

Michael gestured him over. "I don't think he's going to last very long. You better come here quickly. He wants to say something to you."

Arel's mind jumped ahead. If Rolphe died, Arel's opportunity to mete out justice would be lost. His rage resurfaced, pressing him into action. He rushed to where Rolphe lay, knelt down and grabbed the man's shirt. "Do you know what a monster you are? You're a contemptible swine! A despicable blight on the earth!"

Rolphe gazed back, trying to get his breath. "But before I die, have mercy on my soul, please."

"Mercy? What mercy have you ever shown anyone?"

Rolphe shut his eyes. "Tell William that I asked for his forgiveness. I tried to persuade him, but—"

"Stop! Never speak his name, never even think about him! Never!" Arel shook Rolphe's massive bulk roughly with a strength that surged through his body, but the man had passed out.

Foiled and still fuming, Arel sat back in confusion. He'd come to Paris, seeking out Rolphe with one purpose, to kill him. But he'd wanted to make Rolphe atone before he died. He wanted the man to feel the pain he'd caused William and himself.

He glared at Michael. "I can't believe this is happening. That he's going to die!"

Michael gave him a look of surprise. "That's what you wanted."

"Yes, but what good will it do? You've told me that you don't believe in a hell. So how's he going to pay for what he's done?"

"Arel, it isn't your place to—"

"Please, not now, Michael, I have to think." Arel stared at Rolphe's ashen face with disgust. He'd been cheated. William had been cheated. But what could he do? That's when his eyes brightened. "Unless he doesn't die."

"What do you mean?" Michael asked.

Arel thought about his healing abilities. "I mean I'm not going to let Rolphe leave the earth without facing what he's done."

Carey came over and stared down at him. "Remember, Arel, you've deeply regretted keeping William earth bound."

"That was an entirely different situation. I cared about William. I couldn't stand the thought of him dying. And no matter what I did, it all turned out for the best. He's got Annabel and a wonderful life ahead of him."

"But that's not what you want for Rolphe."

"No, you're right, but—"

Michael cut in. "Do you want my opinion?"

Arel's eyes flared, but he kept his temper in check. "Yes, of course."

149

"Rolphe isn't dead . . . yet. Perhaps you could take some time to reflect before you do anything to interfere. You might call William and ask him what he thinks."

"Please, listen to Michael," Carey chimed in. "William is the one who almost died. Shouldn't you include him in what's going on?"

* * *

William held the phone close, making sure that Arel was getting his message. "Let him die, Arel. Am I making myself clear? Don't do anything one way or the other. Simply let Rolphe move on."

"I hear you," Arel answered. "But I'm going to stick around until he's gone. I want to make sure the bastard doesn't have any more surprises in store for either of us."

"Fine, just let me know when you're coming back."

"I will. In the meantime, take care of yourself."

"I'm doing a lot better. I feel more like myself." William ended the call and turned to Annabel. She was sitting next to him in bed. They had taken Arel's suggestion to move upstairs into the master bedroom. With the sun streaming in from the double windows, everything was so much brighter. And yet, when he looked at Annabel, he felt like her glow came from an inner source. Her radiant face made him smile with appreciation.

"What is it?" she asked.

"I have good news. From what Arel just told me, this whole thing with Rolphe is finally coming to an end."

Annabel reached out for his hand. "That's wonderful."

"I wish Arel felt that way."

"What do you mean?"

"He's disappointed that Rolphe won't be sticking around long enough for Arel to punish his misdeeds."

"I wish Arel could let go of everything and just live a more peaceful life."

"That's the problem. I don't think he knows how. In fact, I had a sort of epiphany recently. I realized something about the situation I had with Rolphe. I thought I'd just drifted into a fog of sorts and lost my way. After some reflection, I knew that it was Arel's fog."

"I don't understand."

"No matter how good Arel's intentions are, they're always tainted with his negativity. After tuning into him repeatedly, I think I got drawn into his twisted way of thinking."

Annabel pulled back and picked at the bedcovers. "That may be true, but I'm learning that we have to be responsible, no matter what."

William laughed and snatched up her hand. "Don't worry. I understand that. I've lived by that principle most of my life. It's just that Arel can make anyone slightly crazy if they're not careful."

Annabel leaned into his shoulder. "I see your point. In fact, when I stayed with Peggy and Tim, I kind of came to the same conclusion."

William let out another huff of laughter.

Annabel glanced up and studied his face. "What's that look mean?"

"It means that if Rolphe does live for any length of time, and Arel is around, the guy is going to pay for his wrongdoing."

"How?"

"Let's just say that the name, Arel, and the word, hell, kind of go together."

Twenty-Nine

After an all-night vigil, Arel didn't know if he was happy that Rolphe didn't die straight away or not. He was tired of sitting in Rolphe's bedroom. The place was run down and depressing. The dismal wallpaper looked like it dated back at least fifty years. The furniture was shabby, and the windows were a disgrace. Paris didn't look nearly as beautiful when staring out through windows coated in dirt and grime.

Then there was Rolphe. Arel might have been a little hasty in declaring his intent to stick around. Michael said the man was still in serious danger, but the angel withdrew his declaration about a fast demise. He thought Rolphe might hang on for an extended period of time. Arel's shoulders slumped at the updated information. As he watched Rolphe's chest rise and fall repeatedly, he scowled. If Rolphe lingered, dispensing justice could be a very long, drawn-out affair.

But Arel wasn't alone with his task. Carey was sitting in another bedroom chair, reading a book he'd found in Rolphe's small library. Even if Carey was an angel, Arel had decided to return to their previous relationship as much as possible. Carey had made it clear that he enjoyed the role so why should Arel make it a big deal.

As for Michael, the angel had bowed out for the time being. Rolphe was overwhelmed enough with one angel keeping him company. Since Carey was perceived as the less threatening of the two, Michael kept his distance.

After a night of contemplation, Arel's emotional status was less overwrought than when he'd arrived. As Rolphe's heart continued ticking away, Arel's vengeful wrath was beginning to flatline. It was dawning on him that he was the only one in his group who seemed to make everything a problem. William constantly reminded him of the fact. Everyone in Chicago kind of suggested the same thing.

He cleared his throat. "What do you think, Carey? You've been around me for quite a while. Do you think I'm capable of adopting a lighter approach to life?"

Carey closed his book and smiled. "Of course, and if you did relax a little more, we could go back to Hawaii. Maybe you'd even try surfing."

"I don't know about surfing, but the sun and beach were nice."

"Nice? I loved every minute of our vacation."

Arel stood up and stretched. "You're right, if I let myself admit it, Hawaii was perfect."

"How did William sound when you spoke to him?"

Arel went to the window. He used his handkerchief to rub away enough of the dirty film to get a better look at the city. A thick layer of clouds hung low and dark in the sky. He turned back to Carey. "William sounded good. It's surprising how fast he's regaining his footing after what happened. And I'm sure having Annabel by his side is adding to his good cheer. So I'm hanging out in this dump while they're blissfully strolling through the park."

"I'm happy for them. I bet you are too."

"Yes, I am." Arel pocketed his kerchief. Carey's enthusiasm was contagious, and he liked the feeling. He wanted to go back home. He wanted to put Rolphe behind him. "You know something, Carey, if William can get a fresh start with everything, I can too."

"What about Rolphe? Should we call for medical help?"

Arel looked at the bed again and shook his head. "No, Michael said the man refused to go that route."

Carey got up. "What do you want to do?"

Arel grabbed his jacket off his chair. "We should head back to the hotel. I'll book a ticket home." He was almost at the door when he heard Rolphe moan and call out in a weak, hoarse voice.

"Arel! Please, don't leave me!"

* * *

With his heart barely able to find its next beat, Rolphe knew he didn't have much time left. The thought left him sweaty and desperate. He couldn't face death on his own. Even having his tormenter with him was better than having no one.

But Arel didn't look happy about Rolphe's request. The man stood next to the bed with loathing eyes. "How dare you ask me to stay? Did you stay with William?"

"I know," Rolphe begged, "but don't you understand. William had nothing to fear if he died. I have hell waiting for me."

Carey moved into Rolphe's line of vision. "Rolphe, if you want, I'll stick around."

Rolphe threw up his arm, shielding his eyes. The quick movement made his heart speed up and waste what precious few beats were left. It couldn't be helped. The angel was blindingly bright, and just the sight of him reminded Rolphe of how many sins he'd be paying for. "No! Go away! I'm not ready for Hades yet!"

Arel's scowl deepened. "Stop your whining, you lucky bastard. From what I know, there'll be no hell waiting for you."

Rolphe's fists closed on themselves. "You're wrong. Every time I shut my eyes, I see the fires burning."

Arel looked at the angel. "Carey, what's he babbling about?"

Rolphe watched the angel wave Arel over to a corner of the room. He had to strain to hear what Carey was saying. He was telling Arel that when people believed in punishment, they could experience a hell of sorts.

"Listen to him, please," Rolphe cried out in a gasp.

Arel's frown slipped away, and he smiled. "I am listening. Finally, some good news."

Carey sighed. "Arel, maybe you could try to understand that underneath Rolphe's wrongdoing, there is a part of him that wants redemption."

Rolphe nodded as a little spark of hope made his heart ease. The angel was pleading his case.

Arel's scowl came back. "Please! The man is evil, through and through!"

"It's not your place to judge," Carey insisted.

"Fine." Arel grabbed his jacket again and started to leave. "But I'm not sticking around, listening to him."

"Not even you can be that cruel, Arel," Rolphe groaned. "You know the pain of fire. You've felt it—"

Arel stopped abruptly and glared back at him. When their eyes met, Rolphe knew his words hit their mark. But they did much more than that. Rolphe felt Arel's mind explode into flame. But he didn't just feel Arel's shift, he became part of the scene that Arel was reliving from a past life. Dozens of torches lit up the night. An irate mob's slurs and spittle corrupted the heavy air. Then Rolphe saw the person that Arel had been in that long ago time. He was still so young and unformed. He'd scarcely begun to know manhood. His broken face was blameless and beautiful despite the blood and bruises. Nothing could stop his soul's light from shining through.

The young man's only sin was trying to save his sister from those who defiled her. Now, he was defiled. He'd been battered and torn at the hands of those whose work was to torture and maim. Helpless, he was bound to a stake and engulfed in fire. Rolphe heard his screams and felt the man's skin burning as if it were his own. His visions of hellfire had never affected him physically until now. He had to quickly shut down his gift of sight. If he didn't, he feared that the flames would engulf the bed where he lay.

Gasping, he battled to come back to the bedroom. When he managed to leave the past behind and ground himself in the present moment, he noted Arel's reaction. The man looked dazed as he stumbled to his chair. His persecutor's golden eyes still blazed with the memory.

In that moment, Rolphe began to understand who he was dealing with. Like Rolphe, Arel had been filled with bitterness after what he'd gone through. Yet, he'd found a way to care again. That was why Arel fought so hard for William. His heart was capable of love, a virtue Rolphe had put aside long ago.

When he'd lost everything that he cherished, Rolphe had cursed his ability to hurt so deeply. He'd taken his rage out on others. But now, when he remembered the young man's face in the flames, he knew he couldn't hurt anyone again. He couldn't endure their pain. It belonged to him too.

"Please, Arel, I'm begging you, forgive me!" As Rolphe spoke, he saw his boys. Their ghostly forms stood next to his bed. For the first time, since they'd been visiting him, they smiled as they reached out to him.

Rolphe's children had always been that part of his life that was sweet and faultless. When they had died in his arms, his heart became a stone, a hard, mechanical part of him that did its job of pumping blood. But it lost its true connection to loving the gift of life. Now, his beautiful sons were showering him with their understanding and sweetness again. It was the final straw that broke his heart.

He felt the vessel shatter, falling apart, as broken as the young man in the flames. But the condition of the vessel didn't kill him. When it broke apart, something else happened. More pain rushed in, unbearable pain that seized his entire body. He didn't have to die to enter hell. It came to him. Again, he looked to Arel. This time when their eyes met, Arel's gaze softened the slightest bit. "Go to sleep, Rolphe!" he ordered.

It wasn't the forgiveness that Rolphe yearned for, but something in the way Arel continued to stare at him helped. He felt a little relief. Then he fell asleep. When he woke up hours later, much of the pain was gone. He was sure that Arel had intervened, that his tormentor had taken pity on him.

Thirty

William stood at the kitchen window, appreciating the warmth of the sun streaming in. Chicago was leaving the chill of winter behind. Soon the city and suburbs would be decked out in spring's lively, green wardrobe. Michael's garden would also come alive. Peggy had shown William photos she'd taken the year before. Michael was an enthusiastic tiller of the soil. Beds of daffodils, crocus, tulips and hyacinths would soon turn Arel's back yard into a showcase of color.

William wouldn't be around to witness the splendor. He was taking Annabel back to London. They needed to start planning their life together. If Arel wanted to stay in Paris and wait for Rolphe to leave the earth, that was his decision, and William would respect it.

"I'm sorry you won't be here for the change of seasons," Michael said.

William turned as Michael sat down at the table. "I wish I could, but Annabel and I are both intent on putting the past behind us. We need to start fresh. Annabel has even suggested some changes to my home. She's probably right. Some feminine touches might be just what's needed."

Michael gave him a generous smile. "Good. I'm sure both of you are ready for something different."

William turned to the window again. Some of the tree branches were swelling with buds. There was also a hint of green in the lawn that bordered the garden. "So when is Arel coming back?"

"He wants to return. In fact, he was going to leave even if Rolphe hung on, but that's changed."

"What do you mean?"

157

"Rolphe has begged Arel not to leave him."

William swiveled. "And Arel is letting Rolphe bully him into staying?"

"Arel doesn't know what else to do. Besides, Rolphe has had a change of heart. He's very sorry for what he did to you, William."

William pulled out his phone. "Who cares? Let him repent on his own time. I'm telling Arel to get out of that hellish place."

"I thought you wanted to be free of what Arel is doing?"

William hesitated. Hadn't he recently told Annabel about getting caught up in Arel's insanity? "You're right. Why am I involving myself again?" He returned his phone to his pocket.

"I know you care about Arel—"

William laughed. "Yes, and where did it get me? I can't do it anymore. If Arel can't let go of all the trauma-drama, I can."

"So when are you and Annabel leaving?"

"I want to wait a couple of days, and let Annabel enjoy her new friends. We should be gone by the end of the week."

* * *

Arel came to a decision after spending time in Rolphe's flat. If he was going to remain in the appalling place, he'd have to do something to make it bearable. It needed a deep down cleaning for starters. Thankfully, he was feeling much better physically. It was particularly helpful that his arm was almost well. He needed some muscle if he was going to put his surroundings in order.

Armed with gloves, disinfectant, sponges, and cleaning rags, he began with the walls of the bath. They were still streaked with William's blood. Carey had offered to take care of the chore, but Arel declined his offer.

"But Arel, you should let me do this," Carey argued back. "Working in here will just fuel your anger."

Arel snapped on a glove and snatched up a wet sponge. Scrubbing as vigorously as his recently wounded limb would permit, he began to clean a section of the wall. "I want it to be fueled. I want every square inch I wipe down to remind me of what Rolphe did. I may have to stay with him, but that doesn't mean I'll ever forget what he is, a murderous villain."

"Arel, you can gauge his energy just like I can. He's changed. I don't think he'll ever go back to being so callous again."

"So what? Even if I don't want him to burn in hell anymore, I won't let him think he can just say he's sorry and forget what's happened." He turned to Carey. "Now, make yourself useful, please. Take the supplies I gave you and get those bedroom windows clean."

"But Rolphe doesn't like me around. I scare him."

Arel smiled. "Perfect, he needs some scaring. So take your time and make sure you do the job right. When you're done, call me. I want to see the panes shining again."

When Carey hesitated, Arel put down his sponge, shook his head and grabbed Carey's cleaning supplies. He started for Rolphe's bedroom. "Fine, I'll go in there with you and get you started."

As soon as they entered Rolphe's room, Rolphe's eyes grew wide with fright. He targeted Carey with his petition. "Please, Angel, leave me in peace," he gasped.

Arel grimaced back. "Forget it, Rolphe. He's going to help clean up this pig sty you call your home. Your windows are filthy!"

Rolphe blinked back innocently. "I suppose I got used to the way it looks."

Arel put the cleaning supplies by the window and came over to the bed. "And I'm sick of seeing you just lying there on those detestable sheets."

Rolphe shrugged. "What do you want me to do?"

"Carey and I will get you to a chair so I can change the bed."

Rolphe returned a weak smile. "Thank you for caring."

"It has nothing to do with caring. Unlike you, I find everything here abhorrent and foul. Don't you have any self-respect?"

"Yes, of course I do. When I visit—"

"Visit who?"

Rolphe looked away. "Never mind."

Arel waved to Carey. "I want you to use some of your angel strength and help me get this derelict to the chair."

Carey smiled at Rolphe. "Don't worry, I won't harm you, Rolphe."

Arel tightened his jaw. "Oh, for goodness sake, Carey, like you're going to be a threat?"

Rolphe caught Arel's reproachful eyes and stared back. For the first time since he'd had a heart attack, his gaze was challenging.

159

"Arel, how can you be so disrespectful around one of God's special messengers? They are holy beings."

Arel stiffened. "I am not disrespectful! Right, Carey?"

Carey stepped back and smiled. "You try your best."

Rolphe slowly rolled himself up into a sitting position. Holding his chest, he blinked at Carey as he tried to steady himself on the bed. "I'm sorry if Arel has done anything irreverent. I guess he wasn't brought up to honor God's blessed ones."

Arel skewered Rolphe with a hateful look. "Don't try to ingratiate yourself with Carey by accusing me of ignorance. Is that clear?"

Rolphe nodded and averted his eyes. "I just don't want you to get in trouble. You've had enough of that already, haven't you?"

"What are you talking about?"

Rolphe kept his eyes downcast. "Nothing, I'm sorry." He tried to stand up and had to hold on to the nightstand to steady himself.

Arel signaled to Carey. "Let's get him over to the chair. After that, we'll strip the bed and get the bedding in the wash."

Rolphe looked up apologetically. "You'll have to go to the laundromat."

Arel recoiled when he gave the bedlinens another quick inspection. "Forget that. This filth is going in the dumpster." He reached in his pocket and held out some bills to Carey. "Get a cab, find a store and buy some sheets, blankets, and towels. In the meantime, Rolphe can rest in the living room."

* * *

Rolphe lay on his oversized sofa. Physically, he was just above invalid status, but his powers of observation were functioning just fine. As he watched his visitor working, he realized that he'd never seen anyone as driven as Arel. The man spent hours working fervently on Rolphe's bathroom. When the angel named Carey came back from his shopping trip, Arel continued with his quest for tidiness. He insisted they put the clean linens on the bed at once. He also made sure the angel started washing the windows. Rolphe's home had never been such a hub of activity.

Rolphe smiled to himself. Arel might be a tyrant, but he'd also make a great officer in the army. The man had an iron will when it came to his goals. He could also issue orders to others in no uncertain terms. When he wanted to achieve his objective, he made others around him follow suit.

Yet, Rolphe could also see that Arel had another side. In spite of his harsh and unbending traits, the man's spirited energy had a youthful edge to it. It was an animated vitality that was rarely seen in adults. It was a welcome addition to Rolphe's flat. It changed the mood of the place and opened his mind to happy memories.

As he watched Arel rushing in and out of the kitchen, rummaging for more supplies, he thought about his life as a father. His two boys had been excitable too. When he played the balalaika and sang songs, they danced and clapped their hands. They made their humble home a place of happiness and joy. At night, when Rolphe sat by the fire pondering his life, he knew he was a fortunate man to have sons who made him so happy.

But there was more to consider when he thought about Arel's youthfulness. Perhaps that young man who had been burned at the stake wasn't totally dead and gone. A part of him seemed to remain in Arel's personality. Just like the young man, Arel didn't seem to be fully mature.

Now, Rolphe suspected that Arel was still searching for the man he was supposed to be. Yet, Arel didn't give that part the time needed for the task. He kept himself busy instead of attending to his own needs.

Rolphe sighed as he thought about his children. Would he have been able to guide them successfully into manhood? If they had lived and he'd never been embittered by their deaths, would he have helped them mature? Under his guiding hand would they have found their strength yet held on to their caring hearts?

Rolphe didn't know the answers, but he did feel a growing desire to help Arel in some small measure. The man hadn't abandoned him. Rolphe was even beginning to think he might hope for forgiveness on the part of the Creator.

Arel dismissed his gesture to stick around, but for Rolphe, it was a monumental act of kindness. That singular act gave him another chance in life. It deserved some kind of reward.

Thirty-One

With William away at the park with Tim, Kevin and the two babies, Annabel sat at Peggy's kitchen table, sipping tea. Carol sat across from her, talking about her little boy, Ariel. Annabel was grateful to be spending time with the two women, learning about their take on life. She'd be returning to London soon. William would be there for her, but he was in a state of flux and dealing with his own problems. If Annabel was going to be a well-adjusted ex-angel, she needed to observe other people. She glanced up as Peggy put a plate of scones on the table and sat down.

"I got these at that new shop," Peggy said. "Bon appétit."

Annabel smiled and reached out for one. After taking a bite, she looked at Peggy. "Thank you for getting these treats for us. They're wonderful."

Peggy smiled back. "How do they compare with the ones you get in London?"

Annabel swallowed her bite and returned a puzzled look. "Compare? I guess I didn't think about comparing them. Is that something I should do?"

Carol laughed. "Of course not. It's great if you can just enjoy them and leave it at that."

Peggy picked up a scone, examined it and narrowed her brow. "Carol's right. I think people have gotten too judgmental about everything. Maybe it's because there are so many choices nowadays. In the past, when people lived their lives on a farm, I guess there wasn't much to compare."

Carol patted her mouth with her napkin. "I wonder if people were happier back then."

Annabel took another sip of tea, put her cup down and avoided looking at her new friends. "Do either of you ever think that today's world is a bit challenging?"

Peggy let out a laugh that was a little too loud. "Are you kidding? Half the time I feel like I'm headed for the looney bin."

Carol nodded. "I agree. Who can keep up with all the changes? The world's spinning faster and faster, and on a personal level, I'm barely able to keep my head above water."

"What do you mean?" Annabel asked.

Carol shrugged. "Besides being a wife and mother, I guess I want more out of life. If I deny my own needs for very long, I get cranky." She looked at Peggy. "Right, Peggy?"

"I think what Carol is trying to say is that women today need more of themselves. We can't just clean and cook for our families and be happy."

"That's right," Carol said. "As I get more confident and try new things, I'm more content. I don't always need Kevin to be a certain way. I was very independent before I married, but then I kind of regressed."

Peggy shifted in her seat. "Yes, but now all that's behind you."

Carol grinned. "What Peggy is trying to say is that if I'm not happy, I don't blame Kevin anymore. I know it's my problem, and I deal with it." She reached out to Annabel. "Your William was a big part in helping me change my attitude. He made me look at myself differently and take a chance on myself."

Annabel felt her cheeks flush. "My William—"

"We're going to miss you both," Peggy said.

*　*　*

William gave the baby swing a gentle push. He was rewarded with young Ariel's loud squeal of delight. The little boy's body filled out the seat of the swing, and his high-pitched voice filled the airways. William's ears weren't used to Ariel's exuberant cries, but what could he do? He was on child-care duty once again. He hadn't wanted to accompany Kevin and Tim to the park, but Annabel insisted that he accept the men's invitation. He suspected she needed some time with just her women friends.

Kevin stood a couple of feet away, talking to Tim. Tim was in charge of the baby swing next to Ariel's. He was pushing little Sara. Sara wasn't as happy as Ariel. In spite of swaying back and forth in the warm, spring air, she wore a scowl, a narrowed look of annoyance, as if swinging was an activity she detested. After a couple of minutes, she started to cry. Tim reacted at once, quickly slowing the swing and trying to retrieve the unhappy, little girl. He gave William a quick glance and an explanation. "I better pick her up before she really starts in. When she gets herself worked up, she's very difficult to calm down."

Kevin slowed Ariel's swing to a stop. "It's time to head back anyway," he announced. He tried to disengage Ariel's chubby hands from the safety bar. The baby had a firm grasp and refused Kevin's efforts. Kevin seemed to be used to such reactions. He pulled out a package of apple slices from his pocket and dangled them in front of the little boy. When Ariel let out another squeal and reached out for a treat, Kevin handed him a slice of fruit and lifted the baby from the swing. After the baby was settled in his arms, he smiled at William. "I promised to help Carol with dinner tonight. I think she needs a break. She practically lives in the kitchen trying to keep up with Junior's appetite."

William looked at the two fathers holding their offspring. Tim and Kevin were similar in height and build, but their babies were drastically different. Sara was small for her age and delicate. Little Ariel recently had a first birthday, but he was wearing clothes made for a two-year-old. The last time the baby's godfather, Arel, held the little boy, he looked overwhelmed by the task.

William sighed at the thought. He wondered how Arel was faring in Paris.

Kevin glanced at him again. "Are you okay? You look kinda worried."

William shook his head. "I'm fine."

Tim cuddled baby Sara. "Come off it, Will, you always have that look when you're around Arel. I bet you're thinking about him, right?"

William's scowl deepened. "I didn't realize I was that easy to read."

Kevin laughed. "What is it with you two? I guess you're friends, but whenever I've seen you together, you're always griping at each other or worse."

Tim added a puzzled look. "Kevin and I can't figure it out. When we first saw you in New York, you looked great, a confident man of the world. What happened?"

William narrowed his eyes. "You were there? I never saw either of you—"

Kevin looked away and busied himself with Ariel's shoe, readjusting the Velcro tab. "If you have to know, we weren't supposed to be there, but Peggy had one of her weird dreams and—"

Tim cut in. "What Kevin means is that we were worried about Arel. He seems to get himself into situations that—"

William held up a hand. "Please, don't explain. I get the picture. In fact, I'm living proof of what happens when a person tries to help the guy. Like you just pointed out, I was fine until our little reunion."

"We're not trying to knock Arel, he's great," Kevin insisted. "He was different before that meeting. He smiled and had great dinner parties for us. After he got back from that trip, he went downhill. I don't think he's ever recovered."

William let out a laugh too. It had a hard edge. "That makes two of us. But that's all going to change. Annabel and I are going back to London. We're going to settle down. Hopefully we're going to enjoy a normal life."

Kevin handed little Ariel another apple slice. "And what about Arel? He's still not right."

William shrugged. "I don't know what else I can do."

Tim looked down at baby Sara. She was falling asleep in the crook of his arm. "The only thing I know is that a friend doesn't desert a friend. When Arel comes back, we'll be here for him, right Kevin?"

Kevin straightened his shoulders, making his six-foot-three physique look even more imposing. "Look, Will, you do what you have to do, but Tim and I aren't going to let Arel drive himself into the ground. I tried to follow Peggy's lead to give him space when he got back the last time. It was a mistake. The guy almost died. That's not going to happen again if I can help it."

Thirty-Two

Arel shifted the groceries in his arm and unlocked the door to Rolphe's apartment. It was nice to get out for a brisk walk and do some shopping. After almost a week at the Paris flat, he was tired of working from morning to night. On the plus side, he'd managed to clean up Rolphe's apartment. Carey had helped. For once, he hadn't played the unruly youth. Instead, he'd tried to follow Arel's directions, cleaning windows, rugs and cupboards. With both of them working together, things had gone quickly. Even with his strict code of cleanliness, Arel had finally deemed the flat suitable for habitation.

Carey had been such an enthusiastic volunteer that Arel felt the need to show Carey how grateful he was. He even went against his better judgment when he thought about what to get Carey.

Recently, Arel had banned sweets from the flat. It was plain that Carey had ethereal connections, but he wasn't always the best at handling his physical body. He was crazy about sugar. It was a habit that Arel tried his best to curtail in favor of healthier food. However after Carey's recent dedication to helping out, Arel thought it was time to let him indulge his sweet tooth.

Arel smiled at the thought as he opened the door and carried his groceries to the kitchen. As usual, Carey quickly joined him, eyeing the bag that Arel set on the counter. Arel's smile broadened. "Check out what I found at that little bakery down the street."

Carey's eyes lit up as he started removing the bag's contents. He paused after pulling out a white box tied with white string. He gave Arel a puzzled look. "Is this a box of donuts?"

"Not donuts, Carey. Those are Napoleon pastries. I think you're going to like them."

Carey didn't hesitate. He quickly untied the string and opened the box. Grabbing one of the pastries, he took a generous bite.

Arel laughed when Carey's eyes went from bright to almost glowing. He was mesmerized by their blissful sparkle. In that moment, he couldn't deny that he was looking at an angel. "So they meet with your approval?"

Carey nodded. "They're the best!" he sputtered.

Arel started to unload the rest of the groceries. "Good. I'm glad you like them. You deserve a reward after all you've done to clean up this place. I also got you some of your other favorites. But I guess almost anything sweet is great, right?"

Carey swallowed his bite and shook his head. "It's interesting. I was recently talking to Annabel about sweets. She asked if I had a preference. Now, after tasting a dessert like this, I realize all desserts are not created equal."

Arel pulled back. "Oh, that's a shame. I guess I'll have to return this cherry pie." He picked up the dessert box on the counter and started to put it back in the bag.

Carey reached out to stop him. "Really? A pie too?"

Arel sighed. "Yes, and there are cookies in that third box. Please don't eat all of it at once. Angel or not, you need to take care of your body."

Carey's face went instantly youthful and repentant. "Of course."

"By the way, where's Rolphe? Is he resting in his room?"

"No, he's in his studio. He said he felt a little better and wanted to try painting."

Arel braced against the counter and sighed. "The bastard is never going to die at this rate."

Carey dusted off his hands, avoiding Arel's eyes. "So you still hope he doesn't make it?"

"I just want all of this to be over, don't you understand that? I'm tired, Carey."

"I know you are. You haven't stopped since we got here. You need to rest."

"That's not what I mean, and you know it."

Carey walked over to the kitchen table and sat down. "What do you mean? Please, tell me what you're thinking."

"You're an angel. You know what I'm thinking."

"That's not true. I've stayed out of your thoughts. I wanted you to feel that you could confide in me like another person. So let's talk."

Arel rubbed the worn counter. Days before, in the middle of his cleaning frenzy, he'd scrubbed it repeatedly until it was smooth and sanitized. "Look, it's not that I want Rolphe dead. I know he's changed. But I don't want to have to look after him forever. He treats me like one of you guys since I agreed to stay. But I'm not an angel. I'm not even a decent human being. And I can't be responsible for Rolphe or what he does in the future."

"Why should you be responsible for him?"

"You know why. He has my blood, Michael's blood. It's up to me to make sure he doesn't misuse it like—" He stopped rubbing the counter and closed his hands into fists.

Carey sighed. "Like you misused it? Is that what you were going to say?"

The question made Arel's jaw go rigid. He'd made such a mess of everything since he'd begged for Michael's blood. "In New York, I was so determined to get back at William. Even when he wanted to leave and return to London, I taunted him until he couldn't take it. Once he'd tasted my blood, his life as he knew it was over. Like he said, he's lucky to be drawing breath after what he's been through."

"You made a mistake with William, but—"

"Mistake? When you foul up on the job and get fired, that's a mistake. What I've done is way beyond a mistake."

Carey returned to where Arel was standing. "Hang in there. I know things seem really bad right now, but maybe there's more to it all than you know."

"Like what?"

"Your life is just getting started. I'm sure of it. But you have to stop criticizing yourself."

As soon as Arel thought about giving life another chance, he felt his gut flare with a searing pain. "I remember how hopeful I was when Michael gave me his blood. I thought I had a chance to be free of all the misery. If only I'd simply blown my brains out instead of wanting something that I couldn't handle."

"No! Don't say that!" a voice called out from the hallway. It was Rolphe's voice. It was strained but forceful. He came forward slowly, using the wall to steady himself. "If you hadn't been brave enough to do what you did, I never would have changed what I'd become. I would have remained a monster forever!"

Arel stared back mutely at the tall, imposing man. Even though Rolphe had lost weight and was slightly bent as he tried to get his breath, he could still impress Arel. His physical presence and deep, booming voice seemed to fill up the room with his reprimand. Yet when Arel looked deeper, if he allowed his heart to connect with what Rolphe was trying to say, he knew the man was trying to be decent and honorable again. Still it was hard to admit after he'd hated Rolphe for so long.

Rolphe moved closer, putting a hand on the counter next to Arel's. It was paint spattered and big like the rest of him. He put his other hand on Arel's shoulder. "I'm sorry for all the pain I've caused you," he blurted out. "And I swear on the grave of my boys that I'll never hurt anyone again."

Arel instinctively wanted to pull away from Rolphe's grasp, but he couldn't. He was exhausted from all the effort it took to right his wrongs. He didn't have the energy to do anything but stand rooted to the recently polished kitchen floor.

Rolphe seemed to understand how worn Arel was. "Rest, please. I don't want you to work another minute cleaning up my mess. If it will make you smile, I'll hire people to come in to strip the wallpaper, to paint and refurbish this place."

Arel scowled back. "Why should I care about that?"

"Because being here hurts you. I can feel it. Your soul needs beauty, or it withers. That's why you've been working so hard to put things right."

Arel jerked back, suddenly finding more strength. "How do you know anything about me?" he demanded in a rough voice.

Rolphe stepped away and smiled weakly. "Because I see what you can't see. I see who you are when you only see your failings. But you're not those failings, Arel. And I promise, someday, if I have strength left in my body, I'll find a way to express who you are with my paints. Maybe then, when you look at my canvas, you'll get a glimpse of what I see."

Thirty-Three

William walked around the lower level of his London residence, letting the familiar surroundings fill him with the comfort of homecoming. Checking out the laboratory area, he appreciated how functional the space had been. Cabinets that were filled with a wide assortment of equipment lined the walls. A well-designed work counter sat in the middle of the space. As he ran a hand over his microscope, he thought about all the long hours he'd spent there studying the physical aspects of life. He missed those times. Even if it took years to solve a problem, like understanding the virus that Rolphe had passed on to him, it was a rewarding pursuit. There were answers to his questions.

But his life didn't revolve around the material world anymore. It had become a mystery that went beyond what could be seen, even with a powerful microscope. He had to accept how drastically different life had become. He put the cover back over the microscope and turned off the overhead light. The lab was useless now. He'd probably tear it all out when he remodeled the lower level.

"William!" It was Annabel's voice, cheerfully calling to him from the head of the stairs.

"Down here," he replied in as pleasant a tone as he could muster. He knew he should be happy. He might not have his research anymore, but he had so much more to celebrate. Annabel was a treasure, a beautiful woman who loved him with a totally, open heart. So why was he feeling anything but joy? Why couldn't he relax and let himself think about their future?

The answer slipped in when he thought about Paris. Arel was there, trying his best to keep Rolphe in line. It sounded like a miserable job, but never once did Arel try to involve William in what he was going through. In return, William had tried to put the entire matter out of his mind, as if he'd had no responsibility in bringing Rolphe into their lives. What kind of friend was he? Did he have Kevin and Tim's sense of loyalty?

As he stiffened at the questions that kept coming, Annabel skipped down the stairs and hurried over to where he was standing. She was still wearing the smile she'd had when they returned home. It was clear that she didn't feel the uneasiness that was troubling him. Instead, she took hold of his arm and gave it a satisfied squeeze.

"How are the mice?" she asked.

William blinked back. "The mice?"

Annabel's smile broadened. "Yes, how are they doing? I didn't get a chance to check on them after you picked them up at the neighbor boy's house. Did he do a good job taking care of them?"

William walked over to the mouse habitat. It sat on a table near his recliner. He gave the three occupants a quick scan. "They seem fine. Maybe a little fatter if that's possible."

Annabel looked in on the small, rotund rodents too. "I'm so glad we have them. They're always so playful and happy."

William opened the cage and lowered his hand to the cage floor so that the mice could sniff his fingers. All three tried to climb onto his outstretched palm, making him smile in spite of his uneasy conscience. "I think they missed us."

Annabel let out a contented sigh. "Well, they won't have to miss us ever again, will they? Everything is finally settling down. We can all enjoy ourselves at long last."

William frowned. "Absolutely."

* * *

Arel watched the last of the painters file out of the apartment. Rolphe had hired a crew of professionals to remove the wallpaper and repaint the walls of both bedrooms. The painters were a sour-faced, but efficient group who made short work of the project. After only a couple of days, Arel's bedroom had been transformed into a lighter, brighter space. A new mattress, gold bedding and white curtains complimented the look.

The bedroom would have been almost comfortable if Arel didn't feel like he was a prisoner. He knew it was a self-imposed sentence, but something told him that he shouldn't leave Rolphe to his own devices. Maybe it was Arel's paranoia coming up with the arguments, but he heeded them none the less. Besides, he was too tired to return to Chicago. Friends and babies took energy he didn't have. He'd have to conserve his strength and get his mind quieted before he went back to any kind of normal life.

Thankfully, he seemed to finally be having a positive effect on Rolphe. The man was coming back from years of dysfunction. He looked to Arel for help as he trod the path to "goodness" and a life without "sin".

As Arel shut the door after the painters, Carey came over and joined him. The young man's eyes had a certain spark that made Arel pull back and cross his arms. "Is there something you need, Carey?"

Carey laughed and crossed his arms too. "I was just thinking about how different this place is since you arrived. If Rolphe continues with the improvements, it's going to feel almost like a made-to-order retreat for anybody who loves Paris."

The idea made Arel blink back a few times. He hadn't thought about the apartment in positive terms, but Carey's assessment was intriguing. He walked into the living room and gave it a quick evaluation. "I suppose the place does have potential." He stamped his foot a couple of times. "The hardwood floors are still sound, but the old paneling on the walls doesn't hold much promise. Restoring it would be very costly. It would probably be better to tear it out. Rolphe might consider—" He stopped himself and frowned. "What am I talking about? Why should I care about what Rolphe does or doesn't do with this place?"

Carey shrugged. "I don't know, but I think we both enjoyed seeing something so neglected come back to life a little. I even liked cleaning the windows when I saw what a difference it could make."

Arel's irritation flared. "I wish you could have discovered your ideas about cleanliness when you were back in Chicago."

Carey put out his hands in a conciliatory gesture. "Sorry, I know I wasn't the neatest person around. But cleaning up after me did help you to work off your worries. When I talked to Michael about it—"

"Michael," Arel interrupted. "I miss his maturity. He was always such a steady influence."

"Are you still angry at him for giving you his blood?"

Arel walked over to the sofa and sat down with a sigh. "We both know that Michael wasn't to blame for any of this. He believed in me—"

"He still believes in you," Carey said.

"And so do I," Rolphe said as he joined them in the living room. Every day he looked a little steadier on his feet. Now, he paused and stood quietly next to his piano.

Arel stared back crossly. "Dammit, Rolphe, do you realize that you're always butting in on private conversations?"

Rolphe lowered his head. "I'm sorry. I don't mean to, but if I may, I'd like to ask your permission to do something."

Arel crossed his arms again. "What now?"

"I wonder if we could invite Michael to visit. After talking to Carey and getting his advice on some things, I realize I could learn a lot from his fellow angel."

Arel felt a spark of excitement at the thought of seeing Michael again, but he kept his body in check and his voice even and calm. "If that's what you want and Michael agrees, why should I object?"

Rolphe kept his eyes averted and nodded. "Thank you, Arel."

"Don't thank me," Arel shot back. "I have nothing to do with Michael's comings and goings. He does as he pleases."

Rolphe's dark eyes turned sharp and focused for a brief moment before he lowered them again. "Oh, but I disagree. From what Carey has said, Michael only goes where he's invited. He never interferes if he isn't asked."

Arel sighed again as he remembered how fervently he'd been when he begged Michael for his help. "You would have to remind me of that fact, wouldn't you?"

Rolphe shrugged. "I'm sorry. Did I say something to offend you?"

Arel drummed his fingers on the sofa arm. "Never mind, if you want him here, why should I care?"

Rolphe's face lit up with a smile. "After the life I've lived, I never thought I could be so blessed."

"Be careful what you wish for," Arel barked back. The warning came from experience. When Michael first came into his life, Arel felt like he had a caring friend, one who guided him back into the warm waters of hope and expectation. But nothing had worked out like Arel thought it would.

Rolphe came over and looked down. "What's wrong? Why do you look so sad?"

Arel shook his head. He didn't know how to answer the question. All he knew was that he suddenly felt so alone. His friends back in Chicago were raising families. William had Annabel and a bright future. Rolphe and Carey were getting to be pals. Next, Michael would join them and start tending to Rolphe's needs too. But where did that leave him? He had no place in the world. He didn't really matter to anyone, not in a significant way.

He got up, pushed Rolphe aside and started out of the room. As he retreated, he couldn't hold back his bitterness or his words. "You have Michael's blood now, Rolphe. You can be his new pet project. Goodness knows, I'm beyond his help."

His brooding mood was in full swing as he closed his bedroom door. For a long moment, he couldn't move. He stared at the newly painted door in a kind of daze. His future was a blur too. He didn't know where to go or what to do.

"Arel?"

His eyes sparked with recognition as he turned and saw Michael waiting for him. A smile brightened his face. Seeing the angel banished all thought. It was replaced by a moment of anticipation, almost like what he had when he still had a firm grasp on hope. "Michael, I—"

Michael came forward. "It's good to see you again," he announced with a broad smile.

Arel straightened his shoulders. "Really?"

"And I hoped you'd be happy to see me. I hoped we could talk again, like we used to talk when you were home."

Arel shrugged as his thoughts started up again. "Home? I don't know where that is." He walked over and sat down on his bed. "I feel like I've been searching for home forever, since I was a little boy. I've always wanted a place where it's okay to be me, where I can find some peace. But the more I search, the more I lose my way."

"That's why I'm here. I want to help you."

Arel laughed. "Your intention has always been perfect. But I keep wondering why it hasn't helped. Why do I still feel like I'm always out on the edge, and I'm all alone?"

Michael tapped his chest. "This place you're searching for is inside of you, Arel."

"Yes, that's what you've always said, but I don't feel any comfort in the thought. When I look inside, when I search for a cozy fire to warm myself, all I find is cold, hard facts. I'm not a nice person, Michael. For weeks I've lived with my hate for Rolphe, which is understandable I guess. But why am I bitter when I think about William?"

"I thought you and William were past those old issues."

Arel rubbed the scar on his palm. It was a reminder of a bonding ceremony with the man who pledged himself as a brother. "The guy has proven his loyalty. I know he's done everything he can to support our ties. Yet, I look at him and Annabel and wonder how he got so lucky, how he can find happiness, and I'm left out in the cold again? I try to be different. I try to be better. I try to do whatever it takes to have what he and others have, but it doesn't seem to work."

"Arel, it can work, but you have to—"

"What? I have to try harder? I have to ferret out some hidden pearl of wisdom that will turn it all around?"

"No, it's just the opposite. You have to stop trying and let yourself rest for a while. You're exhausted."

"You're right. Help me to sleep, Michael. Help me stop the thoughts that never stop, please."

"I'll do everything I can, but I have a suggestion."

Arel looked up and sighed. "What?"

"Maybe you need to express yourself in a more creative way. Try something new, like painting. Rolphe has a big studio with everything you need. Using your imagination might be fun."

"Fun?"

Michael laughed. "Yes, you know what I mean. Let yourself do something that's enjoyable for a change."

Arel had to stop and ponder Michael's advice. "It seems so long since I've thought in those terms. But I guess I could give it a try."

Thirty-Four

Rolphe sat at his easel listening to the quiet. After almost a month of constant noise and turmoil, peace had been restored. The renovations to his apartment were complete.

The angel named Carey had definitely helped with the project. He'd located a group of skilled laborers who'd recently formed their own company. They were eager for work. Once they started the renovation, they functioned very efficiently. A job that could have dragged on for months was completed in less than thirty days.

When Rolphe first inspected his updated, living quarters, he hardly recognized the space. He'd purchased the apartment many years before. At that time, the rooms and fixtures were already out-of-date. Rolphe didn't mind their condition. He'd grown up in a poor village and learned to ignore his impoverished surroundings. As an adult, he'd remained more or less oblivious to his outer environment. He experienced beauty through painting and music.

Arel's feelings about Rolphe's home came as a bit of a shock. Arel found the apartment disgusting. In the end, Rolphe had to agree. When he realized how negligent he'd been, he even wanted to go a step beyond Arel's thorough, cleaning job. It was a good choice.

After the remodeling was over, Rolphe knew that even Arel couldn't object to the finished product. The bedrooms, kitchen and baths were updated and fresh. The once dingy living room was a showpiece of comfort and style.

Rolphe felt a sense of pride as he hung his artwork on the beautiful, refurbished wood that replaced the old splintered paneling. When he walked across the oak floors that had been sanded and refinished, he appreciated the beauty that had been hidden under grime and the ravages of time. Now, the floors were adorned with thick, fashionable area rugs. The carpeting softened the look and added color to the room. Rolphe's old furniture gave way to handsome pieces that Arel suggested during trips to the shops. Even the balcony had undergone a facelift.

But it wasn't just Rolphe's apartment that had been renewed. He'd undergone a transformation too. With the help of Michael and Carey, he'd found ways to release much of his fear and self-condemnation. He was also getting stronger physically. It was a relief to be able to walk around the apartment without needing to lean against walls for support.

Arel's condition was a different matter. He seemed to be going in the opposite direction. On rare occasions, when Rolphe was able to tap into Arel's thoughts, he recoiled. A heavy gray curtain of failure and regret had settled over Arel's mindset. For the most part, the man lived in a world of self-inflicted demons.

However, there was one bright spot in Arel's activities. Arel had taken up painting. After making it clear that it was Michael's idea to try something new, Arel began to assert himself as an artist. For an hour each day, he entered the studio and gave his emotions a way to express themselves.

Rolphe stepped back in amazement when he observed Arel's painting method. Arel didn't use brush strokes. He lashed out at the canvas. His body went from docile and withdrawn to combat ready. With a wild, feverish intensity, he covered every inch of canvas with primal colors. After one canvas was finished, another was quickly snatched up and placed on the easel. Rolphe was worried about keeping enough canvases on hand.

Rolphe was also worried about what was fueling Arel's manic style. There was a ferocity in Arel's approach. Rolphe had witnessed something similar on the battlefield. But those were brutal times when lives were at stake, not a studio where a person could enjoy a peaceful pastime.

The situation made Rolphe uneasy. Arel had been brooding for weeks on end, bottling up his feelings and the demons behind them. Painting gave him a brief respite, but Rolphe knew it wasn't enough to change Arel's negative attitude about himself and life.

So what would the future bring? As soon as Rolphe asked himself the question, a sudden chill grabbed hold of his body. It wasn't an ordinary chill. It was the kind that accompanied his premonitions of impending danger. He decided to ignore it. If the angels, Michael and Carey, could remain positive, he had to find a way to remain optimistic too.

* * *

As the weeks slipped by, Annabel felt like she was getting the hang of being a human. At first, the experience was the most frightening thing she could imagine. Her heart raced. Her breath was often shallow and sometimes gasping. She cried a lot. But all those reactions stemmed from fear. Once she had a chance to relax and enjoy her days, her mind and body settled down. She was free to explore the positive side of things.

An angel certainly knew joy, but it was so consistently a part of being an angel that it was taken for granted. The gift of being human came from the inconsistency that the physical offered. A person ate a meal in the morning, but by noon, there was hunger, a need to be filled again. Taking care of that need was something to look forward to. Like Carey, she loved food. Simply savoring a bite of cake, letting the sweetness and delicate flavors linger on her tongue could be an incredible experience.

One of the best parts of being human was being with William. Lying in his bed, glancing over at him while he slept, her heart soared. She knew she'd made the right decision to give up her wings. William was deliciously handsome, gentle and wise. When he showered her with his love, she felt as if her ability to experience pleasure expanded beyond anything she could imagine.

When she'd first returned from Chicago, her only fear was that William wouldn't settle down to an ordinary life. After all that he'd gone through, he might still feel affected by the high drama that seemed to be a part of Arel's world. Thankfully, William didn't talk about Arel. When he was with her, he kept his promise. He concentrated on their life together.

Of course, she did notice that if she caught him off guard, his eyes could be troubled. But that was probably because he needed time to come back to himself. He'd suffered some very traumatic experiences. She didn't have a problem with being patient. They were both making adjustments. The bottom line was that William loved her, and she loved him. She decided it didn't need to be any more complicated than that.

* * *

William sat at the downstairs computer, staring at the various room arrangements displayed on the monitor. When he remodeled the home's lower level, he wanted to maximize its functionality.

The lab area would probably be turned into a large guest facility. It could also be used as a library. The upstairs guest bedroom could then be converted into a studio. Annabel said that she might like to try her hand at pottery or sculpture. The room's natural lighting would be perfect for her artistic endeavors.

The lower level of the home would lend itself to nighttime pursuits. William was planning an entertainment area for those cozy evenings when he and Annabel watched movies or simply wanted to enjoy being together. A fireplace might be added, but would they use it enough to warrant the expense?

The other end of the space would be reserved. If children came along it would be a play room. Annabel liked the idea of a family, but she didn't know if she was ready to be a mother quite yet. She said she wanted to wait until she was really comfortable with her role as a person not an angel.

William needed time too. No matter how much Annabel wanted a normal life, he wasn't normal. Sure he could act the part. He could play the devoted lover with Annabel, but that didn't change the fact that he felt other forces at work inside of him.

Annabel seemed oblivious to the fact that it took all his concentration to remain calm and passive when they were together. While she was chatting away, listing the reasons for raising marigolds in a front porch flower box, he was trying his best to keep his mind from flying off into the ethers. Paris and Arel's welfare were often the targets of his wandering mind.

Was Arel faring well? Why didn't he call or at least text and let William know how things were going? Was Rolphe, the blood-sucking monster, behaving himself?

After weeks of not hearing from Arel, William was worried. He kept thinking about how devoted Arel had been after William's near fatal encounter with Rolphe. His brother in blood couldn't have been kinder or more supportive. After all that he and Arel had shared and the bond that they'd formed, his concern for Arel was natural.

"So why don't I feel like Arel still cares about me?" William mumbled to himself.

He knew it was a crazy thought. One moment, he was happy and grateful for Arel's support. The next moment, doubts about Arel's loyalty plagued him.

As he contemplated the matter, he decided that his moods swings probably had their basis in his recent trauma and the helplessness he'd felt.

"So I'll put my anxieties to rest. I'll check on Arel's activities and be done with it."

He settled back in his chair and concentrated. He was getting very proficient in projecting his consciousness to other places. So a quick mental visit to Rolphe's apartment wouldn't be too difficult. In this instance, it was very easy. He was able to connect with his target location almost immediately. As he continued to focus, he tuned into a strong energy signature coming from Rolphe's studio.

He was surprised to find Arel with a brush in his hand, sitting in front of an easel. The image made him smile. "Arel? Painting? I can't believe it. But at least I know that he's okay."

He was about to break the connection when he saw Rolphe walk over to Arel and begin talking to him. Arel's eyes brightened. He seemed pleased by Rolphe's words.

The interaction made William stiffen. His jaw tightened with disgust. "How can Arel let that ogre near him?" William's next thought was even worse. "Arel hasn't contacted me because he's getting chummy with Rolphe!"

The idea was beyond William's understanding. Arel hated Rolphe and with good reason. Arel nearly died trying to stop Rolphe from lusting after William's blood. So how could Arel forget all that and befriend the fiend?

William needed to investigate further. Shutting his eyes again, he tuned into Arel's energy signature a second time. Again, he was repulsed by what he saw. Rolphe and Arel weren't just having a conversation. Rolphe was smiling at Arel and patting his back. And Arel was nodding back as if they were long lost buddies.

As William came back to himself, he was in shock. But as his numbness wore off, a deep seething anger took its place. He'd gone through hell since Arel gave him Michael's blood. But he'd tried to be forgiving. He'd tried to tell himself that Arel came through in the end. But he'd been fooling himself.

From what William had just seen, the truth was clear. Arel liked playing the hero, but he didn't have the maturity to be truly loyal. He was too needy, and in that neediness, Arel was reaching out to Rolphe.

William jumped up, instantly outraged. Arel had found another person to call his brother. After all William had gone through, Arel was shutting William out and aligning with someone else. The next thought was too much to bear. Arel was buddying up with the vicious brute who had tried to kill William.

It was such a revolting idea that William snapped the pencil he was holding in two. But snapping a pencil did nothing to satisfy his wrath. He'd been betrayed by the one person he thought he could trust. His face flushed hot and red at the thought.

"I'll kill both of them!" he gasped in a seething voice.

He grabbed hold of the first thing that was close at hand, a unique, blown glass vase. He'd destroy it like he'd destroy Arel. His white-knuckled fist was poised in midair when he stopped himself. It took all his willpower, a strength forged over a lifetime of being rational, to replace the vase on the desk.

But he couldn't stop the raging energy that was coursing through his body. As he fought for breath, a hot flash of light exploded outward and lit up the room. The display was enough to prove just how "not normal" he was.

Afterwards, he nearly collapsed. He was suddenly so weak that he barely made it to his recliner. As he held on to the arms of the chair, his teeth chattered and his brain buzzed. His body was vibrating erratically from head to toe. For a long moment, he thought he'd shake apart.

He took slow, measured breaths like Raphael had taught him. It helped. His body began to calm down. His mind regained a small measure of clarity. Arel wasn't betraying him. It was the blood,

Michael's blood. It was intensifying his emotions. It was still bringing up old energies to the surface, especially his paranoia.

Arel often complained about how the angelic substance affected him. William had also experienced the same emotional upheavals. Fortunately, his mind and body evened themselves out over the course of several months. But what he'd just experienced was drastically different than anything he'd felt before.

More purging was obviously taking place. But now, William was much more powerful. He had more energy at his command. If he used it to reinforce his negativity, he could end up traveling the same road that Arel had taken. That road was treacherous. He could become an emotional cripple. Only a vigilant, balanced attitude would save him.

"Arel, old friend, you were so ill-equipped to handle what you were given. With your constitution, it's a wonder you're not locked up in some loony bin."

He felt better as soon as he let his insight sink in. It prompted him to make a silent promise to himself. Whenever any insane feelings of betrayal tried to take over, he had to remember that Arel had proven himself as a steadfast friend and brother.

Thirty-Five

Tim won the battle, but his nerves were shaky when he handed baby Sara to Peggy. "Next time, it's your turn to wipe her mouth," he announced. "I don't think I have what it takes to do it more than a couple of times a week."

Peggy tried to cuddle their frowning baby, but Sara was still in fighting mode. "Now you know why I'm exhausted every night. She's already going through her terrible twos."

Tim retrieved a dish cloth from the sink and wiped up the pureed peas and carrots that covered a good portion of the high chair tray. "I hope she got enough to eat."

"She's teething, but the doctor says she's healthy. And she is gaining weight."

Tim let out a relieved sigh. "That's good. Trying to force her to do anything she doesn't want to do is impossible."

Peggy picked some applesauce out of Sara's hair. "When Carol and I compare notes, we agree that first-time parents worry more."

"I'm sure Carol doesn't worry about their baby's appetite."

"No, in fact she's beginning to list to the side every time she holds him. When Arel gets back home, he's not going to believe how big his godchild is."

Tim rinsed the dish cloth and dried his hands. "Did you tell me that Arel called this morning?"

"Oh goodness, I did, but you had to get back to work before I could tell you what he said."

"How's he doing?"

"I'm shocked to say it, but he sounds happier than he has in months. I guess Paris agrees with him. He said that he's learning to paint."

"Paint? Paint what?"

"Pictures, silly. He sent me an email with a photo he took of a recent canvas he's working on. It was a little rough, but he's never painted before."

"Good for him. I'm glad that he's finally giving himself a break."

"I just hope he can keep doing what he's doing."

"Why wouldn't he?"

Peggy shrugged. "You know Arel. Just when you think he's fine, something always seems to throw him into a tail spin."

Tim reached out to Baby Sara and let her grab hold of his finger. He spoke to her in a soothing voice. "Tell Mommy to stop worrying."

"I guess you're right," Peggy said as she handed Tim the baby.

Tim held Sara close, but he also made sure to connect with Peggy's eyes. "Honey, listen. From what we know, it's always been Arel's friendship with William that's proved difficult. But that's behind them. William has Annabel, and Arel has Paris. Seems like the perfect solution to me. So let's wish them all well."

Peggy nodded. "If you say so."

*　*　*

Peggy stared out the kitchen window. The house was quiet. Sara was down for a nap, and Tim had gone out to take care of some errands. She used her alone time to admire the back yard. It seemed like spring had just arrived, and yet, spring greens were quickly deepening into the dark rich colors of summer. Day by day, the flowers were steadily growing and getting more established in the garden that she'd planted. That was nature's way. The seasons flowed effortlessly, one into another. But people were different. Most of the time, they resisted change. They held on to what they knew.

She'd been thinking about Tim's advice to stop imagining the worst when it came to Arel. And Tim had a point. During their phone conversation, Arel sounded different. Maybe it was the cheerful tone in his voice. But instead of celebrating that new development and flowing with where Arel was now, she held on to the past. But why? She'd seen Carol change very quickly. Couldn't Arel change just as fast?

She retrieved her empty coffee cup and put it in the sink. As she turned on the water and started to rinse the cup, she had another thought. Maybe she was the one who wasn't changing. Maybe she'd inherited what her mother referred to as the "worry gene." Her grandmother was a big worrier. So was an uncle. Both relatives were obsessive about what could go wrong in life. Would she be added to the family's list of obsessive worriers? She frowned at the thought.

Or maybe there was a different explanation. When it came to her relationship to Arel, maybe their ties were so close that she understood him. She knew how his mind worked. He took the idea of resisting change to the extreme. Instead of flowing with life, he examined it. He took it apart and looked at every facet. And if something happened that activated his guilt or anger, he could panic and freeze. He could become a rock in the stream, being buffeted about by the current, even sinking below the surface when the water got too high.

Peggy glanced at the back window. Rain was in the forecast. A dark, dreary sky marred the beauty of the backyard. The grass and plants needed a good shower, but the clouds could be depressing when she was in a contemplative mood. She grabbed her phone. When it came to examining the situation and finding out if she was worrying too much, she needed someone else's opinion. Maybe she'd invite Carol over to tea.

* * *

Carol sat at Peggy's kitchen table feeling a little uncomfortable. As soon as she saw her friend's face, she knew that their chat wasn't going to be about babies or a recent discovery at the mall. Peggy had an agenda. "Is something bothering you, Peggy?" Carol asked in her bravest voice.

Peggy ran her finger over the rim of her tea cup and shrugged. "I wondered if you've talked to Arel recently."

Carol let her shoulders relax a little. "Yes, he actually called this morning. I nearly dropped the phone when I heard his voice."

"I had the same reaction. When does Arel call anyone?"

"Yes, and he sounded almost happy, especially when he talked about learning to paint."

Peggy returned a mischievous smile. "Did he send you what he's working on?"

"Yes, I got a photo in a text message but I wasn't sure what it was at first. It was kind of a muddled composition of non-descript forms with all these colors mixed together. I'm glad that he didn't want me to go into detail when I told him it was unique."

"I blurted out something about it being very expressive, a feeling piece. I hope he bought it." Peggy sighed. "What do you think is going on with him?"

"I don't know, but he sounds like he's finally letting go a little. After these past months of seeing him so upset, it would be wonderful if he could just enjoy Paris. I know I loved being there."

"Yes, you finally got to take a honeymoon. I was so glad when you and Kevin got some time to yourselves."

"Then I came home and everything fell apart again. But maybe it all worked out for the best. I was miserable for a while, but something good came out of it."

Peggy leaned in. "You transformed, Carol. You became a new person."

Carol frowned as she recalled how she'd had a miscarriage and gone into a tailspin. Life felt so bleak and hopeless until she found something to care about again. Helping William when he was gravely ill gave her purpose. She discovered strength that she didn't know she had. "Or maybe I just became the person who was always there, a person who'd hidden herself behind so much fear. But my fear was ruining my life. According to William, I had a choice. I could remain afraid forever, or I could believe in myself again."

Peggy's face lit up. "That's exactly what I wanted to hear."

"What do you mean?"

"Arel's big turn-around! Maybe he sounds happy for the same reason. Maybe he's starting to believe in himself. And painting must be part of the process."

Carol hesitated. "I'm no art expert, but his painting scared me a little."

Peggy sat back and put her hands in her lap. "Yes, it scared me too. When I said it was a feeling piece, it was true. But I didn't get good feelings when I studied it. The colors were really dark and foreboding. It reminded me of my nightmares."

Carol sat up straighter. "Maybe, but shouldn't we concentrate on the fact that he sounded happier?"

"Yes, that's what Tim said too. I have to remember the good stuff and not project the bad. It's just so hard after almost losing Arel again. And part of it was my fault. My pride got in the way. I convinced all of you to back me up when it came to not checking on him like I usually do. And look what happened."

"Hold on, Peggy. You had a right to your feelings. Arel put you in a tough spot. He made you feel like he didn't want your help."

"But he's like a baby! He's like Sara. When she gets in one of her moods and screams bloody-murder, I don't let her cry her eyes out. I comfort her and make sure she knows I love her."

"I understand, but no matter how much you love Arel, you can't make him love himself."

Peggy put a shaky hand to her cup and grabbed hold. "It's just that I do care so much."

"So let's join forces and keep an eye on the situation. We'll share notes. If Arel seems like he's slipping again, we'll figure out what we can do. Is that a plan?"

Peggy nodded. "Thanks for being so understanding."

"And remember, William and Annabel are available too. We can always call them for information."

"Yes, we can. In fact, William and Arel seem to be good friends again. When they were here, they quibbled a lot, but underneath I could feel that they cared about each other."

"I felt the same thing. They seem to enjoy arguing, but I think they've resolved any real problems."

Thirty-Six

Arel held up the empty tube of paint, and looked at Rolphe. Their easels sat about six feet apart. "Do you have any more of the cadmium red?"

Rolphe quickly put down his brush. "There's a new tube in the supply drawer. Do you want me to get it for you?"

Arel looked at the tube again. "I think I used it already."

Rolphe's brows arched with surprise. "Oh, I see."

Arel threw his brush in a partially filled container of turpentine. "What do you see? That I'm a lousy student who wastes paint?" He stood up and started for the door. "I told you that I couldn't do this!"

"Arel, please, stop. I would never think that. You're doing a wonderful job. But you have to give yourself time. You're a beginner."

Arel jerked around and studied Rolphe with laser-sharp eyes. He searched the man's thoughts for any sign of deceit. He found only confusion and slightly wounded feelings. "Fine, I'll send Carey out to get more paint."

"Arel, paint is the last thing I'm worried about."

"What's that mean?"

"I worry about you, about how hard you are on yourself."

"What choice do I have? I've exhausted my friends with my constant drama and as for—" Arel paused, letting his thoughts travel to London. He hoped all was going well.

"William?" Rolphe whispered the name reverently.

Arel glared back. "You know you're not allowed to mention his name!"

"Sorry."

"Never mind."

Rolphe had his head down as if he was afraid to look at Arel directly. "About your friends, I thought I heard you laugh when you were talking to them. I'm glad they bring you comfort."

"I laughed because I want them to think I'm fine. They need a break. They're worriers, especially one woman who doesn't know how to let go of people who are in trouble."

"Are you referring to yourself?"

Arel's gaze flitted about the room. "Do you see anyone else in this studio?"

Rolphe picked up his brush and stared at his canvas. "Everything I say is wrong, so I'll stop talking to you if that would make you feel better."

Arel swallowed hard, let out a heavy sigh, and took his seat again. "The only thing I want is for you to teach me to be a decent painter."

Rolphe stood up and approached Arel's painting. "As I said before, painting is about expressing what's inside of you."

"It's about more than that. It's about creating something to be proud of, like what you do."

Rolphe laughed. "Do you know how many canvases I've burned? Now, when I think back, I wish I still had some of those pieces."

"Why? If they were like mine, they weren't worth keeping."

Rolphe ran a careful finger over a recently dried section of Arel's picture. "Do you see this deep red? When I look at it, I can feel your desire, that part of you that wants to experience life in a passionate, inspired way."

Arel's lids narrowed as he stared at his earlier efforts. When he'd been painting, he'd thought of Michael and how much he'd wanted to succeed at being someone worthwhile. Yet he'd failed. "I was angry when I painted it."

"Yes, because you don't want to acknowledge the greatness inside of you."

Arel jerked up his head. "That's a ridiculous statement, Rolphe! You might know how to paint, but you don't know anything about me."

Rolphe backed away, nodding. "Like I just said, I'm better off keeping my thoughts to myself."

Arel stood up and went to the doorway. "I need some air. While I'm out, I'll get more paint."

"Arel, while you're at the store, maybe you should get several tubes of red."

Arel was about to comment when he saw Rolphe's smile. The gently teasing gesture lit up Rolphe's face and eyes with a kindness that Arel knew was genuine. The man was obviously trying his best to show his good will.

He smiled back before he could stop himself. It was such an unexpected reaction. What was happening to him? Since he'd been staying with Rolphe, he couldn't help but notice the man's efforts to atone. Carey was right. Rolphe had changed. But that didn't excuse him from what he'd done. He'd tried to kill William in a brutal, savage manner. Afterwards, William was so badly shaken that Arel was afraid he'd never be himself again. He'd thought he'd lost his strong, confident brother forever.

Now, thinking that he'd smile at Rolphe was unacceptable. Any form of liking the man meant that forgiveness might follow. And there was no way in heaven or hell that Arel intended to forgive Rolphe for his actions. The idea was so repulsive that he stormed out of the apartment, slamming the door behind him.

* * *

While Arel was busy at the shops, Rolphe took the opportunity to talk to Michael. As usual the angel was reading. He sat in a corner of the recently, refurbished living room, dressed in t-shirt and jeans. At first, Rolphe had difficulty accepting Michael's outer apparel. As a child, he'd seen too many pictures of angels decked out in robes. But after weeks of seeing Carey and Michael dressed like regular people, Rolphe was acclimating to their appearance. Besides, if he allowed himself a more expansive view, neither angel needed robes to be identified as God's messenger. Their inner glow was frighteningly bright.

Rolphe approached Michael slowly. "Dear one, could we talk?"

Michael glanced up and returned a generous and welcoming smile. "How can I help you, Rolphe?"

Rolphe shuffled over to the new sofa and sat down. Gathering up his thoughts, he hesitated. It was one thing to ask Michael about heavenly matters, but he didn't know if it was appropriate to talk to the angel about other people. He blurted out his problem. "I don't know how to comfort Arel. Everything I say seems to irritate him."

Michael's smile broadened. "If you ever find a way around that response, please share it with me."

Rolphe pulled back. "I don't understand. Are you saying that you don't have the answer? Don't angels know everything?"

"I'm not saying that every problem doesn't have a solution. However, that doesn't mean that people are willing to allow that solution to help them with their problem."

Rolphe scratched his head and sat back. "I don't think I understand what you're trying to tell me."

Michael put his book aside and leaned forward. "I know your desire is to find a way to aid Arel in seeing who he really is."

"Yes, that's exactly right. When I look at him, when I look into his heart, it's magnificent. It's almost as bright as the sun. Yet, he denies that fact. He tortures himself constantly with what he calls his faults. But why? He has your blood." He gave Michael a hurried frown. "I've heard him say that you made a mistake. But I don't believe that an angel can make a mistake."

"Rolphe, tell me how you feel about what's happened to you? Are you sorry about Arel's plan to pass on the blood to you?"

Rolphe grabbed hold of his chest. The question made his heart do a little leap of excitement, but there was also a seizing pain. When he thought about what had happened since his encounter with Arel in the London park, he had to take several breaths to calm himself. He kept his eyes downcast as he spoke. "Dear one, I was so angry at first, and terrified. Every sin I've ever committed began to rise up from the depths of my soul. I was swimming in darkness. I was terrified when I thought about the punishment that would follow when I died."

Michael nodded. "Humans often define themselves with what they call their sins and shortcomings."

Rolphe's heart tightened even more. He began to rock himself, like he used to rock his little boys when they were hurt or crying.

"Dear one, I've killed my fellow man. I've been callous and unfeeling. Now, at times, all the pain that I've caused is waiting for me, wanting to crush the life out of me. And I can't bear it."

"But I thought you were learning that who you really are has nothing to do with those negative actions. You lost your connection to your true self, to your spirit."

Rolphe took in a ragged breath. "You and your fellow blessed one, Carey, are helping me to see that more clearly. But at times, I fall back into my old ways of thinking."

"And when that happens, you don't want to feel anymore, do you?"

"No, but I won't allow myself to become callous again. I can't go back to being a monster. Instead, I want to be the person I was when I was with my wife and children. When I provided for them and gave them my love, I felt fulfilled and happy. I try to do that with Arel, but he's so angry that he doesn't let me. And I know it's my fault. What I did to William—"

"Would you do it again?" Michael asked softly.

Rolphe's eyes lit up with the answer. "No! I lost myself to hate and self-loathing once. Never again."

As Rolphe made the declaration, he had a flash of insight. Arel had never known what it was like to be truly happy. Unlike Rolphe, he'd never been a happy husband or father. He'd tried to be a brother, William's brother, and yet he saw himself as a failure in that role.

Rolphe looked at Michael with more understanding. "I have to find a way for Arel to know happiness, true happiness. If he experiences that, perhaps he'll know it's a good thing to stop punishing himself."

"Why is he so important to you?"

Rolphe smiled. "You know that answer. I'm sure you do."

"Yes, but I'd like you to talk about your relationship with him."

"Like me, Arel has known so much pain. Yet, he didn't strike out at others. I can't imagine how much strength he has to accomplish that. I took out my anger and misery on whoever I could. Arel's known hatred too, but he's always kept it contained."

"Until William came back into his life."

"Yes, I know that Arel passed on your blood to him. But it wasn't just because he needed revenge. Some part of him needed to put things right."

Rolphe glanced around the flat. It was so different since Arel moved in. Not only was it clean, it was beautiful. The windows were shiny. There were fresh flowers on the piano. And Rolphe's paintings hung on walls that were fitting for his beloved pieces of art. When his eyes came in line with Michael's understanding gaze, he looked away. "I made William a monster. Arel gave him a chance to soar again. No matter what either of them thinks, that's the truth I know."

Thirty-Seven

Arel stood on Rolphe's balcony, wondering what kept him rooted to a foreign city, living with his worst enemy. Well, the last part wasn't accurate. Rolphe's track record as a villain was a known fact that neither of them ever forgot. However, he didn't hate Rolphe as much now as he once had. In fact, the man could be a source of comfort. He felt better around Rolphe than he did around William. With William, he was always failing in some way. But Rolphe didn't seem to notice his faults. Instead, the man went out of his way to tell Arel about his redeeming qualities.

But Arel's improved relationship with Rolphe didn't explain why he hadn't left Paris and returned home. On a number of occasions he'd gone to his closet and retrieved his suitcase, only to put it back and shut the door on the idea of leaving. Every time he queried himself about the why of such an action, he couldn't stay focused on getting the answer. Instead, he found new ways to distract himself. He even spent time at the piano. With Rolphe's help, he was mastering the idea of hand coordination and the basic mechanics of playing. At other times, he barely touched the keys. He went into a restful state where he simply sat there, letting some inner music play out. He didn't know where it came from, and he didn't care. It was soothing. His body shifted from stressed and tense to a state of calm.

His experiences in the art studio were a different matter. When he took up the brush and heaped generous amounts of paint on his palette, all his feelings came alive. After a lifetime of restraint and exacting control, he could safely express his raging angst in heavy, bold strokes. For a brief period afterwards, he felt like someone had turned down the flaming emotions that usually racked his body.

194

The obvious question was why he still had so much emotion to purge. What fueled the constant pain in his gut? Hadn't he forgiven his father and mother for their ignorance? Yes. Hadn't he accepted his brother, Aldwin's death? Yes. Hadn't he made some kind of peace with William? Yes. Thankfully he was beginning to put aside some of his guilt and failings with the man. So who did that leave? Rolphe? No, Rolphe's sins might fuel some of his anger, but the bulk of it came from another unknown source.

As he gripped the iron railing and thought about his life, he felt worn and weary. His energy dipped so quickly that he had to sit down. He settled into the comfort of one of the new, outdoor chairs that Rolphe had recently purchased. Its stylish design and mesh fabric were pleasing. In fact, the balcony was becoming a favorite place to think and unwind. As he admired the space, his gaze came to rest on a pot of petunias. A display of white and pink flowers nearly obscured the plant's greenery. A dozen branches, laden with blooms, overflowed the pot. The little seedlings that Michael brought home two weeks before had flourished. They had changed so drastically that Arel was astounded by their growth. Yet, why should he be surprised. It was the way of everything that Michael touched.

So why wasn't he thriving? Why was he painting pictures that demanded so many tubes of cadmium red and black paint? Shouldn't there be signs that he was blossoming too? He closed his eyes, searching for indications that he was on the right track. Maybe he was missing something positive about his current state. After a few moments, he let out a sigh of disgust. The truth was all too evident. He was more of a train wreck than ever, and there could only be one explanation for his present condition. He was beyond Michael's help.

As usual, Michael disagreed. He offered an alternative reason for Arel's inability to flourish. Unlike plants, those open and receptive facets of creation, people had the ability to resist life's flow. When Arel argued he was doing his best to be open, Michael gave him a kindly smile.

Arel knew what was behind that angelic expression. Michael didn't make an out-and-out accusation, but his thoughts were easy to read. Arel's resistance came from another hidden agenda. Arel insisted that Michael was mistaken. Yet, he'd already been proven wrong not once, but twice.

The first time, he'd lured William into a trap. In a state of manic oblivion, he'd reaped his revenge by giving the man angelic blood. William was nearly destroyed by the chaos that followed.

The second time Arel's secreted schemes were more complex. Before meeting Rolphe in a London park, he'd told Michael that he was going to simply meet Rolphe and talk to him. Instead, he'd made sure to give a second person Michael's angelic blood. He'd also used Rolphe for his own gain. The man became a vehicle who would fulfill Arel's death wish. But William intervened before that could happen.

Arel smiled at the thought of his savior. William could be insensitive and aloof, but in reality, he had a warm and generous heart. Now, like the petunias, it was flowering too. William was in love with a beautiful ex-angel. His future was bright.

"I'm the one who still hasn't a clue," Arel mumbled aloud.

Was Michael right about him? Did he have some new and crazy hidden itinerary? It was scary to think that something was lurking in his subconscious. But no matter how determined he was to get at what it was, his couldn't manage to ferret out any secrets. Instead, he started to get a headache.

He gave up and sat back in the lounge chair, wishing he could just let it all go. A warm breeze caressed his face and helped to soothe him a little. After a few moments he unclenched his fists. He tried to get his shoulders to relax, but his body wouldn't cooperate. It seemed to know that there was a battle brewing in the ethers. That part was readying itself for what was coming.

* * *

Annabel hadn't seen Raphael in weeks. Her old friend was giving her space, letting her adjust to her new life. When he showed up for a visit, she was happy to see him again. She'd come down to feed the mice and saw him standing by the mouse cage. "Raphael, how nice of you to stop by."

Raphael looked back at her with eyes that didn't have their usual spark. "I thought it might be a good time to talk," he said quietly.

Annabel continued over to the mouse habitat as if she hadn't heard the concern in his voice. In truth, she didn't want to acknowledge any possible problems on the horizon. She wanted her life with William to continue on in the blissful daze she'd been enjoying since coming back to London.

Raphael returned his attention to the mice. Two of them were sniffing the air and looking up at him. The third one, Wolfie, was asleep in a corner. "I'm sorry, but I think one of these little creatures is ill."

"What?" Annabel peered into the cage and felt a twinge of fear. Raphael was right. Wolfie's coat looked dull, and he was shivering. She quickly unlatched the cage door and put her hand in next to him. She held her palm open. It was an invitation for the mouse to climb aboard. Whiskers and Squeaky responded, but Wolfie barely opened his eyes.

Ignoring the two healthy mice, she carefully gathered up Wolfie and lifted him out of the cage. Holding him close, she glanced at Raphael. "Can you help him? William is going to be so upset if anything happens to the poor, little guy."

"I'll do what I can, but you know I can't interfere. If the mouse plans to cross over—"

Annabel shook her head. "No, Wolfie can't do that. As a child, William was devastated when one of his favorite foxes was killed by his father's hounds. I think Wolfie reminds him of that little fox."

Raphael hesitated. "Annabel, please, are you letting your fear take over?"

"I can't help it. William and I have been so happy. We're both settling into a perfect relationship. I don't want anything to change that."

"A perfect relationship can weather a mouse crossing over, can't it?"

Annabel walked to the recliner and sat down. Cradling Wolfie, she carefully ran her finger over his tiny head. She knew she'd exaggerated when she said things were perfect with William. She hadn't wanted to think about some worrying aspects in his behavior. William tried his best around her, but she often saw the stress behind his smiles and easy banter. At night, he often tossed and turned. He even called out in his sleep, as if he was trying to fix some problem. "All that I know is that things will get better with time if William has a chance to relax."

Raphael pulled a chair over and sat down in front of her. "He's troubled over Arel, isn't he?"

Annabel continued to pet Wolfie. "I thought our relationship would be enough, but maybe I was wrong."

"Arel has become William's family. It's natural for him to care about a brother."

"But we both agreed that Arel wasn't good for William."

"Are you sure that William is happy shutting him out?"

"I think it's for the best."

"Would that be your best or William's best?"

Annabel paused, remembering how disruptive Arel's presence could be. She stiffened, hoping to shift the dialog in a different direction. "Maybe it's best for Arel too."

"I don't understand."

"He hasn't called or contacted William for quite some time. Maybe it's his way of making it easier on himself. He doesn't have to worry about William now."

"It sounds like you've made up your mind about him."

"Yes, I suppose I have."

When Raphael didn't comment, Annabel held Wolfie out to him. "Now please, Raphael, help this little mouse."

Raphael hesitated. "As I said before, I think Wolfie has other plans."

"But why would a mouse that is loved by us and his little cage mates decide to die?"

Raphael gave her a surprised look. "Surely you remember that for an animal there is no death."

Annabel sank back into the recliner and took a deep breath. Ever since giving up her wings, she'd felt like she was forgetting everything that she'd known as an angel. But had she really forgotten everything? Or had she become so focused on fear or avoiding anything that scared her that it clouded everything else?

She looked at Wolfie again and tried to put aside all her concerns about William and herself. The mouse was curled up in her hand, sound asleep again. When she let herself connect with his mind, she smiled. His spirit was already in flight. He was dreaming of where he was going. It was a beautiful world filled with green fields, abundant, delicious food and the companionship of his fellow mice.

He wasn't dying at all. He was transiting to another glorious experience.

Annabel sighed. "Oh Raphael, how am I going to put the fear behind me so that I can see life more clearly?"

* * *

William couldn't believe how quickly things could change. He'd gone out for only a short time. When he returned home, Wolfie was dead. It was such a shock that he had to sit in his recliner, holding the mouse's still body in his hand. He examined its tiny ears, thinking about how the animal had learned to respond to his voice. He could put Wolfie down on the carpet, let the mouse explore for a few minutes, and give him a command to return. Wolfie would instantly stop, gaze back with his bright, beady eyes and scamper over to William's outstretched hand. People didn't know how smart a mouse could be. They had no idea that a creature so small could be very intelligent, social and capable of bonding with a human.

If only William had come home sooner, maybe he could have intervened. He had healed the mouse once. Perhaps he could have used his powers again. Now, it was too late.

Annabel tried to maintain a positive attitude. She told him how she'd had a vision of Wolfie on the other side. Her recollection didn't help. It couldn't stop his mind from racing forward, thinking about how the parts of life that a person loved could easily be snatched away in an instant.

The only good thing that came out of his dark musing was that he began to comprehend Arel's attitude a little better. He knew that Arel was a control freak, but he hadn't realized the scope of what that entailed. It took the pain of Wolfie's passing to make him stop and consider Arel's real pain.

Arel didn't just try to keep his home immaculate. He tried to do the same thing with his life. Everything was supposed to stay within certain carefully defined parameters. They were parameters that agreed with Arel's idea of a perfect existence.

The more William thought about it, the more he understood the reason behind Arel's desire to let Rolphe kill him. On some level, Arel was willing to forfeit his life rather than live with events and outcomes that he couldn't control. Besides harboring guilt about what went wrong in the past, he needed to stop life from sending new and unpleasant surprises his way.

William had always felt like Arel's opposite. He imagined himself to be very flexible. He could quickly adjust to adverse circumstances. Yet as he stared at Wolfie's body and felt it growing cold and stiff, he wondered if he was fooling himself.

In the past, he'd been able to put aside his feelings and go on with life regardless of the injuries he endured. Now, with angelic blood in his veins, he didn't seem to have the same ability to ignore his feelings or the pain, especially when it came to those he cared about. Again Arel came to mind.

It was one thing to lose a pet mouse. But there was another bond that was slipping away. His connection to Arel was rapidly dissolving. With each day that passed, they were drifting apart. And it wasn't that Arel wanted it that way. Before the recent difficult events, hadn't he begged William to be his brother?

Their ties were being severed because Arel was trying to put William's welfare above his own. William had never experienced that kind of loyalty before. He wasn't the only one that would go to hell and back to rescue a friend. Arel was just as determined.

The thought eased William's mind enough for him to say his final goodbyes to Wolfie. As he stood up and reflected on Annabel's earlier vision, he smiled. Annabel said that Wolfie was with his friends on the other side. It was a nice concept. Even mouse friends were there for each other.

In Arel's case, William knew that he needed to visit Paris. He wouldn't get involved with past issues. He'd simply let Arel know that he wasn't on his own. William would make sure that his brother would always have someone he could depend on too.

Thirty-Eight

Arel lay on the living room couch with his eyes closed. Earlier, when he woke up that morning, something felt wrong. Perhaps he was still reeling from his dark nightmares. They were overshadowed by loss. It permeated the dream landscape with a sorrow-filled dirge of mourning. Visions of the grim reaper and graves being dug left him so depressed, he didn't want to get out of bed that day.

Rolphe and Carey seemed determined to help. They'd coaxed him from his covers and practically dragged him out into the living room. They told him that Rolphe had composed a piece of music on the piano that needed Arel's critique.

Arel reluctantly agreed to listen, but he hadn't expected a lot. Rolphe was a decent piano teacher. He was patient and did his best to help Arel understand the instrument, but the man had never played much himself, just a couple of simple songs for beginners. So as Arel tried to get comfortable on the couch, and he thought about how long he'd have to listen to Rolphe's efforts, he wasn't prepared to be profoundly moved by the man's abilities.

At first the composition was soft, a whisper of sound. Yet, as Rolphe's fingers gently coaxed a melody to take on life, the air was stirred. The notes came together like a gentle breeze that brought in a sense of harmony and flow. Arel's body responded, giving in a little, letting itself be drawn into lingering, resonant chords. The music felt effortless. It offered an ease that soothed and appeased the tension in his muscles and the often frantic workings of his mind.

As his thoughts relaxed, the nightmares he'd had began to dissolve. All the melancholy of the night before slipped away into a misty fog. He began to forget where he was.

As the melody continued on, the stirring went deeper. It searched in places that Arel had forgotten. When was the last time he'd felt his soul? He'd been so focused on the harsh reality of life that he'd lost touch with any idea of something greater within. Now, that elusive part of him seemed to be calling out.

At first the sound was soft, like the music. But as he acknowledged how long he'd gone without peace or joy, he listened more attentively. The music became a vehicle. Each note was delivered like a prayer being sent heavenward. Each note asked for surrender to something nurturing and giving.

Sound buoyed him up until he felt himself opening his fists. He let go of all the hardness in the world of matter. Stones that could make one trip and fall became elements in a dream. He walked on a smooth path with beautiful gardens. The scent of jasmine and rose filled the air. Color was everywhere, vibrant and alive.

He felt his own vitality and well-being. It was the substance that infused everything he saw around him. He felt free, stripped of burden and basking in a sunlit place where nothing ever went wrong.

As he relaxed in that elevated garden of bliss, he had a moment of clarity. He wasn't an idiot always making mistakes. He wasn't an angry, vengeful mortal. He was so much more than what could be contained in a fleshy vessel. He was something as gentle and giving as the birdsong that filled the garden.

As he drifted further and further into a place of rapture and euphoria, the music stopped. The beautiful sounds of the piano fell into a hush of silence. As soon as that silence invaded the heavens, he had another bout of clarity. He might have slipped out of the world for a few moments, but those moments couldn't last. As soon as he had the thought, he began to fall. His descent from the heavens was so fast that he screamed out in protest. "No! I don't want to go back!"

Yet it wasn't so fast that he could forget what was waiting for him. Instead of being the embodiment of calm and serenity, his earthly nature was a bundle of raging emotions. He was always on edge, watching everything with a critical eye, ready for some slight annoyance to ignite his anger. Neither angel nor human was spared his violent moods and reactions.

He didn't want it to be that way. He'd done his best to change, but William was right to label him an idiot. His personality was fatally flawed. That's what his hidden agenda was all about. He'd been secretly harboring his death wish after all. But after what he'd just experienced, it made sense. Why should he be chained to a life of misery when death could reunite him with perfection?

His flash of insight was useless to stop the world from swallowing him up again. Flesh and bone wouldn't be denied. The feeling of being so light and expansive quickly gave way to the dense heaviness of his physical form. It was such a painful contrast that he didn't think he could go on. He was trapped again, cursing and fighting the life-force that kept him tethered to the earth.

* * *

After Rolphe played the last note of his composition, his fingers slipped from the keys. He bowed his head and offered thanks for the gift that he'd just been given. As he played, he'd felt the Creator's light flowing through him. His hands became divine instruments, gracefully executing every note with just the right touch. As he surrendered to the power of that amazing energy, he and the piano joined forces to express the love that Rolphe felt in his heart. When he finished, he was blissful.

But his jubilation was cut short when Arel started shouting. The man's protests were voiced with so much anger that Rolphe abandoned the piano and rushed over to the couch to help. He knelt down in front of Arel. "Arel! Why are you so upset?"

When Arel opened his eyes, they were wild and raging. Their glaring intensity reminded Rolphe of a soldier he'd known when he was a young inductee in the army. His friend had completely lost it on the battle field. Rolphe tried to stop the man from running into enemy fire, but the young soldier was too quick for him. The man was killed before Rolphe could save him. Again, he felt just as helpless. All he could do was try to understand what Arel needed. Thankfully, Carey was there too. Both of them tried to calm Arel's sudden display of dread and panic. "Tell us what's wrong," he begged.

Arel's frenzy suddenly slowed. He slumped back on the sofa. Only his golden eyes remained active. They darted about like those of a caged bird throwing itself against the bars.

Rolphe tried another appeal. "Arel? It's okay, you're safe. Talk to us, please."

Rolphe's entreaty seemed to get through to Arel. The man reached out with a shaky hand and grabbed Rolphe's shirt.

"How could you understand what I feel?" Arel asked. "You've always pushed death away, trying to stave off hell and damnation. But hell is here, Rolphe, all around you and you're too ignorant to know that. But I crave that moment when I'll forever leave this world. I want to go back to that state of bliss where I'll be free of my faults and what you call sins."

Rolphe bowed his head. "You're right, I don't understand. I only know that your intentions have always been good, my friend."

Arel stared at him. "Friend? Is that what you consider me?"

"I'm sorry if that offends you."

Arel paused and let out a sigh. After a moment of hesitation, he moved his hand to Rolphe's shoulder. "I'm tired, so tired of judging the actions of others when I've failed so completely. But maybe you'll find a way to honor Michael's blood. Do you promise to do that, Rolphe?"

Rolphe swallowed hard. He'd been hoping that Arel would adopt a more lenient attitude towards him. Now he'd been offered so much more. "I promise."

Arel squeezed Rolphe's shoulder a little harder. "I truly hope you succeed."

Rolphe didn't know how to respond, especially when he felt the energy coming from Arel's hand. It was like a mild electric current that went directly to his heart. The pleasing sensation made the vessel pound more vigorously. As the moments passed, Rolphe knew his heart had been restored.

Arel's eyes brightened a little. "Use your strength to do what I can't, Rolphe. Be that vessel Michael has tried to make of me. Be that holy one that your god wants on this earth."

Rolphe was overjoyed. First of all, he hadn't dared to think his heart would ever beat normally again. But more than that, he could feel how much Arel was counting on him. It gave him the inspiration he needed to go forward. He'd try his best to be the man he'd failed to be for so long.

He kept his head bowed as he made a second proclamation. "Dear friend, I also promise to dedicate whatever time I have left to carrying out the will of the Creator.

Arel sighed and nodded. "Michael and Carey believe in you, in your ability to be a good man. From now on, I want to believe in you too. I'll try my best to be a friend, Rolphe."

The words made Rolphe's spirit soar. His gaze was bright and teary as he glanced up, but a movement caught his eye. Before he had a chance to convey his gratitude, he saw a man waiting in the doorway. "Mon Dieu! It's him!" he gasped.

William was standing no more than ten feet away. The man's face was frozen in horror and revulsion. When their eyes met, Rolphe's smile turned into a grimace of shame. He remembered the last time he'd seen William. He'd attacked the younger man, laughing at William's helpless panic. With glee, he'd thrown William to the floor and began feasting on his blood. Afterwards, he'd been in such haste to dump the man's nearly lifeless body in a back bedroom.

As the memory flashed through Rolphe's mind, Arel got to his feet and turned to look at William. When he spoke, it was a whisper of disbelief. "Will? What are you doing here?"

When Rolphe looked at Arel, he quickly forgot his disgrace. The man who'd just reached out to him was surprised and shaken. Shock and panic paled his face. But Rolphe saw what Arel was hiding behind hooded eyes. Arel had spoken about the relief of death, but in life, he valued his friendship with William above any other. It seemed to help him go on with life. It was a comfort when he was hurting and alone.

But William didn't seem to see what Rolphe observed. His numb features came alive as he glared back at Arel. When he found his tongue, his words were fast but deliberate. "I cared about you, you traitor! I wanted to make sure you were alright. I should have known you'd forget what brotherhood was supposed to mean. You disowned me to align with a monster. You've accused me of selfishness, but your cruelty has no boundaries!"

Without waiting for a reply, William turned and walked briskly from the room. He didn't stop at the door. His loud curses could be heard as he made his way down the outer hall.

Rolphe looked to Arel for direction. When the man stood stiff and unmoving, Rolphe spoke up. "Aren't you going to go after him?"

Arel's fists closed on themselves. "No, it's better this way," he said in a barely audible voice.

Carey spoke up. "Do you want me to talk to him?"

Arel turned, censuring the angel with a scowl. "Didn't you hear me? I said let him be."

Carey hesitated. "What do you mean? William doesn't think you care about him. But we both know how mistaken he is. His welfare is always on your mind."

Arel walked forward a few feet and stared at the space where William had stood. "That's why I have to let him think the worst about me. I have to sever all ties. I realize that it's the only way he'll truly be safe."

Rolphe wanted to offer some kind of aid, but he felt helpless again. Arel was saying goodbye to the closest thing he had to family. But Rolphe knew what loss could do to a man. When his wife and children died, it destroyed him. He didn't want to think what it might do to Arel. The man hadn't just lost family, he'd lost all faith in himself.

* * *

As William left Rolphe's flat, he tried to stem the flow of obscenities that had hold of him. He tried to restore some kind of order to his thoughts, but he failed completely. Fires were burning, and it wasn't an easy matter to put them out. He'd been betrayed by the one person he'd always cared about. His paranoia was grounded in truth. Arel's allegiance had shifted. He'd chosen a ogre to take William's place, as if their bond meant nothing.

The thought was so vile that he couldn't allow himself to dwell on it. He'd explode on the spot if he let his anger get any more volatile. Somehow he had to cool the rage that wanted venting. Yet, the day had started with such good intentions on William's part.

After burying Wolfie in the back garden, he couldn't get Arel out of his mind. The man's makeup and personality had always been unstable. Even in the beginning days of their friendship, William had recognized how quickly Arel's mind could swing out of balance. Recent events proved that Arel hadn't changed. He might be carrying the blood of angels in his veins, but it didn't change his basic makeup. Arel and anxiety were almost synonymous. If left to himself for very long, Arel could quickly head for the nearest suicide booth.

After Arel's trip to Paris, he busied himself with keeping Rolphe in line. From what little William knew about the situation, it seemed almost therapeutic. It gave Arel something to do other than obsess over himself. But William knew Arel. How long would it be before Arel went back to his melancholy self? The answer was easy. Not very long.

That's what prompted William to visit Paris. He didn't want Arel to lose himself to depression again. Unfortunately, William ran into some of his own problems. He'd thought he was over his trauma with Rolphe. He'd had the cocky idea that he was sound of mind and self-confident again. It was a total miscalculation on his part. Before he could raise his fist to knock on Rolphe's door, all the helplessness he'd experienced with Rolphe returned.

It took a hasty retreat out of the Rolphe's apartment building to get his body to settle down. His mind was something else. It remained steadfast in holding on to what had happened to him. The traumatic event played out in detail all over again. When Rolphe grabbed hold of him, William had no time to think or act. His fate was sealed. He was in the hands of an uncaring, heartless animal.

The memory had William leaned against the building. He tried to breathe. He tried to remember that Rolphe hadn't won out in the end. Arel had come through and brought William back from death's door. Finally, it was concentrating on Arel's unyielding support that helped William get a grip. In spite of all of Arel's flaws, he'd been totally devoted when needed.

William kept that fact in mind as he returned to Rolphe's flat. He held on to Arel's steadfast loyalty as he climbed the stairs. He held on to the bottom line. Arel was worth the trouble that William usually endured when he was around the man. That's what he kept telling himself as he knocked on Rolphe's door. When no one answered, he took the liberty of trying the knob and letting himself into the apartment. He'd barely had a chance to glance around and notice how different the place looked when he heard Arel talking to Rolphe. Arel's words were clear and direct. "I'll try my best to be a friend, Rolphe."

It took a moment for William to feel the impact of that short declaration. Maybe that was nature's way of comforting its creatures when disaster first strikes. For a long moment, William's ears buzzed and his mind stopped working. When the world started up again, the blow was delivered. Reality hit with an incredible force. Arel had betrayed him.

While William was worrying about Arel, the man was casting him aside. Arel had formed a new bond with the most detestable human being imaginable. The only thing missing in the scenario was a knife in William's back. Arel's method was slightly different than that of most villains. When Arel knifed a person, he did it straight on. The victim definitely knew who was stabbing him.

Thirty-Nine

Arel sat in his bedroom, letting his thoughts drift, each one a lifeboat trying to survive in a tempest. For days, he'd been nursing his wounds, but they weren't going away. He needed something, anything, to help him forget the latest William disaster. No, it was more than a disaster. He and William were finished.

When he'd tapped into William's thoughts, they were filled with outrage and disgust. William found the idea of Arel's friendship with Rolphe unforgivable. William's mindset was so volatile that Arel had to quickly disengage from the link. If he didn't, he'd be consumed by William's hatred and loathing.

To allow William to think the worst was one of the hardest things that Arel had ever done. It was even harder than making peace with his brother Aldwin's death. But it couldn't be helped. Deceiving William was the only way that Arel could ensure William's freedom. The event hadn't been something he'd planned, but when William showed up, when he saw William's face and the horror it expressed, he knew it was an opportunity. In a flash, he knew how to send William away permanently.

At first, the aftermath was almost too much to bear. He knew he'd done the right thing, but he couldn't endure the emotional trauma that came with it. Later, as he accepted what happened as necessary, as the door to their relationship closed, something in Arel's psyche responded. He understood how cut off he was from the one person who'd always had faith in him, but he didn't panic. He became very still. The thoughts came, but he controlled their intensity by taking them one at a time. He isolated each sting and arrow, processing it in slow motion, so that all the pain didn't hit him at the same time.

It helped, but as the days passed, he needed more. He had to find a better method to help him move on in his life. One suggestion came to mind. Michael often encouraged meditation. A person wasn't only his or her thoughts. Perhaps he needed to give those deeper parts of himself time to work things out.

In a quiet moment of desperation, he shut his eyes, hoping the angel was right. It took a number of slow, deep breaths to strengthen his intention. He wanted relief. Gradually, he was able to give himself over to an all-encompassing quiet, one that calmed his body and slowed his thoughts. They were still there, but they moved into the background. He pressed on. He kept breathing and intending, breathing and intending until it became kind of a game.

After days of sitting in a sort of calm, a strange thing happened. The muddied waters of loss and pain began to clear. He began to see his life from a much broader perspective.

In the past, he'd tried to end it all. That didn't work. Some force, be it angel or human, always intervened. Life itself, it seemed, wouldn't give up. It kept holding on to him. So where did that leave him? What was he supposed to do with that life?

If he was going to go on, he had to cut the ties to his past, just like he'd cut his ties to William. He had to find a way not to look back at what he'd lost. Two brothers were dead to him. Justina, the woman he'd loved so completely, was gone too. Those facts usually kept him tethered to pain and misery. Now, he had to relinquish it all. He had to have a fresh start. But it wasn't in Chicago. He knew it wasn't in Paris either. So where would he go for his new life?

That's when he remembered Rolphe's solution. When Rolphe needed to escape the torment that life threw at him, he'd fled to another world. His way out wasn't great. His sanctuary was a dank, rocky cave carved out of a frightful landscape. But at least Rolphe had somewhere to go. When Arel found him, Rolphe might have taken the form of a mangy wolf, but he wasn't suffering like he had when he was in the world he normally inhabited.

As Arel contemplated how he'd destroyed Rolphe's cave and the world itself, he had a twinge of regret. Did he have the right to put an end to another person's safe harbor? Fortunately, his remorse quickly passed. The place was foul, and William had almost died there. There was no reason to keep such a sordid place in existence. But what if he could create a better place? What if he could get a fresh start in a world customized totally to his needs. It was an intriguing idea, one that repeated over and over in his head.

* * *

Carol stood at the kitchen counter, fixing Kevin's lunch for the next day. He'd been complaining about the cost of always eating out. Since Carol loved bargains and saving money, she had no problem coming up with a solution. When she heard Kevin coming into the kitchen, she glanced back with a smile. "Is little Ariel asleep?" she asked quietly. She'd gotten into the habit of thinking she had to whisper whenever it came to sleeping babies.

Kevin stretched and gave her a nod. "He's dead to the world, so there's no need to be quiet. And I don't think you need to call him 'little' anymore, do you?"

Carol grabbed a large paper bag and laughed. "No, you're right. It's just that he's growing so fast. Maybe I want him to stay little for a while."

Kevin walked over and put his hands around her waist. "You love babies, but big guys can be fun too."

Carol giggled, "Yes, I know."

Kevin squeezed her a little tighter. "Thanks for making my lunch."

"I hope you like tuna salad. I made you two sandwiches."

"One will be fine. Save the other one for your lunch."

Carol put the bag aside and turned around to face him. "I don't think so. You'll be starving by the time you get home. Just eat both of them."

Kevin let her go and patted his stomach. "In case you haven't noticed, I've been putting on a few pounds."

"Then I'll leave out the cookies."

"What? No dessert? Forget that. I'll trim down if I start running again."

"That's a good idea. You always seem to feel better when you get some exercise."

"It's too bad Arel is still in Paris. He can be a great jogging partner."

Carol gave him a squinty-eyed frown. "Kevin Bailey, I know why you like jogging with Arel. You like to relive your coaching days. But I don't think Arel appreciates your constant comments on what he's doing wrong."

Kevin picked up a stray cookie crumb off the counter. He popped it in his mouth thoughtfully. "Arel can be just as pushy."

Carol returned to packing Kevin's lunch, putting in baggies of carrot sticks and apple slices. "I guess you're right. You're both very hard-headed at times."

Kevin laughed. "I may be hard-headed, but Arel takes the cake when it comes to stubbornness. You know that."

"I suppose. Anyway, what do you think about that text he sent to all of us? He sounds very occupied, but he didn't really explain what he's up to."

"Before I comment, what did Peggy think? I'm sure you two have already discussed it."

Carol hesitated. "If you must know, she thinks he sounds evasive. We ask him questions about painting and stuff that he's supposed to be doing, and we rarely get a straight answer."

"Straight answer? From Arel? Forget it."

Carol closed the lunch bag and walked it over to the refrigerator. "Aren't you being a little hard on him? I think he believes he's looking out for us. You know he's afraid we'll worry about him."

"Or maybe he can't help but be devious. Some people are—"

"Some people are what?"

"I'm not trying to criticize him, but let's face facts. Arel is a fibber. His track record proves it."

Carol went back to the counter and started to wipe it down. "He tells white lies, so what? But you still haven't told me what you think about his email."

Kevin reached into the cookie jar and retrieved the last cookie. "Were you saving this?" he asked as he waved the cookie aloft.

"Stop avoiding the question."

"I think he's up to something, but at least he doesn't sound depressed. There was something almost upbeat about his tone."

"I hope you're right."

"If you're worried, call your old buddy, William, and get his opinion?"

"Kevin, I swear, sometimes I think you're jealous of that man."

Kevin shrugged. "No, not really, I just wish I could have been the one to help you out when you were hurting."

Carol smiled back. "Honey, you were wonderful and very understanding. You should be proud of yourself."

"Good, so if you call William—"

"I don't know if that's a good idea. Remember when we talked to him last Saturday? He only mentioned Arel very briefly, but there was something in his tone. It reminded me of when he was recuperating here, and he was on the outs with Arel."

"Do you think they had another falling out?"

Carol frowned. "If they did, Annabel would know. Maybe I'll call her sometime soon."

Kevin sighed. "Great idea. Now for my last question, when are you going to make more cookies?"

"I thought you were watching your waistline."

"Can I help it if all this talk about Arel and William has me hungry?"

"I think you're using this conversation as an excuse. However, if you look in the cupboard over the microwave, I think you'll like what you find there. I baked this afternoon."

Kevin's face brightened at once. "You little minx! I thought I smelled a faint scent of cookies when I came in from work."

Carol crossed her arms. "And I thought I aired out the house. How silly of me."

Kevin pulled her close again. "Can I help it if being around you makes me ravenous?"

Carol braced her hands against his broad chest. "Ravenous for cookies or for me?"

Kevin's smile broadened. "For both!"

* * *

Rolphe wiped his hands, content that he'd gotten most of the paint off. He'd been in the studio all morning, enjoying the distraction of putting oils to canvas. When he walked into the living room, Arel was sitting on one of the two matching couches. Blank-faced, he was busy studying something on his tablet. It had been over a week since William's visit.

Perhaps Arel was in auto mode. It was a state that often accompanied denial. Arel refused to discuss his feelings. Michael had tried to talk to him and been turned away. Carey was forced to keep his distance too. So maybe Arel wanted to forget the whole affair and not deal with the repercussions. Or maybe the man was good at keeping his thoughts and feelings hidden.

Arel had a way of shielding himself more powerfully than anyone Rolphe had known in his long life. The barriers he erected around his person were as thick as fortress walls and much more resistant to any form of intrusion.

Rolphe cringed at the thought of prying, but he couldn't put his own welfare above helping his friend. Shields or not, Rolphe knew that Arel had to be hurting. When Arel looked up and gave him a relaxed smile, it challenged his assumption. Arel's expression of well-being was so genuine that Rolphe was forced to smile back. "It's a beautiful day outside," he mumbled, trying to recover from his surprise.

Arel nodded blissfully. "Yes, it is."

Rolphe stepped closer, drawn in by how handsome Arel could be when his features weren't marred by unhappiness. His dark curls were growing out a little, framing a face that was the picture of well-defined symmetry and classic bone structure. The man could be a painter's delight when he was calm and stress-free, a perfect model of humanity at its best.

Rolphe almost grabbed for his phone, anxious to capture Arel in a rare moment of ease. He stopped himself before his hand found his pocket. Arel hated the idea of pictures of himself. When Rolphe had secretly taken a few, he later found them missing from his phone. Arel was vigilant when it came to his privacy. Rolphe never got away with any deceit, even if it was innocent and well-intentioned.

"So what are you studying?" Rolphe asked.

Arel closed the cover on his device and broadened his smile. "Paradise."

Rolphe scratched his head and sat down. He stretched out his legs, enjoying the comfort of the new couch. His gaze traveled around the remodeled flat and out the open balcony doors. "Why would you look elsewhere for paradise when it's all around us?"

Arel's eyes narrowed. "Maybe for you. But tell me about something. That cave where you hung out, where did that world come from? Who created it?"

"That's a long story, but basically the woman who took me under her wing was responsible for its existence. Chessa and another man, a powerful man, knew enough about such things to find a way to make it real in some way. When the man was killed, Chessa didn't want to go there by herself. But sadly, no one could make the journey with her . . . until I came along."

"Was it always so hideous?"

Rolphe scowled. "Certainly not! It was a kind of paradise too until—" He didn't want to go on. He didn't want to remember how everything fell apart when Chessa died.

Arel drummed his fingers impatiently. "So what happened, Rolphe? Talk to me."

Rolphe shrugged. "Places like that need a certain kind of energy. Chessa had so much vitality. She loved life. She expressed it in the colorful way she dressed and how she conducted herself. That world was an expression of how she felt. Without her passion, it decayed. But I had to have someplace to go after you gave me the blood and—"

Arel looked away. "Thank you. I won't ask you about it again."

"Why did you want to know about—"

"Never mind." Arel stilled his fingers. His eyes became dreamy and fluid as he stood up. When he spoke, his voice was distant too. "I need to lay down for a while. Don't disturb me, is that understood?"

Rolphe watched Arel walk slowly from the room. When Arel paused for an instant in the place where William last stood, a fortunate thing happened. Arel let his guard down, as if his dreaminess and the pain of William's visit collided and made him negligent. With the man's shields out of the way, Rolphe allowed himself a peek at Arel's aura. As he suspected, dark expanses of pain could be seen, but they were buried. A layer of another kind of energy dominated Arel's auric body. It felt like excitement, but the excitement wasn't pure like that of a child. It had heavy, dense overtones.

When Rolphe tried to go a little deeper, Arel glanced back at him. His golden eyes were so intense that Rolphe felt an attack of nausea. He had to put up a few of his own shields to keep from getting sick.

"Don't go there again," Arel ordered. "It's none of your business."

Rolphe nodded and looked away. After Arel left the room, he felt a little better physically. But his intuitive senses were anything but appeased. Arel was hiding something. It wasn't a small something. Whatever he was doing was going to change everything, including the peaceful life that Rolphe was finally enjoying.

Forty

Annabel put her phone on the table and went to the living room window. The weather was wet and windy. Her trip to the shop would have to be put off to the next day when the weather was supposed to improve. After talking to Peggy, she didn't feel alone in her need for sunnier days. With Chicago having a rainy spell too, her friend sounded a little down. Annabel understood why. Peggy and Carol liked to take the babies out every day and visit the park. Being cooped up in the house was more difficult when there were children involved. "I wonder if I'll be pushing a stroller someday," Annabel sighed aloud.

"Are you saying something to me?" William asked as he came in from the hall.

Annabel smiled. "No, I was talking to myself."

William walked over to the window and stared out too. "What's going on, something I should know?"

"I guess I was thinking about Peggy and Carol's babies. They're so adorable."

William gave her a quick scowl and retreated to the sofa. "I'm sorry, but I can't think about children right now."

Annabel studied William's furrowed brows and the hard set of his jaw. He'd been wearing the same expression for almost two weeks. She had tried to talk to him about what was troubling him, but he refused to discuss the matter. "I'm sorry about the difficult time you're having, William, but you can't keep dwelling on what happened in Paris."

William crossed his arms and stiffened even more. "Fine, explain to me how I'm supposed to get over being betrayed by someone I trusted more than anyone else on this earth."

"Maybe you're making a bigger deal out of what happened than you should. Maybe you should open the emails that Rolphe has been sending to—"

"Annabel please, don't mention that fiend's name in this house!"

Annabel hesitated. When William first returned from Paris, she found herself being secretly happy that he'd had a falling out with Arel. She knew it was selfish to feel the way she did, but her needs seem to overshadow everything. She yearned for a happy life with the man she loved, just the two of them. Later, when they were both ready, children might come along. They'd raise a wonderful family together.

Now, looking at William, seeing him so miserable, she knew her wishful thinking wasn't very smart. She should have known William was going to be deeply affected when he thought Arel had cast him aside. Loyalty was a foundation stone in William's nature. It was part of the code he lived by. He didn't extend that loyalty to very many, but when he did, it was forever. To find out that it was abused was shaking him to the core.

But would she really want it any other way? One of the reasons she fell in love with William was because of his allegiance to those he cared about. "I'm sorry. I only want you to feel better. That's all."

William relaxed his arms and gazed back at her. His eyes softened a little. "No, I'm the one who's sorry. I shouldn't be around you when I'm in such a foul mood."

Annabel walked over and sat down next to him. "Is there anything I can do or say to help you get over—"

William stood up abruptly and cut her off. "Get over what? Get over being an idiot? Is that what you're asking? Do you know how many years I've invested in that ingrate, Arel? Do you have any idea how much crap I've ignored, thinking that self-serving bounder deserved my indulgence?"

Annabel stood up too. She could try to understand William, but at times her fears got the better of her. Was she going to lose William to his bitterness over Arel? "Then forget him, William! Don't spend more of your life holding on to your grievances."

"You'd like that, wouldn't you?"

"What do you mean?"

"Oh, come off it, Annabel. Do you think I don't know what's going through your head? It's so obvious. Ever since you gave up your wings, you only think about yourself."

Annabel backed up, stunned by her own stupidity. She'd never thought about William being privy to her secrets. "What do you mean? Have you been reading my mind like you read Arel's?"

William let out a sarcastic huff of laughter. "I don't have to read your mind. You're the most transparent person I've ever met. When I got back from Paris and told you what happened, you practically glowed from head to toe. I knew you disliked Arel, but I never suspected that you'd be happy to see me disown him."

Annabel frowned, trying to stop the tears she felt welling up. "I don't want to be like this. I know it's not right, but I don't know how to stop feeling what I feel."

William took a deep breath, reached out and pulled her into his arms. "It's not your fault, my angel. As soon as you decided to join the human race, you were immediately thrown into an impossible situation."

Annabel pushed William back enough to look up at him. "I'm so relieved to hear you say that. Because I want to help you again. I want to be wise and caring like I was when I was truly your angel. And I don't want either of us to push Arel away—"

"Please, you were right about him! I'm the one who made a grave error in judgment about that—"

"No! Stop it, William! I may not have my wings, but everything inside of me says that Arel is innocent." As soon as the words were out, Annabel cringed. She'd been holding back so much because of her fears. Now, everything spilled out before she could stop it.

William let her go and pulled away. "What do you mean?"

"For two weeks I've let you curse Arel, but all that time I knew you were wrong. I should have said something sooner, but—"

"Annabel, you weren't there! You didn't see what I saw! You didn't hear—"

"I talked to Rolphe, William. He called here before you even got back. He explained everything, and I believe what he said. I also talked to Carey and Michael. Arel never betrayed you. It was all a misunderstanding."

William looked like she'd slapped him. His pale, blue eyes were wide with disbelief as the color drained from his face. He turned and started out of the room. "I can't talk about this now. Excuse me."

* * *

A few minutes earlier, when Peggy heard her phone ring and saw Annabel's cell number, she knew something wasn't right. Annabel never called twice in one day. Then she heard Annabel's panicked voice and almost panicked herself. She only relaxed a little when she found out that there was nothing seriously wrong on Annabel's end. At least no one had died or anything like that.

"Sweetie, slow down, please," she instructed. "Carol is here with me. We're having a chat over coffee. I'm sure she'll want to help you with your questions too. So I'm putting you on speaker, okay?"

Annabel's voice was quivering when she replied. "Carol's there?"

Peggy nodded automatically. "Yes, is that okay with you?"

"Yes, that's fine," Annabel said.

Peggy gestured to Carol to move her chair closer. "Say 'hello' to Carol."

Annabel responded a moment later. "Hi, Carol, I'm sorry to interrupt."

Carol leaned in. "Annabel, it's good to hear from you. Can I help in any way?"

Annabel didn't say anything at first. Finally, she managed a few words. "I'm a terrible person!"

Peggy gave Carol a concerned frown. "Tell us why you feel that way."

There was another long pause on Annabel's end. "William has been having a very hard time, and I could have helped, but I didn't. I should have tried to make him understand things a little better, but I was too selfish. Like he said, I only think about myself."

Carol leaned in even more. "William said you were selfish?"

Annabel started to cry. "Yes, and he's right."

"Can you tell us a little more about what happened?" Peggy asked.

Annabel sniffled. "I just want us to be happy. Then William went to see Arel and . . . and everything was horrible after that. You see, they had a misunderstanding, and William got very upset."

Carol gave Peggy a knowing glance. "Annabel, those two don't always get along, but that's not your fault. It was a real mess when William visited a while back. William was upset that time too. And Peggy and I kind of got in the middle of it. It got a little dicey, but things worked out. And in the end, Arel and William patched it up, or at least they seemed to have come to some kind of truce."

Peggy reached for the phone and pulled it closer. "Annabel, listen to me. You have to give yourself a break. You got caught up in something that's probably been going on for a long time."

Carol nodded this time. "Peggy's right. You're blaming yourself when you shouldn't be. And I'm sure William didn't mean it when he said you're selfish. I think he was probably taking his frustration out on you."

Annabel sniffled again. "Really? So I'm not a totally, horrible person?"

Peggy pursed her lips. "I hate to tell you this, Annabel, but you're probably always going to have your hands full with those two. My advice is the same as Carol's. You have to give yourself a break."

"I don't think I know how to do that. I don't want to be selfish again," Annabel said.

Carol gave Peggy a knowing look. "Maybe this will help. I used to think Kevin was the problem in our relationship. Then William helped me realize that I needed to have more confidence in myself. When I worked on appreciating myself more, things changed for the better. Now I don't worry about Kevin so much. I find ways to be happy with myself."

"Do you understand what Carol is trying to say?" Peggy asked.

Annabel sighed. "Yes, I think so, or at least I think I know more about what I need to do."

"Good," Carol said.

Peggy snatched up the phone. "And remember, you can always call us if you feel discouraged. We're here for you."

"Thank you," Annabel said. "Thank you both so much for being so understanding. Now I'll let you get back to your visit."

"Talk to you soon," Peggy said just before she hit the disconnect button. She put the phone back on the table and looked at Carol. "That poor thing, I feel for her."

Carol sat back and smoothed out her napkin. "I can only imagine trying to cope with Arel and William when they're going at each other. It got pretty ugly when we were involved."

"I know. Arel practically disowned me at one point. He thought I only cared about William. In truth, I was simply trying to help both of them."

Carol smiled. "I think William believes he's the rational one, but he can get pretty upset too."

"They're both very intense, but they express it in different ways."

Carol started to giggle. "Thank goodness our guys are as easy going as they are. Can you imagine being in love with William or Arel?"

"Heavens, no!" Peggy laughed. Then she sobered and gave Carol a beseeching look. "Carol, I'm serious, we have to start praying for Annabel. Otherwise, she might not survive those two if they go nutty with each other again."

* * *

After Annabel's revelation, William walked stiff-kneed down the steps to the lower level. He didn't know how to deal with what she'd told him. He was barely aware of where he was as he slumped down into his recliner. He tried to take stock of himself, but he felt scattered. He'd sown so many fields of anger and abandonment that he couldn't think clearly. After weeks of allowing his emotions to rule his thoughts, he needed sleep, but he knew it wouldn't come. There was too much chaos wanting his attention. After the incident in Paris, he thought he'd had Arel figured out. Now, he knew he hadn't figured out anything. He had to start all over again. This time he'd go all the way back to the time when he and Arel first met.

William recognized something extraordinary about Arel shortly after they became friends. The man was self-centered and constantly playing the victim, but that was only a small part of who he was. The real person, the real Arel, lay hidden below his miserable personality.

It took a lot of digging for William to access the soul of the man or should he say, boy. In those days, Arel looked more like a child trying to play at being an adult. With his unruly curls, and his thin, still-developing frame, he often lacked any sign of maturity. But William didn't let that stop him from searching for Arel's true identity. After a couple of months, he thought he'd made a mistake. Arel was quarrelsome and difficult to be around most of the time. How could he be special?

Then, on the most unlikely of occasions, William's hunch paid off. One night, he and Arel were sitting on a rooftop, smoking cigars and getting drunk. As the night wore on, Arel put the whiskey aside and extinguished his cigar. He sat back to study the night sky. William wasn't paying attention. He was in a good mood, laughing at some joke he'd just made. He was surprised when Arel turned to him and wouldn't stop staring at him. At first, William thought Arel was just being his usual annoying self. He wasn't prepared for what happened next. Arel's persona suddenly shifted. He was neither man nor boy. William couldn't classify Arel at that moment. He was too busy staring at Arel's eyes. They began to glow as bright as liquid gold.

While William was wondering how eyes could be that brilliant, Arel began to talk. His voice went from sluggish and slurred to crisp and clear. He asked William if he believed in mysteries. Before William could answer, Arel turned back to examining the heavens. In time, he also began to share what he saw. But he didn't talk about starlight or the crescent moon, he described incredible worlds beyond. He talked about the universe and how it was dreamed into reality. His voice became a whisper when he explained how beautiful a star nursery could be. He expounded on the vast number of galaxies that lay beyond man's telescopes and how they were created.

As William listened in awe, Arel became a grand storyteller. But where was he getting his information? Arel made it sound like he was accessing the Creator's handbook. His detailed accounts were poetic to the ear and dazzling to the imagination. William knew a little about astronomy, but it would be many years before science caught up with Arel's explanations about the unseen world of space.

Afterwards, as the night wore on, Arel fell into a deep sleep. When he awoke and William queried him about what he'd seen, Arel claimed he didn't remember anything. He even claimed to have a disinterest in the idea of space and galaxies.

It was always that way with Arel. At rare moments, he'd leave reality behind and turn his focus on whatever caught his fancy. It could be a grain of sand or the song of a bird. But while he was in that altered space, his vision was expansive and beautiful. It was the exact opposite of how he normally saw life. Later, Arel never remembered anything.

In the end, it was William who was always left with the task of holding on to Arel's visions. Otherwise, they would have been lost forever. Arel himself would have been lost forever if William hadn't saved him from himself.

William sighed as he thought about his rekindled memories of youth. He had placed so much value on Arel's life, but how much value did Arel place on William? Was Annabel right about Arel still caring about a brother?

He sat up and retrieved his laptop from the side table. For two weeks, he'd ignored the messages that Rolphe had sent. Now it was time to see what the man was trying to tell him. He started to tap open the mail program, but his hand was shaky. His thoughts vacillated. Two weeks of playing the trauma/drama game was hard to put aside. When his nerves calmed a little, he opened the first email that Rolphe had sent. He groaned as he read the words that Rolphe had written. Like Annabel, he believed Rolphe. The man might have been an ogre, but William knew in his gut that he wasn't lying now. William read the message a couple of times.

"You were the final straw, William. Now Arel has lost everything and everyone he loves. Please help him before he tries something crazy."

William heard the urgency in the message. It hit him so hard that he had to swallow a lump of fear closing up his throat. He couldn't imagine what Arel might be like after two weeks of feeling that he was the object of William's hatred. The guy was probably on some kind of death wish campaign again.

He closed the laptop and grabbed his phone. After punching in Arel's number, he waited. He held the phone close to his ear as it began to ring. After a half dozen rings, Arel answered. It was William's cue to brace himself for what was coming. Arel could be so depressing. Would his mood overshadow William's intention? He wanted to have a receptive attitude, but that meant putting aside two weeks of anger.

Before he could make sure his emotions were stable, he got a shock. He almost dropped the phone in disbelief. Arel sounded cheerful. He was more welcoming and excited than William could remember. But it wasn't an insensitive cheeriness. Arel began to apologize for any misunderstanding in the most sincere of voices. He went on to say that William was and would always be his closest friend. He made it clear that William was the brother he'd always wanted and no one would ever be more important.

William was left speechless as Arel went on. Arel extended an open, heartfelt energy that warmed William's being. All the ugliness he'd experienced since leaving Paris dissolved so completely, he couldn't remember why he'd ever been upset. When he hung up the phone, he didn't know why he'd ever worried about anything. Arel was happy and content at long last. Everything felt perfect. He could finally turn his attention to Annabel and have the wonderful relationship they both wanted.

Forty-One

Rolphe didn't mean to keep spying on Arel. But as he crept closer to Arel's open bedroom door, he knew it was for Arel's best. Something very strange was going on. As the days passed, Arel went from being at his lowest to suddenly acting animated and happy. He was painting pictures that still had somber tones, but patches of green and blue were creeping in. Sometimes Arel sat at the piano. Besides painting, he allowed Rolphe to teach him a little about playing the instrument. Arel didn't practice much, but he did smile wistfully as his fingers caressed the keys.

Rolphe didn't trust the sudden mood swing. He was even more wary as he listened to Arel's conversation with William. Arel wasn't pushing William away anymore. He was renewing their bond, making sure it was stronger than ever.

Rolphe scratched his head, trying to clear his thoughts. When that didn't work, he knew he had to seek advice from a higher source. Slowly, backing away as quietly as he could, he turned and started for the doors to the balcony. Michael was sitting outside, enjoying the day.

Rolphe approached the angel carefully, as he always did, trying to show respect. He'd been told that he could drop all formality, but it didn't feel right. He liked using some of the old ways that he'd been taught. He bowed his head as he spoke. "Blessed one, could we talk?"

Michael looked up and smiled. "Please, sit down."

Rolphe hastily took a seat. "I don't want to interfere, but I think something is wrong with Arel."

Michael's smile broadened. "Are you saying that he shouldn't be happy?"

Rolphe stiffened. "No, of course not. Every day I pray for that. But I'm afraid it won't last, that he's hiding something."

Michael sat back mutely and stared out at the city. His eyes seemed to flit about from rooftop to rooftop.

Rolphe looked out at the view too. He noticed the many gardens growing on the rooftops. The plants appeared as tiny dots of green, flourishing under a sunny sky. "Blessed one, am I wrong to think of such things?"

Michael stirred a little and turned his gaze to Rolphe. "I didn't mean to make you uncomfortable. I smiled because I understand how you feel. It's unusual to see Arel like this. He can be so bright, can't he? Almost like a small star in our midst."

"Yes, yes! He makes me feel even more alive when he's like this—"

"But?"

"But I don't think it's going to last. That's why I needed to speak to you. Am I wrong? Is my gift of knowing leading me down the wrong path?"

"I can only tell you that Arel believes he's found a way to be happy again. Has he made the wrong choice? That's not for me to judge. However, you need to trust what you feel, Rolphe, not in a critical way, but in a way that allows you to adjust to what Arel's put in motion. You have to decide what's best for you."

"Blessed one, I've already made that decision. I want to help Arel in any way that I can."

"Does that mean you're willing to let him go?"

"What do you mean?"

"What if Arel believes his path to happiness is to leave this world?"

As soon as Rolphe heard the question, he knew what Arel was up to. He'd been confused up until that moment. Now, he had a flash of clarity. Arel was pursuing a plan that he thought would solve all his problems. But his solution was going to do just the opposite. Rolphe let out a gasp of horror as he got a glimpse into the future.

Michael looked at him. "Are you thinking about your past again?"

"No, not this time. It's what's coming that scares me. Oh dear one, I think there are very troubled times ahead. Will you help us to get through them?"

Michael nodded. "I'll always be there for you."

Rolphe sat back, holding his chest, trying not to let his fear swallow him up completely. "No, not just for me, blessed one. You have to be there for all of us. If my gift of sight is true, there's going to be war, a terrible war, with brother against brother. I'll have to watch as one fights the other. Both could be lost in the end."

Michael reached out and put a hand on Rolphe's shoulder. "I promise that I'll do everything I can to prevent that from happening."

Rolphe shook his head. "If only you could, but I know the ways of man. Our human failings and bad decisions have a way of binding the power of angels."

* * *

Arel put his phone aside and breathed a sigh of relief. He'd had to switch tactics with William. It was unfortunate, but the man found out the truth. He knew Arel hadn't betrayed him. Luckily, Arel had felt William's change of heart before he got his call. He'd had time to prepare himself.

If pushing William away didn't work, he had to pacify his old friend. William saw himself as Arel's protector. Arel had to convince him that there was no one to protect. Hopefully, he'd accomplished his goal. William got off the phone with not a care in the world.

He let out a sigh of contentment as he stood up and went to the mirror. There was still a slight glow coming from his eyes. His heart felt strong and energized too. Sometimes, when he wasn't making some stupid mistake, his power could come in handy. Besides, it wasn't hard to love his brother. Hadn't they been twins in a past life? And in this life, William had tried his best to be steadfast and true. He'd gone through so much trauma on Arel's behalf.

Just the thought of William's suffering made Arel's contentment slip away. "The poor guy never knew how to back off, even when it was for his own good."

He frowned at the mirror as he started to go over his faults. He stopped himself before he got very far. Maybe it was time to give himself a break and look at where he'd come from. Ignorant, cruel parents and the ceaseless pain he'd endured in life hadn't prepared him to be a good friend. But the scope of what he'd suffered rested on a bigger problem. If he delved deeper and thought about what it was like to live on the earth, his heart wanted to stop in mid-beat. Mankind could be an abomination. History was full of all the horrors man could inflict on his fellow man. Life could be a terrifying experience. The nightly news validated that fact.

He walked over to his chair and sat down again. "If only William would have let me die—"

Sometimes, when he thought about William, he only felt love and appreciation. But sometimes, a deep resentment could take hold. Hadn't William made mistakes too? The man refused to mind his own business. He refused to let Arel bow out of life. But did he have that license? Was it right for William to decide another man's fate?

His hands closed on the arms of the chair as he thought about being forced to stay in a world he detested. There was so much ugliness, so much hurt. The only thing that gave him hope was creating his own world. He'd already begun to fashion a place where there was no pain, a place where everyone was happy and thoughtful. Every time he added details, they expressed the best that creation had to offer. When he finished the project, he'd have a world that righted the wrongs and offered only bliss and delight to its inhabitants.

A knock on the door interrupted his thoughts just as they were moving into a positive direction. He looked up and saw Michael in the doorway. He had to be very careful around the angel, just like he was with William. He'd have to keep his shields in place at all times. Neither of them could know what he planned.

"Is this a good time to talk?" Michael asked.

Arel laughed. In the past, every time Michael said they needed to talk, he'd expected the worst. Now, with the idea of escaping to his own world rapidly becoming a reality, he didn't have much to fear. He looked at Michael with peaceful eyes. There was no stress clouding his vision, only a vision of paradise. When he waved Michael forward, his voice was cheerful and inviting. "Come in and sit down. Tell me what you've been up to. You haven't been around much."

was being very conciliatory. Was there
something behind his casual, non-confrontational manner? "You're
right. I feel happy overall."

"Excellent, so maybe you're ready to return to Chicago. Your
friends—"

"No, I like it here."

"Don't you miss the children? Don't you miss your godchild,
Ariel?"

"Poor little guy, he's going to have to grow up in this miserable
world."

"Why would you say that? You know his parents are—"

"Carol and Kevin can't protect him forever."

Michael clasped his hands, gazing back with surprise. "I thought
you left all those feelings behind, that you could see the good things
about life. What's made you feel differently?"

Arel paused, reflecting on how he'd treated Rolphe when the
man threatened William, how he'd even been determined to kill
Rolphe if necessary. "I always thought all the violence was on the
outside. But it's not true. It lives inside each of us. But it's not the
fault of us poor demented humans."

"Then who is responsible?"

"Your boss, Michael. You're working for the ultimate, bad guy."
Arel hesitated. "I know that seems harsh, but I don't want to
sugarcoat anything. I want you to know the truth. Because I don't
think you're capable of seeing it yourself, not the way you're
programmed."

Michael blinked back, still looking confused.

Arel could see that the angel was trying his best to understand.
"I probably sound irrational to you, but I've been giving all this a lot
of thought. You might say I've even put myself in the Creator's
shoes."

Michael's voice became very deliberate. "Go on."

Arel shrugged. "It's simple. Your kind, the angels, have to do what you do. You have to live by the rules handed down from the Creator. The difference with humans is that we're supposed to have free will. But that's a joke. Look at William and myself. We're very different in how we approach life. And we're supposed to care about the other's welfare. But the bottom line is that we always end up hurting one another. No matter how hard we try, our brotherly love isn't enough. It doesn't 'conquer all' as the saying goes. Like I said before, humans are basically flawed from the start."

"And the Creator's role in all this?"

"That's just it! The Creator set this hellish existence in motion, then abandoned the project. He . . . She . . . It . . . just bowed out and left us in the soup, killing each other!"

Michael remained very still as he asked his next question. "You mentioned something about being in the Creator's shoes. Could you tell me how you would have handled it?"

"I would have kept all of us angels!"

"And since that hasn't been the case, what now? Do you have any advice for—"

"Your boss? No, I don't have any advice."

"Arel, have I totally let you down? If I am a stooge of the Creator, as you seem to think I am, what can I do to show you that I want to be more than that?"

Arel studied Michael's inquiring eyes. He didn't think about it very often, but Michael had stuck by him no matter what. When he considered how devoted the angel had been, he was overcome with sadness. "You haven't been a stooge, Michael. I'm sorry I lumped you into that category. I was talking about angels in general. You've been a friend . . . you've been the father I never had. And I believe you're a very different angel than most. I think you went outside the boundaries that you were given, hoping to save me from being a complete failure."

As Arel tried to apologize to Michael, he didn't expect Michael to leap out of his chair and kneel down in front of him. The tall, refined angel always conducted himself with the uppermost dignity. "Michael, what are you doing?" he asked, suddenly panicked by the angel's unusual behavior.

"Please, Arel, promise me something," Michael pleaded. "Promise me that if you find yourself in trouble again, if you feel like everything and everyone is against you, that I have your permission to help you. Please, promise me."

Arel's breath caught. He'd never seen Michael act so strangely. Yet, the angel's petition was totally unselfish and sincere. "Michael, dear friend, get up. You shouldn't be—"

Michael bowed his head. "Please, Arel, promise me, and I'll know I haven't acted in vain. I'll know that you believe in who I am and that I care about you. Carey feels the same way, please let us be there for you."

Arel hesitated for only a moment. How could he refuse this blessed being? The Creator might have botched the job when mankind was created, but Michael was totally unflawed and pure. And Carey could act a little childish, but he was also an innocent. "I promise, Michael. You have my permission, okay? Now get up. This is embarrassing."

Michael did as he was told and stepped back. "I just want you to know that I'm still here for you."

Arel rubbed his forehead. He was a little flustered after only a few minutes with Michael. "Yes, well, I'm glad we had a chance to talk, but I think we've said enough for now. In fact, I should never have said some things—"

Michael started for the door. "No, I like knowing how you feel. It gives me a chance to see things from your point of view."

Arel gave him a final nod. "Good, but don't try to figure out things that angels don't need to worry about. I do enough of that for both of us."

Michael nodded back. "Thank you, I'll remember that."

* * *

After talking to Arel, Michael returned to the apartment's storage room. Since his arrival, it had been turned into a makeshift bedroom. His roommate, Carey, was waiting for him. The room was only large enough to accommodate two small beds, a chest that hosted a lamp, and a chair. However, it provided privacy from Arel's watchful eyes and ears. Arel's bedroom was located on the opposite end of the apartment. Still, Michael always shut the door just to make sure. After he sat down in an aging, wooden chair, he gave Carey a playful glance. "So I take it that Rolphe isn't the only one who spies on conversations. Did you hear everything, my fellow stooge?"

Carey laid back on his cot and laughed. "Now, now, Michael. Only one of us has to go by that label. Arel did say you're an exception to the rule."

"Yes, that was quite a talk we had, but I was grateful for the opportunity. Arel has avoided being in my presence, but I had to do something before—"

"Yes, I know." Carey grabbed a tennis ball and began throwing it in the air and catching it. When he stopped and studied the fuzzy outer surface, his brows were creased. "Things are moving so fast. Arel's abilities are very powerful at this point, and he'll soon be using them to carry out his plan."

"And he doesn't want any interference. His shields are up about ninety-five percent of the time. Thankfully, between Rolphe's vision and what I've been able to learn when Arel's shields are down, I have a pretty good idea about what he's up to. I'm sure that you do too."

Carey frowned. "He has such a cynical view of just about everything."

"I'm glad that Rolphe was out for a walk this afternoon. If he'd heard Arel's description of our 'boss,' I think he might have had another heart attack."

"We don't want that to happen. When Arel really revs up his power and sets things in motion, Rolphe will want to help in any way that he can."

"Yes, and I told him that he has our total support."

Carey paused, squeezing the tennis ball thoughtfully. "I was impressed with how you got that promise out of Arel. Really, Michael, it wasn't easy, was it?"

Michael shrugged. "Like Rolphe, I'll do whatever it takes to help Arel, but I had to get his permission first."

"Thanks for throwing my name into the bargain."

"The frontlines will be a difficult position to manage if things go south, my friend. I'll need you by my side."

Carey stared back. "It's interesting. Arel really believes he can leave all his negativity behind and create the perfect environment."

"He has a highly developed sense of control. With all that's happened, he needs something to make him feel safe again."

"And what if he thinks that his ideas are being challenged, Michael?"

"If that happens, we better be prepared for the worst."

Forty-Two

Annabel felt the need to avoid being around William. After admitting she hadn't been completely honest concerning Arel, she experienced the true meaning of shame. Talking to Peggy and Carol helped, but their support wasn't enough to excuse her behavior. William was very forgiving. He didn't bring up the fact that she'd withheld information. In fact, he seemed very relieved after a call to Arel. In a way, it might have been easier if he'd taken issue. Maybe if they talked about her self-serving attitude, Annabel wouldn't have had to handle the burden of her emotions by herself. Now, she needed time. If she was going to go forward, she needed to know how to handle her powerful feelings of fear.

When William needed space, he usually disappeared to the lower level. She decided the guest bedroom would be her place to retreat. She even slept there. After a couple of days, William confronted her and asked for an explanation.

She had stayed in her room all afternoon. Towards evening, her stomach got the better of her, and she needed food. William was waiting in the hall when she came out of her bedroom. His arms were crossed and his eyes were narrow and questioning. "William? How long have you been standing there?"

He answered her question with his own.

"Why are you acting like this, Annabel?" he asked.

She hurried past him, determined not to discuss her feelings. Her thoughts were still too muddled to try to explain herself. "I don't want to talk about it," she said quietly.

William stood, statue-like, studying her as she made her way to the kitchen. After a brief time, he joined her, still watching her as she scanned the cupboards and decided on canned soup.

"I think you need something more nutritious," he said as he approached the refrigerator. "Would you like me to fix you some eggs?"

She couldn't help but smile. "You don't know anything about cooking."

He gave her a backward glance as he opened the door. "It can't be very difficult, can it?"

"William, please, don't worry about me, I can just open this soup."

"Arel was right when he said you need to properly care for yourself. For now, I'll scramble some eggs for you. Tomorrow we can go to the market and get some fresh vegetables and whatever you need for salad and—"

"William, I'm not a child. I can take care of myself."

"I know that, but—"

"But what?"

William paused and put a carton of eggs on the counter. When he looked at her, his eyes softened. "I love you, Annabel. I know I haven't been there for you, but I want that to change. Do you think you can forgive me for being so distant?"

Annabel felt her heart do a little leap of joy, but immediately quelled the feeling. She couldn't let it interfere with her desire to be her own person. She looked away, holding on to the counter. She searched for the strength she needed to help herself. "Please, William, there's nothing to forgive. You were only trying to take care of a brother. I was the one who was wrong. But I'm learning, albeit slowly, to stand on my own. Truly, I want to be your partner, not some needy ex-angel."

William walked over to her and reached out for her hand. "Do you know how beautiful you are?"

She gave him a squinty look. "What does that have to do with the way I've let my feelings get out of hand?"

"Annabel, don't you understand that there's so much more to you than feelings?"

She shrugged. "All that I know is that I'm confused about everything."

236

William pulled her closer. "I'm not. Everything is very clear to me. As an angel, you didn't know anything about neediness. But you fell in love with a human being. You took a chance on a totally different experience. You gave up your wings because you wanted us to make a life together. That was a very brave and courageous thing to do. So stop being so hard on yourself."

"I do want that, more than anything. But I don't seem to make the right choices."

William smiled. "With all that you've had to face? Believe me, you're doing very well."

"Your convictions are so strong. You're so unwavering in how you see yourself. I hope I can be like that someday."

"Remember, as a human being it takes time to know who you are, to separate yourself out from the fear. Look at Arel. He's still struggling."

Annabel sighed. "I remember viewing him from a loftier perspective. He came into the world with such great plans. Life has been quite the challenge. I hope he doesn't give up again."

"When I talked to him, he sounded renewed, even hopeful. Maybe a different environment is helping. No matter what, I wish him well."

Annabel was about to agree when she felt a pain in her stomach. She hadn't eaten much all day. Maybe it was time to let William fix her some eggs. Anyway, she hoped that was the problem. She hoped the pain she was feeling didn't have anything to do with Arel.

* * *

With Annabel by his side, William lay in bed thinking about the evening he'd just had. Instead of fixing eggs for Annabel, he'd taken her out to a very nice, Italian restaurant. As she ate her lasagna, he couldn't stop looking at her. She was so happy and satisfied. Her face was radiant as she enjoyed the taste of the food and the quaint, friendly atmosphere. The experience seemed to restore her spirit.

It reminded him of the first time he'd met her. After introductions, they spent some time at a little shop that served tea and desserts. Looking back at who Annabel was before she took off her wings, he realized she hadn't been exposed to many of the physical pleasures of the world. She delighted in the smallest things. A bite of cookie or a sip of tea could make her blush with pleasure.

Returning to those feelings was what she needed. She had to have time to feel how rewarding life could be. But would she be able to enjoy life enough to balance the fear that could eat at her. It was too soon to know. Annabel was strong and capable, but she did have a tendency to think about what could go wrong. Therefore, it was up to him to make her journey easier from now on. He had to focus on starting over like Annabel wanted.

Even if he had angelic blood in his veins, he also had to stay centered in reason. Annabel wasn't the only one who'd recently gone haywire emotionally. He'd allowed himself to wallow in self-pity for two weeks. And for what? Arel was loyal. He hadn't betrayed anyone. In truth, Arel sounded like he was starting over as well. He was finally making a life for himself. He was doing what Annabel wanted to do. He was becoming his own person.

The thought was a comforting one. He'd been concerned for Arel for far too long. But Arel wasn't a boy. William had to look at his friend and brother as someone who could handle himself. Arel was a man, a man with tremendous power. If he wanted, he could create something wonderful for himself.

Forty-Three

Arel's secret world took shape even faster than he had hoped. It was an ambitious project, but it quickly became everything he'd dreamed it could be. He wanted a perfect world, one that wouldn't take billions of years to create. He didn't have the Creator's patience or the time. He skipped preliminaries like the Big Bang and anything that involved the idea of evolution. If he was going to play god, then he'd create his world his way.

He let the thought of a paradise fill his mind a little more each day. "A new world," he'd repeat to himself. It helped him to let go of his role as an earth inhabitant. He still did a little painting. He spent a few minutes at the piano. But in the background, he was preparing for his exit from the life he'd known. Every day he spent more time in his room, in a kind of sleep mode. But he wasn't simply dreaming. When he closed his eyes and drifted off, he had a destination in mind. He traveled to a utopia that he'd created.

Beautiful stars, a galaxy full of them, graced the heavens. The planet itself was flawless. Pristine oceans and waterways, fertile green lands throughout, gardens of Eden on every continent, these were the specifications that he'd insisted on. He didn't have the know-how to plan cities, but he did make small towns. He used memories of places he knew. When it came to people, he didn't make the Creator's mistake. His people were special. Every one of them was angel material. Each one displayed a permanent air of contentment. No one on his world would ever know anything but love and bliss.

When he got down to details, he made a very special park, a park for mice. It was inspired by Wolfie's demise. When William told him about the little mouse's death, it hit Arel much harder than he'd

239

expected. But by some miracle, he discovered a means of interacting with the departed mouse. It had taken a bit of dream searching, but Arel located the mouse's soul on the other side of life. It was a joyous reunion.

Afterwards, he'd decided to fashion a place for all kinds of mice. It was a place where the small inhabitants would never have to worry about sickness or hunger. They could gorge themselves on treats and play to their heart's content.

The first mouse that he invited to Mouse Park was Wolfie himself. "Welcome to eternity, my little friend," Arel said as he greeted the tiny rodent. Wolfie was sleek and handsome again. When he looked up at Arel, his small, black eyes were bright and sparkling. When invited, he quickly leaped onto Arel's outstretched hand. Arel spoke to him in a soft, quiet voice. "Let me show you what I've made," he said as he put the mouse on his shoulder.

* * *

The afternoon light was fading fast as Rolphe put a few last touches on his painting. It had been a quiet day. Michael and Carey had decided to do a bit of sightseeing. Carey in particular seemed anxious to check out the art galleries. After watching Rolphe paint and trying his hand at it, the angel wanted to study the works of masters. Arel had spent the afternoon sleeping. Rolphe was left to work on a piece that he hoped Arel would like.

Rolphe had never finished his original portrait of Arel. He'd put it aside for some time. Now, it was an active project again. Since the beginning of the week, he'd been altering it. He'd added William to the painting.

When he heard Arel's bedroom door open, he put down his brush. Each day, Arel took frequent naps even though he slept late each morning. He also went to bed early. The extended periods of rest didn't seem to help. When Arel came into the studio, he still looked drowsy. His appearance was disturbing. Arel had always been impeccable about how he presented himself. Now, he looked like he hadn't shaved in days, his clothes were rumpled, and his dark, thick mane of hair was wild and unkempt.

Rolphe stared at his houseguest with concern, but he didn't dare voice it. Arel was more sensitive than ever. The slightest remark could set off a sudden and often volatile reaction. Instead, he offered a friendly greeting. "Arel, you've slept most of your day away. You must really enjoy your slumber."

Arel came forward slowly, yawning and looking like he was trying to get a kink out of his neck. "Sleeping can be the best part of life, don't you know that?"

Rolphe grabbed a rag and began to clean his brushes. "I prefer painting."

Arel glanced around the studio. "That's obvious. Maybe you should sell a few pieces. Your finished canvases are stacked a foot deep everywhere I look."

Rolphe smiled. "I do sell some of them. There are a couple of galleries that have been exhibiting my work for years. That's how I was able to pay for the remodeling."

Arel walked over to stand in front of Rolphe's easel. "I wondered where the money came from. That said, you do have a remarkable talent. What are you working on now?"

Rolphe smile deepened. "Don't you recognize yourself and your friend—"

Arel stiffened. "William?"

"Yes, it's coming along very nicely."

Arel squinted and gave the canvas a closer look. "Why in the world would you paint William and I?"

"Because when I think about the two of you, I feel like you represent brotherhood. You both care so deeply about each other."

Arel huffed. "Brotherhood? That's all in the past."

Rolphe looked up and was surprised by the change in Arel's face. The drowsiness had quickly turned hard and menacing. "But I thought—"

"Thought what? That a bond between two people lasts forever? Think again."

"What do you mean? Brotherhood is something a person can count on. It's the kind of tie that's lasting and true."

Arel's mouth twisted into a contemptuous sneer. "Let me enlighten you, Rolphe. William is committed to Annabel now. He has no time for brotherhood."

Rolphe returned his gaze to his canvas, not wanting to look at Arel's eyes. All the kindness that could shine through the golden portals had given way to a flashing anger and resentment. "You've always wished him well."

"And I still do!" Arel shouted as he grabbed the canvas off the easel. For a long moment he studied the two men who stood shoulder to shoulder. "That's why I want you to burn this damnable canvas! It has nothing to do with reality. William has Annabel, and I have—"

Rolphe glanced up. "You have what?"

Arel tossed the canvas to the floor and raised his chin. After a moment, his eyes slowly returned to a dreamy gaze. When he looked at Rolphe, he laughed. "I have myself at long last. For years, Michael has been preaching about how a person needs to be responsible for who they are. I guess I finally found a way to do what he was talking about."

"I'm happy for you, Arel. I know life hasn't been easy—"

"Easy? No, it hasn't, but what else can you expect? As soon as you enter this world, as soon as you take your first breath, you find out what you're up against. You're cold and alone and vulnerable. With that first breath, you learn that you have to fight for existence."

Rolphe felt a chill grab hold. The light from the window was gone, and the room was losing itself to dark shadows and an eerie feeling of gloom. "Is that how you see the world?" he stuttered.

Arel looked back with kindness. His face softened with compassion. "Yes, it is. And I understand it all now. At last, I have enough power to see things clearly."

"Can you explain it to me? I know I don't have your power, but—"

"It's all so simple, really." Arel paused and put his hand on Rolphe's shoulder. "The sovereign being you petition, the one you think of as all-knowing and all-loving, that being made a terrible mistake, Rolphe. Now all of us have to pay for it. Our only recourse is to find a way to—"

"Find a way to do what?"

Arel shook his head and backed away. "Never mind. Maybe it's better that you don't know what I know. Hold on to your innocence if it serves you. Paint your pictures, but don't include me in them, is that clear?"

242

Rolphe nodded and stared at his empty easel. As Arel left the studio, his gaze moved to the canvas that Arel had discarded. It lay on the floor, forever unfinished. The vision that prompted the painting had been so beautiful. To capture it and put it on canvas had been a wonderful idea. It sent a rush of excitement coursing through Rolphe as soon as he took up his brush. He'd wanted to capture the light that sometimes radiated out from Arel and William's bodies. When he'd glimpsed the phenomenon a couple of times, it always lifted his spirit. The two men made him feel hopeful about his future. After all, he had a little angel blood in his veins too. Now, he needed a blanket to warm his bones. They felt stiff and unmoving as the temperature in the room continued to drop.

He had to take hold of himself as he began to shake. He tried not to let what Arel had said penetrate too deeply, but the man was powerful, like he professed. He had an ability to shine or to cast darkness wherever he went.

After Arel's visit, Rolphe's gift of sight took hold, too. He could see into that darkness. The war he'd feared was quickly becoming something real and tangible. Arel stood on a field, clothed in battle dress. He was a terrible sight to behold. When the vision shifted, Rolphe saw himself. He was in a prison of sorts. His head was downcast, and he was praying.

Forty-Four

William hung up Annabel's coat in the hall closet and smiled. Taking Annabel out to dinner was becoming an everyday affair. It was fun for both of them. William thoroughly enjoyed watching Annabel's reaction to different kinds of cuisine. Each time Annabel tried a new style of cooking, she didn't hold back. Every bite made her face melt into an expression of bliss. The pleasure she felt became a vicarious experience for William. But it didn't make him want to eat anything himself.

He remembered eating being an enjoyable affair, but he'd never thought about food after becoming a vampire. Now, he had no desire to eat. He was never hungry. When he'd tried eating, it didn't sit well. His body had changed. Food was too dense for its needs. William didn't know what kept him energized, but he hadn't had time to question the whole affair. Maybe someday, his curiosity might spark an investigation.

Annabel was the opposite. She often got hungry and scoured the cupboards for sustenance. She did have a problem with certain foods. She didn't have a palette that could accommodate foods that were too spicy. Other than that, she rarely tasted anything she didn't enjoy. Now she was in the kitchen, squirrelling away the leftovers from her Chinese dinner. The portions had been generous, and Annabel was thrilled to think there would be enough for her lunch the next day.

"Annabel, throw out anything that's been sitting in the refrigerator for more than a day, please," he advised as he approached the kitchen.

Annabel immediately peeked out of the doorway. "But William, it's all perfectly good. Why should I throw anything away?"

William gave her a stern look. "Annabel, please, just because you had a tough time at Arel's house, you know that I promised not to let that happen again. You'll always have enough to eat."

Annabel frowned. "I know, but—"

William moved her aside and went to the refrigerator. "The last time I looked in here, there were containers everywhere."

"That's because I save a little of each thing for later."

William gave the refrigerator interior a quick inspection and closed the door. "Fine, but if you get sick because you ate something that spoiled, don't say I didn't tell you so."

Annabel grinned back. "Thank you for all the delicious meals I've had. It's been the most wonderful week ever."

"You're welcome," he said, smiling back.

Annabel reached out for his hand and pulled him forward. "It's getting late. Are you ready for bed, my sweet William?"

William felt a current of excitement move through his body. Annabel could enjoy other physical pleasures even more than eating. In that respect, William could be just as hungry, especially when he considered the tight grip she had on his hand. She didn't have any problem expressing her desires.

Once they were in his bedroom, he was about to undress when he saw a blinking light on the answering machine. He'd forgotten to take his cell phone to the restaurant, so whoever was trying to reach him, must have dialed his home phone.

He almost ignored the blinking light. Annabel was slipping out of her dress and giving him backward glances as she got ready to let it fall to the floor. Everything told him to take her into his arms, but some small nagging feeling in the pit of his gut wouldn't grant him that pleasure. "Sorry, my darling, but I better see who called."

Annabel's expression went from playful to worried. "Yes, of course. I hope our friends are okay."

William pressed the playback button and hoped for the same thing. Unfortunately, the voice that came through sounded very upset. Rolphe was calling with a message that he said was urgent. "I'm so sorry to bother you, but I have to talk to someone. Michael and Carey can't help, but I think you can."

William looked at Annabel. "Before you say anything, there's a second message. Let's listen to that one too." He pushed the playback button again. Rolphe's voice was a little calmer this time. His message was very different.

"Ignore everything I told you. Forget I called. Get on with your life. Be safe. At least that way I'll know there's one bright light left in the world. Please don't call me back. I won't answer."

William didn't know what to say. The feeling in his gut was getting stronger, but he didn't know what to do next.

Annabel snatched up a robe, put it on, and came over. "Call Michael or Carey," she advised.

William nodded and did as she suggested. He called both angels on their phones, but neither answered. Frustrated, he sent out a call to Raphael. The angel didn't have a phone. He communicated the old fashioned way, on ethereal airways. He usually appeared within a few minutes of a summons by William. This time he didn't show up in person. William heard Raphael's voice clearly on an inner channel.

"William, for your own good, do as Rolphe suggested. Don't ask questions. Put the past behind you and make a life with Annabel."

Annabel seemed to hear Raphael too, but she didn't say anything more to William. She walked over to a bedroom chair and sat down.

William stared at her, but she remained very still and quiet. "Do you know what's going on, Annabel? Because I sure as hell don't have a clue."

Annabel looked away. "Isn't it clear? Everyone is telling you to get on with your life, our life."

William could see that Annabel was struggling with the current situation. She wouldn't even look at him when he walked over to her. "And I suppose that's what you want too, isn't it? You want me to forget everything but you, right?"

"Yes, that's true, but—" She jerked her head up, staring back with emerald eyes that looked as bright as they'd been when she was an angel. "But I also want what's best for everyone, not just me."

William knelt down in front of her. "Really?"

She returned a weak smile. "Remember how I told you about Arel's plans for this life?"

"Yes, what about them?"

"You had great plans too, William. You wanted this life to be so extraordinary. You both wanted that. You both knew it wasn't going to be easy, but it didn't matter. The two of you are very similar when it comes to courage and determination."

Annabel's statement resonated with something William had always felt. He could almost remember a time when he'd stood next to Arel, planning a life where they would be more than friends. Their bond would be so strong that nothing could break it. At least that's what they hoped.

Annabel put her hand on his cheek. "Forget about me, William, and tell me what you want."

William stood up. It took a moment, but he was finally able to quiet the chatter in his brain. When he felt clear, he let the answer to Annabel's question come from his gut. "I want to know what Arel is up to now. First thing tomorrow, I'll check into it."

Annabel sighed. "I see."

William smiled. "No, you don't see, my beautiful Annabel."

"What do you mean?"

"You think I'm choosing Arel over you, but I'm not." He held out his hand and helped her up. "Maybe my desires are too grand, but I don't think so. I want it all, Annabel. I want you to always be by my side. I also want Arel to be in my life, as my brother. And I'm not willing to trade one for the other. Whatever I have to do to make that happen, I'll do."

Annabel smiled too. "And I promise to do my best to help you realize your grand dreams."

"Do you think that they could be *our* dreams?"

Annabel reached out for him again. "I'd like that."

William untied the belt on her robe and carefully opened the garment to look at her. "You're the most beautiful woman I've ever seen."

Annabel giggled. "I think I've put on a few pounds since I've given up my wings."

William began to kiss her neck and paused. "I love everything about you. In fact, I'm suddenly ravenous. I think I'm going to devour every one of those pounds."

Forty-Five

Tim sort of shuffled his way into the kitchen. He couldn't remember the last time he'd felt so exhausted. He headed for the coffee maker and gave Peggy a quick glance of appreciation. "Thank goodness you made a whole pot," he said as he grabbed an extra-large mug.

Peggy yawned and nodded. She was sitting at the table, looking like he felt. Her droopy lids were at half-mast. "The nightmares just wouldn't let up. I'm sorry you're having them too. Maybe it's catching."

"I don't think so. My problem started when I had that terrible dream that Arel had to help me resolve. That particular nightmare went away, but now I think I'm prone to having them."

Peggy stretched out her fuzzy-slippered feet and yawned again. "It's weird, but we're not alone. Kevin said he's been having restless nights for a while too."

Tim ferried his coffee to the table and sat down. "I don't know what's going on, but thankfully it's Friday. Maybe we should all get together tonight and compare notes."

Peggy's eyes brightened. "Maybe it should be a pajama party, in case one of us falls asleep on the sofa."

"I'll stop off at the store after work and pick up some snacks."

"And we can order some pizzas. What do you think?"

"Great, if I'm going to make it through the day at the office, I need something to look forward to."

* * *

Kevin sat back in his chair and patted his stomach. "Wow, that was the best pepperoni pizza I've ever had. The sausage one was good too, but the pepperoni was outstanding."

Peggy piled up three empty, pizza boxes and started for the kitchen. "It's a good thing I ordered that extra pizza. I had a feeling that two wouldn't do it."

Kevin smiled. "I wasn't the only one who was hungry. Tim did a pretty good job of polishing off a few slices."

Tim held up a hand. "Guilty as charged. When I don't sleep, I eat more."

Kevin tried to get comfortable, but he knew he should have left that last piece for someone else. "I guess that explains why I had to eat so much," he said. "At best, I only clocked a few hours last night."

Carol hadn't said much during the meal. Now she looked around the dining room table with a frown. "Why am I the only one who can sleep? I always thought I was as sensitive as the next person."

Kevin bent over with a groan and put a hand around her shoulders. "Believe me, Carol, I can't imagine anyone more sensitive."

His statement was delivered in a serious tone, but it made the group laugh.

Even Carol grinned back at him. "Alright, alright, I guess I should be very thankful that I'm the exception this time."

Peggy sat back down at the table. "I'd trade places with you in a heartbeat."

Carol glanced around at the group. "So is everyone having the same kind of nightmare?"

Peggy shrugged. "I keep seeing someone falling down a rabbit hole, sort of like Alice did in that Wonderland story. But she doesn't have a happy landing. She feels like something evil followed her down. I know it doesn't sound that bad, but the dream is really scary."

"It sounds scary," Carol said as she looked at Kevin. "But Kevin's nightmares might be a tad worse."

Kevin groaned again. "Yeah, I'll take a kid's tale anytime. I dream about this horrible battle. Let's just say it's dark and brutal."

Tim leaned forward and put his hands together. "Mine are more like Kevin's, with lots of fighting. I even got a glimpse of the man who was in charge of this dark army of brutes."

Peggy leaned forward too. "You did? Why didn't you tell me about that part?"

Tim hesitated. "I didn't think you'd want to know the person I saw. He was really a villain."

Peggy scowled. "Oh no, I think I know who you saw. I refused to believe it could be true, but my kid's story kind of morphed midway through. Alice looked so sweet in the beginning of the dream, but when the dream shifted I saw a kind of evil overlord instead. It was weird but the guy looked like—"

"Arel!" Kevin blurted out the name before he could stop himself. "Sorry sis, I love him dearly, just like you, but now that we're all seeing the same thing—"

"But none of this makes any sense," Peggy said in a forceful tone.

Carol smoothed out her napkin. "Maybe it does. Remember those pictures that Arel sent us? The ones of his paintings? Maybe he was trying to let us know how he really feels, deep down. The last time he was here, he tried his best to be congenial around everyone, but I don't think he's come to grips with some inner demons."

Peggy's brows shot up. "You're absolutely right. Something has been troubling him for a long time."

Kevin cleared his throat. "If that's the case and my dreams mean anything, maybe Arel needs to get some professional help."

Tim clasped his hands tighter. "What I don't get is why three out of the four of us are dreaming about Arel and his inner demons. I know he's like family, but still—"

Carol continued to pick at her napkin. "The first time I had a conversation with him in that chat room, I almost felt like I knew him. As time went on, he felt like my protector."

Kevin gave Peggy a quick glance. "It's like he's more than family, like our connection goes further back."

Carol stared at him for a long moment. "Further back? Like how?"

Peggy spoke up before Kevin could answer. "You all thought I was crazy when I first met Arel. But Kevin's right. I felt like we'd shared another life. It still sounds strange, but—"

Tim locked onto Peggy's eyes. "Honey, strange or not, we all seem to have some special connection to Arel."

Kevin picked up a piece of leftover crust from Carol's plate and chewed it thoughtfully. "I think someone else has a connection to Arel. But we never talk to him about it."

Peggy's eyes widened. "Michael, right?"

"Yeah, Michael," Kevin replied. "I think we should call him tomorrow and get his take on what's happening."

The words were barely out of Kevin's mouth when his phone went off. Kevin took it out of his pocket and stared at the screen. "This is really weird. Michael's calling."

Peggy winced. "Answer it, Kevin. Something might be wrong."

Kevin quickly took the call. "Michael, how'd you know we were just talking about you? Hold on. Let me put you on speaker. The gang's all here, and everyone has questions for you."

* * *

After a conversation with Michael, everyone around the table was looking at Kevin. He put his phone on the table and stared back. "Well, what do you think about what he said? Any comments?"

Peggy sat up straighter. "First of all, Michael admitted that Arel is going through some emotional difficulties. Secondly, when we asked him about our nightmares, he said we might be focusing too much on negative stuff."

Tim jumped in. "What he said made sense. Ever since we've known Arel, we've tried to help him. We always acted out of a fear that he couldn't take care of himself. Kevin and I even went to New York after you had those nightmares, Peg."

"Yeah, that was a fun trip," Kevin added with a scowl.

Carol looked at Peggy and sighed. "I think what Michael was trying to say is that we've been concentrating on Arel's problems. Maybe it's time to think about what's right with him. At least that's how I got my life back on track. I had to start thinking positive stuff about myself."

Kevin patted her back. "Maybe that's why you're not having nightmares. Maybe you don't think about Arel in the same way as the rest of us."

251

"Thanks," Carol said with a smile. "But don't forget all the hours I talked with Arel before any of you knew him. He could be so funny and so sweet. I think I got a different take on who he is."

"Until I got involved," Peggy grumbled. "Everything went straight downhill after that. All I could do was see Arel as this poor, wounded person who needed saving. I dragged all of you down too."

"Stop blaming yourself, Peg," Tim insisted. "I'm sure Arel had lots of problems before you got involved."

Kevin reached out and took Peggy's hand. "Listen sis, I think you saved the guy's life. He even admitted that he'd almost done himself in with his depression."

Peggy's eyes brightened a little. "He did seem really happy there for a while."

Carol reached out too. "You gave Arel a chance to know somebody cares about him. He was alone for a long time from what we've learned. Now he has friends, family."

"Exactly," Kevin said.

Tim spoke up again. "I think we should talk about what Michael advised. He asked us to stay positive. Even if Arel is still struggling, it's not going to help if we don't believe in him."

"That's so true," Carol said. "When I was with William, he didn't see me as broken. He said that I was strong and capable and that—"

Kevin cut in. "William again?"

Carol laughed. "Oh, stop it, sweetie. I think William could help me because he wasn't so close to the problem. Period. End of story, okay?"

Kevin's frown softened a little. "You're right. I guess I should be grateful."

Peggy gave Kevin a playful but stern look. "Please, Kevin, maybe we should listen to what Tim was saying." She looked at Tim. "What were you trying to tell us, honey?"

When all eyes were turned on Tim, he smiled. "Why don't we try an experiment tonight. Let's all think about Arel finding a way to handle his problems in his own way. Let's see him as happy again. Tomorrow, we'll report back to one another. Hopefully there won't be any more nightmares."

Forty-Six

The blaring, two-tone sound of a siren outside his window
threatened to bring Arel out of his deep slumber. It was such
an abrupt and sharp intrusion into the peaceful serenity of his own
world that he almost lost his connection. Sheer willpower helped him
to stay seated in the lush, green gardens of Mouse Park. He'd been
watching dozens of small rodents scampering about the large
expanse. They were so playful. Running and chasing each other, they
reminded him of tiny children. They came in all varieties, spotted,
black, white, curly haired, and straight. Arel had been experimenting
with various forms that he found pleasing.

Arel already knew each mouse by name and family. He was
about to pick up the newest arrival, a plump youngster named
Wiggles, when a second siren sounded. It was followed by the
repeated honking of an automobile. He opened his eyes in protest.
As his bedroom slowly came into focus, he made himself look at the
clock. He was surprised that it was already past noon. He'd been
asleep for over fourteen hours.

Mouse Park still beckoned to him, but as he looked around the
room and listened to the traffic outside, he had a moment of
complete confusion. The divide between the two worlds was getting
more and more pronounced. When he went to sleep and poured his
energy into his own wonderful creation, he often forgot there was
any other reality. And when he was awake in the normal world, he
couldn't remember the details of Mouse Park and its creatures.

Just waking up was becoming a tricky business. The old world
felt fuzzy and out of focus, just like his mind. He had to sit on the
side of the bed and work at thinking clearly. He used facts to help

253

him adjust to the world that most people called reality. When he finally got settled into the idea that he was living in Rolphe's apartment, and he thought about some of the mistakes he'd made recently, he didn't know why he bothered with normal life. So much of him wanted to go back to sleep.

It was a small responsible part of him that offered a reason for venturing out of his bed. Before he gave himself fully to his own creation, he needed closure with his friends in Chicago. That would take some careful deliberation on his part. Then there was Michael. When he thought about how rough he'd been on the angel, he wanted to smooth out their relationship a little. He had to make sure that Michael knew that his care and concern hadn't been in vain. Arel had moved out of despair and into a better life. Soon he'd move into paradise.

As he got to his feet and made his way through the hallway, he reminded himself of his obligations repeatedly. If he didn't, he could easily get sidetracked. If his mind wandered and he took up his role as a creator too quickly, if he remembered an improvement he wanted to make on the look of a tree or a stream, he'd quickly become too sleepy and return to his bed. This time he'd make sure to take care of business in the waking world.

As he approached the studio and noted a one-sided conversation between Michael and another party, he realized that Michael was on the phone. The tall angel was just signing off when he saw Arel. Michael beckoned him forward with a friendly wave and sparkling, bright eyes.

Arel let out a soft sigh. He didn't usually take time to study Michael. Now he knew he had to commit to memory everything wonderful about the angel. He had to hold on to Michael's virtues, his giving spirit and compassion.

Michael wouldn't be a part of Arel's new creation. He couldn't be invited there for one very specific reason. Michael belonged to the old world. Prime Creator had set it up that way. In general, angels were friends who had one job to do. They tried to guide humans through the trials and tribulations they endured. Michael was proof. He'd tried his best to help Arel.

But helping humans was often a thankless task. Humans, including Arel, rarely gave angels their due. But their selfish natures weren't their fault. The gift of "free will" that the Prime Creator bestowed on humans came with a terrible price. Unlike angels, humans were cut off from feelings of continual bliss and contentment. Instead, they used anger and resentment as tools as they tried to survive in a world that could be harsh and punishing. They didn't have the time or energy to be thankful to beings like Michael.

But Arel had been given more than the usual assistance. He'd been given Michael's blood. The damnable stuff was nearly impossible to use successfully in the old world, but it would give Arel the power to create and maintain a new one. With that thought in mind, Arel came forward and reached out for Michael's hand. "Dear friend, please listen to me. This is very important, and I want you to remember every word I say. Is that clear?"

Arel's words seemed to affect Michael. His eyes became so bright that his face shone with light. "What do you want to tell me, Arel?" he asked.

Arel had to pause. There was such child-like innocence and good-will in the angel's voice, such a desire to help and nurture. When Arel gave himself totally to his new world, he'd never be the object of Michael's radiant love again. On the other hand, he'd never have to endure his own flawed nature or the cruelties of the old world either.

He closed his eyes and used the tradeoff as a vehicle. The thought of what he'd be gaining gave him the courage to go on. "Michael, thank you for being there for me all these years. You've tried so hard and diligently to help me lift the burdens I've carried. Given what you had to work with and the restrictions that you've labored under, you've been an outstanding credit to your kind. Is that clear? Do you understand my gratitude for what you've done?"

"Yes, but—"

"Relax, there are no buts about it, only my appreciation. And that goes for Carey too. Both of you are magnificent examples of what is good and pure. At least your boss got that much right."

Michael took a step forward. "Arel, the Creator knew what he was doing when he brought you forth too."

Arel smiled back indulgently. Michael only saw the good in creation. Perhaps that was the angel's one failing. "Yes, yes," he said, patting Michael's shoulder. "But let's move on. Tell me who you were talking to. Anyone I know?"

"Our friends in Chicago. I promised to keep in touch."

"Yes, our friends—"Arel felt his chest tighten even more. Everyone he knew and loved lived in the old world. Would he ever forget them or how kind they'd been to him? He carried their picture in his wallet. Carey had taken the photo at one of the dinner parties that Arel had hosted. Tim and Kevin stood on either side of Arel. Their massive bulk made him look small, but their generous smiles were those of friends who cared about him. After all, they considered him family. In the photo, Peggy and Carol stood in front of the men, holding the babies. They were smiling too.

Arel hadn't allowed himself to look at that photo for quite a while. What was the point? Chicago was so far away. He wasn't going to host any more parties. He wasn't going to play with the children or take them to the park anymore either. Instead, he had to remember that he had another park that he could visit. Just the thought helped him to recall little Wiggles and how he'd make sure the young mouse got an extra special treat.

"Arel, are you okay?" Michael asked.

The question interrupted Arel's wandering mind. He looked up at Michael and made himself smile. "I'm fine."

Michael pointed to Arel's easel. "Are you going to paint today?"

Arel walked over to the picture he'd recently started. He fingered the cloth that was draped over it. "I don't know if I'll have time."

"Would you like to show me what you've done so far?"

"No, it's not important."

Michael took a step forward. "You said that you appreciate my helpfulness. Is there anything more I can do?"

Arel rubbed his forehead, forcing himself to be resolute. He had to stay the course he was on. He didn't need the angel's help anymore. He didn't need anyone. "No, not a thing. Now, go water your flowers or do whatever makes you happy. As for me, I have some duties to attend to. Since you brought up our friends, maybe I'll call them too, or maybe I can send them a photo of my latest attempt at art. Kevin and Tim can have a good laugh."

"You might give William a call too. I'm sure he'd be happy to hear from you."

Arel returned a hateful look without meaning to. "William has nothing to do with my life or me with his."

"Really? Am I wrong to think that you consider him your brother?"

Arel tried to recover his good humor and failed. Instead, he remembered how naïve he'd been when he convinced William to engage in a blood brother ceremony. The ritual might have seemed childish to some. It might even have seemed childish to William. But for Arel, it meant unity and dedication to something greater than one person alone could embody. He envisioned what Rolphe had started to paint, two men who would stand shoulder to shoulder and create a life that was infused with harmony and goodwill.

But nothing worked out the way it was supposed to. Trying to be a good brother had nearly killed William. And Arel was left feeling responsible. All in all, brotherhood ended up being the worst of ideas. "I don't believe in the word, brother. I believe what you've been teaching, Michael. I believe in self-reliance and independence."

"Yes, that's very important," Michael said. "But once you achieve that ability to be your own person, it's wonderful to join in with other like-minded people. Don't you agree?"

"Maybe for some, that's an option. For others, a singular existence is best. In my case, I've released William from any bonds or ties. He's free, just as I'm free."

An unexpected response came from someone Arel hadn't dared to think about.

"What if I don't want that? What if I still want brotherhood, Arel?"

It was William's voice. When Arel jerked around, William was standing in the doorway, and he was smiling. Arel had to grab for a chair to keep his balance. His thinking had been so focused on creating his own separate world that he kept all thoughts about William locked away. He'd been fashioning a place where there were no attachments to people he cared about deeply. Yet now, seeing William standing a few feet away, his heart raced back to a time when he was a boy and his only desire was to align himself with Aldwin. Aldwin was his older brother and his hero. In some ways, William had taken Aldwin's place. "Will! What are you doing here?"

William walked over and clasped his shoulder. "Why wouldn't I be here? We're still blood brothers, aren't we?"

William's touch was strong and reassuring, just like Aldwin's had been. When Aldwin came home from university, he made Arel feel like he mattered to someone. It was such an exhilarating thrill that Arel's seven-year-old heart could barely contain its joy. Life suddenly felt bright and welcoming. Then Aldwin died. It was a crushing blow that extinguished all his hopes and dreams. The moment, Aldwin left the world, the world went black.

William stepped back and shook Arel's shoulder. "Arel, are you alright?"

Arel's mind blanked out before he could answer. For a moment, he was sitting in Mouse Park, having a conversation with Wolfie. The little mouse was so easy to love. So were all the little creatures that played on the grassy lawn. Then William's voice broke in and the park slipped away. He looked up and saw that William was staring at him. There was concern in his eyes. Arel smiled and let go of the chair. He pulled his shoulders back and took a deep breath. "I'm fine, Will. In fact, I can assure you that I'll always be fine from now on. It's just that I'm rather sleepy. If you'll excuse me, I need to take a little nap. When I get up later, we'll talk."

Forty-Seven

The morning after William got the phone message from Rolphe, he woke up early. Annabel lay snuggled up close to him, dozing peacefully. After their discussion the night before, it was a relief to know that she supported his desires. She seemed to understand that if she wanted true happiness, she needed to allow herself to be more expansive. Their relationship might be a central part of her life, but there had to be room for another person that William felt connected to. There had to be room for Arel. When fear took over, Annabel couldn't see that. However, as she tapped into more of her wisdom, she knew what needed to be done. She told William to return to Paris and check things out. He would have done so anyway, but it was nice to have her blessing.

He didn't know what to expect as he made the journey. He kept trying to tune into Arel and never succeeded. Arel's shields were strong and effective, but there was more to it. William sensed that Arel was somehow absent, that behind the shields there was a void of sorts. The idea of connecting with that void left William cold and uncomfortable.

When he arrived at Rolphe's apartment, the place felt empty too. Rolphe was clearly absent. He finally discovered Michael and Arel in the studio, but their presence didn't make him feel any better. Then, Arel saw him and time stopped. The moment lasted long enough for Arel to perform a bit of magic. All the stress Arel usually carried around on his person melted away, and his face morphed into that of a young boy. It was so innocent and sweet that William almost forgot that he was looking at an adult who had been on the earth for a very long time. All that he saw was a child who wanted happiness, who wanted to know that there was a bright future waiting for him.

It was a stirring moment for William. He knew that he'd always known that part of Arel. He'd always tried to protect that part. He wanted to protect that part again. But the moment passed quickly. Without any time for a meaningful conversation, Arel made some excuse about needing a nap.

* * *

William sat on the sunny balcony, trying to calm himself. Michael was checking on his plants, touching a bright flower here or there, and testing the soil for moisture. The angel didn't seem to share William's feeling of impending doom. When he took a seat, he looked relaxed. William gave him an impatient glance. "Why wouldn't you answer my phone call last night?"

Michael didn't respond. He gazed out at the city with a seafarer's eyes as if he was looking far beyond the housetops and steeples that were spread out in front of him.

William knew enough to tread carefully. Angels never tried to be obstinate. If Michael was avoiding a question, there had to be good reason. William had to approach the subject from another angle. "Arel looks like he's in good health, so why is he so tired?"

Michael hesitated again, but he shifted ever so slightly. "Why did you come here, William?" he asked in a solemn voice.

"Because Rolphe called. He said—"

"He called twice. In the second call, he asked you to ignore his first message."

"Like that's possible? He said I could help, but with what? I don't want to play games, Michael. Tell me what's going on."

Michael glanced behind them, scanning the living room with searching eyes. When he looked at William and spoke, his voice was a whisper. "Oh, but it is a game of sorts. That's what's going on."

William felt a shiver grab hold. The temperature was pleasant, but his body acted as if he was sitting under a dark cloud. Instinctively, he glanced around too. "What are you afraid to tell me, Michael? What's the big secret?"

260

Michael stood up. "Rolphe is at a park nearby. I think he should help explain the situation."

* * *

Rolphe kept chastising himself for what he'd done. Why did he have to panic and act so impulsively? Why did he contact William? For hours he'd been going over the questions that had no satisfying answers. It was a useless cycle to pursue. On the other hand, he couldn't change the past, so he had to try to deal with the consequences.

He could feel William's presence in Paris. That meant the man would pay a visit to Arel. After their initial meeting, how long would it be before the two of them came to blows? It wouldn't be that day or even the next. Some period of time would pass before the inevitable happened, but a battle was coming. And no matter how much Rolphe wished it otherwise, he was partially to blame. Why hadn't he let William remain ignorant of Arel's plight? Without Rolphe's urging, William would never have come to Paris.

He looked down at his hands. He hadn't done a very good job of getting the paint off of them. But how could he think about Arel's need for cleanliness when lives were at stake? He had to give his full attention to the most important of matters. He had to figure out how to save the two people he really cared about. He had to find a way to mediate between Arel and William. But was that a possibility? In his vision, he'd seen himself in a prison. He'd felt his mindset. He was praying in a most desperate way.

As he continued to go over what was coming, Rolphe felt a tap on his shoulder. He jumped back and saw William and Michael standing a couple of feet away. "Mon Dieu, no!" he cried out.

William scowled back. "Steady yourself, Rolphe. You look like you're seeing a ghost."

Rolphe balled his fists, trying to block out a new vision. It played out in his mind, giving him access to a vivid scene of violence and chaos. The sound of men fighting was in the background. William was on a battlefield, but he'd been struck down. His face was so pale as he lay immobile on the field. The vision passed quickly, but its effects left Rolphe mumbling to himself. "Please, no, don't let that happen, dearest Creator," he prayed. "Show me a way to help them both."

William intruded on his prayerful petitions. "We need to talk."

Rolphe looked around the little park. There were a number of joggers and visitors in the area. "I have to pick up my kitten. She's at a friend's house. Let's talk there."

Forty-Eight

Rolphe stood at Myra's door, hoping she wasn't upset about his months of absence. He'd called her a number of times, but he'd always avoided seeing her in person. As for explanations, he could never come up with one that didn't sound evasive. Myra, being the indulgent soul that she was, didn't push the matter. However, one time, she came up with an explanation of her own. She told him that he was going through a mid-life crisis. He didn't fight her reasoning. It was true. He had been going through a crisis, one that was a little more serious than most men experienced.

When Myra opened the door, Rolphe forgot everything but how lovely Myra was. Her thick, off-the-shoulder hair was stylishly cut and tinted red. It contrasted beautifully with a modest, gray suit that accented the beautiful curves of her body. She also wore dangle earrings that hinted at her more passionate side. They were adorned with tiny silver bells that jingled when she reached out for him. Rolphe rushed forward and embraced her, holding her close, inhaling the delicious scent of her perfume and thanking the Creator for giving him such a patient girlfriend.

Myra was laughing when he let her go. "So you missed me, didn't you? But look at you. What happened? You're so thin, and your hair is shorter and—" She reached up and ran her slender hand over his cheek. "Your beard is so much shorter too. It's not as thick now, but I like it."

Rolphe averted his eyes for a brief moment. "Yes, there have been changes since I last saw you."

"I want to hear all about it, but I don't have time right now. I wish you could have gotten here a little sooner. I have to leave. I have a plane to catch." She paused, tilting her head to look past his bulk and pointed. "And who is this handsome man?"

"Oh, I'm sorry," Rolphe said as he moved aside. "Let me introduce you. Myra, this is—" He stopped himself. Even when Arel wasn't present, Rolphe honored his promise not to utter William's name. The exception was when he was talking to the angels. Michael and Carey said it was better to be direct with them.

William stepped forward and held out his hand. "Hello, my name is William. Very nice to meet you."

Rolphe smiled. "Myra, I know you have a spare room you sometimes let out, and my friend needs a place to stay for a few days. He could stay with me, but he's bothered by the smell of paint. I wondered if he could stay here while you're gone."

Myra shrugged playfully, her cheeks rosy with a bit of rouge. "Of course, the place is all his while I'm visiting my sister for two weeks." She looked up at William. "Please help yourself to whatever is in the kitchen, but I'm afraid there's not much."

William gave Rolphe a questioning look, and turned to Myra. "Rolphe is full of surprises, but I couldn't think of putting you out."

Rolphe scowled back. "It's better this way, my friend. You know my apartment offends you."

Myra took William's arm and briskly led him into the living room. "You're staying here, William. I insist. My place is small but I like to think it's cozy. You can water my plants while I'm gone."

Before William could reply, Myra turned to Rolphe. "Dantela is going to be thrilled to see you. I think she missed you terribly. I have to put her in the bedroom whenever anyone visits. Otherwise, she tries to escape as soon as I answer the door."

Rolphe doubted that Myra was right. The last time he'd seen his kitten, she was suffering from injuries that he himself had inflicted. "Thank you for taking care of her all this time. I've been so busy—"

Myra put up a hand. "Stop it, please. You know I love her dearly. She was never a minute's trouble." She turned, went to the window and peered out. "I see my cab waiting. I have to go."

Rolphe followed Myra back to the hall and grabbed two suitcases. "I'll help you with these."

Myra laughed. "You've always been such a gentleman, Rolphe." She gave William a final wave as she gathered up her jacket and purse. "I hope to see you again, William."

Myra's farewell to William made Rolphe's breath catch. Would William still be alive by the time Myra returned? As soon as he could get Myra on her way, he'd have a serious talk with the man.

* * *

William had barely settled back on the sofa when he heard a light knock on the door. It had to be Michael. The angel had temporarily stayed out of sight, not wanting to overwhelm Myra with too many visitors. "Come in," William called out. "The door's unlocked."

Michael obeyed and let himself in. "Rolphe should be back soon. I saw him helping his friend into a cab."

"Good, I'm tired of all the secrecy and waiting around. And I don't know why Rolphe thinks I should stay here—"

"He's trying his best to make sure you don't get involved."

William stood up. "Involved with what?"

Rolphe had let himself back into the apartment in time to hear William's question. He came forward and stood next to Michael. "You have no idea what Arel is doing, and you don't want to know, not if you value your life."

William crossed his arms. "I just saw Arel. He looked fine. He was very cordial."

Rolphe wrung his hands nervously. "Good, you're right. So go back to London," he pleaded.

"I'm not going anywhere until you tell me why you look so scared, Rolphe. Has Arel been threatening you again? Did you do something to make him think you're a problem?"

Rolphe pulled back. "No, I swear, it's nothing like that."

Michael patted Rolphe's shoulder. "Please, William. Rolphe has been doing his best. He's been Arel's friend, and he's trying to be your friend."

William grabbed his jacket. "Fine, if neither of you will talk to me, I'll go back to the apartment and get some answers from Arel."

"No!" Rolphe yelled. "You can't do that!"

William advanced on Rolphe, suddenly angry at the man who had tried to take his life. "Don't you ever talk to me that way! Do you understand?"

Michael moved forward. "Please, calm down, William."

265

Rolphe dropped to his knees and reached out for William's hand. "I pledge my allegiance. I swear that as long as I have the ability to guide my own actions, I'll never harm you."

William yanked his hand away and looked to Michael for help. "Do something. Rolphe has obviously lost touch with reality."

"No, that's not true," Michael said as he helped Rolphe up. "It's Arel who's lost touch."

Rolphe stood with his head bowed. "I think I'm making things worse," he said to Michael. "I think it's best that you explain what's going on. I'll go check on Dantela."

Michael watched Rolphe leave the room and took a seat across from the sofa. "It's quite simple, William. Remember the cave you visited and what happened—"

William had just sat down too, but the mention of an experience that could still send chills through his body made him jump up. "Tell me that Arel hasn't found another hellish place—"

"No, no, nothing like that. He's created his own world, and I'm sure it isn't hellish at all. I think it must be beautiful."

William sat down again. "What do you mean he's created a world? How's that possible?"

"Game programmers do it all the time. Only in Arel's case, he has the power to project his intentions so completely that a person or persons can visit that world just as you visited the cave. When they go there, everything in that world feels as real as this." Michael bent forward and tapped the coffee table that sat between them.

"So what's the problem? If Arel's world is a great place, maybe I'll have him show me around."

Michael pulled back and shook his head. "No, that's not possible. This is Arel's creation and his alone. No one is supposed to even know what he's done. He's very protective of what he sees as an act of perfection. He believes it's the kind of world that my boss should have created."

"Your boss?"

Michael pointed upwards and smiled. "That's how Arel refers to—"

"You mean he has an issue with God?"

"He believes the Source has made a big mistake giving people free will."

William sat back for a long moment letting the situation gel in his mind. "Maybe you and Rolphe were right to tell me to go home. Maybe Arel needs his little paradise to recuperate. After all that's happened, he needs time to let his emotions stabilize." He looked up at Michael. "Right?"

Michael's gaze was steady and unwavering as he looked back, but he didn't comment.

"Oh great," William protested. "I'm not right at all, am I?"

Rolphe came back into the room carrying a young, black cat. "Would you like to meet your savior?" he asked as he walked over to where William was sitting. Without hesitating, he put the cat in William's lap. "Her name is Dantela, and she stopped me from killing you."

William didn't know what to say or do at first, but the cat responded very quickly. She stood up, turned and gingerly put her two front paws on his chest. Her toes were white-tipped and reminded him of the white marking on his mouse, Wolfie. As they gazed at each other, William was taken with Dantela's beautiful, blue eyes. They were filled with an intensity that was mesmerizing. Without thinking, he smiled and ran his hand over her thin, frail body. "Rolphe said you saved my life, Dantela. I guess I owe you a big debt of gratitude."

Rolphe stood back and smiled too. "She's telling you that she's here to help you again," he said quietly.

Forty-Nine

Arel stared out the kitchen window enjoying the bright greens that dotted the city. It inspired him to put more color into his own landscapes. Everything about his world was already dazzling, but there was always room for a few new, creative touches. When he visited Mouse Park, magnificent, tree-dotted hills could be seen in the distance. The next time he visited his world, he'd make their leaves a little brighter.

Just the thought of being so powerful a creator was thrilling. It was such a thrilling feeling that he almost nodded off. He caught himself just in time to hear the apartment door open. Soon there were voices in the hallway. Carey explained that Rolphe and the others had gone to pick up Rolphe's pet at a friend's house. Arel had been relieved that he'd had time to wake up fully before their return. Now, he had to blink a few times to stay awake.

When Rolphe walked in with a small, black cat, Arel felt himself pulled into a memory. He'd last seen the feline in an awful vision. When Rolphe was in the process of killing William, Arel had managed to spur the cat into action. She'd suffered for her bravery. She hadn't grown much since the incident. She still looked delicate and thin.

"So this is Dantela," he said as he walked over and took the cat from Rolphe. She felt feather-light in his hands. How could anything so delicate have the courage to take on the brute that Rolphe had been? Arel held her to his chest, silently thanking her for what she'd done. She began to purr contentedly. As he patted her head, he felt wistful about the small animal. She wouldn't fit into his beautiful world. "Too bad that you're a mouse catcher," he sighed.

268

After a moment, he handed Dantela back to Rolphe and turned his attention to William. He hadn't really given the man a proper welcome. "Come and sit down, Will," he said as he headed for the living room. Once everyone was seated, he smiled at his old friend. "Tell me all about Annabel, and how she's doing."

William returned a half-hearted smile. "Annabel is doing quite well. She loves going out. I think we'll eventually be acquainted with every eatery in London."

Arel laughed. "She does enjoy her food. But that's good. She's finding a way to make peace with her new circumstances. And what about you, Will? What have you been up to?"

"I've been working on plans for the lower level. I'm getting rid of the lab—"

"Really? I thought you enjoyed delving into the physical mysteries of life. So how can you leave all that behind?"

William's smile broadened. "Of all the people, why would you care about physical mysteries?"

Arel shrugged. "Maybe I'm changing. Maybe I understand why you've been fascinated by how the world functions. Maybe I think we can improve on how it works."

"Maybe so, but for now, I'm thinking in terms of Annabel and—"

"Starting a family? That's wonderful. I'd love to think of a little William running around in the world."

William sighed. "And a little Arel?"

Arel frowned. "Are you crazy? The world didn't want one of us. Why would it welcome in a second?"

"I thought you used to talk about having a relationship someday?"

Arel sighed and looked at Michael. The angel had taken refuge in a chair in the corner. "Like I told you earlier, Michael has emphasized the importance of being content with oneself. I didn't believe it was possible, but I like my own company now."

William stared back. "But Arel, you could come back to London with me and visit. I could show you my plans, and you could tell me what you think."

Arel stretched, feeling suddenly weary of the conversation. He wanted to return to the restful oasis of his own world. He never had to answer any questions there. Well, that wasn't strictly true. Wolfie was often curious. But his questions were about the stars or how Arel felt about creating a new kind of wheel for the little mice to play on.

"Arel? Are you falling asleep? Arel!"

When William called out his name a couple of times, Arel roused himself. He tried his best to focus on William, but he had trouble keeping his eyes open. "I'm sorry, Will. I can't think about London. I think I need to rest again. But don't worry, we'll talk tonight."

William looked at his watch. "But we've only had a few minutes to chat."

Arel started out of the room, ignoring William's protest. "Sorry, but you always have Rolphe and Michael to talk to." He paused in the hallway. "And Will, if you need to get back to Annabel, I understand. Give her my regards."

When he returned to his bedroom and shut the door, Arel felt relief, like a burden had been lifted. The normal world was so exhausting. He was about to lay down when a soft meow made him glance down. He had company. Dantela had followed him into his room. "What are you doing here, little one? You should go back to Rolphe. He's your master."

Dantela paid no attention to his remark. She made a rush for the bed, tried to jump up on it and fell back. She didn't seem to have the strength to scale its height. After a second failed attempt, she looked up at Arel with soulful eyes.

Arel couldn't help himself. After spending so much time with animals, he couldn't deny Dantela's wish to take a nap too. He picked her up, lay down on the bed and let the cat find a spot next to him. He went to sleep with his hand cradling her small body.

* * *

After Arel left the room, Carey came in from the studio. When William asked him if he wanted to join the conversation, he declined. He said he wanted to stand guard close to Arel's bedroom in case he woke up unexpectedly. He didn't want Arel to find out what William and the others were discussing. William was left wondering about all the secrecy again. He was also trying to sort out his feelings about Arel. Staying positive seemed like a wise way to start out. "Finally, Arel wants to be his own person. That has to be a good thing."

Michael abandoned the corner where he'd been sitting and took a seat on the sofa. "Being one's own person is perfect when you love who you are. It's the natural state for everyone, whether they're human or angel."

"Luckily, I've never had a problem liking myself," William said.

"Arel thinks the big error was giving people choices."

"Who's error is he talking about?"

"Like I told you before, Arel claims that the Creator acted recklessly. He says people shouldn't have been given the ability to make mistakes."

William shrugged. "So people make mistakes and learn from them, so what?"

"For Arel it's not that simple. Every time he does something that goes against his true nature, his loving nature, he suffers more than most people. Like many children, he grew up in an imperfect world. But the imperfection he witnessed was very harsh. There was only one person in his life who was different."

"His brother, Aldwin. I know the story," William said.

"Yes, but when the brother died, Arel's father blamed Arel for being the worthless son who lived. In time, he came to believe in his father's hatred and started hating himself." Michael stopped and stared at William before going on.

"What is it?" William asked. "Why the look?"

"When you were a young man, you knew that Arel wasn't long for this world. You did what you thought best, you tried to hold on to him by intervening. But when you gave him your blood—"

William's face reddened with a sudden anger. "I loved him. I tried to be the brother he lost, but all he could do was rage against me for what I did."

Michael returned a knowing smile. "I understand."

William drummed his fingers on the sofa arm. He couldn't believe he'd reacted so strongly. "Sorry, I guess all those years took more of a toll than I thought."

Michael continued. "The bottom line is that you made Arel face his self-hatred. Having to live with that fact, day in and day out, made his life a hellish burden to bear."

"I guess that's why he felt I cursed him. But that's all behind him, isn't it? When you gave him your blood, he felt differently."

"He thought I gave him a chance to become what I am."

271

William laughed. "He wanted to be an angel? Arel?"

Rolphe stood up, looking towards the hall and Arel's bedroom beyond. "He is an angel. At least he is in my eyes."

William stared up at him. "Sit down, Rolphe. You don't know what you're talking about."

Rolphe shook his head. "You're wrong and so is Arel. Neither of you can see what I see, the light that's inside both of you. It's God's light and—"

Michael stood up too and went over to Rolphe. "It's okay, my friend. I believe you."

William's first inclination was to tell Rolphe and Michael that they were both crazy. Instead, he steadied his hand and maintained a sense of self-control. "All that I know is that this angel you're talking about threw me out of heaven. And as for you, Rolphe, he battered you senseless."

Rolphe gritted his teeth. "It was the only thing he knew to do to keep you safe. But when I was dying, and I asked him to stay with me, he did. I'll admit, his outer ways can be harsh, but his heart is good and pure."

Michael returned to his seat. "Yes, it is, Rolphe, but Arel doesn't understand that."

William sighed. "So we're right back where we started when he was shot, right? But instead of retreating to some cave, he's made himself a perfect world to live in. So maybe we should let him stay there. Maybe I have to let him go so he'll be happy at long last."

Neither Michael nor Rolphe commented. Rolphe shifted nervously and averted his eyes. William studied their behavior and frowned. It was obvious that he was missing some vital piece of information. To satisfy his concern, he had to find out what Michael and Rolphe were hiding. "Is there any way I can visit this perfect world? I want to see what's going on."

Carey tip-toed into the room and stopped next to William. "Arel's been very cautious around Michael and me. Neither of us have had any success with actually checking in on what he's been doing."

William looked up at Carey, noting his disheveled clothes and youthful demeanor. He could see why Arel had been fooled by the angel. Carey's face was child-like and wholesome, with a bit of mischief thrown in. Instead of being the picture of confidence like

Michael, Carey looked like a kid who needed looking after. But if William delved a little deeper, if he let himself tune into the angel's true energy, it was the embodiment of strength and daring. "Carey, tell me this. If you can't check things out, how do you know that Arel's playing at creating his own sanctuary?"

"He's talked a lot about the idea to Rolphe, questioning him about the cave and how it came to be. He's also been very pleased with himself a few times. In those moments, he forgot to shield his thoughts. Michael and I caught glimpses of his world. It's quite a stunning achievement."

Rolphe stood nearby, shaking his head. "Yes, but for how long?"

"What's that mean?"

Rolphe's fists tightened. "Nothing, like our angelic friend said, it's a beautiful world."

"Terrific, but how do I get a first-hand look at the place?"

Carey leaned forward and kept his voice low as he spoke. "Are you certain that you want to get involved? Michael and Rolphe have advised you that it might not be a good idea."

"Look, unlike Arel, I like having choices. And presently, I'm choosing to check up on Arel. Is that clear?"

Carey frowned, looked at Michael and shrugged. "Okay, if you're sure."

"Just stop stalling and tell me what to do."

Carey continued. "Since your unexpected arrival, Arel's been too busy with his project to think that you might be a threat. If you act quickly, I think you can follow his energy trail. And if it's alright with you, we'll follow you in."

William blinked back. "Do you think Arel will let you?"

Carey's boyish face lit up with a playful grin. "He won't know. We'll use your energy as a camouflage of sorts."

Fifty

W hile his body slumbered in his bed, Arel explored different parts of his new world. He walked the streets of a neighborhood that looked very much like the one where William resided, minus any sign of city grime. The urban streets were spotlessly clean and the scenery hosted lots of flower boxes and trees that would never know pests or drought. Another favorite place to stroll was modeled after his neighborhood in Chicago. He'd done a very good job with recreating his friends' houses. The Carol and Kevin model even boasted a flowered wreath on the door that matched the original.

There was one rather important modification to the layout of the community. In the area where the playground for children should have been located, he'd built Mouse Park. It was the one place where there were no people allowed. It belonged to the mice and Arel alone.

More than any other area, Mouse Park was Arel's favorite place to spend time. He enjoyed his interactions with its tiny inhabitants. He especially loved Wolfie. Like many of his species, Wolfie was very intelligent. His viewpoint on life was simple and amiable. As man and mouse got to know each other better, they were becoming good friends.

On this particular trip, the two of them were discussing the park. Wolfie sat on Arel's shoulder, a spot that suited both of them. It made communication easy.

"So what do you think about the exercise wheels? Are they the right size? And what about the bedding for the mouse huts? Is it adequate?" Arel asked.

"Everything is perfect!" Wolfie exclaimed in his high-pitched voice. "You're doing a splendid job, Great One!"

"I told you before that you don't have to call me that," Arel replied.

"Oh, but I want to. Look at what you've done for us. We have everything we could possibly want here. To us, you are the Great One."

Arel smiled contentedly. In his world, mice could talk. And Wolfie was a wonderful conversationalist. He had informed Arel about all kinds of things that mice knew. Some things concerned the old world, and how mice managed to survive there. They were very adept at searching out food and finding places to live. Wolfie also discussed his ideas about people. Arel was surprised to learn that mice were great observers of humans.

"Your species carry heavy burdens," Wolfie confided. "In the old world, we watch your old ones and wonder why they look so sad sometimes. As babies you start off like us, cheerful and carefree, but you change."

Arel let out a small laugh. "Yes, I know. But it's different here."

Wolfie squeaked with delight. "Yes! The people in this world are happy like us."

Arel agreed. "And I'll make sure they stay that way."

The words were barely out of his mouth, when he noticed a slight change in the grounds. A shadow replaced the sunlight over a bed of daisies. He looked up and saw a cloud in the otherwise clear, blue sky. "That's strange. I don't remember making any clouds."

"But it is rather nice," Wolfie said. "It's so white and puffy, like a big piece of cotton bedding."

Arel glanced upwards again and rubbed his brow. "Maybe I did make it. I've had so many details to attend to. I might have included it somewhere along the way."

* * *

William tried repeatedly to find a way to Arel's new world. He didn't know if he'd ever reach his destination. He felt like Christopher Columbus, only he was sailing on a vast ocean of energy instead of water.

His home base was the storage room that served as a bedroom for Michael and Carey. He lay on one of the cots, using the privacy of the small space to let go of himself and reality. After numerous failed attempts, his body was restless. Fatigue and doubt were overriding his optimism. When he'd visited Rolphe's cave, Michael had been there to help him. Now he was on his own.

He opened his eyes and frowned at Carey and Michael. "This isn't working."

The two angels sat side by side on the other cot, quietly observing him, but not responding.

William knew he had to be more direct. "Tell me what I'm doing wrong." His request was delivered more forcefully than he'd intended. "Sorry, I think I'm getting tired."

"You might also be resisting the process," Michael said quietly.

William remembered the cave incident and how Rolphe the wolf nearly killed him. The experience left him less than confident. "Maybe you're right. I don't have Arel's power or much experience with this kind of thing."

Michael smiled. "Actually, you're more powerful than you think. But you're right. You don't have much experience. Perhaps it would be best to forget the whole thing."

William considered Michael's suggestion for about two seconds. "How am I going to get experience if I give up? Besides, I need to check on Arel and make sure he's okay. Can't the two of you help me?"

Carey nudged Michael. "The man is asking for our assistance. I think we should oblige him, don't you?"

Before William heard Michael's answer, he felt the angel's energy. It hit him like a massive wave, yet one so reassuring that his body instantly relaxed. A feeling of ease replaced his anxiety, soothing his tight muscles, flushing out the stress in his limbs. Within moments, he was floating in a state of tranquility and calm.

When Michael began to speak, his instructions were fluid too. "Let yourself go, William. Let your inner guide take you to Arel's beautiful, new world."

This time, William didn't think about what to do. He gave himself fully to Michael's directions. A soft, whooshing sound followed, and William's ship of consciousness was on its way. Unlike the arduous trip that Columbus experienced, William's journey was effortless. He felt himself easily swept into a stream of energy, Arel's energy. He soon realized that it was a direct route to Arel's new world.

Within a brief few moments, he found himself hovering over the most beautiful sight he'd ever seen. Like the earth, a small planet sat suspended in space. It was a dazzling, blue jewel. Its exquisite splendor was set off by a black, velvet backdrop containing countless, twinkling stars.

He could have contentedly remained there, contemplating the perfection of what Arel had made, but he couldn't stop whatever it was that propelled him on. As he continued to speed towards his intended target, he felt like a returning astronaut. He saw continents, mountain ranges, and oceans. Everything was coming up fast.

"Too fast!" William cried out mentally. Panic started to grab hold, but he managed to rein in his fear just long enough. After a dizzying descent, things began to level out. When he was stable again, he was situated above a park. Arel sat on a bench in the middle of the green expanse. William almost panicked again. He remembered Michael's warning. He had to keep his energy body at a distance and well hidden. But how? It was imperative that Arel didn't know about his visit.

"It's okay, William," Michael said. "We've taken care of that problem."

William realized that Michael and Carey were right behind him. He also realized that he was in the middle of a mist.

"Actually, it's a cloud," Carey explained.

But William didn't know if their efforts were enough. He sensed that Arel was agitated. He felt a shift in the man's mind and braced himself for discovery.

Again, Michael's voice was soothing. "We're way ahead of you," he replied.

The mist around them thickened enough to hide them from view. When Arel looked up, it was only for a momentary glance. Then he went back to what he'd been doing. The man appeared to be talking to a little mouse that was sitting on his shoulder. When the tiny creature sat up and lifted its head to sniff the air, a white marking could be seen under its chin. William smiled and let out an exclamation of joy. "Wolfie, it's you!"

William woke up, blinked a couple of times and tried to clear his head. He'd had the strangest dream. Arel had been in a park, entertaining mice. They were all winsome, happy creatures who seemed to adore him. Arel was happy too. In fact, his face was a picture of joy and contentment as he left his park bench and sat down in the grass. As soon as he did, the mice that had been playing nearby seemed to know what to do next. They scampered over close to where Arel sat and lined up in a very orderly fashion. As the line moved forward, each mouse leaped onto Arel's outstretched hand. In turn, Arel stroked its head and inquired about how it liked the park. He asked for requests and suggestions. He seemed to know each mouse by name and often told the mouse how handsome it was. Before placing the mouse back on the grass, he gave it a special treat. The exchange was repeated over and over.

As William came fully awake, he was left with a feeling of contentment too, as if he knew that all was right in the world. He started to sit up and saw Michael. The angel was reading his book in a corner chair. "You won't believe the dream I just had. If it means anything, I think it's telling me that Arel is finally on his way to being happy."

Michael nodded. "Yes, he does seem to love his little mouse friends, doesn't he?"

William rubbed the remaining sleepiness from his eyes, wondering about Michael's comment. When Michael smiled at him, William realized that he hadn't been dreaming. "Oh, it's starting to all come back."

William got out of bed and stretched. But as he remembered more of what he'd seen, he had to pause. Visions of beautiful landscapes and tidy, immaculate towns flashed in his mind. The scope of Arel's creation was almost too enormous to comprehend. He looked at Michael again. "I'm stunned just thinking about Arel's handiwork."

Michael smiled and put his book aside. "Yes, I agree. It is wondrous."

"Michael, aren't you excited about what Arel has done? His world is vast. You saw the communities and the people—" He sat down again. His words seemed so incapable of expressing his admiration for Arel's abilities. In London, he'd been working on remodeling the lower level of his home. Arel had taken on the creation of an entire world. He let out a gasp. "It must take so much power and control to accomplish what Arel has accomplished. You must be so proud of him, Michael."

William got up again and started for the door. "Why don't you and I congratulate him? Arel needs to know he's achieved something miraculous, don't you think?"

Michael remained seated. "That might not be a good idea. He might not appreciate the fact that we were curious about his special place."

William let go of the door handle. "That's true. I better not let on since he's felt the need to create his own retreat. I'm sure he needs that after all he's been through."

* * *

Rolphe sat on the balcony, trying to occupy his mind with the way the clouds were gathering over the city. He studied the milky whites and deepening grays and the way they were distributed. He noted how the light pierced through the mistier parts. Painting such a sky could be tricky if the artist didn't take care with his colors and brush strokes.

But he couldn't keep his mind on the sky or painting, not when he knew that the angels and William had been exploring Arel's world. He shifted his body, trying to remain passive, trying not to let his curiosity take over. What wonders had they seen? He'd had brief flashes of Arel's dedicated labors. They were just enough for him to know that Arel had made something unique and marvelous. If only he could visit Arel's creation, he'd put what he saw on canvas. "If I could gaze upon his beautiful world before—"

"What are you mumbling about?" William asked as he walked out onto the balcony.

Rolphe looked down, clasping his fingers together, regretting that he'd been dreaming about Arel's world. He hoped William wasn't accessing his thoughts. The younger man was already too involved. He needed to be guided away from Arel's project. "I was watching the clouds move in," he said.

William sat down in the chair that Arel always used, the one nearest the potted gardenias. They were in flower and their fragrance filled the air. "I wanted you to know that I'm returning to London today."

Rolphe's heart grabbed at the thought that Arel's only hope was vanishing with William's departure. Rolphe ignored the pain. What else could he do? He had to remain firm in what was best. At least William would be safe. "Good. I'm sure you're anxious to return to your lady."

William's eyes flitted over Rolphe's person. "And you can return to your Myra."

Rolphe tried to smile. He tried to remain calm in spite of the fact that his heart refused to behave itself. The pain in his chest was getting worse. Arel had helped to heal the vessel, but that didn't mean it didn't voice its opinion about whatever Rolphe contemplated. When he was happy, its beats were strong and in perfect rhythm. When he worried, that was another matter.

Rolphe had to shift his focus from Arel's plight to something more general. Before he had a chance to talk about the weather again, William commented on his recent adventure.

"You'll also be happy to know that Arel's world is perfect. He's happy there. So whatever you've been concerned about can be dismissed."

Rolphe glanced at the sky. The sun was barely peeking out from the heavy cloud banks drifting in. He stood up and steadied himself as he focused on the storm that was moving in. "Thank you for that bit of news."

He was about to retreat into the apartment when William reached out and grabbed his arm. "Arel's creation is nothing like that hellish cave where I found you."

Rolphe's shoulders slumped under the weight of William's bitterness. The man was clearly letting him know that he hadn't forgotten what Rolphe had done to him. "Chessa's world was once beautiful too."

"Chessa? The woman who—"

"Yes, the woman who made me what I was, the woman whose blood I passed on to you."

William released Rolphe's arm and let out a mocking laugh. "I never understood why you gave me your blood, but I can enlighten you a little. You passed on a virus."

Rolphe nodded. "Yes, Arel explained the truth."

"Good, you need to bring yourself up to date. Stop behaving like a throwback from some bygone era."

Rolphe studied his hands. They were coarse and thick compared to William's slender, refined limbs. "I know you think of me as ignorant. You think my beliefs are those of a person who clings to outdated customs."

When William looked away, Rolphe smiled. "Maybe you're right. I abandoned the values and virtues that I learned as a child. In my long life, I lived in darkness. I lost what was important. Now I've come full circle, and I won't lose my way again."

Fifty-One

William was about to tell Arel that he was leaving when he had second thoughts. He kept remembering something Rolphe had said about the world that Chessa had created. If it had once been beautiful like Rolphe claimed, what happened? How did it become such a dismal, desolate place?

"Are you enjoying your stay?" Arel asked.

The question made William come back to himself. He'd been sitting on the sofa, opposite Arel, not realizing that his mind was drifting. "Yes, my stay has been good," he said half-heartedly.

"Will, is something bothering you?" Arel asked.

William looked up, trying to understand the uneasy feeling in the pit of his stomach. But when his eyes met Arel's, he understood why Rolphe thought the man was an angel. So much of the time Arel hid himself behind a mask of troubled emotions. But on this special occasion, his handsome face lit up with the most beautiful, caring smile. William had never seen another person who could exude such unguarded warmth. In spite of the rainy weather outside, he was left with the feeling that the sun was shining just for him.

Arel repeated his question. "William, are you okay?"

For the second time, William made himself come back from his musings. "Yes, I'm fine. What about you?"

Arel sat back and crossed his arms. "I'm happier than I thought possible."

"It shows. It's been a while since you looked so full of life."

Arel nodded and pressed on. "I'm finding my way to a much better place. Which reminds me, Annabel has faced a lot too. Giving up her wings was kind of a crazy thing to do. Is she adjusting?"

"Day by day, we're working things out."

"She must be missing you."

"Maybe, but I think she needs a little time to herself. You talked about people feeling confident in who they are. She wants that, too. She wants to get beyond her fears."

"She will, with you by her side. You're one of a kind, Will. You have a great capacity to do whatever is needed. I only wish I'd realized that when we were young. You were always trying to steer me in the right direction, and I was completely oblivious to how much you tried to help. Please forgive me for all my blunders and ridiculous behavior."

"Arel, it all worked out, didn't it? We're both fine now."

"Yes, but I want you to get on with your life. I don't want you to worry about me anymore. It's not necessary."

"What about the blood brother pact we made with each other? Do you want me to forget that too?"

"It was one of those blunders I mentioned. I don't know how I could have acted so childishly."

"Why would you say that?"

Arel looked away, appearing more somber than before. "Because I'm finally growing up. I'm learning not to lean on other people. It's time for each of us to—"

"To do what?" William demanded.

When Arel wouldn't answer, William rubbed the scar on his palm. "Please don't do this, Arel."

"Do what?" Arel asked with a frown.

"Make me feel like you're disowning me again."

Arel tried to laugh off the statement, but when he saw that William wouldn't back down, his face paled. Looking away, his fists tightened on themselves. Whatever he was battling seemed to be getting the best of him. His voice was weak, almost a whisper. "Disown you? Never. You have to believe that I'm trying my best to keep you safe."

"From what? Look at me, Arel. I'm fine!"

"But for how long? If something happened again . . . I just can't—"

William sat forward. "What is it? What do you want to tell me?"

Arel started to reach out, but he stopped himself. Within moments, he looked drained and weary. His sparkling eyes went dark

283

and dull as he rubbed his brow with a shaky hand. "I'm so tired. I'm sorry, but I have to rest. Try to understand, please."

Arel's transformation from a state of vibrant health to exhaustion happened so fast that William didn't know what to do. As he watched Arel struggle to get to his feet, his chest tightened. If he left now and went back to London, he'd never see Arel alive again. It was a fact, something that came from that knowing part of himself.

After Arel left the room, William got up quickly and hurried to the storage room. Two could play the game that Arel was engaged in. If Arel retreated to his utopian world, William would follow him. He'd spend more time observing the situation and try to find out what he had to do next.

He lay down on the cot and looked at the scar on his palm again. Annabel told William that he and Arel were united in purpose before they came into this life. They had renewed their agreement in the ceremony that Arel had dismissed. But sharing their blood wasn't a juvenile affair. It was one of the most powerful events that William would ever experience.

William smiled at the memory of that day. When Arel suggested a blood brother exchange, William backed away in disgust. He was already in the middle of a transformation that he didn't understand. He thought Arel had passed on a disease that was killing him. He was grieving over what he'd lost. His body wasn't strong anymore. Instead of being his usual, rational self, his emotions were raging. Arel's ideas about angelic blood and its potential seemed like gibberish to his scientific mind.

But Arel was persistent. He ignored William's foul moods. One day, he allowed his true nature to shine, like a beacon of light. The man exuded a confidence that was profound and palpable. When he held out the blade to William, he was in total harmony with some greater force of well-being. His invitation to join their strengths and power was so tempting that William finally yielded. He couldn't resist Arel's grand belief that something glorious was there for them. They only had to hold on to that vision. When their blood was joined, it formed a lasting bond. When one of them doubted, the other would always be there to stand in the truth.

Now, as William closed his eyes and willed himself to visit Arel's world, he had to be the one to champion the truth. People like Arel could create whatever they wanted with their powerful focus. But if they didn't believe that their life had the potential for happiness, if fear dominated, what good was that power?

No matter what Arel said or did, William trusted that the man he thought of as a brother could find his way back to happiness, not just in his world of mice, but in the real world too. Someday, Arel would stand in his true power again, the power to love and embrace all of life.

* * *

Arel walked through Mouse Park, nodding at the many little rodents who rushed over to greet him. He tried his best to smile, but his hand was hurting so much, it was difficult to be pleasant. It was the first time that he'd brought his troubles with him when he visited his beautiful world. He'd always been able to forget everything there. But after his conversation with William, his hand was a painful reminder of their bond and a deep down desire that things could be different.

He sat down on his favorite bench and waited. He knew Wolfie would be joining him shortly. As if on cue, the little brown mouse scurried up the ramp Arel had provided. It gave Wolfie easy access to the bench seat. Arel usually had his hand waiting to ferry the little creature to his shoulder. On this occasion, Wolfie stood up on his back legs waiting, but Arel couldn't offer that kind of assistance. He was clutching his hand, trying to ignore the pain, but it was getting worse.

"Great One, it's so wonderful to see you again," Wolfie exclaimed.

The mouse's squeaky voice made Arel return a genuine smile. He loved the sweet sound of the little mouse's voice. It reminded him of the squeals of laughter that his little godchild, Ariel, made. "It's nice to see you too, Wolfie. How is everyone doing today? Is there enough food? Are the treats adequate?"

"Oh, yes indeed. Everyone is well-fed and happy. The Field family did have a small mishap. Their youngest fell off one of the exercise wheels. She let out a surprised squeak when it happened, but she's fine."

Arel frowned. How could something go wrong when he'd made sure that everything would always be perfect in Mouse Park?

"But she wasn't hurt?" he asked.

Wolfie's beady eyes sparkled. "Oh no, but her parents are keeping her in the sandbox today. They think it best if she stays away from the more active areas. She is very small, you see."

Arel held his hand closer. "I've tried my best, Wolfie. You do believe that, don't you?"

"Of course, Great One. Why would I ever think otherwise?"

Arel blinked back, trying to redirect his focus. He stared at the wildflower section of the garden. It was more free-flowing than most of the manicured beds. Every month there would be new flowers blooming and many of the mice liked to take afternoon naps under the foliage. After a few moments of admiring the violet-blue bluebells, the pain in his palm began to ease. "You're right. I have to remember that this place is nothing like the old world."

Wolfie crept closer and put his front paws on Arel's leg. "You'll always visit us, won't you?"

"I promise you this, my dear friend. If I have anything to say about it, neither heaven nor hell will keep me from being here with you."

"Great One, what is hell?"

Arel hesitated. "It's a place that no mouse or human should ever have to experience."

"Oh my!" Wolfie exclaimed. His delicate claws tightened on Arel's wool slacks. "Have you been to hell?"

Arel offered him a weak smile. "We won't talk about such things. They have no place here. Instead, we'll talk about the stars. How would you like it if I take you with me when I visit them?"

"The stars!" Wolfie gasped. "I would love to visit the stars."

Arel looked skyward, thinking about how grand it would be to introduce the mouse to the celestial bodies he'd created. He was looking forward to the trip when he noted something out of place. The cloud he'd seen on his last visit was back. It hovered directly above Mouse Park.

As soon as he noted the unwelcome addition, his palm began to throb again. The pain brought him back to his conversation with William. Why did the man have to bring up the blood brother ceremony? It was a foolish deed that came from Arel's childish desires. It was an action he'd taken when he still believed in Michael and the promise of change. But a person couldn't escape being who they were. The old world would always be a place where the flawed and fallible lived. Arel couldn't be the friend that William wanted. He'd always end up using his power in disastrous ways.

Wolfie leaped onto Arel's lap. His tiny paws tugged on Arel's shirt. "Great One, you're making that face that people make when they're unhappy. Is something troubling you?"

"Sorry, my mind keeps wandering today. I was thinking about the old world and how things don't work out the way they should. Sometimes the people you love get hurt, and you feel like it's your fault. No matter how hard you try, you can't make that world perfect like this one."

"Is that what hell is like?"

Arel nodded. "I'm afraid it is, my little friend. But it's none of your concern. I'll make sure of that."

Wolfie leaned against Arel's shirt and closed his eyes. "I believe you, Great One. We all appreciate you so much."

Arel felt the adoration and caring that came from the mouse. Physically, Wolfie was tiny, but the capacity of his heart to love and give seemed boundless. It was a comforting feeling until he looked skyward again.

He didn't like the cloud spoiling the look of the otherwise blue sky. He needed to dispose of it once and for all. Thankfully, he had the power to do whatever he wanted. "Go away," he ordered.

Wolfie sat up again, his eyes blinking with concern. "Were you talking to me?"

"No, I'm getting rid of that cloud. It's a nuisance."

"It doesn't seem to be listening to you, Great One."

Wolfie was right. Instead of conforming to Arel's wishes, the cloud remained stationary. A feeling of panic surged through his body. Why wasn't his world behaving the way he wished? First there was the little mouse falling off a wheel. Now the cloud over his head refused to disappear. The more he focused on getting rid of it and being foiled, the angrier he felt. The angrier he felt, the darker the cloud became. In the end, the obstruction got the better of him. He had to wake himself up.

Arel opened his eyes and stared at the ceiling. Instead of a cloud, he saw ugly cracks in the plaster that a coat of paint couldn't cure. But he didn't care about cracks. There was something wrong in the paradise he loved.

"What in blazes is going on? It's my world! I decide what happens there!" he shouted as he sat up. Before he could find a satisfactory explanation he noticed Dantela. The kitten was at the end of his bed. She'd gone to sleep next to him again. He enjoyed her company and liked cradling her against his side. Now she was cleaning her fur. It was dark and matted with a reddish substance.

"What the—"

As he reached out to the cat, he saw his hand. Somehow the scar on his palm had opened. The gaping wound was dripping blood. When he examined his bedding, it was soaked with the stuff.

Seeing the blood and the wound made something click.

"Oh hell, that wasn't just a cloud!"

No wonder his hand was hurting when he'd visited Mouse Park. It was his connection to William.

"He found a way to follow me to my new world," he gasped. "William was hiding behind that cloud, watching me."

A flush of anger made Arel's pale face go red. Embarrassment added to his outrage. William must have been chuckling to himself when he saw Arel talking to his mice. William had always conducted himself with self-assurance and maturity. He must have found it amusing and infantile to think that a person was so inept at the real world that he had to create a place where his best friends were rodents.

Arel stared down at the floor as the truth became evident. "But it's true, isn't it? That's what I did."

He stood up too quickly and had to steady himself on the side table. William often referred to Arel as an idiot. William's pet name was often accompanied by a smile, as if he was only joking, but the man was right. The thought made Arel lean more heavily on the table. "I am a fool. I am an idiot."

The feeling that followed was so demeaning and hurtful that he had to sit down again. But instead of giving in to more anger, he began to laugh. It came from an unwanted, but electrifying clarity. Looking at himself from William's point of view, he could see how amusing he was. As William had once suggested to him, he didn't know how to grow up. He was still acting like a seven-year-old boy.

"Again, he was so right." The words came out in a whisper. It was accompanied by a rush of heat. It fired through his body. As his flesh grew hot and feverish, his mind was consumed by the flames of

288

shame and humiliation. The feelings were summed up in one sentence. It was delivered in a measured, deliberate voice.

"My entire life has been a farce, a meaningless sham."

It was an illuminating moment. It was a moment that changed everything.

Fifty-Two

William woke up on his cot and took a deep breath. His first thought was of Wolfie. On his second visit to Arel's world, he was able to pay more attention to the tiny mouse. Sitting next to Arel on the park bench, he was just as he'd been in life. He was a gentle, giving creature, and one that was very easy to love.

Arel's entire creation was inviting. It was a place to restore one's faith in the grand design of life. Arel took what was good and right about reality and demonstrated how mankind should honor it. William had once known that kind of love for nature. It took Arel's vision to rekindle his desire to experience it again. Someday, if he and Annabel had a family, he wanted his children to know such a world.

The only glitch in William's experience was Arel himself. The man seemed upset. He kept holding his hand and talking about why he didn't fit in with the world of men. Then he started getting angry when he saw the cloud that shielded William from sight. William tried to rectify the situation and withdraw, but he wasn't fast enough. Traveling through energy fields wasn't his strong point. The pressure of Arel's emotional outrage didn't help either. Finally, when Arel returned to the normal world, William was able to trail him back.

He sat up and hoped he hadn't distressed Arel too much. As he got to his feet, there was a knock on the door. When it opened, Carey peeked in. The angel looked uneasy.

"What is it?" he asked.

Carey's answer was immediate. "We have a situation."

William followed Carey out into the living area where Arel was sitting on the sofa. The man's hand was wrapped in a towel. His skin was red, and his eyes were hard and vacant. They were so devoid of

290

any expression that William felt a chill. When he was younger, he'd met a couple of ruthless criminals who looked friendly compared to Arel. "Are you alright?" he asked as he came forward.

"Sit down," Arel ordered. "Just keep your mouth shut and listen."

William hesitated, but he held his tongue.

Arel's eyes grew fiercer, glowing like fluid orbs of coal. "Don't worry, I'm not going to bite, yet. But I do want to tell you how much I admire the life you've led. You're a lucky bastard."

William noted that Michael was standing to one side of the room. Carey had taken his place next to the slightly taller angel. Rolphe stood on the other side of Michael. All three of them were watching him as he took a seat on the sofa opposite Arel.

He crossed his arms and sat back. He didn't know what Arel was up too, but his gut told him to be alert and ready for anything. "Go ahead. I'm listening."

Arel sat back too, holding his hand closer to his chest. "You've always given yourself a break, haven't you, old friend? You've always taken the easy road and called me an idiot countless times for my naïve approach. You've given yourself license to kill, while I gave myself more grief, always trying to be the good guy. Now wasn't that silly of me?"

William didn't move or reply, but he did keep his eyes in line with Arel's. There was no life in them. When he reached out with his mind, it was as if he was searching in a void. There was no feeling in Arel's gaze that he could connect with.

Questions came to mind. Had Arel finally snapped? Had he finally lost touch with reality? Was the real Arel even present or had his soul been lost in some distant world he'd created?

Arel feigned surprise, as if he'd heard William's fears. "Oh my, is your little friend gone?" he asked. "Has his soul flown the coop? Is that what's worrying you, William? Maybe he's been possessed! Maybe he went from cavorting with angels to joining forces with the devil. Wouldn't that be a hell of a game changer?"

Arel began to laugh and kept laughing. He'd almost stop and start again, as if he couldn't help being amused by something only he could understand. When he finally quieted, his face was a deeper shade of red. He took a moment to catch his breath.

Still chuckling, he began again. "Just so you don't distress yourself too much, let me tell you where things stand. You were right. I was wrong. But I can learn. It might take me a little longer than you, say an extra century or so, but I can learn. I can be ruthless and cold. I can hate mankind for being selfish and insensitive. I can give myself license too. It's easy. I never knew how easy it could be. I thought I was better than you, but we're all made from the same defective material. Evil is natural to us. When we free ourselves from the shackles of morality, we free ourselves to be who we really are."

Arel started to remove the towel covering one of his hands. As he did, the soiled inner folds came into view. They were soaked with blood. When his hand was exposed, fresh blood was gushing from the wound on his palm. Arel held up his injured limb. "You see what's happening here. When a person finally surrenders to who they are, they purge all the crap that they got from angels and people like you, William. They allow their body to get rid of what has kept them in misery. Isn't that wonderful? We instinctively know to heal ourselves."

William almost voiced an objection, but he reconsidered. His own instinct was telling him not to challenge Arel, even if it was for his own good. He had to be very careful in how he expressed what he was feeling. "Aren't you afraid that you're going to bleed to death?"

Arel began to laugh. "You underestimate me, William. I can't just die. I'm too powerful for that. You've seen what I can do. I can create worlds. Do you think a person who creates worlds can bleed to death? Think again."

William didn't know enough about Arel's power to disagree with his logic. What he did know was that Arel could be dangerous if provoked. Arel's interaction with Rolphe was proof that Arel's methods could even be brutal. With those facts in mind, William wondered what Arel had in store for him. "So what do you want from me?"

Arel shrugged. "Nothing."

William hesitated. Arel sounded aloof and dispassionate, but William didn't feel reassured. His gut was sending out a very clear message. Retreat! When he spoke, he made sure to use a respectful tone. "So you don't mind if I leave?"

Arel began to finger the blood coming from his palm. "I think that's a splendid idea. In fact, I'd advise you to do just that if you know what's good for you."

"What do you mean?"

Arel sat back and narrowed his eyes. "I mean that I'm giving you fair warning. I'm going to make some changes to the new world that you insisted upon violating. It'll be more accommodating to who I really am. There'll be no more pretty flower beds to stroll through, no more idiotic parks for rodents. Instead, I'll design a proper place for a person who likes the darkness, who welcomes it. And anyone who dares to enter my world will find out that they made a very bad vacation choice. Is that clear?"

William nodded. "Very clear."

In spite of his calm, unflustered attitude, Arel stood up with difficulty. He didn't seem to notice that he was having trouble maintaining his balance. His scowl was fixed and unyielding when he looked at Michael, Carey and Rolphe. "As for you three, why bother talking? You're hopeless children. But that doesn't mean you should try my patience. Understand?"

When all three nodded in unison, Arel turned and started to walk out of the room. He didn't get very far. Before he reached the hallway, he staggered against a wall, tried to save himself from falling and failed. His descent was swift. He crashed to the floor in a sprawl. He tried to move and in the next instant, went limp and motionless.

William and the others rushed over to him, forming a circle of concern. William crouched down and shook him gently. When there was no response, he grabbed for Arel's wrist. The man still had a pulse, but it was slow and weak. He put a hand to Arel's forehead.

Looking up at Michael, he wanted the angel's take on what was happening. "Arel's burning up with fever. Maybe that's why he sounds so crazy."

Michael shook his head. "On a deep level, Arel is raging at himself and everyone else. That's what's fueling his fever. But don't be fooled by his physical condition. In some very real ways, he was correct when he said he was powerful. He's removed his consciousness from this world. Instead, he's exercising his authority in a different one. The world he's working on will reflect his new vision of himself. To enter that world could be very dangerous."

William left Rolphe's apartment after Michael instructed him to rest. He needed time to sort things out. In the meantime, Michael and Carey promised to look after Arel's physical woes. William knew what Michael was also advising. William had a decision to make. Did he want to go up against Arel?

When he arrived back at Myra's flat, he realized how exhausted he felt. Thankfully, Rolphe had made sure he had a place where he could have some privacy. He was anxious to take advantage of that privacy. He wanted to talk to Annabel. After dealing with Arel, he needed to hear her voice and express his appreciation. When he thought about how easy it was to love her, even her fears were welcome. Annabel was rational. He could deal with her problems.

When she answered the phone, he let out a sigh of relief. "I am so lucky to have you in my life," he blurted out.

"You've never said that before," Annabel laughed. "But it's a wonderful way for you to start a conversation."

"I mean every word. If nothing else comes out of what I've experienced, at least I know I'm blessed to have you."

"William, tell me all. What's going on there? Are you okay?"

William nodded as he pressed the phone to his ear. "Yes, but Arel isn't."

"Is he ill again?"

"Annabel, when you were an angel, did you ever deal with someone who thinks his only recourse is to shut off his heart and embrace evil?"

There was a long pause. "My dear William, isn't that what you did?"

William sat back on the sofa and rubbed his forehead. "Can you believe I actually forgot about being that way? It's strange, but the memories feel like they belong to someone else."

"My darling, it feels that way because those feelings and the actions you took had nothing to do with who you are."

Annabel was right. When he was a young man, he'd isolated himself from any positive emotion and become cynical. But when he came to his senses, he knew that he'd hidden himself behind a façade of lies.

"William?"

"Yes, I'm here."

Annabel let out a sigh. "I was just thinking about the situation. Arel loves to help those he cares about. When you were ill, he wanted to be there for you. But if he's denied who he is, it's because he must be in a very bad place."

"Yes, he thinks he's wasted his life trying to be the good guy. I think he's afraid that he'll never succeed being that perfect person he envisions. It's easier to give into his faults."

"Oh William, remember how you acted when you were so angry."

"I remember."

"Then you know that Arel is going to lash out if anyone tries to change his mind. And with his abilities—" Annabel paused. "I know how much you care about him, but—"

"Don't worry, I'm not going to go rushing into anything."

There was another long pause on Annabel's end. When she spoke, her voice was soft but direct. "I believe in you. And I told you that I'll support your decisions. But please, promise me something."

"Yes?"

"Remember what's good and true in yourself. You have to believe that's where the true power remains no matter what you come up against. Don't let what Arel is going through make you forget your own light."

William smiled. "Annabel, you sound like your angel self. You must be overcoming your fears."

"I wish that was so, William, but the truth is that I'm scared."

William didn't say it to Annabel, but he was a little scared himself. Arel destroyed Rolphe's cave as easily as if it was a child's Popsicle stick project. "Try not to distress yourself. I have a lot of thinking to do before I take any action."

"You sound tired."

"Yes, I think I need sleep more than anything."

"Remember how much I love you."

"And I love you. I'll talk to you tomorrow."

295

Fifty-Three

Kevin sat at Peggy's kitchen table, fidgeting as his sister brought over the coffee pot. "This feels kind of weird, Peg."

Peggy refilled his mug. "What feels weird?"

"Asking you about my dreams, but you're kind of an expert on the subject."

"Kevin, don't be silly. It's nice to know my big brother respects me enough to want my opinion."

"Yeah, well my nightmares let up for a while after that talk with Michael. Now they're back. I didn't want to say anything to Carol, but they have me wondering if I've got a problem."

Peggy put the coffee pot back and sat down. "You're fine. I've been having them too. Tim hasn't said so, but I think he's having trouble sleeping again."

"You know I care about Arel. I'd do anything for him, but why am I bringing his worst side into my dreams? I keep waking up feeling like he's some kind of crazy nut."

Peggy looked down at her mug and smiled. "You've had some pretty awful feelings about me in the past too."

"What are you talking about?"

"You know, when we've argued, you said I was bossy, that I had to always have things my own way."

"Sorry, Peg, but since we were kids, even though I was older, you tried to tell me what to do."

"Looking back on being a child, I felt like I had to battle the bullies. But I was this little kid. I couldn't take care of the tough guys myself. But you were big and strong. I guess I saw you as the solution to my problems."

Kevin smiled. "That's kind of nice to hear. It doesn't make me feel better about the times I got my face smashed in, but at least my little sister felt I could protect her."

Peggy caressed her cup. "You know how I am. I've always been a worrier. I thought I was worried about stray puppies and kittens, but maybe I was worried about myself too. Sometimes I wish I could have been you, the brave, big brother who never backed down from a fight. Instead, I was just this skinny brat with a big mouth."

Kevin felt his face flush and quickly took a sip of coffee. He wasn't used to his sister saying nice things about him. He didn't know how to respond.

Peggy continued. "Anyway, if I've never said it before, I'll say it now. Thank you for being you, Kev. No matter what, you were always there, helping me fight my battles."

"Aw, stop it, sis. That's what big brothers are for. And you weren't just a skinny kid with a big mouth. Remember all the strays you saved. You even got homes for them all. You found ways to help when most of us were just playing baseball."

Peggy smiled. "I hope I did some good along the way."

"Of course, you did." Kevin paused and took another sip of his coffee. "Which brings us back to Arel and the dreams."

"Yes, I've been giving that subject some thought. I've also been going over the whole idea of being a worrier."

"What's worrying got to do with dreams?"

"When I was a kid, I worried about bullies. I dreamed about them too. And I think I managed to infuriate every one of them within a five mile radius."

"That's true. You were a bully magnet."

"Yes, more so than any other person in school."

"So what are you saying? That your worries have something to do with what's happening?"

"Our worries, big brother."

"Gee, I never thought about myself as a worrier."

"Kevin, please, what about the time I was in the hospital? You nearly went out of your mind worrying about me."

"Oh yeah, that's true. And I have been thinking about Arel and how bad off he's been recently. He looked better when William was here, but underneath—"

"Me too. I had more positive thoughts after Michael's words of wisdom, but now I'm back where I was."

"Makes sense. When I've coached people in sports, they have to practice whatever they're learning or they revert back to old habits. But what about Tim? He doesn't seem like a worrier."

"He's married to me. He'd have to be dead not to pick up on my vibes. So, I'm thinking all three of us have to go back to more positive thoughts about Arel."

Kevin shrugged. "I'll do whatever it takes to get some sleep."

Peggy got up and put her arms around him. She gave him a wholehearted hug. "You're the best."

Kevin laughed. "Take it easy, sis. Those strength-building yoga classes are working. You're stronger than you think."

Peggy let him go and laughed too. "Good to know in case I meet any more bullies, and you're not around."

* * *

Carol scowled as she picked up her phone. She felt like she should call William at once, but Kevin was out on an errand. He'd be disappointed if she called without him. He liked to be in on everything, especially when it came to William. Her loving husband had tried so hard to be the person she could turn to when she was upset. Unfortunately, he didn't always have the skills or the ability to shift Carol's attitudes. William was the one who helped her gain a new perspective of herself. He'd also advised her about living her life with more assertiveness.

As she made changes, Kevin had to get used to the "new" Carol. When she did or said things that surprised him, he made every effort to keep up with the new version she was becoming. Would he get his feelings hurt if she went ahead and contacted William? She decided it didn't matter. Something told her that William needed her.

As she listened to the phone ringing and waited for William to pick up, she felt a chill take hold. Strong feelings of impending doom weren't something she usually felt about other people. That was Peggy's department. But when she heard William's voice on the other end of the call, she couldn't hold back her question. "Are you okay? Has something happened?"

"Carol? Is that you?"

William's voice sounded sleepy.

"I'm so sorry, William. Did I wake you up?"

There was a long pause as if William needed time to focus on their conversation. When he responded, he sounded more like himself.

"I'm fine," he said. "But what about you? Is something wrong?"

Carol hesitated. She clutched at the phone and scolded herself for being impulsive. She'd always been careful not to stick her nose in other people's business. Kevin was the exception, but he was her husband. So why had she let her crazy need to talk to William get the better of her? She should have waited and had more clarity before she phoned him.

"Carol, are you still there?" William asked.

"Yes, I'm here."

"You don't sound quite like yourself."

"I think I just woke you up for nothing. I had this ridiculous idea that you might be in trouble. Isn't that silly of me?"

Another long pause.

"William, I'm so sorry. You encouraged me to have faith in myself, not to go around interfering with other people's lives."

"But my dear Carol, what would have happened if you didn't help me when I was near death's door?"

Carol smiled. "How could I do otherwise? I had to try to help you."

William laughed. "You're a very strong and capable person. Always trust that about yourself."

"Should I also trust this feeling I have? I don't know how to put it in words, but a childish image comes to mind. It's almost like you might open a door, and this horrible bogeyman will jump out. Does that make any sense?"

"Yes, unfortunately it does."

Carol's fingers tightened even more as she held the phone close to her ear. "Please listen to me, William. I know that you're so much more adept in this world than I am, but don't take any chances that might end in disaster."

William let out a mildly, mocking laugh. "But Carol, the bogeyman doesn't belong in this world."

Carol stepped back, trying to understand what he was telling her. "You're right. I've only seen that creature in my imagination. Still, after my miscarriage, I felt like he took my unborn child. I was just lucky that you came along and helped me to see things differently."

"How did you deal with this bogeyman?"

"I realized I was making him up. At first, I was still scared, but you kept encouraging me. So I guess the only way I escaped that monster was by finding a way to live in the real world. Now I don't let myself get caught up in the nightmare anymore."

"Thank you, Carol. You've been very helpful once again."

"Really?"

"Yes, I'm glad you called."

"And I'm always here if you or Annabel need anything."

"I'll remember that," William said as he signed off.

Carol put the phone on the table and smiled. She was still smiling when Kevin opened the kitchen door. She greeted him warmly. "Hi, sweetie."

Kevin stared back. "Why do you look so happy? Did the baby do something special?"

Carol stiffened. "No, I was talking to William."

"William? About what?"

"I was very upset about this feeling I had."

"I'm sorry I wasn't here," Kevin said as he quickly walked over to join her. He looked troubled as he smoothed back a strand of her blond hair. "I guess I let you down again."

"No, you don't understand. I'm okay, but I wanted to warn William."

"What are you talking about?"

Carol told Kevin about her conversation. When she was finished, she was surprised by Kevin's reaction. He took her into his arms and hugged her. "Kevin, did I upset you?"

Kevin pulled back. "No, just the opposite. I've been having those nightmares again. Peggy helped a little, but you made me feel like I can deal with them."

"Goodness, so I helped William and you. That's a wonderful feeling."

"You bet you have. My nightmares have been the worst. There was something evil in them that made me feel like it was going to have me for dinner."

"Why didn't you tell me about your dreams?"

"Look Carol, you're doing so great. I didn't want to rain on your parade."

Carol sighed. "Poor Peggy."

Kevin's eyes turned curious. "What is it?"

"When you talked about rain, I thought about your sister and how much she worries. If I were her, I'd always have an umbrella close."

* * *

William was still reflecting on his phone call with Carol when he heard a knock on the door. He answered it and welcomed Carey in. "I was going to call you or Michael and ask about Arel."

Carey walked over to an overstuffed chair and sat down. "There's not too much to say. Arel's physical condition is stabilized, but he's still in a deep sleep."

"That's good."

"Not necessarily. Michael is sure he's restructuring his world, getting it ready in case anyone visits again."

"So what will become of Arel? Will he dream away the rest of his life? Will he stayed holed-up in his creation like some evil overlord?"

"It looks like it could happen that way. All his energy is going into the world he's holding together. In the meantime, his negativity is cutting off the life force that his physical body needs. So he might not have as long as he thinks."

"Look, Carey, I've already interfered way too much. I think I'm responsible for this whole mess. From now on, I better respect his boundaries. You and Michael are much better equipped to take action."

"That's a bit of a problem. We can't intercede with Arel directly. However, we could support someone like you."

"If you need a human to interface with Arel, Rolphe is your man. He seems to understand Arel's problem."

"Rolphe has volunteered to enter Arel's new world, but we're sure Arel wouldn't allow him there very long. Anyway, we're running out of options."

"I can't help that. I can't help Arel." William let out a hard bark of laughter. "I guess Carol's bogeyman has taken all my courage."

Carey didn't comment. Instead, he sat forward, elbows on knees, hands together. His gaze slowly swept over William.

William scowled back. "I hate when you and Michael do that."

Carey sat back and smiled. "Why? What do you think we're doing?"

"Checking out my deficiencies. Unlike Arel, I fall short in the power department, right? I couldn't even take on Rolphe the wolf. When he attacked me in that cave, I was helpless. Arel, on the other hand, not only took care of the beast, he destroyed that cave and that world. And he didn't even struggle to do it." William snapped his fingers. "Just like that, it was gone."

"William, you're doing remarkably well under the circumstances. After Arel passed on Michael's blood, you lost everything you considered important. Yet, when you were dying, you made peace with it all. You even forgave Arel. Do you realize how much strength and courage that takes?"

"So what did it get me? Arel has enough power to override death itself."

"No, not really."

William froze. Ever since being thrown out of heaven, he'd been convinced that Arel's power bordered on being unlimited. "Explain what you mean."

Carey shook his head. "Sorry."

This time William leaned forward. "What are you hiding?"

"Sorry again, but you have things turned around. You're the one who's hiding information from yourself."

William wanted to protest, but Carey's youthful, animated eyes told him he'd be foolish to argue. Angels couldn't lie. That meant William wasn't allowing himself access to the whole picture. But how could he? He'd been overwhelmed with fear for months. He glanced at Carey again. "Arel is always talking about shields. Now, I wonder if fear isn't something we use to avoid more clarity."

Carey nodded. "Yes, but truth has a way of shining through if you let it."

As soon as William decided Carey was right again, he had to pause. When he sat up this time, he was clasping his hands. "I just got the weirdest feeling about my trip to the afterlife. I think some part of me wanted to come back, that Arel was simply there to help with the part that was resisting."

Carey shrugged. "On a soul level, you knew this life still held great value for you."

"Why hasn't Michael helped Arel remember this stuff? It might help him to feel better about his power."

"It wouldn't help much. Arel is too caught up in what he sees as his flawed nature. He's tried to come to grips with it, but he's never been able to go beyond a certain point."

William thought about the aftermath of feeling forced to come back to life and the helplessness that followed. "For my part, I suppose I needed to blame someone. I might have been courageous enough to embrace death. Soul or no soul, I didn't want to keep living if it meant being a normal human being."

Carey smiled. "You and Arel are both rather unique and extraordinary. That doesn't mean that you're better than any human, but you have the capacity to carry more light than most. When Michael and I scan your energy fields, we're gauging how much of that light is being allowed to shine."

William thought about being a child and loving every creature he came across. In the end, he turned away from fawn and fox. He learned to fight those he hated instead. "I never trusted that light. When I did, I suffered for it. Everything I cared about was destroyed."

"But Arel isn't dead, yet. I think you know that saving him isn't your job, but both of you want to be free to live life without fear. You both want to go beyond the limited definition that humans put on themselves."

William shrugged. "I don't know anything for certain anymore. All I know is that I came here to help him if I could."

"And you still can. You saw Arel demonstrate his power and thought that was the end of it, but it's not. Your faith in yourself came into question, that's all. Now, I'm telling you that you have just as much power, but it's up to you to believe in it."

William's scowl deepened. "I have no idea about how to do that."

Fifty-Four

Arel's mind was swimming in confusion. He knew he must be sleeping, but he couldn't navigate in his dreams like he usually could. When he finally found his way back to a place of comfort, he was in his beloved Mouse Park. Even so, it took a while to get his bearings. He kept remembering a conversation he'd had with William. He kept wondering about his attitude during their talk. It was so cold and unfeeling. But somewhere between the world of William and his own newly-created world, he dropped that persona.

As he sat on his bench and watched the little mice playing and enjoying the beautiful park, he knew he still loved everything he'd created. Yet, in his recent conversation, he had labeled it a ridiculous, fairy-tale world of an immature idiot. The words were so easy to spew out as he sat on the sofa in Rolphe's apartment. After deciding that he'd wasted his entire life, the crushing pain of his decision was too great. Something snapped in his psyche. Instead of feeling the pain, he went cold and numb.

But he didn't bring that numbness back with him to Mouse Park. As he surveyed his glorious world and thought about wiping out all its beauty, he was overcome with so much sadness that he wanted to weep.

"Great One, you look upset again," Wolfie squeaked.

As usual, the mouse sat on the bench next to him. The little rodent had been quiet for a long time, but now he was looking up with curious eyes.

What could he tell his little friend? Could he explain what he was going to do? Could he inform Wolfie that Mouse Park was destined to be leveled? Could he deliver that kind of news to an innocent creature that looked up to him for its happiness? No, he had to make their last moments together an experience that both could remember with fondness. "I look this way because I'm thinking, my little friend. And sometimes thinking can be very stressful."

"Is there anything I can do to make your thinking easier?"

"I'm afraid not, in fact, I have something I need to share with you."

Wolfie's ears tipped forward expectantly. "Is it about the stars? Are we going to visit them tonight?"

Arel avoided Wolfie's eager gaze. "No, I wanted to tell you something very important. You have to leave here and return to the world you used to inhabit."

"Really? But it's so beautiful here."

"But the place where I found you was beautiful too, remember?"

"Oh yes, it was. There were vast fields to explore and lots of grasses and seeds to enjoy. But—"

"But what?"

"But you weren't there. And that was fine because I didn't think about what it was like to talk to someone like you, Great One. Now, our conversations often fill the time when you go away. I ponder the things you've spoken about. They're such happy things, like noticing the color of the sky or the smell of a rose in bloom."

"I'm happy that our talks please you, but times are changing. It's best that you go back to the other place where you'll always be happy and safe."

"Will you visit me there too?"

"No, I won't be able to do that."

"Then I want to stay here. And I'm sure the others feel the same way."

"I'm sorry, but soon this place won't be very nice. The flowers will be gone, and the sky will be dark all the time."

"Great One, it sounds like you're speaking about that place you called hell?"

"I suppose I am, but sometimes a person has no options but to go there."

"But you'll be all alone!" Wolfie squeaked out in his loudest, high-pitched voice.

Arel smiled. "Yes, but I'll remember our time together. That will have to be enough."

"Great One, are you going to lose your power to make this world like you want it?"

"No, but there are people who don't see things the way I do. If they come to this world, I'll have to make it hard for them to stay here. I might also have to fight to keep them out."

"I've heard about this thing called fighting. In the old world, there are stories about great animals who try to eat us. Some of our kind have struggled to protect themselves and their young against these great beasts."

Arel nodded. "I think you're talking about cats."

Wolfie shrunk back. "Yes, that is how they're called. Do you ever have to fight them in the old world, Great One?"

"No, but sometimes humans fight each other."

"Do you think that some of those humans are coming here?"

"Yes, my friend, I think that's exactly what they plan to do." Arel's eyes narrowed with anger as he thought about what he was going to have to deal with. William had interfered when Arel was young and headed towards suicide. The man would most likely try to rescue him again, especially since William had become one of the good guys. He'd also have angelic support. Michael and Carey seemed to think their only purpose was saving Arel's soul. As he considered how to deal with them, Wolfie put a paw on Arel's hand.

"Yes, Wolfie, do you want something else?"

"Please don't send me away. Let me help you with the ones who you'll have to fight."

"You're too little to help me, my friend."

"Then use your power, Great One. Make me bigger!"

Arel was about to object again and stopped himself. "Wolfie! You're right! In fact, I could make you like me. Would you like that?"

Wolfie squeaked with excitement. "Oh yes, I'd like that, Great One! I'd be able to reach the branches of that tree by the pond, and I could pick an apple for one of the others. I could—"

Arel laughed and picked up the small mouse. Looking him in the eye, he realized the potential that Wolfie represented. "You could do and be so much more than that, Wolfie."

Wolfie tilted his head. "Please, tell me more. I want to know what I can do and be, Great One."

Arel paused, letting his mind revel in possibility. He'd told William that his new world was going to be different. The words came from a state of detachment, but if he examined them now, he knew they held great value. From that dispassionate, objective viewpoint, he'd seen a new life. That new life was free and easy because he could do as he pleased. He could even enjoy the flawed nature he'd been burdened with. Without the pain of caring, it could become his greatest asset. And he didn't have to live out that existence alone. He had Wolfie.

He looked at the small mouse again, narrowing his eyes. "Before I can tell you about what you can be and do, I have to let myself do and be something different."

"I don't understand, Great One."

"Don't worry about it, Wolfie. It will all be very clear when I'm finished. For now, go to sleep. And when you wake up, everything will be just as I want it."

"As you wish," Wolfie said as he blinked a couple of times. "I do feel like I need a nap."

Arel watched as Wolfie yawned and curled up in his hand. As he laid the little mouse on the bench, he shivered. A strange feeling was taking hold of him too. The spell that he'd put on Wolfie seemed to also be working on him. As he continued to shut out all thought of trying to be a good person, the world around him began to go dark. The sky was rapidly losing its light as he closed his eyes.

* * *

Annabel sat in the living room of her London home. William was supposed to call, but in the meantime, she was talking to Raphael. She was giving him a sort of progress report. "Life was beginning to stabilize. I was starting to think I was getting the hang of being a human. Now everything is out of control again."

Raphael straightened in his chair. When he wore his hair pulled back, his face looked youthful and lacking in experience. Yet his gaze was a powerful indicator of his true nature. Bright and steady, it held a depth of vision and ageless wisdom. When he spoke, his tone was deep and purposeful. "But you do seem much calmer than you were."

Annabel laughed. "When I started on this adventure, I was what people call a basket case. Now, at least I'm sitting here without my heart pounding."

"So tell me about your new perspective?"

"I understand people's emotions a lot better. I can feel why they get angry at what they perceive as hurtful. When William talked about Arel's decision to give in to what Arel terms his flawed nature, I also had a brief moment of curiosity. After all, that path does provide a sense of letting go of the terrible struggle most people go through."

"Are you saying that you'd consider such a course change?"

"Oh no, I chose being human because I wanted to experience love in the way people experience it. And even though I've been very afraid at times, the happiness I've felt has been worth the struggle."

"And what about Arel's decision?"

"He'll have to give up all the joy if he embraces the idea of evil. So what good is it in the long run?"

Raphael sat forward. "But the Creator doesn't want any of us to suffer."

"I know that, but Arel doesn't."

"Are you prepared for William to take action again?"

Before Annabel could reply, the phone rang. It was William's ring tone. She hesitated, trying to give herself a moment to pull herself together. She'd been expressing views that sounded good on the surface, but how strong would she be if William's life was threatened? Would she still be happy that she wasn't an angel if William ended up on the other side?

She picked up the phone, hoping she could put aside her concerns. She'd made a promise to William. She wanted to be supportive. That meant she had to sound as cheerful as possible. "William, how are you?"

When William responded, she found herself frowning, but only for the briefest moment. Then she was smiling and nodding her head. The conversation was a very short one, with William doing most of the talking. By the time she said goodbye, her face reflected her surprise.

She returned to where Raphael was sitting and shrugged. "I can't believe it. William wants me to come to Paris. I think he wants my help. Isn't that something?"

"Good, you'll have a chance to work together."

"Oh my, so far we haven't done much of that. I've always felt like William had better ideas when it came to worldly matters."

"But you're wise and experienced in how the universe works, Annabel. Aren't those valuable strengths to bring to worldly matters?"

* * *

It had been a day and a half since William left Rolphe's apartment. He'd been deeply troubled by Arel's behavior. Arel had obviously lost touch with reality, but what could William do about it. He found that Myra's flat provided the quiet he needed to consider his options.

At first he'd felt hopeless. Arel seemed to hold all the cards. Maybe the man was weaker than he thought in the real world, but Michael warned that wouldn't be the case in the world Arel had created. As William pondered Arel's current status, his hopeless feeling switched to one of anger. William came to Paris trying to renew their bond. He tried to be there for a friend, and Arel responded with threats, threats that scared the hell out of William. Would Arel snap his fingers and dispose of him like he'd disposed of Rolphe's cave?

Once the questions started, they seemed overwhelming. How could a gifted guy like Arel be so incapable of managing his emotions? Why did he have to be so extreme in his reactions? How could Arel turn into some kind of mob boss who abandoned everything he held dear? How could he turn on William?

Carey's visit helped bring in some clarity. The angel's youthful look and mannerisms reminded William of when he'd been a young man. Rolphe's blood, and the virus it contained, helped turn William into a kind of super human when it came to health and aging, but he'd been fearless before he ever met Rolphe. He'd walked around with the feeling that no one could take away his belief in himself. So what happened?

During Carey's visit, the angel pointed out that William had lost sight of that belief. His statement was dismissed at first. But, now, as William sat in Myra's living room, thinking about Annabel arriving very soon, he knew Carey was right. He was puffing himself up, thinking about how he'd bolster Annabel's self-confidence when his own was almost nonexistent.

That fact was reinforced every time he retold stories about his experiences. He was always talking about what Rolphe had done to him, what Arel had done. He was like an old woman repeating the same tales over and over.

The thought made him grab hold of the sofa arm. "My god, I'm turning into a bigger victim than Arel, if that's possible."

When Annabel arrived a short time later, she looked her bright self, but William couldn't appreciate her beauty or smile. He was too upset about continuing down a road to complete uselessness.

Annabel seemed to sense his concern. She reached out to him with a radiant face and carefully spoken words. "William, you always think of yourself as very rational." She paused. "You know what I mean, a person with a scientific viewpoint, but you're so much more than that. In spite of the pain that Arel has caused you, you came to Paris anyway, still championing what's important. Do you know how much I admire that?"

William stalled as he went over his recent discovery and how he'd been kidding himself. "I know you mean well, Annabel, but can we stop talking about it?"

"Of course," Annabel said quickly. She hesitated and stood back, her green eyes sweeping over him with unease.

"And please stop doing that."

Annabel's gaze went from scan mode to looking back with surprise. "Doing what?"

"You and your ex-buddies are always looking for my weaknesses. I'm sure it's warranted, but it's tiresome."

Annabel paused. "William, has something happened since I talked to you last."

"I said I didn't want to talk about it."

Fifty-Five

When William returned to Rolphe's apartment with Annabel, he tried to appear as normal as possible. He was doing his best to ignore the sinking feeling in his gut. He kept telling himself that even if he'd been playing the victim, he could change his attitude. At least he hoped he could. Otherwise, he'd have to join Arel in his demented world. They'd be brothers alright, a couple of broken-spirited beings who were utterly pathetic and useless.

Trying to get on with the business at hand, he wasted no time in calling for a meeting with Rolphe and the angels. It was held on the balcony because of the need for secrecy. Once everyone was seated, Michael, Carey and Rolphe looked to William to start the conversation.

William cleared his throat, his hands clasping each other. "First of all, what's Arel's physical condition?"

Michael spoke up. "He's in a kind of very deep sleep. Sometimes, he starts to wake up, but usually falls back to sleep very quickly. As for the loss of blood, we've been able to help in that department. So physically, he's stable. However, emotionally, he's still in a very negative space. He's living out that negativity in the world he's created."

Annabel gave William her sweetest, most supportive smile. "We've talked things over and decided we both want to help Arel if that's possible."

Rolphe shifted uneasily in his chair. "I don't mean to be too forward, but do either of you have any idea about what you're facing? Arel's world is vastly different now. Anyway, that's what I've seen in the visions I've had."

"Different how?" William asked.

When Rolphe hesitated, Carey raised his hand. "Michael and I got a personal invitation, you might say. We've had an up close look at the new version of Arel's creative endeavors."

"What do you mean by a personal invitation?" Annabel asked.

Carey straightened in his seat. "Arel communicated via our airways. He's indicated that he knows we'll want to get involved. That being the case, he's decided to make it a kind of contest. He's invited us to check out the provisions he's provided if we decide to intervene. Anyway, Rolphe is right. Arel's world isn't what it used to be. The people and nice neighborhoods are gone. It doesn't look like anything in today's world. The landscape looks like something out of the *Lord of the Rings* movie, minus the nice, scenic parts."

Rolphe nodded. "It's very dark, but there is one spot that's still beautiful. There's a hill with a crystalline castle perched on top, complete with turrets."

William grimaced. "Let me guess. It belongs to Arel."

Michael shook his head. "No, it's ours. Arel's castle is dark and quite foreboding."

"What do you mean when you say it's ours?" William asked.

Rolphe rubbed at some paint on the back of his hand and looked at William. "He means that the beautiful castle is flying two flags, Michael's flag and your flag, my Prince."

William found his patience at an all time low. He grimaced at Michael. "Why is he calling me that?"

"During one of his lifetimes, Arel was a very capable knight. He's fashioned his present world to reflect the medieval period. Now, he's taken on the title of king, the powerful sovereign ruler of his lands. Rolphe feels like you should have a title too."

Carey smiled. "Prince William does seem appropriate."

Annabel stood up, her face suddenly flushed with emotion. "I said I want to help, but I think we need to remember how dangerous this is, everyone. William doesn't need a title. He needs protection if he's going to challenge Arel."

Carey sobered immediately. "Of course, Annabel. We all plan to do everything we can to help him."

William glanced up at Annabel. "Please, don't chastise Carey. I need as much levity as I can get." He meant it. He'd seen his face in the hall mirror at Myra's. If he looked any grimmer, he'd end up on a poster for the lame and downtrodden.

Annabel took her seat again, letting her bunched brows ease a little. "Sorry, I sometimes get—"

William patted her hand, trying to use the wit that had always been there when he needed to be entertaining. "Here's a nice thought. If I'm Prince William, you could be my Lady Annabel."

Annabel sat up straighter. "Do you mean you want me to visit this castle we're discussing?"

"If Michael and Carey think it's safe, of course."

Michael nodded. "It is for now. I think Arel wants us to acquaint ourselves with the place. He's welcomed us there so we can get used to the idea of what's coming, even prepare for it."

Annabel looked around the table. "What are we preparing for?"

Rolphe's eyes clouded over. When he spoke, his words were delivered in a quiet, somber tone. "A war, my Lady, a war that decides who's the more powerful, Arel or the prince."

"That's not exactly what's going on, Rolphe," Michael corrected. "What Arel really wants to discover is the truth about human nature. He wants to find out if darkness can extinguish the light."

Rolphe pulled back. "That sounds even worse."

William had to avoid letting Rolphe's despairing attitude pull him down any further. He held up a hand. "If that's the case we need to know what we're dealing with. Before we make any plans, I suggest we all visit Arel's world."

When everyone nodded in agreement, Michael stood up. "I think one person should stay behind with Arel." He looked at Rolphe. "While we check on what Arel has set up, you can monitor his condition here. If he looks like he's waking up, you can alert us. And please don't discuss what we're doing. Even when Arel's awake, he seems to be in a state of confusion. I don't think he's very capable of remembering what's going on in his new world. I'm sure it's more like a fuzzy dream."

Rolphe clasped his hands together. "I won't say anything that might upset him."

William stood up too. Despite a feeling of deep-down agitation, the thought of visiting Arel's newest handiwork had engaged his curiosity. He gave Michael a quick nod. "Let's get started."

Annabel felt like she was standing in one of the great castles of Europe. Her eyes widened with wonder as her gaze traveled up the soaring walls of the great hall. When she crouched down and ran her hand over the floor's stone surface, it was hard and cold to the touch. Everything appeared so real that she had to remind herself that this castle belonged to a world that Arel had created.

The space was also on the chilly side, making her gravitate to the massive fireplace on one end of the hall. A well-stoked fire was burning, giving off enough heat to help her warm up a little. As she briskly rubbed her hands together, she thought about how easy it was to switch realities. Michael, Carey and William were all very helpful. With a few simple instructions and Michael's energy boost, she relaxed and quickly slipped into a light trance. Following Michael's directives, she soon found herself in Arel's world.

She had shuttered when she'd first seen the landscape. She hadn't been prepared for the barren fields or the muddy, stagnant waterways that greeted her. Not a bird or any kind of beast was visible. The only signs of life came from two opposing hilltops. Each boasted a fortress. William and Michael's structure was beautiful, with white granite walls and elegant turrets that graced the upper level. Arel's abode was made of stone too, but it was blackened like the fields. Seen from above, there were fires burning inside the thick outer walls.

Just the thought of Arel's depressing stronghold made Annabel edge closer to the fire. William was still investigating some of the other parts of the castle. Since it would be his base of operations in Arel's world, it was important that he familiarize himself with the layout. When he came striding into the hall, he was with Michael and Carey. All three were animated and talking with each other.

William had never looked more handsome. Decked out in boots and breeches, he wore a gleaming, silver breastplate over his white, linen tunic. A golden, royal crest was stamped on the breastplate's polished surface. The emblem was a winged, jeweled crown set in a sunburst. A long, finely woven, scarlet cloak was draped around William's shoulders. His head was adorned with a small crown encrusted with small diamonds.

As Annabel watched William walking over, she noted that he was in a good mood. When he laughed and patted Carey's shoulder, she scowled. Obviously, the man she loved wasn't too worried about the situation he was facing. It was only when he tripped over the edge of a rough stone in the floor that his laughter turned to expletives. Annabel tried to hide her reaction as he regained his composure. Hopefully, William would soon come to his senses and realize that he was dealing with a world that wasn't only real, it was dangerous and potentially deadly.

* * *

William snorted his displeasure as he recovered his footing. He'd been caught off-guard when the edge of his boot caught on a paving stone. It was enough to remind him of a similar mishap that had happened months before. When he'd been approaching the cave where Rolphe was hiding, he'd tripped too. He was wondering about the two incidents when he looked up and caught Annabel's gaze. Her reproachful eyes were letting him know that she was concerned about him.

His first reaction was an impatience bordering on anger. Taking a couple of breaths of the chill air, he managed to hold in his temper. Still, he couldn't hold in all of his resentment. Annabel was an ex-angel. Couldn't she use a little of her old intuitive angel sense to know they both had to remain positive? He tried to ignore the anxiety in her gaze as he approached her. "You're doing it again, Lady Annabel."

"What am I doing?" Annabel asked.

"Letting your fear get the better of you."

"Fine, but it's hard not to feel like this when I look around this room. Do you know how much power it took to create something so magnificent? Look at the stone work. Look at these elaborate furnishings!" She crossed her arms. "Look at you, William, and what you're wearing."

William stared at her, suddenly taken by Annabel's beauty. For a moment, his heart raced with desire. "Me? What about you?" he asked. Annabel was gorgeous in her red, floor length, silk taffeta dress. The becoming, cinched bodice was embellished with gold cord

315

and lace. Her auburn hair was pulled back and adorned with a pearl and diamond headpiece that showed off her regal, high cheekbones. "You belong in a fairytale."

Annabel ignored his compliment. "William, are you listening to what I'm trying to tell you? Arel is playing at something that could end up being very dangerous!"

Annabel's panicked voice echoed in the high-ceilinged room, making William back away. He gave the hall another quick sweep, taking in the incredible details of the structure. He was surrounded by evidence of Arel's powerful abilities. Those creative abilities had the potential to also be used in lethal ways. He hoped Carey was right about his own potential. Would he measure up when it came to being as powerful as Arel?

As he wandered around the room, the chill began to seep into his bones. It made him wonder about the real motive behind Arel's 'medieval game' theme. When historians referred to the period as the Dark Ages, there was a reason for the label. It was a brutal time.

He paused in front of a larger-than-life tapestry that hung on one of the walls. William was familiar with things of beauty, and he could appreciate the finely woven piece. The scene was something else. It depicted a village setting, populated by a large number of peasants. Many wore agreeable faces. Their pleasant attitude made William let out a sneer of disapproval. There was nothing pleasing in the daily fare of people who lived in such a village. They were mired in ignorance and harsh realities.

After reliving a past life in the middle ages, he hated the thought of what he'd suffered. Yet, he was drawn in by the tapestry's subject matter and examined it with care. He zeroed in on one of the details. Was that a child hiding in the shadows?

If he narrowed his eyes, he could make out a boy. The boy's face was pathetically thin and dirty. William stepped closer and put a hand on the woven cloth. He became fixated on the child's beseeching eyes. They were dejected and wanting, filling his mind with a deep despair.

When William had been visiting Arel in Chicago the first time, he felt that same despair. He was deathly ill and delirious most of the time. For days, his hallucinations kept him trapped in a past life. He felt like a helpless child, one who was being burned alive by a cruel, uncaring mob. In the midst of the experience, he'd blamed Arel for the episode, thinking that Arel had abandoned him in that life.

Now, as he tried to distance himself from the pathetic boy in the tapestry, the scene he was staring at began to shift. The light was lost as a nighttime scene unfolded. The people changed. They were holding torches. Their smiling faces turned angry and savage.

"Oh god no, not again," he groaned as the tapestry began to take on life. He tried to turn away as the object of the crowd's hatred came into view. A man was tied to a stake. He was so young, barely more than a boy himself, and he was engulfed in flames. Before he'd been burned, he'd been tortured. There was no light left in the young man's eyes, only torment and pain.

William shuttered as he connected with the man. "Arel, I'm so sorry for blaming you," he whispered. "You gave up your life trying to save your sister. You had nothing left when they got through with you. Yet, I couldn't see past what they did to me. I'm sorry that I never forgave you."

William couldn't move as he thought about how much hate he'd reaped on Arel during his stay in Chicago. Again, he realized how he'd played the victim. It was a shameful memory that made his face flush with heat. As that heat spread to the rest of his body, he was pulled deeper into the tapestry. Flames lit up the village square and threatened to engulf him next.

Again, he tried to shift his gaze, but he couldn't control his focus. When he tried to step back, he realized that he couldn't move. The more he struggled to disengage, the hotter the fire became. He could feel the heat coming off the blaze. As he was forced closer and closer, the heat became almost unbearable. Panic grabbed hold of him, but he had no voice to protest what was happening. It was only someone else's hands, pulling him backwards, that saved him from a fiery demise. Everything faded after that.

Later, when he woke up, the scene replayed like something out of the worst of his nightmares. He quickly glanced around, relieved that he wasn't in Arel's realm anymore. He was in the small space that served as Carey and Michael's bedroom. Annabel sat on the edge of his cot, looking white and pale. Michael and Carey sat on the other cot. His heart was still pounding as he looked at Michael. "Tell me what just happened to me."

Michael sat up straighter. "Remember when we visited Rolphe's cave? I told you that you had to watch your thoughts and feelings. The same advice applies here. When you looked at the tapestry, you allowed yourself to be drawn into a frightening memory."

William pushed himself up. "So it was all my doing?"

"Yes, that's what I'm saying. Arel's world reacts to whatever you think or imagine."

Annabel grabbed William's hand. "Do you understand what Michael's telling you?"

William frowned and pulled away. "Give me a break, Annabel. Of course, I understand." He sat for a long moment realizing he'd just told a lie. He wasn't clear about anything. He'd once imagined that life was simple. A person grew up and fought the ones who tormented them. They became so tough that no one could override their determination to survive and thrive. Now, that role had been snatched away. All the hatred that once fueled his life didn't work anymore, not with angelic blood in his veins. Yet, as he learned to see himself in a different light, he'd become weak, even helpless on a number of occasions.

Carey stood up and smiled down at him, knowingly. "This process needs time. To go from one way of life to another requires patience."

William sat up. "We don't have time. Arel isn't long for the world." As soon as he heard the harsh edge in his voice, he knew he was being too hard on Carey. Obviously, he needed to be grateful for the help that both Carey and Michael were providing. He gave each of the angels a quick nod. "Thank you for pulling me out of that nightmare I created."

Michael smiled. "It wasn't me. I never got a chance to help."

"Neither did I," Carey added.

William frowned. "Then who saved me?"

* * *

Arel twisted the large ruby ring that adorned his finger and gritted his teeth. He could hardly control the rage and disappointment that surged through his body. He'd been privy to William's visit to his world and observed the man's blunder. "You almost killed yourself, you fool!"

He threw back the velvet cloak that sat on his shoulders and began to pace. He'd intended to give William every chance to understand how to play the game he'd set up. He'd made sure that the rules were unbiased, but William almost burned himself out of existence before the game even started. Only Arel's quick intervention had saved the man.

"Now your stupidity has doomed us both, Will!"

At first, Arel had been relieved to give up his quest for goodness and virtue. The thought of not caring, of being cold and heartless seemed like such an easy way to live. His little speech to William rolled off his tongue so effortlessly. As he made threats to use his power to destroy anyone who got in his way, he felt like a great burden had been lifted. He could do whatever he wanted. He'd never feel any guilt or remorse.

But afterwards, as he tested the concept of being evil and distanced himself from his heart, a great emptiness took hold. That's when he came up with a new idea. The game he'd fashioned was supposed to give William a chance to be the Creator's new champion. Surely, William would demonstrate what it meant to be strong and unbending. Surely, William would succeed where Arel had failed.

Instead, William didn't last long enough to prove anything. He quickly became another victim of the Creator's foul-up. That deity who had given man a flawed nature was responsible for William's weakness.

"I'm sorry, Will," he whispered to himself, "for all the years when I argued with you, when I insisted that we lived in a world that could be redeemed. But I was wrong. Like you told me, good never wins over evil!"

The damning statement made his knees go so weak that he had to sit down. He made his way to an ornate chair that occupied a corner of his bed chamber. Made of oak, it wasn't nearly as comfortable as the recliner in his Chicago living room. Instead, it was hard and unyielding, a perfect reminder of how he had to be if he was to survive the role he'd recently chosen.

He put his finger tips to his temple and closed his eyes. After a moment, when he knew he had a clear connection to William's mind,

319

he sent out a message. "I recently saved you from yourself, Will. I let myself care about you one last time. But I can't keep caring about you. It hurts too much, and I can't stand the pain anymore. So I'm asking you . . . no . . . I'm begging you to stay away. Never enter my world again. If you do, you'll face who I really am. You'll face evil itself, my brother. And it will destroy you."

Fifty-Six

A somber silence hung over Rolphe's living room as William stared at Arel. It was a special meeting. After slumbering most of the time for days, Arel had rallied. He'd managed to stay awake long enough to respond to William's request. "Thank you for talking to me, Arel," William said in a cautious tone.

Arel remained mute, staring back with an expressionless face.

William studied Arel's physical condition and found it hard to believe that the man was a powerful creator who could fashion an entire world. In the real one, the man's body was rapidly declining. He was thin and boney, with a face that had no color, just sunken cheeks and hollowed out cavities for his dark, brooding eyes.

William offered an encouraging smile. "All you have to do is let me in, Arel. I promise to help you if you stop pushing me away."

Arel held a bony finger to his lips. "Don't!" he hissed in a low, husky voice. "I've made my choice. Now, do as I told you and leave."

"And if I refuse to listen to you, what then? Will you use your power to kill me?"

Again, Arel hesitated. It took a long time for his eyes to take on any life. When they did, they glowed for a brief moment. He shook his head and lifted his hand. He pointed at the scar on his palm. It was still raised and red, almost healed but still oozing a little blood. "Never, not in this world, my brother. I could never harm you here. But—" He paused and took a heaving, wheezy breath. "But I meant what I said. If you try to fight me in my world, you'll die. I hope I can make it a quick death. I only wish I could promise that you won't suffer, but I can't even guarantee that outcome if you insist on a battle."

William looked at his own hand, at the scar that he bore. It was red and inflamed too. It had been painful ever since he'd returned from Arel's world. "You make everything so difficult. I don't understand why you insist on thinking the worst about yourself."

Arel started to laugh, but ended up coughing. "This isn't about me or you, Will. This is about Michael and his blood, that accursed stuff that ruined both of us. As soon as I took that first sip, I was damned. When I passed it on, you were damned too."

"What are you talking about? Michael has always tried to help you."

Arel took in another gasping breath. "Michael is a good salesman, the best in creation. He's the carrot in front of the donkey, urging mankind on with a promise of virtue. Supposedly, if we humans try hard enough, we'll be like him, pure and innocent." He hesitated and closed his eyes, but there was a discernable struggle in the way he tried to keep his face from showing any emotion. When he continued and opened his eyes again, his voice was strained and on the verge of breaking. "And I did try, Will, you know I did. I tried my best to be something worthwhile, but that will never happen. Michael's perfection only makes me realize how ugly and inadequate I am in comparison."

William kept wondering what he could say to pull Arel back from the place of despair he was in. "I've been doing a lot of thinking recently. I've come up with some ideas I think might help."

Arel shook his head and slowly got to his feet. "No, no more ideas. No more talking. I'm exhausted. I'm going back to bed."

"Arel?"

Arel paused and glanced back at him. "Yes?"

"If our positions were reversed, would you let me give up on myself?"

For the first time since their conversation began, Arel became almost animated. His bent body straightened a little. "If you were suffering, Will, I'd put you out of your misery. I'd put a bullet through your head so you wouldn't be in pain any more. But unfortunately, you'll never be that kind and generous when it comes to me. The tables have turned. You're the good guy now, a champion of life. And I'll pay for your goodness. I'll go on suffering forever."

William knew Arel's strange proclamation came from the bond that still existed between them. Arel was trying to be gracious in his own, irrational way. He cleared his throat. "Yes . . . well . . . thank you, I guess."

Arel didn't seem to hear his comment. He continued out of the room. As he left, Rolphe hurried in.

"Sir?" Rolphe asked in a hesitant voice.

William sighed, feeling how uncomfortable the man always looked around him. At times, the feeling was mutual. He was still trying to forget the trauma he'd experienced at Rolphe's hand. But all in all, the man no longer felt like a threat. Maybe that was an indication that William was taking back a little of his courage and fortitude. He could view Rolphe as simply an annoyance. Now, he gave that annoyance a scowl. "Listen, Rolphe, you can call me William, okay?"

His request made Rolphe bow his head. "I can't do that."

"Yes, I know. You promised Arel, but when it's just the two of us, I'm telling you to call me William. Is that clear?"

Rolphe nodded. "Yes . . . William."

William's mind kept going back to Arel's declining condition. After finding out that Arel had saved him again, he was determined to rally his own strength. He didn't have time to chat with Rolphe, but the guy was hard to ignore. "What do you want, Rolphe?"

Rolphe quickly took a seat on the sofa. "It's Arel, sir, I mean William. He's in a very bad way."

William glared back. "I can see that."

"I just thought you should know how much he cares about you. He's keeping himself confined to the world he created for a reason. He wants to contain the evil inside of him. But he's not evil. He's so much closer to being like Michael than he knows. He just can't manage his power properly. It really scares him. But, in time, he'll shine brighter than any of us can imagine."

William sat back and touched his palm again. "He won't live long enough to shine."

Rolphe let out a ragged breath. "I know that."

William glanced up and saw the strain in Rolphe's face. "You really care about him."

"If I could, I'd take his burdens on myself, but I don't have the strength. The weight he carries is too much."

"He's completely lost touch with reality. He's mentally ill."

Rolphe's heavy brows came together. "You can see his condition in any way that you want, but I believe he can come out of the darkness he's in."

"How? I can't reason with him. And if I try to enter his world, I don't think I'm strong enough to fight him."

"Of course not. Fighting him would never work. It would mean your death."

"Thanks for that vote of confidence."

Rolphe's eyes came alive with a sparkling passion. "But I do have confidence in you. After watching you, I've come to realize that you're very powerful, too."

"Right, I was in Arel's world for two seconds and nearly killed myself."

"Exactly! If you weren't powerful, you could never have brought that tapestry alive."

"That's not what Michael said. My fear got out of hand and nearly did me in."

"Sorry, but I have another point of view."

"What are you trying to tell me?"

Rolphe dropped his head again. "I have a little experience with alternate worlds. Remember the cave?"

William sucked in a breath. "What about it?"

"When you saw me there as that repulsive animal, I didn't want to look like that. My wolf body was beautiful when my mentor, Chessa, and I roamed that world. Then she died, and I cursed those who'd killed her. When I returned to her world, it was up to me to keep it going. But my anger and rage were too great. It corrupted me. I couldn't maintain the vibration I needed, and Chessa's world turned foul."

William shrugged. "So how does that help? Arel destroyed your cave in an instant. How do I control my fear when I'm dealing with that kind of power?"

Rolphe looked up again. "Fear is like darkness. It's the absence of something. You can call that something faith or just believing in yourself. But fear can't exist in the light. If you turn on the light in yourself, the darkness will disappear." Rolphe's eyes widened, and he smiled. "And sir, when you look at Annabel, the light in you is so bright that I have to turn away."

Fifty-Seven

Arel sat in the throne room. After trying so hard to earn some wings, a crown he'd never wanted sat on his head. It was simple and tasteful. The gold base was inlaid with a circle of beautiful rubies that matched his ring. He'd chosen rubies as a reminder of the fire that burned in his gut. Even though he hoped he'd chosen an easier path, his gut was still a constant discomfort. The painful, burning sensation seemed to be letting him know that his power would always be a terrible affliction. Keeping himself busy helped him forget the pain.

It wasn't hard to occupy his time. The game he'd created demanded readiness and preparation. But he had support. After his talk with Wolfie in Mouse Park and explaining that the world was going to change, Wolfie had wanted to help. He was excited by the idea of being like Arel in size and form. But Wolfie wasn't the only one who wanted to be there for him. An army of mice from Mouse Park had volunteered their services. At first, Arel had put them all to sleep and transported them to the castle he'd created. Later, their transformation into human form became Arel's finest creative act of all.

"You'll all be like me," he had declared. "You'll all be the most intelligent and amazing of humans. And you will be my warriors."

After that announcement, mice with curly black fur became men with curly, black hair. Blond mice became blond-haired men, and so on. Each reflected aspects of their original mouse characteristics, and at the same time, each became a striking example of the human form.

Wolfie was the last to be transformed. Arel wanted to make sure that his friend was still happy with the idea. "Are you sure, Wolfie?" he asked as he crouched down in front of the mouse.

Wolfie looked at his fellow mice who were now tall and handsome men. "Oh yes, Great One, please."

"Very well," Arel replied as he snapped his fingers. In an instant, the small rodent became a man. Wolfie became General Wolf. His dark hair and well-muscled, lean physique looked perfect in the battle dress Arel had designed.

After Wolfie got over looking at himself and striding back and forth in his new body, he smiled and thanked Arel numerous times. However, the former mouse was puzzled by his weapon. A beautifully made sword hung at his side. "How do I use this implement?" he asked innocently.

At that moment, Arel realized that he'd need to educate his new warriors. He was quick to remedy the situation. He gave all his new recruits the knowledge that he had about fighting and warfare. But it wasn't only the information that he possessed presently. He reached into another lifetime for additional skills. He'd once been a knight, a cunning, victorious knight. He knew how to defeat his enemies and win battles. He shared everything with his friend, Wolfie, and his beautiful army so that their minds were transformed too.

Wolfie's expression and mannerisms changed at once. He took out his sword and examined its blade. He tested it a couple of times, slicing the air with precision strokes. "It's a fine weapon, my Lord, well balanced and suited for battle." He paused and smiled. "It's suited for winning, my Lord!"

"Yes, and you will be my Commander-in-Chief."

The winsome, new soldier knelt down before Arel. "It will be my great honor to serve you, my Lord."

Later, after all of his new soldiers were bedded down in their barracks, Arel had a moment to ponder what he'd done. His actions weren't honorable. He'd corrupted innocent mice. Yet, he took comfort in a very important fact. The spell he'd cast wouldn't be permanent. Once the game he was planning was over, the mice would return to their normal mental and physical natures. Anything unpleasant that they experienced would be forgotten.

But what about his part in it all? He'd always hated conflict. Yet, he was preparing to behave like a villain. But what choice did he have? He'd left his virtues behind him.

His final wish was that his preparations would be for nothing. He had to hold on to the idea that William would remain the rational, level-headed person he'd always been. If the man wasn't capable of being a champion of goodness, maybe he'd go back to London and forget their bond.

Arel sent out a last warning, just in case William had second thoughts. "Stay away from me, William! You can't win this battle."

* * *

William sat on the balcony with Michael. The angel didn't have much to say so they remained contemplative, each absorbed in their thoughts. Carey's entrance helped to break the silence. "Any luck?" William asked.

Carey shook his head. "Rolphe tried to wake Arel up again, but he couldn't manage it. Anyway, Rolphe will let us know if anything changes."

Michael's eyes shifted to the sky. "At this stage, Arel doesn't have the energy needed to connect to this reality anymore. He's completely focused on his own world."

William sat back with a scowl. "From what I can tell, his mind is gone. He's finally snapped."

Carey pulled out a chair from the patio table and sat down. "You did everything you could under the circumstances."

William let out a wistful laugh. "I keep thinking about my last conversation with him, how he said he'd put a bullet in my brain if our roles were reversed. But I knew his feelings were genuine. He thought such an act would be his gift to me. I've had thoughts like that too, about someone ending my life when I was in pain. But it was a self-serving idea. Arel's viewpoint feels different."

Michael smiled too. "He can't bear the idea of suffering, and he'll do just about anything to keep those he loves from pain."

William crossed his arms. "Except in Rolphe's case. He beat the hell out of that guy. Not that Rolphe didn't deserve it."

"Yes, but Arel broke his own rules. Being ruthless isn't something he could abide. Afterwards, his actions pushed him over the edge."

William studied the angel. "He says you're a con man, Michael. What do you think about that?"

Michael laughed. "I've been called worse."

William squinted back, his eyes suddenly dark and angry. "He's going to die. Doesn't that upset you? Maybe you should have stayed out of his life instead of involving yourself. At least he might have had a chance of surviving."

Michael's gaze remained steady. "I don't think so. In all probability, he'd be dead by now."

"But at least when he took that last breath, he wouldn't think of himself as the devil incarnate."

Carey straightened. "William, please believe that Michael has always wanted Arel's best. He's trying to be as helpful as possible."

William glared back. "Help? Arel is beyond help!"

Carey took another deep breath. "What I'm trying to say is that maybe Michael can help you."

"Help me do what?"

"Bring Arel back."

William got up, braced himself on the table and laughed. "Bring him back? Maybe I could have attempted a daring rescue if I still had the guts, but I feel as crippled as Arel at this point. Hell, I can't visit his world without almost doing myself in."

Michael stood up and looked at Carey. "William's right. We can't ask him to intervene again."

Carey didn't reply. He remained in his seat as Michael went back inside. When he was alone with William, he looked up. "I'm sorry if I was out of line."

"You don't look sorry, Carey. You're staring at me like you want something. And I'd be happy to oblige if I thought I could actually do something."

"It's just that I know Arel. No matter what you think, he hasn't lost his mind. He's just—" Carey paused.

William watched Carey's smooth, youthful face settle into a frown. "Arel was right about you. You can really play the role of the disappointed youth."

Carey sat back. "I'm not acting out some role for you. But perhaps I am allowing myself to feel the situation from a more emotional standpoint. Arel has tried his best to be a model for me when I pretended to be a lost kid. I don't want his life to end this way."

William shrugged. "Neither do I, but Arel is right about failure. When it grabs hold of a person, fear takes over."

"If you believe evil has the upper hand in this world or in Arel's latest approach, please reconsider. Every time Arel's used his power in some extraordinary way, his intention was to preserve your life. I'm not saying that his actions were good or bad, but his power came from his heart."

William paused and reflected on his past. "Maybe you're right about the idea of power. At times, my hatred seemed to have no boundaries, but it didn't stop Arel. When I wounded myself and he showed up, my rage and insults didn't deter him at all. He sat in a chair, refusing to budge. Nothing I did could change the fact that he cared about me."

Carey's eyes sparkled brightly again. "Yes, and in the end, you reached out to him. Now the positions are reversed."

When William didn't comment, Carey continued. "Do you think that the angelic kingdom is lacking in strength? Do you think that those who embrace the light are weak?"

"I never thought about it in quite that way, but—"

"We aren't without power, my friend. I assure you that Michael and I could assist you in ways you might consider grand."

"What do you mean by grand?"

"Arel is preparing his forces just in case you decide to play his game. He's left it up to Michael and me to come up with an army for you."

"I can't fight Arel. Rolphe assures me that I'll be a dead man if I try."

"What if you only had to have faith in yourself again? What if you only had to believe?

"Believe in what?"

Carey stood up and walked over to where William was standing. He tapped William lightly on the chest. "Believe in what's in here."

Carey's touch made William's body wobble unsteadily. He staggered back and collapsed into his chair, buzzing from head to toe. The effect wasn't unpleasant. When he put a hand to his chest, his heartbeat was strong and spirited. It pounded against his chest wall with an unbridled enthusiasm.

William took a deep breath. He hadn't felt so alive in a long time. But the feeling was one that he recognized. Whenever he'd excelled in some way or persevered when he'd been challenged, his physical vessel always felt exhilarated afterwards. If he gave himself to the feeling more completely, a sense of warmth, even joy surged through his body.

His joy gave way to a sudden understanding of how he'd been approaching life since he'd been given angelic blood. 'Loss' had become a keyword in how he handled his new life. It tainted everything, making it impossible to see himself in a way that was tangible and concrete. He was sure that loss was a part of the darkness that Rolphe had mentioned. The man was right about it feeling empty. Darkness housed fears, but nothing of substance, nothing that could be useful in creating a life that William wanted. Shame and guilt were part of the nothingness.

He looked at Carey with questioning eyes. "I want to ask about an experience I had. When I looked at the tapestry and remembered being that child who was burned, I was able to study Arel in those awful flames. His eyes were full of pain and suffering. There was nothing behind them that I could connect to."

Carey sighed. "That was a very unfortunate time for humanity. I'm sorry that you experienced what you did."

"When I first had that memory, I held Arel accountable. I know it seems ridiculous, but I felt like he should have been able to reach out to me in some way. After reliving it recently, I know he was beyond reaching out. So why can't I put the whole thing behind me?"

"Arel gave up at the end of that tragic life. In a way, his inability to hold on to who he knew himself to be, is still haunting him. That same feeling is haunting you too, especially now, when you feel like your life is out of control. The wonderful thing about the two of you is that you've always helped each other. That changed in that life when you both burned. Since that time, you've found it almost impossible to find a way back to cooperation. You want to be there for the other, but you need more of yourselves to accomplish that goal."

330

William put a hand on his chest. His heartbeat was still strong. "Maybe, and it's a big maybe, I might be remembering a little more of who I am."

When Carey smiled agreeably but looked away, William laughed and shook his head at the angel.

Carey glanced back. "What is it? Did you want to discuss anything else?"

"Don't worry, Carey, I might be talking about myself a lot, but I haven't forgotten Arel's situation."

Carey's usually gray-blue eyes sparked a bright, summer blue. "We can do this, William. Together, we can get him back."

William nodded indulgently. "I'm listening."

* * *

William watched Dantela as the small cat rubbed against Annabel's legs. Annabel responded with a smile and reached down to pet the kitten. "You have to watch her," he warned. "She's always trying to stare into people's eyes. I almost dropped her twice when she jumped up too fast."

Annabel laughed. "If you look closely, you'll see that she's special. She's one of Michael's friends."

"She's what?"

Annabel laughed. "Animals can be very loving and non-judgmental. In this situation, Dantela has been doing a very good job since Rolphe adopted her. She's helped him get in touch with his caring nature."

William squinted at the kitten again. "It seems there are always surprises in this crazy business."

Annabel picked up Dantela and held her close. "When you say crazy business, are you thinking about Arel again? William, please stay out of—"

"How can I let him die thinking he's a complete failure? What if he becomes a tormented ghost?"

"That's not how I understand what happens when a person dies. They—"

"Normally, dying is not a problem, even if a person is unbalanced, but Arel's case is a different matter."

331

"Is that what Michael or Carey told you?"

"Not exactly, but it's what I know."

"You think you know more than they do? How?"

William looked away. "I just do. Leave it at that, okay?"

"I thought you gave up on fighting Arel, that you'd lose if—"

"It's not about fighting."

Annabel set Dantella on a cushion and stood up. "Then what are you trying to tell me?"

William stood up too, letting his eyes meet Annabel's frightened gaze. "I won't leave Arel in some dark, forsaken world. Can't you understand that? I won't let him think that goodness never prevails. If I do, then maybe he's right about mankind and about me."

"And if you try to help him, wouldn't you be in danger?"

William cleared his throat. "Possibly, but I wouldn't be alone. I'd have Michael and Carey there too and—"

"Michael and Carey? Are they in on this too?" Annabel's eyes flared as she glanced at the balcony. With hands on hips, she issued a loud order. "Carey, come in here, please! I want to talk to you."

William stepped forward. "Annabel, let Carey be. This is my decision."

Carey came in from the patio and looked at Annabel, then William. "How can I help?" he asked quietly.

Annabel closed the distance between them. "Please tell me that you're not encouraging William to do something that could put his life in danger."

Carey remained calm, but his voice was tinged with enthusiasm. "I believe in William, don't you?"

Annabel's eyes glared even brighter. "I saw Arel's world, and I know what can happen there. So did you!"

William quickly moved between Carey and Annabel. "Listen to me, Annabel. Carey is trying to help Arel, but he's also trying to help me. This fear that I've been experiencing, that you've been running from, is ruining our lives. Even if Arel weren't involved, I can't be happy if I go on like this."

Annabel stepped back and put her hand to her chest. "That's fine for you, but I'm not that strong!"

William reached out for her and pulled her close. "Yes, you are. You're very strong. You just don't know it."

"But how do I stop this horrible dread I'm feeling? I've tried, but—"

William held her closer. "If you can't trust yourself, trust my decision. Help me to do what I need to do so we can have a life that's worth living."

Fifty-Eight

Rolphe lay on the bedroom floor in Myra's apartment, trying to get comfortable. He'd made a decision. After days of sitting quietly at Arel's bedside, he couldn't remain passive. Arel's life force was slowly ebbing away. He had to act before it was too late. He didn't dare use his own home as a base for what he was planning. William, Annabel and the angels were there. One of them might hinder his movements. No, he needed to be away from them when he visited Arel's world.

He glanced around Myra's bedroom. It had pretty flowered wallpaper and smelled of perfume. He'd spent many wonderful nights in the soft bed that boasted a half-dozen colorful pillows. He sighed wistfully. He might never see his lady love again. But the thought of death didn't affect him like it used to. If he didn't come back from Arel's world, the risk was acceptable. Arel needed to know the truth about himself. The man wasn't evil. He was misguided, but his heart was good and pure. Rolphe had to find a way to convince Arel of his worth. If he died trying, he'd end his days honorably.

He shut his eyes and concentrated on his target. It would be an easy task to find Arel's world. When Arel traveled there, Rolphe had secretly followed on a couple of occasions, never allowing himself to fully enter the world. He saved that trip for a time when he didn't have any other options. Now that time had come.

As he let his breath ease and he felt himself slipping into a trance, he smiled and began his prayers. "Dear God, help me to be a comfort for Arel in this time of darkness."

334

Arel was pacing around the throne room, trying to go over his list of tasks when Wolfie came rushing in. His friend's face was filled with alarm. "What is it, General?"

"An intruder showed up in our camp, my Lord. Two of my men are bringing him here."

"An intruder?"

"Yes, my Lord."

Before Arel could reply, two of his soldiers entered the room. They had hold of a tall, stocky man, dressed like a monk. His robe was rough and coarse, tied at the waist with cord. His tonsured hair, with its bald spot, reinforced the idea that he was a man of the cloth.

Arel stiffened. "Rolphe! What are you doing here?"

Without answering, Rolphe looked right and left, taking in his surroundings with an attitude of surprise and astonishment.

Arel approached him, snapping his fingers. "Rolphe! Are you listening to me?"

Rolphe's wide-eyed stare came to rest on Arel. "I knew you created something amazing, but I never expected—"

"How dare you trespass on my world!" Arel shouted. "I don't have time for tourists!"

Rolphe fell to his knees and directed his gaze at the floor. "I'm sorry, but I was so afraid for you. I wanted to let you know that I'm here to help."

"Help? How?"

"Rolphe clasped his hands in prayer. "I'm beseeching the heavenly Father and the angels to bring you out of darkness. I'm here to let you know how much I believe in you."

Arel backed up. "Great! Like I don't have enough to worry about, you show up trying to save my soul."

Rolphe raised his eyes just long enough to glance back. "Your soul doesn't need saving. It's pure and beautiful."

Arel heaved out a heavy sigh. He knew Rolphe. Once the man set his mind on something, he was like a tenacious bulldog with its jaws clamped shut. Now, the man had come on a mission, thinking he'd do something good. But Arel had no time for Rolphe or his mission. He looked at Wolfie. "Throw him in the dungeon, General Wolf!"

Wolfie blinked back in confusion and cleared his throat. "My Lord, I'm not aware of any dungeon."

Arel stared back for a long moment, realizing his mistake. Then he turned on Rolphe. "Hell and damnation, Rolphe!" he shouted. "Do you think that I have energy to spare coming up with accommodations for you?"

When Rolphe remained mute, Arel started pacing. "Oh, never mind. Why do I waste my breath?" He snapped his fingers a couple of times and glared at the two soldiers. "There, now we have a dungeon. Take him away."

When the two men still looked confused, Arel walked over to Wolfie. "Why aren't your men doing as they're told, General?"

"Again, I'm sorry, my Lord, but how do we find the dungeon?"

Arel looked away, cursing the fact that he had so many things to think about. William's mood had shifted. The man was planning on playing Arel's game. It was a disturbing situation that had Arel staying up all night with worry. Would he end up killing his brother, the man he cared about more than himself? He cursed again, wondering if being evil was any easier than being the good guy he'd always tried to be.

When he looked up, he saw the two soldiers holding on to Rolphe. They were waiting for directions. With all that was happening he'd made a second mistake. He'd forgotten to create stairs leading to the newly fashioned, lower level. After a moment of collecting his thoughts, he snapped his fingers again. When he turned back to Wolfie, he forced himself to keep his tone civil. "You'll find a new flight of steps by the entrance. Please have your men use them, General Wolf."

* * *

Carey approached William cautiously. The man had been edgy for the last couple of days, trying to prepare himself for an encounter with Arel. Unfortunately, he wasn't sleeping much and his temper could be short. Now, he was sitting on the living room sofa, deep in thought. Annabel was next to him, keeping herself busy with a knitting project. Carey gave her a quick smile before he tapped William's shoulder.

"What is it?" William asked impatiently.

"I thought you'd want to be informed. It seems that Rolphe left in the early hours of the morning. He had his shields up so we wouldn't notice his absence. When I went into Arel's bedroom to give him a break, I found a note." He handed it to William.

William looked at his watch. "It's noon. That means he's been gone for at least a half a day." He unfolded the note, read it and tossed it aside. "Great. He told us that he was going to side with Arel. Now he's gone and done it."

Annabel put her knitting on the cushion and picked up the note. After she read it, she looked at William. "I don't think Rolphe wants to hurt anyone. It says he wants to do God's work, William."

Carey nodded. "I agree. Rolphe's intentions were good. Unfortunately, his plan has backfired. When Michael looked into the matter, he found out that Arel locked Rolphe away in a dungeon."

William stood up. "But he's not really locked up, is he? So if we find Rolphe and wake him up, he'll be all right." William started for the door. "I bet he's gone to Myra's. Let's go see if we can get him back."

When Carey and William arrived at Myra's flat, Carey tried the door and found that it wasn't locked. William pushed him aside and quickly started looking for Rolphe. He didn't have to look very far. Rolphe was sitting on the sofa. He was clearly disoriented and mumbling to himself.

Carey rushed over to the man and tried to get his attention. "Rolphe, are you okay?" When Rolphe didn't answer, Carey knelt down in front of him. "Rolphe, it's Carey. We're here to take you home."

William came over too. "What's he saying?"

Carey looked up. "He's praying for Arel."

William frowned. "Look deeper, Carey. See if you can find out why he's acting like this."

After a moment, Carey stood up. "I think I know what happened. After Arel imprisoned him, Rolphe started beseeching God to help Arel in a prayer ritual. Unfortunately, Arel heard his continued supplications. He couldn't get them out of his head so he banished Rolphe from his world. In his haste to get rid of Rolphe, he kind of affected Rolphe's mind. I don't think Rolphe will be returning to Arel's world any time soon."

"I see. Then I suggest we leave him here for the time being, if you think he'll be okay."

"Yes, I believe he's in a kind of trance. It's rather incredible that he's still praying. Arel tried to stop him, but Rolphe wouldn't back down. Trance or no, Rolphe is determined to help."

"And I'm determined to finish this game Arel's playing. Let's go back to Rolphe's apartment. I need to talk to you about something."

Carey nodded as they started to leave. "Of course."

As they were about to shut the door to Myra's apartment, Rolphe's murmured prayers rose in volume. "And bless William! Keep him safe from fear and darkness."

* * *

When they got back to Rolphe's flat, William turned to Carey. "I know I can't put off Arel's game any longer. However, I haven't been wasting time these past days. I've been thinking about what Arel has planned. I also visited his world briefly."

Carey sat down across from him. "Do you want to tell me about what happened?"

"It was very disturbing."

"Did it have to do with Arel?"

"No, not with Arel directly. I saw what he was doing, and it affected me in a way I hadn't expected." William paused, thinking about how he'd stood in one of the towers of the beautiful castle that Arel had made for him. It was the perfect place to observe Arel's dark fortress.

But William had also been given a means of viewing Arel's actions close up. He'd found a large, viewing screen waiting for him. The device didn't belong in a medieval world. Neither did the modern glass in the windows of the castle, but Arel took license when he wanted.

William sighed. "I think Arel wanted me to see what I'd be up against if I dared any opposition."

He hesitated again, recalling Arel's training exercises. They were splendid and horrible. He'd watched Arel, astride his great, black stallion that he called Frick. The man had an ability to instill order and discipline and even looked like a sovereign lord. He wore shining armor and a long, flowing, purple cloak that streamed out behind him as he rode back and forth checking on his men. He corrected any soldier who was out of place or not paying attention. He seemed harsh, but fair. It was clear that his men looked up to him with admiration and a blind need to serve.

William barely recognized Arel's chief supporter. The mouse known as Wolfie had been turned into a tall, impressive man known as General Wolf. He was never far from Arel's side, riding a huge, reddish-brown, chestnut horse. With its heavy, black mane and tail, it pranced excitedly and snorted with impatience, wanting to do what it was trained to do, prove its power and fighting abilities in battle.

But seeing Arel and his army wasn't what bothered William as he recounted his visit. He gave Carey a troubled glance. "Something happened to me when I was in Arel's world."

Carey sat back and nodded. "You look like you're still upset."

William shrugged, but he couldn't shake the unwanted feelings that had attached themselves to his mind and body. "While I watched Arel, I had a vision of myself. I'm sure it was from a past life." He twisted in his seat as vivid details of a warrior filled his mind. As he allowed the vision to take hold, his bones grew heavy. They were a warrior's bones, and they were weighed down with the blood of the men he'd killed on the battlefield. "It's like I've tapped into some inner resource of knowledge I shouldn't have."

"About what?"

"About conducting a war." William studied his clasped fists. He'd never thought about how to plan a campaign or command an army. Yet, he knew so much about the subject. More importantly, he knew that he'd once reveled in the power, in the sensation of having authority over others. The feelings left him wanting relief from a time he should never have remembered.

He looked at Carey, meeting the angel's searching eyes. "In the vision I had, I killed my brother. He was the heir to the throne, and I wanted to take his place. In a particular battle, we fought shoulder to shoulder until victory was ours. Then I turned on him and ran him through with my sword."

Carey sucked in a breath. "That is a terrible memory."

"My triumph was short and bitter. My best friend stabbed me in the back, literally. I lost all that I'd lusted after. The throne, the lands, the woman I loved, everything was gone in an instant. While I lay dying, I thought about my brother. He was a good man. He taught me everything about being a warrior, about being honorable. But his values didn't take hold. I let myself be corrupted by my greed. Before he died, he opened his eyes and saw me lying close by. There was so much pain and disappointment in the look he gave me."

Carey's eyes brightened. "That was another life. It's not who you are now."

William looked away. What if he lost control when he came up against Arel? What if Arel was right about evil? What if it still lived in William's bloody bones? Could he entertain corruption again? After a moment of reflection, he put an end to the questions. He unclasped his fingers and stood up. "Whatever happens in this game of his, I won't fight Arel. And I won't hurt his soldiers. They're mice, being ordered around by a madman. I won't raise a weapon against them."

"I agree with you," Michael said as he walked into the room. He smiled. "But what if you could free them from the spell they're under? Would you agree to that?"

Fifty-Nine

Tim stood outside the spare bedroom and listened. Peggy had come up with a plan for Kevin's sleep problems. Tim hadn't thought Kevin would agree to her proposal, but he'd been wrong. Brother and sister were getting along better than Tim could remember. He suspected that Kevin was trying to be supportive when he said he'd let Peggy help him. And maybe Peggy could help. She'd been reading up on hypnosis and suggestibility. Tim was pleased to note that her new project had unexpected benefits. Peggy was worrying less and seemed generally more positive. All her extra energy was directed at helping Kevin.

Tim wondered about the first session that Peggy was conducting. In the end, his curiosity won out. It was an interesting situation. Kevin seemed to be letting Peggy use him as a guinea pig. Tim didn't know what to expect, but he carefully pushed the door open a couple of inches and peeked in.

At first glance, everything looked very tranquil. Kevin lay stretched out on the guest bed. Peggy sat in a chair with her back to Tim. Her quiet manner and soft voice made Tim smile. It was a well-known fact that Peggy could be very vocal when she had an agenda, but not this time. After a couple of minutes, he heard Kevin begin to snore. Peggy didn't seem to mind. In fact, she continued on as if Kevin could still hear her.

After a few more minutes of observation, Tim found that he was getting sleepy too. In fact, his eyes wanted to close as he continued to listen. He felt so tired that he decided on a nap.

He backed away from the door as quietly as possible. Once he was in his own bedroom, he didn't bother to take off his clothes. He fell onto the bed with a deep weariness. He dozed off at once.

What happened next was strange but intriguing. He woke up in a garden. It wasn't one he recognized. He glanced around, taking in the flowers and trees. Nearby, a squirrel scampered around in some dry leaves. It took a moment to acclimate, but he let out a low whistle. "I think this is a lucid dream!"

Peggy had read about such a phenomenon and explained that a person could do what they wanted in such a dream. Tim had never given the idea much thought, but he tested the theory by crouching down and touching the grass. It felt as real as the stuff growing in his front yard. He checked out the clouds next. One of them reminded him of what could be a chubby elephant. As he concentrated on it, the cloud changed and became more defined. Soon the shape of a very large pachyderm came into view. As he enjoyed the idea of making more just like it, a parade of elephants could be seen traipsing across the sky.

Tim tried to contain his excitement. He didn't want to wake himself up. Instead, he intended to do something more meaningful than creating elephant clouds. Arel came to mind. Peggy was always wondering how he was. Tim wondered about his friend too. William and Michael didn't offer much information during their phone calls.

Tim sat down on a bench, letting his mind expand with possibilities. If he could connect with Arel in his dream, maybe he could assure Peggy and himself that the man was doing okay. He'd no sooner had the idea when everything shifted. He wasn't sitting in a park anymore. He was in a large room, sitting at a table. Arel sat at the head, staring at him as if he was a ghost.

"Tim? Is it really you?" Arel asked.

Tim couldn't answer. Instead he was fixated on Arel. The man had a crown on his head and an outfit that belonged in a movie about knights. "Where am I?" he asked. "And why are you dressed like that?"

Arel's face went pale, and then he flushed with embarrassment. "You're dreaming, aren't you?"

Tim nodded. "I think I am. But I've never had this kind of dream before." He rubbed his hands over the arms of his chair. The wood was smooth to the touch. When he glanced around, he scowled. "This is the first time anything like this has happened to me."

Arel removed his crown and set it on the table. He slumped back in his chair. "I don't understand it. I try and try to keep people out, but nobody pays any attention. I feel like I'm running some ridiculous bed and breakfast."

Tim pushed back his massive, oak chair with difficulty and stood up. He approached Arel with a smile. "It's okay. This is just a dream. Don't upset yourself."

Arel nodded, but his eyes were filled with so much anxiety that Tim was concerned. "So anyway, I think it's time to wake myself up. Maybe we can talk soon. Peg and I have called you on a number of occasions, but Michael keeps putting us off. I'll insist on speaking to you the next time."

Arel's eyes flared. "No, don't do that. Michael's right. I need time to rest." He stalled for a long moment. "And Tim?"

"Yes?"

"Maybe the next time you do any lucid dreaming, you'll think about visiting a motorcycle shop instead of looking for me. You can take a bike out for a spin."

"Good idea, I'd like that. But before I go, I want you to know that Peg and I will be happy when you return home. I hope it's soon."

Arel managed a genuine smile. "Thanks. Now wake up in your bed, my friend. Forget about me."

Tim wondered about how to get out of the dream when Arel snapped his fingers. It seemed to do the trick. When he opened his eyes, he was in his bed again.

* * *

Tim sipped his beer thoughtfully as Kevin waited for an answer. After he placed his drink on the table, he frowned. "I don't know what to say, Kev, except that lucid dreaming is different. It feels as real as this place. And I guess you can go where you want to go or visit anybody you want. I just thought about Arel and I was instantly sitting at a table with him. Of course, like I explained, he didn't look like the Arel we know, but he acted just as nervous and jumpy."

Kevin fingered his empty glass. "Would you do it again?"

"I don't know. Maybe it's better if we don't mess around with stuff like dreams."

"I disagree. Do you think I'd be letting Peggy monkey around with my mind if I wasn't desperate?"

Tim smiled. "I thought you were trying to be the nice, big brother."

"I'm not that nice. But ever since I told Peggy about my nightmares, she's been trying to find a solution. Now I'm kinda stuck with letting her help."

"Is she helping?"

"Yeah, I guess she is. I'm sleeping pretty good again. But I'm not doing what you're doing, visiting Arel in some grand castle. That could be fun."

"I didn't plan on it. It just happened after listening in on Peggy's suggestions."

Kevin returned an annoyed scowl. "You listened in?"

Tim laughed. "Yeah, I love my wife dearly, but you are a friend. I thought I better make sure you didn't go into some sleep coma if Peggy got carried away with her ideas."

"So why didn't I get to do what you did?"

"I don't know, but maybe you could."

"How?"

Tim laughed again. "Ask Peggy. She's the dream expert."

* * *

Peggy closed the front door with a smile. Tim would be busy for a couple of hours with a list of errands. Now she could talk to Carol without any interference. Not that Tim ever interfered, but still, she wanted her conversation with Carol to be a woman-to-woman talk. "Coast is clear," she announced as she returned to the kitchen.

Carol was at the counter, refilling her coffee cup. "What's that smile?" she asked with one of her own. "Why did you want to get rid of Tim?"

Peggy sat down at the table. "For the same reason that you left Kevin at home, taking care of Ariel."

Carol gave her a narrowed gaze. "You want to talk about what you're doing with Kevin, don't you?"

Peggy sat up proudly. "You bet I do. I'm so happy that I've been able to help him. I didn't think the day would ever come, but we've found a way to be great friends, not just brother and sister."

"I think it's wonderful too. So why don't you want Tim around?"

"Because I also want to talk about Tim too. He never hides anything from me, but recently he's been acting funny, like he doesn't want me to know something."

"Like what?"

"Kevin gave me a clue. We've had a couple of sleep sessions recently, right? Then all of a sudden, he started asking me about taking charge of his dreams, and if I knew how to help him. I think he wants to know about lucid dreaming."

"How's that a clue?"

"Because I heard him talking to Tim outside the other day. And Tim said something about dreams too. He said he was thinking of trying something again, but I didn't hear the last part clearly enough to know what he meant."

Carol folded her arms across her chest. "So you've been spying on them?"

Peggy avoided Carol's eyes. "Oh please, if I do overhear something once in a while, it's for everyone's best. I need to stay informed."

"So just ask Tim about what you heard."

"But I don't want him to know I'm listening."

Carol laughed. "Trust me, Tim will understand."

"I know, but he tries his best to keep me from worrying. Maybe he's afraid to confide in me."

"Peggy, as your friend, I think you should come clean. It'll be best in the long run."

* * *

Peggy took Carol's advice that evening. She asked Tim about what she'd overheard. When Tim explained everything, Peggy didn't know how to react. She sat on the edge of the bed waiting for him to finish

345

brushing his teeth. When he came out of the bathroom, she sat up straighter. "First of all, like I said before, I didn't want to pry. So I hope you understand my—"

Tim walked over to his side of the bed. "It's fine, honey. In a way, it's a relief that you know what happened. And let's face it, I was spying on your session with Kevin in the first place. I want to apologize for that."

"It's nice that you were interested."

Tim smiled. "You're not the only curious person around. I was impressed with what you were saying. You really know your stuff. Kevin said he's sleeping better now."

"Well, after all my nightmares and Kevin's recent problems, I think knowing more about sleep and dreams is necessary. In fact, after Carol's visit, I did some more research. I learned a lot more about lucid dreaming. And it's something a person can learn to do."

"Really? Kevin will love hearing that. I think he wants to do some exploring."

"I hope he doesn't get his hopes up too much. You slipped into one naturally, but with some people, it can take quite a while to learn to do it." Peggy paused. "You said you visited Arel, only he was in some dream kingdom."

"I don't know what more to say about my visit."

"But Arel was alright when you saw him."

"Yes, he looked different in the way he was dressed, but he looked fit enough."

Peggy lay back on the bed and pulled up the cover. "At least he's fine in your dreams. In real life, I have my doubts. It's been too long since we got to talk to him."

Tim reached out for her hand. "I promise that if I have any more dreams with Arel in them, I'll make sure to tell you about them."

"And maybe I'll give myself a few suggestions. If I'd known I could reach Arel in the dream world, I'd have practiced lucid dreaming instead of worrying about him."

Tim squeezed her hand. "Can you imagine Arel's reaction if we all started visiting him in some dream world?"

Peggy snickered. "It would serve him right. If he won't keep us informed about how he's doing, I say that extraordinary measures are in order."

346

Sixty

Arel sat on his throne, appreciating the comfortable seat. It seemed pointless to try to be too authentic with his surroundings. Who would really notice or care? So he'd enhanced the chair with a soft, foam cushion. But nothing could soften the fact that he was losing control of his world.

First, Rolphe, and then Tim, proved that he didn't have enough energy to keep everything going without a hitch. Their sudden appearances made him wonder about his power. Maybe he didn't have as much of the stuff as he thought. On the other hand, he had to look after all of the soldiers in his army. Keeping them well-fed and housed properly required a lot more focus and effort than maintaining Mouse Park with its tiny inhabitants.

"My Lord!" Wolfie called out from the other end of the hall.

Arel noticed his friend's masculine voice. It filled the room with a deep, forceful tone. It wasn't anything like the squeaky, high-pitched voice that Arel had enjoyed before Wolfie became a man. As the days passed, the former rodent was becoming quite the formidable soldier.

Of course, Arel had changed too. He wasn't caring for tiny mice anymore. He was in charge of battle-ready warriors. As Wolfie approached, he gave his general a quick nod of acknowledgement. "Yes, what is it, General Wolf? Is everything alright with the men?"

"Yes, my Lord, I made sure everyone was bedded down for the night."

"Good, now you should get some sleep too."

"Thank you, but if you don't mind, I have a question before I take to my quarters. I wondered when the battle is going to begin."

"That's not up to me. It depends on William."

"William? My William?"

"Yes, that's right."

"But he's our friend."

"This is not about friendship. It's about something much more important."

Wolfie stiffened and stepped back. "Is there something more important than friendship?"

Arel hesitated. What was he supposed to say? How was he supposed to explain the idea of good versus evil? In Wolfie's natural world, such concepts didn't exist. "Never mind all that, General Wolf. We'll talk about it another time."

Later, when Arel retired to a small room that adjoined the great hall, he tried to relax. He succeeded in some small ways. He even managed to calm his breath. His chest rose and fell in a steady rhythm. Only his mind jumped from rock to rock in its fast-moving stream of thought.

He began by going over his military plans. Next, he'd reflected on how much he missed Mouse Park. Finally, he'd doubled back to his actions on the training grounds. He was playing out the role of an exacting, military marshal who was preparing for battle.

He wondered how things got so out of hand. His plans had started out so innocently. He created his world because he was in love with all things beautiful, yet he'd ended up with a tough, no-nonsense militia.

Sometimes, he didn't recognize Wolfie. More than just the mouse's physical form had changed. Under the strain of training soldiers for long hours each day, Wolfie became very serious. His sweetness was lost to his dedication. He prided himself on carrying out Arel's orders, his need for self-control and discipline. The innocent creature that Arel had treasured was long gone. In fact, there wasn't a sweet, former mouse in the lot.

Of course, it was all Arel's doing. He'd made men out of mice, fighting men. He excused himself with the idea that the mice were under a spell. But what if something happened and that spell was never broken, what then?

He began to reconsider his harsh judgments about the Creator. He'd jumped to conclusions about how things came to be. But maybe the Supreme Being blundered into something unplanned too.

Maybe evolution took an unexpected turn, and the Creator had to bravely go forward from the Garden of Eden, hoping for a better day.

In any case, he was faced with a situation, and he didn't feel like he could turn back. The day of reckoning was at hand. He could feel it. In fact, as he let himself tune into William's mind, his heart sped up with unwanted anticipation. Events were in motion. The battle that General Wolf had asked about would commence in the morning.

Sixty-One

Annabel followed William into the storage room. After a discussion with Michael and Carey, William decided it was time to engage Arel. Annabel didn't agree with his decision, but she'd stayed quiet during the round table meeting. She shut the door behind her, with a hand on her pounding heart. "William, before you do anything, you have to know that you can't save Arel. People have to want help and ultimately help themselves. That's one piece of wisdom I still retain."

William glanced at her and walked over to the one, small window in the room. "I care about Arel, and I'll do whatever I can to help, but I'm not trying to save him."

Annabel walked over to where he stood. "Then why are you going to play his game when it's so dangerous? You almost died just looking at that tapestry scene. You got pulled in so quickly."

"But I've learned a lot from that experience. However, you're right, sometimes I'm almost as bad as Arel when it comes to holding on to fear and pain."

"So you're human like everyone else."

William turned and glared back. "That's the last thing I want to be. I've always hated the idea of weakness and acting like some frightened fool. It's never served me to let life or tough situations intimidate me."

Annabel turned and sat down on the bed. "We've had this discussion before."

"I guess we have, but I'm more determined than ever to prove something to myself."

"What is more important than protecting your life? What makes you want to put yourself at risk?"

"I have to feel good about who I am. I have to know I'm still capable of determining my destiny. Besides, if Arel is right about evil and fear being more powerful than anything else, life isn't worth living, not to me. I'd rather be dead than live in a world where I'm powerless."

Annabel's brows furrowed as she let out a sigh. "Then I want to help. I'll help you play this stupid game."

William sat down next to her. "You can help, but I want you to do it here."

"How?"

"Don't let yourself give into your fear. If you believe in yourself and in me, I'll feel your strength no matter what I'm facing."

Annabel knew William was right, but when she heard a knock on the door, she panicked. The knock was Michael's signal that the game she'd been dreading was about to begin. What she didn't know was how strong she was or wasn't. She'd developed a very bad habit of thinking the worst when she was scared. She grabbed hold of William's arm. "You're better off without me. So don't let yourself connect with whatever I'm feeling, promise me."

"No, I won't promise that. I believe in you. That's why we're together."

"But, William, what if—"

"No excuses, Annabel. Arel has given us both a gift. It's not the kind of gift anyone wants to find under the Christmas tree, but it's still a gift. We can use it as something that strengthens our faith in ourselves or we can let it destroy us. But no matter what happens, I have a feeling that the outcome is up to us."

* * *

Tim tried not to let Peggy see his excitement as he climbed into bed. He was careful to follow his normal routine. He wished Peggy sweet dreams and kissed her cheek as he usually did before he turned out the light. Fortunately, Peggy was tired and ready to give herself over to a restful sleep. She kissed him back with her eyes half closed. After Tim was sure she was asleep, he went over his plan. First, he needed to relax as much as possible. Second, he set an intention to be aware in his dreams again.

Being aware in his sleep had been one of the most amazing experiences Tim had had in a long time. If he could perfect the art, he saw lots of opportunities for more adventure. Kevin was working on a similar goal. He was anxious to see the incredible world where Tim had met with Arel. They had even come up with a possible scenario. If one of them had a lucid dream, they would contact the other in the dream state. They would try to bring the other person along for the ride.

Tim had been practicing relaxation and intention-setting each night since he'd had his first experience. Now, as he settled into the soft comfort of his bed, he had an unexpected feeling surge through his body, a powerful sense of well-being. It was so inviting that it shifted his focus. Instead of thinking about dreaming, he listened to Peggy's steady breathing with a new sense of appreciation. He realized how fortunate he was. He had the most loving of women as his wife and a daughter he adored. As he counted his blessings, dreaming didn't seem nearly as important as being happy with what he already had. It was enough to make him forget about intentions and doze off with a smile on his face.

* * *

Kevin didn't know he was dreaming until Tim showed up. As soon as he saw his friend, he smiled. "You did it!"

Tim laughed as he came over and shook Kevin's hand. "I think I stopped trying so hard, and look, here I am. Then I thought of you."

Kevin stared at their clasped hands. "It feels so real." He glanced around. He was in a garden. "And listen to the birds! And the sky is a deeper blue than I've ever seen before."

"Would you like to see Arel's place?" Tim asked with a grin.

Kevin didn't have time to answer before the scene suddenly shifted. He stood on a lofty scaffold of sorts. He was fortunate not to have a fear of heights, but he grabbed hold of the railing anyway. From his vantage point, he could look out over a large expanse of barren field. The dark, lifeless land lay between two hilltop fortifications. One fortress was unsightly, with a charred exterior.

The other castle was the most beautiful structure Kevin had ever seen. Its walls were fashioned from a white crystalline stone that sparkled in spite of the gloomy atmosphere. As he tried to take it all in, a familiar voice called out a welcome. He turned and saw Michael. The man stood a few feet away, clad in gleaming armor. Kevin stiffened when he noted the glow coming off of Michael's face. "Why are you dressed like that? Is this some kind of dream festival?"

Tim seemed just as surprised by Michael's appearance. "How do you get your eyes to sparkle like that?" he asked in an uneasy voice.

Michael smiled back as Carey joined them. The younger man reached out to shake hands with Tim, then Kevin. "Hi guys! Nice to see you again," he said in a cheery voice.

Tim's brows were bunched as he gave Carey a quick inspection. "I've never seen you out of jeans. Now, you look quite impressive in that armor."

Carey smiled back. "So you two found us in your dreams. Isn't that something, Michael?"

Michael nodded to Tim and Kevin. "Remember the dream part if you experience something you don't expect."

The advice was barely out of Michael's mouth when a trumpet blast assaulted the airways and Kevin's body. He jumped back as shock waves from the sound made his hair stand on end. When he looked to Michael for an explanation, Michael pointed to the field below.

Kevin stepped up to the rail again. Grasping it with tight fists, he watched as large numbers of soldiers marched out of the two fortresses. Both sides appeared to be well-armed and ready for battle. He recognized the leader of the dark fortress. "Tim! Check it out! I think that's Arel riding some giant horse."

Tim's wide-eyed stare was trained on the troop movements too. "And look at the other side. That's William. His hair is long, and he's wearing armor, but I still recognize him."

As Kevin continued to observe the two armies taking their positions on the field, the feeling of an impending battle took hold of him. Like the soldiers below, he stood at attention. Even if it was part of some crazy dream-pageant, he couldn't contain his excitement. He yelled out to the man riding the large, black stallion. "Arel! Arel! This is some kind of show! People would pay big money to see something like this. Good for you, old buddy!"

Far below, the knight he was shouting at seemed to hear him. Instead of waving back, the man quickly lowered his visor and trotted off behind one of the barricades.

Kevin shrugged. "That's Arel for you. He's really rather shy when you think about it. Right, Tim?"

When Kevin glanced at Tim for an opinion, he noticed that his friend and the surroundings were getting fuzzy. He rubbed at his eyes, but it didn't help. The scene began to fade. In the next moment, he woke up, back in his bed. His heart still raced with the thrill of what he'd seen. He almost woke up Carol, certain that she'd love to hear about his exploits. He stopped himself just in time. He decided to contact Tim the next morning instead. It was a Saturday, and they could take the babies to the park. While they were there, they could compare notes.

Sixty-Two

Arel straightened in his saddle, observing the scene in front of him. The battle had been raging for hours on a field of mud and muck. Horses screamed. Weapons clashed. Warriors used raw courage to grimly push themselves beyond what they thought they could endure. The field itself was barely lit as a diminished sun limped across the sky, looking like it too was a victim of the sword.

But this wasn't an ordinary battle. It might have looked like a scene from the days of knights, but there were no corpses or severed body parts scattered about the battlefield. The weapons, be they sword or lance, didn't slash flesh or shatter bone. Their effectiveness was measured by a different standard. In this unique kind of warfare, everything centered around energy.

Arel let his gaze settle on the person in charge of the army he was fighting. When the battle began, William had appeared strong and more capable than Arel had imagined. It gave Arel hope that he'd be proven wrong. He'd championed the idea of goodness for too long to really want evil to win.

His ego did suffer a little when William immediately cut through one of his energy barriers. He'd let his mind wander for a moment and hadn't sufficiently maintained the shield that protected his front lines. His men were soon under attack. Quite a number were lost. Well, not exactly lost. They disappeared.

The rules were simple and part of an agreement between Arel and William. Whenever William bested any of Arel's men, they would be ferried away by Michael's helpers. Afterwards, they would be released from Arel's spell. Michael promised that all would be relocated in a very suitable and heavenly mouse world.

If Arel's men got the upper hand, William lost his angelic helpers. They had to immediately leave the field. Focus and keeping one's mind on what was needed was everything. It was what directed the energy involved in the battle.

At first, Arel comforted himself with the fact that none of his men actually suffered physically. However, something shifted when his men all looked to him for help. Each one of them had promised to fight valiantly. Each one had trained for long hours. As those training sessions wore on, individuals bonded and became a cohesive group of warriors. That closely knit army expected Arel to lead them to victory. When William seized the upper hand, they didn't understand why Arel was hanging back and not being more aggressive.

Arel knew that they were right to question him. He'd set up the game, and he was supposed to do whatever it took to win. He tried his best to dissuade William from taking up the challenge. If William ignored his warning, Arel had no choice but to ignore their ties. Leniency had no place when one was unleashing darkness. As soon as he made a decision to give the battle his best, he began to fight for real.

* * *

As the day and the battle wore on, William felt his mind and body losing ground. When he'd entered Arel's world, he hadn't expected everything to move so quickly. He'd barely had time to acclimate to the foreign surroundings when he was told to bring his troops forward onto the field of battle.

Earlier, he'd refused most all the armor plating that a knight normally wore. It felt clumsy and burdensome. The only piece he retained was the breastplate. As for the rules that governed the game of battle, he'd been given clear instructions. They prompted him to update his attitude very quickly. Doubt about his abilities had no place on the battlefield.

Arel was a master of focus. William would have to be just as capable. His confidence was bolstered when he thought about his scientific aptitude. Annabel said he was so much more than just a scientist, but he knew that being a man of science could be helpful. It meant staying attentive to solving a problem. It had taken years to understand the virus that Rolphe had passed on to him. During all that time, William never let himself falter in his quest. His mind maintained a fixed ability to stay solution-oriented while never giving into crippling doubts.

When entering a field of battle, he had to be just as unbending in his resolve. After Michael's briefing on what to expect, William couldn't let anything weaken his belief in himself or those who would help him.

William was in charge of an army of angels. When he first saw his warriors go into formation, he was overcome with their splendor. All were suited up in luminous armor. Each one of them proudly bore William's red and gold colors. Their flowing hair and glowing faces were resplendent against the ugly, sterile grounds where they would fight. He didn't think their kind belonged in such dismal surroundings. Angels were meant to adorn shimmering, crystal cities where ascended masters walked the streets.

But he'd underestimated his forces. He soon found out that angels could be tough, no-nonsense fighters. When they locked on to a purpose, they were almost unstoppable. The 'almost' snag in their drive was William. If he lost focus, if his energy was diverted by fear or anger, they were not only stoppable, but he could lose them completely. They vanished individually or in groups, depending on how much energy he squandered on negativity or inattentiveness. Unable to stay on the field, the angels rejoined Michael, their Commander-In-Chief.

William had help from another unexpected source. He sat astride a magnificent, white mare named Boda. Being of angelic origin, the horse was acutely tuned into her rider's every thought and emotion. Each time she'd felt William faltering in weariness and fatigue, she'd swung her head round and had used her teeth to get his attention back where it belonged.

William was both grateful and irritated by her actions, not knowing whether to thank her or cuss her out when his leg suffered from her painful nips. But she was sure footed, fast and nimble, turning on a dime when he had to change directions. Still, William needed more than an angelic horse if he was going to successfully meet the challenge he faced.

Arel and his forces weren't there to play nice. After all, Arel was testing out the powers of darkness. He seemed to have given himself wholly over to being the bad guy. William wondered if he was enjoying the role. When Arel appeared on the field, he looked damn scary. He and his men had worn shiny armor during their drills. Now they were decked out in blackened suits. Arel's helmet had an added black plume. A flash of color was displayed in his flowing, purple cloak. When he cantered about the field on his grand horse, his men couldn't miss his presence or ignore his orders. They were bellowed out in a strong, commanding voice.

There were supposed to be rules that governed conduct, but Arel ignored them and so did his men. Even if there was no bloodshed, it wasn't easy for William to watch one of Arel's brutal soldiers trying to take the legs out from under one of his noble, cavalry steeds. Because the game was supposed to be realistic, there was always the compulsory scream of the horse as it disappeared from the field.

Sound could be a terrible device on a battlefield. William lived in a modern world of car horns and traffic, but as a child, he'd known the terrified cries of animals in pain. His father hunted with dogs that weren't above tearing apart an innocent fox. Arel was aware of that fact and used it to his advantage when he trained his soldiers. William's only defense was to remind himself of the truth. The brutes in Arel's army were brainwashed innocents. They were following orders and trying to serve their master. Unfortunately, they were really good at doing just that.

Arel also used other tactics. Fireballs were catapulted through the air and exploded on impact. The energy shields that William maintained around himself and his comrades were the only things that protected them from the blasts. William's controlled inner rage and anger wanted to explode too when he was caught off guard and lost dozens of his warriors. But he couldn't allow any such weakness to be expressed. It would only strengthen Arel's position.

The strain shown on William's pale face as his belief in himself and his abilities was battered and pounded by his relentless foe. When he feared that he would fall, he'd call out to Michael. Over and over, the magnificent angel would instantly be there for him, with his hand on William's heart, strengthening it, readjusting it's rhythm like a divine pacemaker. It helped, but William wondered if anything would be enough to get him through a battle that seemed to go on forever.

William didn't dare focus on another pressing issue. He and Arel were exceptions when it came to actual bodily harm. If injured, he'd carry that injury back into his normal world. He'd promised himself not to harm Arel, but would Arel and his men respect his person?

* * *

Rolphe was barely aware of Myra's apartment as he continued to pray. He repeatedly asked for the assistance of the Creator and His angels. While Rolphe's lips moved in reverence, his gift of sight was focused on Arel's world. The war that he'd feared had started. As he zeroed in on the battlefield, his prayers increased in volume. He hated looking at the violence, but he couldn't make himself turn away.

Amid the battlefield's ugliness, he located Arel. The man sat erect and sure on his black stallion. He traversed the field of battle confidently. In return, his men looked up to him with veneration. When Rolphe tuned into their minds, he felt how deep their devotion went. They knew Arel was their protector, and they were willing to give him everything in return, even their very lives.

The most fervent among them was a man who rode at Arel's side. Arel referred to him as General Wolf. As Rolphe watched the intent man go about his duties, he had a new respect for this mouse turned soldier. General Wolf had a true and faithful nature. He was always attentive to Arel's safety, constantly making sure to keep his master out of harm's way if at all possible.

When Rolphe readjusted his focus to the other side of the field, he didn't see William at first. He was nearly blinded by the splendor of the angels who were fighting under the man's command. They were resplendent in the dreary world of warfare, and they were trying to protect someone in their midst.

Rolphe panicked when he finally located William. Unlike Arel, the man looked tired and worn. There was no enthusiasm in his stricken face, only a look of struggle and need to do what needed doing. Rolphe understood how difficult it was for William. When a person's heart wasn't in something, it made them weak and vulnerable. He feared for William's life.

He'd no sooner had the thought when he saw William's horse rear back. A ball of fire exploded nearby and debris was flying in all directions. William wasn't prepared for his mount's sudden reaction. He tried to keep his seat and failed. He fell backwards, flailing helplessly at the air and then slamming to the uneven ground. When his head struck a rock, he stopped moving.

The scene was so upsetting that Rolphe lost his focus. He was back to praying even more desperately, trying to block out what he'd just witnessed.

* * *

A great shout of elation made Arel pull Frick up short and turn around. His troops were all celebrating. A quick scan of the energy on the field validated their elation. The balance of power had tipped dramatically in his favor. He urged his horse into a fast canter and headed towards the front lines. The stallion felt the excitement too and leaped into action.

General Wolf was soon riding alongside Arel on his capable steed, Whisk. Arel's general had been checking on the battle from an elevated position on the field. He was eager to deliver his news.

"It's happened, my Lord. He's down. The prince is down," he said in a gasping voice.

Arel's eyes widened with surprise and confusion. General Wolf and his men were reveling in a great victory. His side was winning. Yet the thought of what that meant nearly took his breath away. He spurred Frick forward. He knew his adversary, William, was in trouble. The man's energy was definitely waning, but how badly was he hurt? What if he died?

In his heart, Arel shouted out his concern. "Dammit, Will, you can't let it end this way!" But even as he made his declaration, some darker part of him knew he had to stay true to what he'd started.

"Alert the men, we have to finish this now!" he shouted at his general.

* * *

360

William lay very still. He was afraid he was going to pass out. His head was a blinding spasm of pain, but he couldn't let his condition deter his focus. He needed to properly direct his energy if he wanted to maintain his army. A multitude of angels on the ground were depending on him.

He'd been shouting out orders when a fire ball had exploded close to his position. In his distracted state, he'd forgotten to maintain his personal shields. But his mount, Boda, was very aware and quick to react. Throughout the battle, she was lightning fast on her feet and constantly positioning her body as a buffer to keep him safe. When she reared, she was trying to protect him from flying debris. William was caught off guard and lost control. Horsemanship had never been one of his strong points.

After William fell, Boda swiveled round and nudged him with her muzzle. Her encouragement and energy helped. William pulled himself back from the pain enough to steady his resolve. Fortunately, when he looked up, Michael was rushing over.

"Hold on, William, hold on for a little while longer," Michael said in a calming voice.

William didn't have the strength to answer him. A number of his troops were quickly gathering around him, protecting him like Boda tried to protect him. But he was the one who had to stay clear-headed and remember why he was on the battlefield. From the very start, he'd needed to prove something crucial to himself. Fear could only overpower him if he let it. As he tried to stay alert, the concept weaved in and out of his wounded head.

Unlike William, Michael never lost his poise or focus. He was always vigilant and attentive to whatever was required. He gave William a reassuring smile, then turned his attention skyward. His eyes were bright and expectant.

* * *

While Michael was on the ground, Carey was high above the field, standing on a viewing platform. When he'd seen William fall, he wasn't surprised. The man was exhausted.

William was a powerful and willing leader, but he didn't have any experience in directing an army of angels. It was like a teenager trying to drive an eighteen wheeler with eighteen forward gears. Learning to handle a truck like that took time and practice. So did directing a large battalion of angels.

Boda was also a problem for an inexperienced rider. She was an excellent mount, the best there was when it came to being battle ready. Her responses to both the conditions on the field and her rider could be almost instantaneous. She'd done her best to adapt to William's lack of skill. However, she had to protect him even if it meant he might not be ready for her sudden responses. Of course, if he'd been riding a lesser horse, it wouldn't have been as able to protect him as effectively as Boda had. It wouldn't have been as capable of boosting William's energy either. All in all, Boda had been an excellent choice on Michael's part.

Carey smiled as he nodded down to his fellow angel. Michael was comfortable in just about any situation. As Arel once observed, Michael had been around longer than dirt. So had Carey. They'd been there to watch the earth evolve and become a place suitable for life. Now, they were eager for humanity to continue on its quest for happiness.

The battle that William and Arel were fighting was significant. It was a kind of marker denoting what was possible for people like William and Arel. The two men had been comrades and sometimes enemies in many lifetimes. In this life, they were seekers who needed to define themselves in a way that went beyond the norm. Michael felt they had a very good chance to succeed.

However, as Carey studied the two armies, he saw Arel and his troops advancing very quickly towards William's position. It was a decisive point. If William lost hope, he'd do more than suffer from a head wound. A little help was needed. With William's petition and focus in place, Carey heeded Michael's signal to proceed. It was time for a different kind of angel to come forth. It was time to call upon an angel named Grace. She'd demonstrate how versatile an angel could be.

For an angel, changing their appearance was like putting on different clothes. Grace normally looked very sweet in her role as Carol's angel. She wore matronly dresses. Sometimes, her hair was pulled back in a bun. She'd adopted that particular look when Carol was a little girl and had caught a glimpse of Grace. Since the child had imagined Grace to be her fairy godmother, Grace appeared in grandmotherly apparel. But grandmothers had no place on a field of battle. Grace needed to be a much more impressive angel to engage Arel's army.

Sixty-Three

As Arel spurred Frick down the field, one thought took hold and repeated itself over and over. It was his father who had won the war he was fighting, not him. That hard, wooden cane that the man had used to beat a small boy, had never stopped punishing Arel. As a man, he was still feeling the blows of being the child who had no value. Only now, those blows had taken hold of his mind. They'd become a terrible filter that didn't allow him to see anything properly, including who he really was. In the end, he'd lost touch with anything valuable in his make-up.

The worst part was that his twisted vision hadn't allowed for good decisions. Arel had broken and defiled everything he'd held sacred. Despite his efforts to survive and seek out what was good and true, he'd let his father's venom poison him. Its toxic nature made him weak when it came to holding on to what really mattered to him. Now he was surrounded with the result, and it sickened him.

He wanted to blame the Creator for the darkness, for the ugliness of battle, but the Creator hadn't started the war he was fighting. The Creator had never made him turn against a brother or train innocent creatures to fight and battle someone he'd chosen to make an enemy. If evil was more powerful than good, he'd been the one to give that evil its power.

As he closed the distance between himself and William, he saw Michael looking at him. The angel was standing close to where William lay, but his eyes were trained on Arel's eyes. Even though Arel wore a helmet, it couldn't stop Michael's gaze from penetrating the metal and seeking him out. But there was no judgment or condemnation in Michael's eyes, only understanding and kindness.

It was Arel who still harbored a sense of failure, a failure to leave his past behind. He'd dragged it along throughout his life, a dead thing, a corpse that didn't belong in the present. There was no life in his father's hatred. It needed to be given a decent burial, a final resting place. Instead, Arel had been too angry to let it go.

The thought drained more of the blood from his face as he rode. Yet a few words slipped out before his despair took hold completely. "Help me, Michael!"

As he uttered the words, he was shaken out of his morbid mood by his men. They were screaming in panic all around him. His horse, Frick, was screaming too, fighting the reins and coming to a sudden stop. All eyes were on the horizon. A dragon was silhouetted against the meager remains of daylight.

Arel watched as the beast rose up slowly. Her emerald green scales glistened in spite of the dim light. Her massive wings were a much darker green, almost black. Even from a distance, her bright, yellow eyes were visible. They remained steady and unwavering.

As she stared back at Arel and his army, she began to fan her wings with more determination. She ascended higher into the fouled atmosphere. Her breast glowed with the fire she carried within. When she'd reached a sufficient height, she hung in the air for a moment. In the next, she began her dive, leaving tendrils of smoke in her wake.

Arel's mind froze in horror. The old memory of being burned consumed him, making the reins slip from his hands. Frick tossed his head and backed up. The horse was gripped in fear and panic too, moving erratically, stumbling on the uneven, deeply-rutted ground. When Frick's back hoof got stuck in a hole, the horse began to fall, taking Arel with him.

Arel's armor saved his leg from being crushed. Frick didn't seem to fair as well. When the horse managed to get to his feet, he was limping badly. But even in his injured state, he returned to where Arel lay and stood over him. Wolfie was there the next instant. He'd thrown off his helmet and tossed it aside as he knelt down and positioned his body over Arel.

"Great One, tell me what to do," he asked in a shaky voice. "How can I protect you?"

Arel knew Wolfie was terrified, just like all his men. Not only was their leader cowed by the winged monster, but their basic rodent nature was in total survival mode. An aerial attack activated their need to run for cover. But they didn't scatter like he thought they would. They ran towards him, forming a great circle, protecting him against the alien creature in the sky, covering their heads with their shields.

Arel's face turned to the heavens as he waited for the end. "Michael, please, help these innocents! I'm the one who started all this! I'll pay for anything I did, but don't let harm come to these brave creatures!"

As his prayer was leaving his lips, Arel saw the dragon appear directly over him. She stared down with her hard, unblinking eyes. The smoke from her massive exhalations filled the air around her. But instead of using her fiery breath, she shook her head, as if she was a great mother bird chastising a fledgling. Then she rose up again and slowly left the battle field.

Arel tried to get up and couldn't. Everything about him felt broken. Even if his armor saved his leg, he felt himself slipping away. He had to act quickly. He told Wolfie to order the men to remove their helmets. After they did, he used what breath he had to thank them, to tell them they had served him well. With a snap of his fingers, he released them to Michael's care, knowing they'd soon be in a glorious, mouse heaven. Only Wolfie remained a soldier, but not for long.

Arel reached up and touched the face of his beloved friend. "I'll never forget you, Wolfie. I promise you, there's never been a better man than the man you have been. But now, I want you to go back to those who have served with you, not as their general, but as that amazing creature you've always been."

Wolfie didn't say anything. He nodded and smiled back. When Arel snapped his fingers again, Wolfie was gone.

Arel noticed that Frick had wandered over to where William's white horse was standing. Wolfie's horse, Whisk, was with them too. The three horses looked back at him, as if they needed permission to move on. He smiled as he released them too. "Go with her, you two, enjoy perfect health and green pastures again."

* * *

William pushed himself up into a sitting position, ignoring his head. He needed to kno why there was so much discord coming from Arel's men. They were all looking to the skies and screaming out in fright. The reason was soon obvious.

William had only seen dragons in books and in the movies. But the one flying over the field made him forget his pain. His mind and thoughts were transfixed by the size and powerful energy of the amazing creature. She was alternately gliding and flapping her wings in purposeful manner. She was flying directly to the spot where Arel had fallen. She did glance in William's direction briefly. It wasn't a comforting glance. The great winged reptile seemed rather annoyed with him. At least, that's what he felt when he tried to tune into her mindset. Thankfully, she kept moving. William gasped. "Oh hell, what's she going to do to Arel?"

He didn't have long to wait for an answer. Once the dragon reached Arel's location, she hovered in midair. But she didn't stay very long with Arel either. She moved off after a brief visit. A few minutes later, she disappeared over the horizon. When she was gone, William wondered if he'd been hallucinating. Dragons weren't real. Then he saw Michael smiling at him. It was the kind of smile that made a lump stick in William's throat. As he tried to swallow, he realized how little he knew about the power that Michael was capable of wielding.

As he sat wondering about the battle's outcome, a very strange thing happened. One minute, Arel was surrounded by his men. The next minute they were gone. A little while later, his horse, Boda, and a couple of other horses disappeared too. When William glanced around to check on his own troops, the field was empty. Even Michael had left. Only two people remained on the field.

William succeeded in getting to his feet and steadied himself against his dizziness. He slowly made his way across the rough ground to where Arel lay very still. "I think it's over, don't you?" he said with a frown.

Arel looked up and sighed. "Yes, it's done, and so am I."

William's frown deepened. "Don't start. I'm hurting too much to have you acting like the king of drama."

"I'm not kidding. I can't hold on much longer."

"You're fine."

"How would you know what I am?"

William chuckled in spite of the pounding in his head. "I've always known you were fine. You're the only one who thinks he's broken."

Arel's face lit up. "Are you sure?"

"Yes, I'm sure. Just be thankful that you don't have a concussion like me."

Arel shook his head. "You don't have a concussion. I checked." He paused and slowly scanned his surroundings. "Maybe I'm not broken, but I am crazy sometimes, aren't I?"

"Of course, but I've always known that too." William held out his hand. "Let's get out of here. Even if I don't have a concussion, I'm tired. I want to sleep for a week."

Sixty-Four

Arel woke up with the sun shining in his eyes. Then he realized it was Michael standing over him. "Why do you do that?" he complained.

Michael shrugged innocently. "Do what?"

Arel hesitated. "Oh, I see. It's me. My angel filter is slightly off. I'm seeing who you really are."

Michael nodded. "You'll adjust after a few minutes."

Arel sat up, glancing around the bedroom, happy that it was newly painted and bright. He needed reality to be inviting. The world he'd created and everything that followed seemed like a bad dream. He decided it was in his best interest to leave it at that. He wouldn't think about it for a while. He needed time to feel normal again. He wanted to enjoy feeling good for a change. "How long have I been asleep? I feel like a new person." He stretched out his arms and did a couple of neck rolls. Then he remembered his hand. When he looked at his palm, the scar had faded again.

Michael walked over to the window. "You've been recuperating for a bit. But you're getting very good at quickly coming back to health."

There was a knock at the door. William looked in. "Finally, you're awake."

Arel smiled. "William, come in. Michael was just complimenting me on how fast I am at healing."

William rubbed the back of his head. "He said the same thing about me." He paused and folded his arms over his chest. "That was a day and a half ago."

"You had a bump. I was at death's doorstep. So I think I'm doing remarkably well."

William looked like he was going to comment, but he held his tongue. When he spoke, his tone was light and sincere. "I'm glad to see that you're looking better."

Arel stared at his palm again and lowered his voice. "Thank you for everything, Will."

William took a deep breath and sighed. "You're welcome, but I didn't do what I did just for you. I did it for myself, too."

Arel felt himself getting dreamy again, but he threw back the covers and stood up anyway. Straightening his shoulders, he tested his balance. Satisfied that he was fit enough, he put out his hand to William.

William stared at it for a moment, then clasped it with his own. He raised his eyes to meet Arel's and smiled. "So we're still brothers?"

Arel's heart did a kind of jump start. It propelled his consciousness into skies of happy bliss. For a moment, he felt like he was soaring. As he gazed at a shimmering landscape below, he heard himself saying something to William. "We've dived very deep, my brother, but nothing will stop us this time. Nothing will keep us from the freedom that we've sought for so long. I'm sure of it."

"What are you talking about?" William asked.

His question brought Arel back to himself and the moment. When he realized he was still staring at William, he let go of the man's hand and stepped back.

"Arel, are you sure that you're alright?" William asked with new concern.

Arel glanced at his palm. There was a faint trace of blood there. Arel knew the blood belonged to both of them. The scars on their hands had a way of opening and closing on their own. But there was no pain. In fact, his body felt the thrill of renewal and vitality. He grinned at William. "I've never felt better. I'm also ready to go home. I want to relax in my own house and have friends over."

"You could visit London first."

Arel shook his head. "That's very kind, but I need to do some fence mending with everybody in Chicago." He paused and rubbed his beard. It needed tending. There was also something else that he needed to take care of. Finally, a thought made its way through his energized mood. "Oh hell, I almost forgot Rolphe. I think I left him in some kind of weird spell."

Rolphe peeked in from the doorway. "I'm okay."

Arel returned a censuring frown. "Listening in from the hall again, Rolphe?"

Rolphe studied his hands, then dropped them to his sides. "Carey came over to Myra's apartment to help me after . . . after . . . you know, everything went back to normal. I snapped out of whatever came over me."

Arel walked over to where Rolphe stood in the doorway. "Your incessant prayers nearly drove me out of my mind. Do you know that?"

Rolphe backed up. "I'm sorry. I was trying—"

Arel clasped his shoulder. "In the end, I think they also helped me remember who I am. So thank you." He held out his hand.

Rolphe grabbed hold with both of his much larger hands and squeezed enthusiastically.

Arel allowed the giant of a man to pump his slender limb for only a few moments before he pulled away. "Right, now go paint something while I get showered."

After Rolphe turned and hurried back to his studio, Arel worked his fingers, then held them up to Michael. "Do any of them look broken? Rolphe has no idea about being careful."

* * *

Annabel smiled when William walked into the living room. "Guess what? I'm almost finished with my project," she said as she examined her knitting. It had taken the shape of a winter hat. Its bright blue and yellow colors were separated by deep green stripes. "What do you think?"

William stopped, going suddenly pale. "You don't expect me to wear that, do you?"

Annabel hesitated and frowned. "No, it's not for you."

William's color returned to normal as he let out a burst of laughter. "Arel is going to have a good time modeling your handiwork, I'm sure."

"It's not for Arel. It's for Carey. It gets cold in Chicago. He'll need something to keep him warm next winter. If I have the time, I want to try a sweater next."

William made his way to the opposite sofa, never taking his eyes off the hat. "Listen, if you have to make something for me, please make a simple scarf, preferably in charcoal gray. Also, the smaller and finer the stitching the better."

Annabel shook her head. "Don't worry, I already have something planned for you. I'm sure you'll love it."

William sat back and let out a sigh. "I see you're really enjoying your new hobby."

Annabel glanced back towards Arel's bedroom. "I think it got me through your trip to you-know-where. We haven't talked about that terrible day, but knitting helped me find a way to stay calm."

William smiled. "I felt your support and energy when I was out on the battlefield. You did a very good job of not letting your fears get the better of you."

Annabel finished the last stitch and tied off the yarn. "Yes, well, I'm very proud of myself." She held up the hat and inspected her work. Then she looked around the apartment. She needed to see what the hat looked like on someone's head. "William?"

William had picked up the morning paper and was studying the front page. "Yes, what is it?"

Annabel stood up and went over to where he sat. "Would you try this on? I want to make sure it's big enough for a man to wear."

William's fingers tightened on the paper. "Get Carey. He's around here, isn't he?"

"Carey slipped out to the bakery."

William's voice got edgy. "What about Rolphe or Michael?"

Without paying him any attention, Annabel put the hat on William's head and pulled it down over his ears. She was surprised that it didn't fit like she'd hoped. It covered half of William's face. She could just see a little of his eyes as he peered out apprehensively.

Arel was just coming out of the bathroom in his robe. His hair was still wet from a recent shower, and his face was relaxed and back to its handsome self. When he looked up, he paused. "William? Is that you under that very colorful hat?"

Annabel smiled. "I could make one for you too, Arel."

Arel tightened the belt on his robe. "Oh, what a nice thought, but I'm kind of allergic to knitted things on my head. It makes my head get too hot."

William yanked the hat off and scowled back. "Nice save, Arel."

Annabel frowned at him and then at Arel. "You two are no fun sometimes. Do you know that?"

Arel came forward a couple of steps, looking contrite. "Sorry, I didn't mean to upset you."

Annabel stared back, noting how quickly he could become the courteous, English gentleman. "What about something in black or charcoal, with very fine stitches?"

Arel nodded. "Yes, that's an idea, maybe a scarf."

Annabel gathered up her knitting supplies and headed for the studio. "At least Rolphe expressed an interest. I'll see if he'd like something handmade, something to keep him warm." She glanced back at William. "Something for those cold nights when he's all alone."

William's eyes widened as Annabel stormed out of the room. "Annabel, please, I'll wear the damn thing if it makes you happy, but—"

Arel began to laugh as William got up and started after Annabel. "Send me a picture when you're wearing your night cap, Will. I'll enjoy looking at it when I need to lighten up."

William stopped suddenly and turned around. "Arel, I just had the strangest thing happen. I think I had some kind of premonition. I saw you with this woman. She had blond hair."

"Woman? For me? Stop kidding around."

"No, I'm not kidding. I got a very clear flash of you and this person meeting. I've never had that kind of feeling before."

Arel smoothed back his hair. "Was she pretty?"

"Yes, I guess so."

Arel sighed. "It's just your imagination. Falling on your head isn't a good idea. You're getting weird."

William blinked back. "Stop resisting what I saw. I think you're going to meet that woman you've been hoping for."

Arel continued on to his bedroom. "I don't need a woman right now. I'm going to get my life in order and start gardening with Michael."

"You hate gardening."

Arel glanced back. "I'm going to change all that. I've taken the cure. No more craziness. I'm going to find a way to keep my life in balance from now on."

Sixty-Five

Carey returned to Rolphe's apartment with enough croissants to last the weekend. He'd be returning to Chicago very soon. Once he got there, he needed to find a French bakery. He'd begun to really enjoy the fineries of what he'd tasted in Paris. After he stashed the desserts away in the cupboard that Arel rarely checked, he smiled. As he turned away, Rolphe was coming into the kitchen.

"Rolphe, I thought you were painting."

"I was, but I heard you come in. I wanted to talk to you while everyone is out."

Carey glanced around the flat. "Where did they go?"

Rolphe grimaced. "You're an angel, don't you know?"

Carey laughed. "I play the human as much as possible."

Rolphe walked over to the table and sat down. "I'm going to miss you and Michael."

"We're always available, my friend. All you have to do is think about us, and if you need something, we're always happy to help."

Rolphe's frown deepened. "Perhaps you're right, but still—"

"What are you trying to tell me?"

"When I was doing all that praying, I realized how much I miss my boys. Now, I think of Arel and William in the same way. I know that they're men, but I see the boy in each of them."

Carey laughed and opened the cupboard, pulled down the bag of pastries and quickly retrieved one. "Sorry, Rolphe, but I imagine Arel will be home soon, and I better have one of these before that happens." He returned the bag to its hiding place and joined Rolphe at the table. "Please, go on."

375

"I think Arel's back on track, but sometimes I worry about William."

"Why?"

Rolphe looked away and twisted uncomfortably in his chair. "A person's blood carries information. I might know more about him than he knows about himself."

"Rolphe, I understand. But Arel and William have to figure out their lives. And you have to keep your energy centered in what you're doing from now on."

Rolphe tried to smile back and couldn't manage it. "I don't know what that means."

"Just enjoy your life," Carey said as he took a generous bite of his dessert.

"Is it that easy?"

Carey swallowed his mouthful and nodded. "It is, but you have to let go of trying to figure everything out. Have fun painting. Take Myra out and dance."

"So you don't think I should try to help Arel and William if they need someone to—"

Carey wiped his mouth on his sleeve. "I'm sure it will be nice to keep in touch, but try to simply love life again."

Rolphe stood up. "Thank you, dear one. You've inspired me to work on a new painting. Arel made me destroy the last one that depicted brothers. Now, I think he'll approve."

Carey laughed. "Yes, Arel seems to be a reformed man since he's been back in the real world. He's even looking forward to seeing Chicago and hosting dinner parties again."

Rolphe smiled too. "Arel actually whistled when he was watering Michael's plants."

Carey frowned. "Arel was watering plants? I better tell Michael. Arel can be a little too enthusiastic about the amount of moisture he thinks they need."

Rolphe picked at his thumb, scratching off a bit of blue paint. "I think he wants to make sure everything is taken care of before he leaves. When he inspected the studio, he decided to give my brushes an extra thorough cleaning. Some of them are quite old and didn't fare too well. But it doesn't matter. As long as Arel is enjoying life, I'm happy."

"Good."

Rolphe waved Carey over and lowered his voice to a whisper. "William informed Arel of something exciting. If William's vision is correct, Arel has a woman waiting in his future."

"Really? That should make life back in Chicago interesting." Carey's eyes narrowed as he pulled Rolphe closer. His voice was a whisper too. "Rolphe, you are a wealth of information. What am I going to do without you when I leave?"

* * *

William felt more at ease than he'd felt in a long time. After their adventures in Paris, he and Annabel were back home in London. As they sat on the couch in the living room, he went over current events. Arel had phoned earlier, and he'd said that he was getting settled in Chicago again. When he and Arel said goodbye to each other, the strain was gone. Each of them seemed to know that a difficult chapter in their life was over. Each of them was ready for a new and better future. They'd stay in touch, but not because of any new problems, but because they were learning to simply be friends again.

Annabel interrupted his thoughts. "Are you happy?" she asked as she reached out for his hand.

William turned and scanned her face. Thankfully, the worry line in her forehead had disappeared. She was beginning to look a little more like her angel self. But he knew he loved her no matter what. "I am," he mused. "I feel like it's time for us now."

Annabel nodded. "You did a wonderful thing for Arel. I think Arel's found himself at long last. He seemed genuinely cheerful when we left. Whatever came out of that crazy world of his seemed to set him on the road to stability."

"It was crazy, but I learned something too."

"What's that?"

"I learned that power needs a very stable person to wield it properly."

"And what do you think Arel learned?"

"I think he found out that he could leave his past behind him. Maybe that's why I had that premonition about him meeting a woman. Maybe it's time for something new in his life."

"When I still had my wings, he once asked me if I thought there was someone out there waiting for him. And when I think about the smile he gave me as I was leaving, I believe there is someone."

William put his arm around Annabel and pulled her close. "Good, then we both agree. Arel is going to meet a woman. Hopefully, she'll be the woman of his dreams."

As he made the pronouncement, he had a flash of his own future. Or maybe it was simply the future that he'd have without Arel causing havoc in his life. He saw himself beside Annabel, walking hand in hand down a quiet street. The moon cast silvery shadows on the buildings they passed. They were talking about the idea of a family.

It was a beautiful thought to contemplate, yet he couldn't give himself over to it completely. Maybe that was to be expected. Recently, he'd been in command of a glorious army of angels. He'd needed to be at his best in order to handle the position properly. To go from such an exhilarating experience to planning a quiet, family life was a challenge.

He also kept thinking about something that happened on the day that Arel left for Chicago. That morning, they'd had time for a brief chat. Arel had been animated at one point in their conversation. He'd grabbed hold of William's hand. For a guy who'd been near death's door only days before, his grip was impressive. But Arel's glowing, fluid eyes grabbed hold of William even more powerfully.

When Arel spoke about all that they'd gone through, William knew Arel was referring to more than what they'd experienced in their current lifetime. Many of their other lifetimes had been overshadowed by darkness. Now, Arel spoke of what he hoped was coming. As William listened to Arel's mellow voice, he found himself mesmerized so completely that his consciousness was thrust upwards. When he looked around, he was floating in a place where the stars and galaxies lived. Below him, he saw the earth. Resting in the caress of infinite space, the blue orb was beautiful, the most exquisite gem in all of creation.

Arel was floating next to William, telling him that better times were coming for the earth and for them. They were going to find the freedom they'd been seeking for so long. When they did, the earth would be their playground in the best kind of way. Beauty would be restored, and the planet would once again return to an elevated state, a paradise that it was always meant to be.

Arel's words and descriptions took root in William's heart, making his chest stir with excitement and wonder. Afterwards, when Arel released him, William's mind blanked. He couldn't retain what he'd seen and heard. He was back in Rolphe's apartment, looking at a friend who was regaining his health and coming to his senses.

But the vision wasn't lost forever. When William returned to London, it surfaced. One morning, he woke up and remembered everything. He was in the heavens again, feeling like there were no boundaries in that place. The freedom Arel spoke about became a living force that moved through his heart and soul.

The vision left him restless. That's when he purged it from his mind. He refused to give in to a feeling of wanderlust that wanted to take up residence in his bones. He was tired of the problems that came with dreams. He needed to simply enjoy being with Annabel. Period.

Sixty-Six

After returning to Chicago, Arel made a promise to himself. No brooding. No overthinking anything. No guilt trips. He was determined to be happy. His stern self-directive was a relief after being overwhelmed by his negative emotions in Paris. On the plus side, he and William were the best of friends again. Whatever had happened during Arel's travels to the dark side was slipping away like a bad dream.

On the first weekend following his return, Arel lost no time reestablishing his ties with the two couples he thought of as family. He'd planned a Saturday evening dinner. He enlisted Michael and Carey in the kitchen to help with preparations. When he bumped into Carey for the third time, he almost let his temper flare. He caught himself. Instead, he stood aside and let Carey retrieve a serving dish out of the cupboard. He even found the patience to smile. "You know, I might have to add an extension to the back of the house. That way this kitchen would be roomier."

Carey paused and returned a thoughtful look. "Maybe I should go finish a few things in the garage and give you and Michael more space to work."

Arel forced himself to continue smiling. Carey had often found excuses for getting out of kitchen chores in the past. However, those were the times when Arel thought he had a real human in his care. Now, no matter how Carey acted, the fact was that he was a very capable angel. Still, Arel wouldn't let himself get annoyed. "No, you're fine, Carey. It's me. I'm just a little excited about this dinner. It's been a while since I've prepared one. I'm a little out of practice."

Michael glanced over after he closed the oven door. "I think the lasagna is done, Arel."

Arel noted Michael's flushed face and realized how warm the kitchen was. He'd suffered from fevers for so long, he sometimes took being too hot for granted. "Michael, I've never seen you look so red. Are you okay?"

Michael retrieved a handkerchief from his jeans, wiped his forehead and smiled. "One of your first suggestions was to always carry one of these in my pocket. Now I know why."

Arel's brows narrowed. "You're sweating?"

Carey laughed. "Even an angel's body can get a little overheated at times. Michael has been working close to the stove for hours. First you had him make up a batch of hard biscuits for the babies. Then he made that cake for dessert and—"

"I get it, Carey," Arel said as he mopped his own forehead. He thought about his guests and how uncomfortable everyone would be if he didn't cool things down. His hand shot out as he looked at Carey and pointed. "Quick, run to the hall and turn down the thermostat," he ordered. He looked at Michael next. "Please, Michael, don't just stand there. Get that lasagna out and turn off the oven."

Michael frowned. "What about the garlic bread?"

Arel patted his face again. "Oh hell, I mean, oh heck, put the bread in, but take it out as soon as the butter melts."

"But you usually wait until you're about to serve dinner before you put it in."

Arel felt his nerves slip a little, but he recovered his composure as quickly as possible. "It can't be helped." He glanced at the clock. Everyone will be here in a couple of minutes. We'll skip any long conversations and serve dinner right away."

Michael nodded. "I think everything is ready. Do you want me to put the salad on the table?"

"Maybe." Arel made a speedy trip to the dining room. He was inspecting the table settings just as Carey was returning. "Carey! You forgot to put the salad bowls out."

"Sorry, I was going to take care of that when you called me in to wash vegetables. And Arel, I have some bad news. I think the air conditioner is broken. Nothing happened when I turned down the setting."

Before Arel could react to the latest piece of information the doorbell rang. He glanced towards the kitchen. "Michael, quick! Come into the dining room! How hot do you think it is in here?"

Michael did as he was told and shrugged. "I'd gauge the temperature to be about ninety degrees."

"Ninety degrees?" Arel gasped. As he tried to think of what to do to rectify the situation, the doorbell rang again. He threw up his hands as he went to answer it. "This is a disaster, and I wanted everything to be so perfect!"

* * *

Carol patted Arel's hand. "See, everything turned out just fine, didn't it?" When she and the others had arrived at Arel's house, Arel looked totally dismayed and embarrassed about his broken air conditioner. Peggy and Tim came up with a quick solution. They insisted that the party be moved next door, to their house. Now, Arel sat at the table looking very relieved.

"Yes, Carol, thanks to all of you, and especially to Peggy and Tim, I'm a happy man."

Kevin leaned back in his chair. "Maybe I should go back to your house and sweat off a little of this weight. I'm sure I've gained another couple of pounds after that dessert. But it was too good. I couldn't stop myself."

Peggy walked into the dining room and smiled. "The babies are sound asleep."

Arel sighed. "I wish I could have spent more time with them this evening, but maybe tomorrow Carey and I could take them for a nice stroll around the neighborhood. I hope it hasn't changed too much since I've been gone."

Tim shoved his empty cake plate back a little. "I wonder who's going to rent the house next to yours?"

Arel hesitated. "I hope they're nice. The people who own the property are great. They liked to garden. Michael used to talk to them off and on. They told him that they're moving abroad for a couple of years."

Peggy sat down next to Tim. "I've seen people looking at the property. I'm surprised it hasn't been rented."

Arel nodded. "By the way, thank you for mowing the grass while I was away, Tim."

Tim looked at Kevin. "Yes, well, it helped to keep me in shape. However, you better tell Michael that the gardens out back might need some looking after. I didn't have time to get to everything."

"It's a shame that Michael didn't join us," Carol said.

Carey returned from the kitchen carrying dessert seconds. "He's hiding out in Arel's downstairs level, cooling off and relaxing after a day in Arel's kitchen."

Arel's face went red. "Yes, well, at least the downstairs is comfortable since it's below ground. We'll use it as our sleeping quarters tonight. Carey, you know where that extra fold-up bed is, right?"

"Sure do," Carey said as he waved his fork and glanced around. "Anybody want more cake? There's lots left."

When everyone groaned, Carey shrugged. "I guess it's up to me to whittle it down a bit more."

* * *

As Arel and Carey walked back home after dinner, Arel pointed to the moon. "Look at how beautiful it is, Carey."

"It sure is," Carey said as he nudged Arel. "And look at you. It seems like you've been very happy since you came back."

"You're right. I feel like a new person."

"See, you didn't need to worry. The Creator, or should I say, our boss, knew what He was doing after all. People can lead wonderful lives." Carey paused and stared at the home next to Arel's. "Look, Arel, there's someone standing on the porch." He waved his hand. "Hi there!"

Arel stopped and leaned forward a little. A blond woman had turned and stared back at them. With the porch light on, he could see her face quite well. She was pretty except for the fact that her brows were bunched. He raised a hand and waved too. "Hello, are you renting that house?"

The woman nodded as she put a key in the lock. "Yes, I am."

Before Arel had a chance to go over and introduce himself, the woman let herself in and shut the door. A moment later, the porch light went off.

Carey gave Arel another nudge. "She didn't say much. She might be shy."

Arel felt his stomach tighten. For some reason, he felt like there might be something special about the woman he'd glimpsed. "Yes, maybe that's good. She'll probably be a nice, quiet neighbor."

"Something tells me that she's single."

"Really? Is that your angel intuition working?"

Carey gave Arel a broad smile. "Yes, it is."

To be continued in Book Five, ## TAINTED BLOOD

Thank you for taking the time to read *Brother's Blood*, the fourth book of my series, THE VAMPIRE RECLAMATION PROJECT. If you enjoyed it, please consider telling your friends. Word of mouth is an author's best friend and much appreciated.
Thank you. – S. S. Bazinet.

To visit S. S. Bazinet's website,
go to SSBazinet.com.

THE VAMPIRE RECLAMATION PROJECT
Book Five
TAINTED BLOOD

Arel thinks that his search for the perfect woman is over when he meets gorgeous Claire. However, perfection comes with a staggering price. Infatuated by Claire, Arel is ready to pay that price even if it means giving up all that he holds dear. He makes plans to marry her when she agrees to his proposal.

When a second woman named Elise comes into the picture, Arel is faced with a dilemma. After being alone and single for a very long time, he suddenly has two women vying for his attention. In the middle of Arel's confusing choices, he must find the truth. Is he really in love with Claire or has he been fooling himself?

Unfortunately, the answers he needs are contained in his heart, a vessel that's been carefully guarded for a very long time. Can he trust that deeper, more informed part of himself? Dare he put aside his fears and commit to that elusive thing called love? And most importantly, will that part help him choose the right woman, one who'll truly love him too?

Other Books by S. S. Bazinet
✧ ✧ ✧

THE VAMPIRE RECLAMATION PROJECT
Book One: Michael's Blood
Book Two: Arel's Blood
Book Three: William's Blood
Book Four: Brother's Blood
Book Five: Tainted Blood
Book Six: Forgotten Blood
Book Seven: New Blood

IN THE CARE OF WOLVES SERIES
Book One: My Brother's Keeper

OPEN WIDE MY HEART
Book One: Traces Of Home
Book Two: Traces Of Angels